PAPER TREES

Paper Trees
Roy Sinclair

CAITLIN
PRESS

Caitlin Press
1999

Paper Trees Copyright © Roy Sinclair

Caitlin Press Inc.
Box 2387, Stn. B
Prince George, British Columbia V2N 2S6

All rights reserved. No part of this publication may be reproduced in any form by any means without the written permission of the publisher, except by a reviewer who may quote passages in a review.

Caitlin Press gratefully acknowledges the financial support of the Canada Council for the Arts for our publishing program. Similarly we acknowledge the support of the Arts Council of British Columbia.

Layout and Design by Patty Osborne, Vancouver Desktop
Cover design by Roger Handling, Terra Firma Graphic Design
Cover photo courtesy of Northern Forest Products Association

CANADIAN CATALOGUING IN PUBLICATION DATA

Sinclair, Roy 1933-
Paper Trees
ISBN 0-920576-78-8
I. Title
PS8587.I55273P36 1999   C813'.54   C99-910684-8
PR9199.3.S533P36 1999

1

I shifted my flatdeck truck down to second gear in its four speed transmission, not because I needed the power but because I wanted to go slow. The switchback marking the halfway point in my climb to the railroad is wide and flat, easy to negotiate. But the sweep of my headlights shows a maze of muddy ruts frozen hard into minor mountain ranges that do their best to split tires or break springs as I bounce from one groove that doesn't fit to another. By two o'clock tomorrow afternoon it will be soft and sloppy, smooth to drive on, with a hard roadbed a few inches under the surface that's still wet from last week's heavy rain. But now, at 1:00 a.m. the cold has it all solid as concrete. I smiled as I reminded myself that it's still only September and winter is a ways off yet. I'm not particularly good at remembering dates or caring much about it but I know it's early in the month for such a hard frost.

Three hundred and sixty-some times a year I drive up this hill in the middle of the night. No one else wants the job so I've never had to explain how much I feel the need to do it. Behind me at the bottom of the hill our little town is sound asleep—or it should be at this time of night.

Town! It's the word used by my employers, the family who own the place lock, stock and a fair bit of the barrel. Most of us irreverent employees call it 'Camp' but being a limber willow in the wind, I can say it either way depending on who I am talking to. Things never change much here and that's partly why I stay. I seldom admit even to myself that there are other reasons. I'm a day-to-day man so as far as I'm concerned this is just another trip up the hill to meet the train to exchange a bag of outgoing mail for a bag or two of incoming letters and parcels. I also have to pick up the shipment of groceries, repair parts and other odds and ends that are always coming to a logging and sawmill town that has no road connection with the outside world. We have only the train, one each way, east and west, seven nights a week and a local mixed freight with one, or sometimes two, old wooden passenger coaches going east one day and west the next but not on Sunday. If we were closer to the city, the local might get more passenger traffic from us but it stops too long, too often and even sits in passing tracks waiting for faster freight trains coming from behind. The local is still well used, it's different, a change of pace downward and travels by day so you can see the country. There seems to be no firm schedule for the daytime train other than knowing it will pass through in the morning westbound and the afternoon eastbound. Best to check its progress by phone before driving up to the track. It too has to be met every day on its back and forth shuttle but usually not by me. The night trains are the ones that reach out across the land and bring the country to our doorstep. To me, they are the ones that count.

Once around the switchback the road resumes its gentle climb and is much smoother. The big diesel logging rigs are hauling on this road every day bringing logs from high on the mountains and faraway valleys down to the sawmill. I could go back up a gear but I'm in no hurry, there's lots of time before the westbound

No. 9 is due, so I dawdle along quite entranced by the sparkling display of frost crystals that wink at me from everywhere.

A train called No. 9 some place far away in a different world than mine is famous in song. It's easy to think of that fabled train while waiting for the long string of express, baggage and passenger cars that slip through our mountains every night as silently as its diesel electric engines will permit. I suppose its only logical that the eastbound train should be No. 8 but it bothers me in a minor way that No. 9 rarely gives us more than one slim bag of mail while No. 8, coming from the coast at Prince Rupert and through the supply centre city of Prince George is our lifeline.

Nearing the top of the hill I catch glimpses of the town lights below me and not far away. In daytime thick timber hides all sign of the settlement but at night a few stray lights find holes between the trunks and branches. Where the road flattens to make a turn to the right there is a line of electric lights hanging from a pair of wires most casually attached to trees along a footpath that goes almost straight down the hill. In this cold, sparkling taste of autumn, the pale bulbs are obviously losing the battle but the trail itself is a winner for it arrives at the edge of the town in a short, steep two hundred yards while the road, built on an easy grade, takes over a mile to wind around to the same place. It means I usually ride alone, both up and down the hill for the local people who go and come by train simply use the trail getting up or down in less time than it takes me to drive by the road. Only strangers coming for the first time to take a job in the mill or on a logging crew ride with me because they don't know the way. Someone has to show them where to find a bunk for the rest of the night, tell them where the cookhouse is and what time breakfast will be on in the morning. That too is part of my job.

The main road goes over the tracks on a timbered crossing then vanishes into the night-shrouded woods. I know it goes a long way back into the mountains, mostly climbing sometimes dropping, but usually by gentle grades and sweeping corners. I also know, to my sorrow, that the branch roads and spurs that climb under, over, and around cliffs and slides looking for the benches and valleys where the timber grows best are little more than goat trails. Most of them are steep and narrow. Some of the old ones are very dangerous.

I don't turn to cross the track but rather go almost straight ahead over a mixture of gravel and cinders toward the shanty that serves as station. I haven't a clue where the cinders came from nor the station either, probably built elsewhere perhaps for other purposes then dropped off here from a rail flatcar long before my time. It's a building that instantly makes you think of an old boxcar but isn't. It's about ten by thirty-odd feet in size with one end being a waiting room complete with a coal-burning stove and even some small blocks of wood to burn in it for lack of coal if you have the need for heat. There's a bench along each of two walls, a door that opens and closes, a window that does neither and three coal-oil lanterns on a wall shelf. One is red, one green and the third is clear. I've heard that in theory you light the lanterns, place them on the outside platform and the train will stop. But in actual practice it doesn't matter because the train always stops anyway. I've never seen the lanterns used except the clear one for simple lighting purposes when for one reason or another the electric light fails to work. The single dirty bulb hangs on an even dirtier cord that escapes the upper reaches of the building by way of a large knothole. It's the last light on the line that comes up along the footpath, Sometimes it works, sometimes it doesn't. By the time the electricity has climbed the hill on those slender wires, it's so tired that burned-out bulbs are unheard of up here. Wind is the problem with swaying trees or falling limbs sometimes breaking a wire.

The other half of the station is for freight storage, I guess, since it has a wide doorway now minus the door and absolutely nothing inside. In the four years I have been here there has always been absolutely nothing inside it. A sign board on each end of the building claims this is Rainy Mountain but like a lot of small sawmill towns off the highways you won't find it on many maps of British Columbia.

I turn around and park my truck along the track near the grade crossing about where I judge the express car will be when the train stops. Then I shut off my headlights and sit in total darkness till my eyes become accustomed to the night light. There is no moon but the stars are bright in a cold, cloudless sky with just a hint of northern lights flickering over the mountains across the river. After awhile I turn off the ignition and listen for any night sounds but there isn't much to be heard other than the usual pops and snaps from my cooling truck engine. As always I am early and the train is not yet close enough to hear. Just before I start the engine again to get some warmth from the cab heater a wolf howls nearby. He starts at a mid range tone then wavers through a couple of breaks downward ending in a long almost inaudibly low moan. An answer almost overlaps from even closer. Such a lost, forsaken sound that I want to feel sorry for them—but why should I when it's me who waits alone.

Nothing catches my imagination like waiting in the darkness for a train to come. There is such room for the mind to wander uninhibited by the realities of daytime. I like to sit quiet in my truck and imagine that some part of me is inside one of those long, narrow boxes of artificial light and warmth twisting its way around the mountain shoulders. There's no worry that it will get lost and take its packaged load of life—and that little part me—to some other place because no matter how it turns this way or that the steel rails beside me will bring it exactly here. I need only to wait and then I will be complete again until the next train is coming.

The fuss of arrivals and departures has an almost mystical attraction for me. I long to see firsthand who comes and who leaves for how long. I itch to know what is in each container or box unloaded and I take great satisfaction in delivering everything the next morning to exactly where it is needed or wanted, from the office or warehouse or store, to one of the shops or engine rooms or even out to a logging show in the woods. I have become, in other words, an incurable busybody with my nose in everyone's business. I've been that way ever since I started recovering from my accident nearly four years ago. I guess we all must have our fun somehow.

The northern lights are building up to a brighter display with a pulsating curtain of colour on three sides of me. I enjoy the spectacle till the westbound No. 9 pulls in ten minutes late and drops its usual flabby bag of mail plus two interestingly heavy crates from a foundry in Edmonton. As the train lights disappear I back along the track past the station to be in position once again but this time for the eastbound express car. It's lucky for me that we live close to Dome Creek where the trains meet each night for it means they arrive so near to each other that I can usually meet both with one trip. And yet if someone comes on the first train who needs a ride to camp, there is time to drive down and come back for the next one. As I watch the shooting lights in the sky I drift into thoughts, as I often do, of my own arrival here just four short years or a lifetime ago depending on the mood I am in.

I was running at the time. I was always running in those days but it's hard to win when you're running from yourself. I like people, I really do and I make friends easily, maybe too easily but I've come lately to like them best at a little distance. As a youth I had as many friends as anyone but as we grew up some differences began to show as they found jobs or got married and many things changed. I began to see friends as a luxury I couldn't afford to keep up with. They seemed to think I should settle down like them or at the very least get a job and show some reliability. And there is the rub because despite growing up in a family addicted to the grindstone, I have never been a subscriber to the work ethic. I know what I like and what I don't, and work of any description is #1on my automatic avoidance list.

The few who still admitted to being friends of mine were, it seemed, all in on a scheme to end my freewheeling ways. I would be invited to share a meal only to discover there was someone else at the gathering; usually someone who knew of a great job opportunity that would be right up my alley. Or worse yet, there would be a girl my hostess hoped would take on the challenge of trying to shape me up. After one particularly close call I simply swore off old friends and became a drifter.

From then on I made it my style to move around a lot. Of course like anyone else I had to work now and then or starve so taking a new job became something I found myself doing rather often though with increasing reluctance. The less I worked the less I wanted to work and the more I wanted to idle about by myself. But since I'm neither smart enough nor lucky enough to acquire my grocery funds any other way, the time invariably came when I had to sign up for another stint as a wage earner. As much as possible I arranged to work during the winter and saved my money toward a summer of freedom when the climate is more agreeable to footloose wanderers.

Despite the fact that I seldom managed to last more than a month or two at any job, for some reason I have never understood my various employers have always seemed to like and trust me. They mistake the curiosity that drives me to ask questions for a genuine interest in my work and that has often led to my moving on all the sooner. If that sounds strange it's nothing new—more than one person has advanced the word strange when trying to describe me. My last employer probably uses stronger wording than that whenever he thinks of me. I can't blame him either for how could he have anticipated my aversion to even tiny doses of responsibility.

He ran a small trucking business from an office near his home in Prince George where he dispatched his dozen or so vehicles. Some of them were long distance highway rigs but I drove a small delivery van for him seldom ranging more than a hundred miles from town. It was an easy run with no tight scheduling, lots of customers to talk to with no fear of forming commitments and generally a minimum of complications. It was made to order for me and could easily have become a bad habit. But one day in

April when I was in the office to shoot the breeze with the boss and as usual to check what was happening with the other trucks, he asked me to take over the dispatching. He also asked me to move into his house and take care of that too while he and his wife took a month's vacation—right over top of all his more senior employees!

I was so appalled that for one of the few times in my life I was speechless. When I finally did regain the use of my voice I read him out as if I were the boss and he the erring hired hand. Then I stomped indignantly out and I haven't seen him since. When my final pay cheque came to my general delivery address I was still so angry that I tore it into little pieces and mailed it right back to him. It was a panicky performance but a fair sample of my reaction when my efforts to do a job well were mistaken as a desire for advancement. Anyway, it was pretty well getting into springtime so I would have been leaving him soon no matter what.

The following autumn I held off as long as I could, a bit too long as it turned out, so when I started checking jobs I found all the good ones were filled. I was now faced with the choice of shipping out to the boonies to pile lumber at a sawmill or, heaven forbid, becoming a logger and earning my pay for a change. So I fought it out a while longer and though my stomach kept telling me I was starving to death, I knew better, I had been hungry before. But the long cold nights of November finally rousted me from my inadequate shelter and sent me to the employment office where having piled lumber before and knowing it's really not that bad compared to freezing hungry, I signed up to go to a place called Rainy Mountain. I thought I knew the country well but this one I had never heard of. I was grumpy and obviously unhappy so as I accepted the advance of a rail ticket to my newest home, the lady behind the desk tried to cheer me up—a lost cause if there ever was one.

"You'll enjoy your job at Rainy Mountain," she said, smiling, "there are lots of pretty girls out there."

I knew she was pulling my leg and I told her so. I also had to ask where the place was. "It's east of here, alongside the Rockies, there's no highway so that's why you get the train ticket."

"Hmff," I snorted, "after six months snowed in out there anything in a skirt will look pretty."

She just laughed at me. "Oh you'll see when you get there why the little town is famous up and down the line."

As I staggered off the train in the middle of the night half sick after being awakened from a poor sleep, there was this flatdeck truck taking on a load from the express car. All around was darkness and forest—let the train and the truck leave—turn to face the woods and one might as well be standing here a century ago. With this disheartening thought in mind I wandered along the track as the train pulled out knowing the truck would be my ride to camp and a bunkhouse I would call home for awhile. It was snowing a wet heavy stuff that clung to everything it touched and a smallish person was struggling to cover the load with a canvas tarp.

A definitely feminine voice called sharply to me. "Come on and lend a hand will you and we'll get down to town all the sooner."

That was different enough to have me wondering as I helped clumsily to spread and tie down the tarp.

"Have you been drinking?" she asked even more sharply.

"No. I just haven't slept or eaten properly for the last few days." Weeks would have been closer to the truth.

There was a hesitation then she said, "Okay, climb in."

That's when I realized she had been going to tell me to ride on the back. As I closed the door she went on conversationally, "A lot of the boys have hangovers when they come from town and I don't like the mess in my truck so if you get sick put it out the window or give me time to stop."

"I won't get sick," I promised, red-faced in the darkness.

"What's your contract?" she asked with confidence and authority in her voice.

"I beg your pardon?"

"Your job. What job have you come to fill?"

"Lumber piler."

"Oh! You'll go on the green chain." Then after a pause she added, "we were also expecting a truck driver tonight, in fact we need one badly, have you ever driven?"

"Just on highway a bit, I've never hauled logs."

"'Fraid that won't do here, we need a driver with wintertime mountain experience." She then proceeded to demonstrate a fair degree of wintertime mountain experience herself on the way down the hill. It was a fast wild ride considering the bad visibility and slippery road but soon we entered the mill yard. She drove up to a huge frame building but swung to the right in front of it and continued along a road, or street, with a lot of small, more or less houses on each side. "That was the office that I turned in front of and the cookhouse is the long, odd-shaped building across from it. Breakfast is on cafeteria style from 6 a.m. till 7:30. After you've eaten, report to the office dressed for work and someone there will assign you to your job."

She stopped in front of one of the bunkhouses. "You will find an empty bunk in there, just be quiet as other men are sleeping."

With my duffel bag rescued from under the tarp on the back of the truck I was about to close the cab door when she spoke again. "Oh, and the commissary is in the east wing of the office building, it's open from seven in the morning to nine in the evening every day but Sunday. If you need any work clothes or boots or mitts you will find we have a good supply in all sizes. Good night."

I kicked the snow off my boots before stepping onto the narrow, covered porch and opened the door to an entry room where a small oil space heater hummed away, its electric circulating fan blowing warm air generously. The place smelled, or at first impression I could almost say stank, of wet wool pants, sweaty flannel shirts, hot felt insoles and drying rubber boots. But after being out of work for longer than was good, the place struck me as downright homey and no more or less than I had expected.

The only light in here came from the open door of the washroom straight across from the outside entry. It was just enough to show the source of the smells as work clothes hung to dry on nails and lines around, above and behind the stove. It also showed a wide open doorway to each side. A glance through the door to my right revealed a sparsely furnished room about ten by fourteen feet in size with two beds in the shadows at the back. Both cots were occupied but a check of the other room turned up an empty bed in which I was soon enjoying the luxury of clean sheets and a soft mattress for the first time in a while. That's when it finally came to me just before sleep did that beyond the faintest shadow of a doubt, I had just met the most intriguing woman in my world.

If pressed for detail I would have to admit that the only women seriously in my world so far are the lovely fictional ladies I'd met in the tons of novels I read every chance I got. But there was mystery here! There had to be or she would not be out in the middle of the night hauling strange men to their new quarters and doing it with such competence and unassailable dignity. She was so bundled up for the weather tonight, parka hood and all that I really hadn't seen her yet but I know that when I do she was going to be the prettiest girl I have met in a long time. In my mind there is no room for it to be otherwise.

My roommate turned out to be an early riser and seemed to think I should be too. His name was Dean, he was probably about fifty, built wide but not tall. He had long greying hair and a thick, wild beard that could be called any of several colours. Without the beard he might have looked only forty for all I can tell.

The two in the other room, I was informed, are Archie and Tag. I never did learn what Tag is short for. Dean and I went to the cookhouse together but the others were in no hurry. I ate gratefully and slowly then when it passed seven o'clock I went looking for the commissary to get some warm mitts and, I guess, just to size the place up.

The office building looked even bigger now that I was close up to it than it did in the truck lights last night. As I walked along the front to get to the commissary I decided it had once been two entirely separate but parallel buildings that were later joined by a large central addition to make one huge structure. A bell rang as I opened and closed the door but no one came right away so I wandered on in. One look around and I abandoned all thought of referring to it as a commissary. It's really a full-fledged general store with everything working men might want, from peanuts to pop, from caulk boots to hardhats and even radios, record players and you name it. But that's not all, they obviously cater to a sizable family trade as well judging by the complete grocery and small hardware lines. Men's clothing and shoes take up a large area but so do women's and children's needs.

To my right as I entered is the cashier's counter and on the left a cubicle with a closed door and a wicket-type window also closed. This must be the post office and sounds of a mailbag being dumped and mail sorted indicate that the postmaster was busy. The rest of the room which overall must measure about thirty by sixty feet, is taken up with crosswise running rows of shelves and display counters.

I found the type of mitts I wanted and walked back to the front where I was startled to find that a young woman had materialized from somewhere, but not from the post office as the sound of letters being sorted into wall slots or boxes still came from that partitioned-off area. Something inside me did a flip-flop for this raven-haired beauty, surely the girl from the truck last night. I nodded to her as I put my purchase on the counter but got absolutely no sign of recognition.

"New account," she said, more as a statement than a question, "what's your name please?"

I told her and watched as she block-lettered it on the end of a new counter bill book. She was much younger than I had thought last night, not more than eighteen or nineteen, but there was a coldness in her coal-black eyes and the line of her mouth was straight, hard and firm. So much for dreams I mentally shrugged, next time I will remind myself to make judgment by full daylight. She entered my purchase onto the first page of the book then stuffed it into a row of others just like it except for the different names printed large on their exposed ends. A noisy group of mill workers pushed in past me and fanned out around the chocolate bar display. I was halfway out the door when the post office wicket banged open and a familiar voice said, "Not much mail today, Jo, nothing at all for you and Terry."

I would have gone back to where I could see her inside the now open post office but the one she called Jo, at the store counter, was looking coolly at me as though wondering if I were stuck in the doorway. I took the hint and left but I was elated to find my truck-driving girl even if all I saw of her was a mop of jet black hair not unlike that which I had already admired on the other girl. Sisters no doubt and sure to be equally attractive.

Now that fact should have meant nothing more to me than that my snap judgment in the darkness last night was correct. Yet in the very back corner of my mind now came the illogical notion —intuition—wishful thinking—that she could be very dangerous to me. That ensured I would not be here long! On that cheerful thought I reported to the office.

Most places I've worked it was easy to tell who the boss was but here I ran into some confusion as there seemed to be four of them. Two of the younger three were shouting insults at each other, mixing in something about lots of logs to move and not enough trucks on the road. I was saved from the dilemma of having to make a choice by the oldest of the four who waved me over to a desk at one side.

"You are the lumber piler who came in last night?"

I nodded.

"Just sit down here and fill out these forms, sign them, then bring them to me over at the counter."

It didn't take long to fill out the forms with my vital statistics, I'd worked briefly at so many different places that I know the routine by heart. The man showed no surprise when I handed him the completed forms so quickly, he just glanced at them to get my name.

"Okay, Byron, I'm John Morrow and these are my three boys. Allan here is plant manager for the sawmill and planer, you stick with him and he will put you to work. The big tall one there is Tom who is our woods boss in charge of the logging crews. You can ignore him and also Terry who is transport manager. The logging trucks and all the smaller rolling stock are his problem."

I knew then that Rainy Mountain was going to be different because nowhere else that I'd worked, had I been treated to an introduction to the brass. And if that wasn't enough they all gave me a handshake and a nod ranging from pleasantly interested to no worse than indifferent. John Morrow smiled in a friendly way that I was not used to seeing in management-type people then continued, "And I just run the office with some help from my girls." When he moved off to the other side of the room, I assumed that I was dismissed.

The argument over logs and trucks that had been in progress when I came in was now shelved but plainly not forgotten. All three of the younger Morrows were glaring at each other like dogs circling hoping for one more good bite but only if someone was foolish enough to turn his back.

Terry was the one that caught my eye, he was not a large man but the air of confidence about him more than made up for any lack in size. He fairly glowed with some inner charge, his reckless eyes saed "look out world, here I come." He had the blackest hair I had ever seen, so black there were blue undertones, it was trimmed long but tidy. Unlike the others his complexion hinted that he had just come from a vacation in the sun. He was in basically the same rough clothing as the rest of us, flannel shirt and wool work pants, but on him everything fit with a neatness that defied description. Though shorter than average he would stand out in any group of men. He appeared to be the youngest of the brothers, probably in his early twenties.

All three of them wore exactly the same type leather-topped, rubber-bottomed boots but that was the only similarity. At first impression, they were certainly different in appearance for brothers. Tom, looked to be two or three years older than Terry and he was big—not fat, just big. Though every bit as well proportioned as his younger brother, at six foot four or five he towered over all of us. I was not used to looking up that far at people so he caught my respect right away. Unlike Terry, his hair and Allan's also, was as yellow as gold is supposed to be and that was the only similarity between them.

Tom was angry and didn't care who knew it. Allan too was angry but only his eyes gave him away, his face was smooth and calm. He was plainly the oldest and came between his brothers in size being quite average in build and for that matter about the same as the father.

The air between them was loaded with something akin to dynamite and I watched with interest to see what might develop. None of them took notice of me but each seemed reluctant to start the ball rolling. I watched Terry, thinking of what the girl in the post office had said to the one at the store counter, "not much mail today Jo, none at all for you and Terry." So Jo must be Terry's wife and a striking good-looking couple they would be. A door closed and after a moment of shuffling noises a woman's footsteps came click clicking from somewhere back of the office but evidently she went into an adjoining room for no one came in sight. One of the women from the store, I presumed, as there were bound to be connecting doors or hallways even though each has its own outside entrance.

The footsteps served for some reason as a signal to the three men for they all relaxed and Allan turned to me, "Byron, is it? Come on, it's just about time to go, I'll show you where your job is." We hiked along one edge of the lumber storage area past a large repair shop with vehicles and machines of many types parked in confusion around it. The sawmill was next with a big log yard adjacent. While the lumber yard appeared to be pretty well-stocked with lumber piled for air drying the log yard is nearly empty. In my limited experience that seemed a normal enough situation for early winter. Since this was a wet country 80 to 90 percent of the year's logging would be done over the next four or five months while the roads were frozen hard and snow and frost made it possible to work on otherwise boggy ground. For people in the sawmill and logging game in this part of BC the busy time of year was closing in.

It turned out that Dean and my other two bunkhouse friends also worked on the green chain and Allan Morrow simply handed me over to Dean for instructions. The four strands of chain that carred the lumber out from the sawmill were covered with a roof that extended over the walkway on which we worked but the lifts of lumber that we hand piled on each side were only partly sheltered.

Dean grinned but said nothing as he handed me a big scoop shovel. It didn't take much expertise to see that the first effort of the day was to shovel away last night's accumulation of snow, after that it was just like any other lumber piling job I'd worked at. Archie was the lumber grader and that surprised me because he seemed very young to have had the necessary training and experience. He stood where the rough boards dropped onto the chains and put a mark on each one after judging its quality. Dean, Tag and I along with a man I hadn't met, raced up and down the walkway stacking boards in their allotted piles as indicated by size and Archie's grade marks.

Every time I got near Dean he enthusiastically did his best to convince me that we had the best job in the world. We were out in the clean fresh air he pointed out, with a roof over us, no dust, a minimum of noise, no responsibility but enough work to make us hungry and all the good food we could eat. Add to that an excellent bunkhouse to live in and what more could a man ask for? He might have been right at that, he probably saw a lot of helpers come and go and, looking back, I like to think he wanted me to stay. At any rate the job was rapidly settling into routine—a tiring routine—by 10 a.m. when the mill shut down to sharpen or change saws whichever it was they did. Dean and I put our coats on and sat on a lumber pile sipping coffee from a vacuum bottle while down at the sawmill end of the chain, the other three were doing the same.

Suddenly I became aware that there is a minor commotion within the mill then two young women sauntered out of the same doorway that Allan Morrow had entered earlier in the morning. Archie, Tag and their friend called good-natured taunts to them but the girls just laughed and waved in reply. The first and most obvious thing about them was that they were dressed identically in long red coats that swept below their knees. A black trim stripe down the front of the coats matched the colour of their high-topped, high-heeled boots. A stray and useless thought flitted through my mind that those boots were too small and neat to have any warmth in them. The necks of the coats seemed to rise straight up, like short stove pipes, to the girls' chins the same way turtle neck sweaters did. Thick waves of golden yellow hair, with odd streaks of darkness mixed in, cascaded over their shoulders and as they came closer I could see that they were openly and frankly examining me. About then I also realized if there was a difference between them it was beyond me to see it except that one wores a white artificial flower in her hair while the other had a red one. The nearest, the one wearing the white flower, fluttered her eyes to Dean. "Hi Dean, who's your cute friend? "

"This is my good friend and roommate, Byron." Then he added, "Now you can both come and toss your boots under our bunks." Until that moment I thought Dean was a pretty decent fellow, but now I felt betrayed. I looked at him wondering if my hearing has suddenly become flawed but he just sat there grinning and seeming quite pleased with himself. I thought I was already surprised and embarrassed but now I found out what the words surprised and embarrassed really mean. The girl squared off to us, blue eyes blazing and cursed Dean out like nothing I'd ever heard before and I'd not led a sheltered life. She cursed him long and loud with obvious growing satisfaction until she finally ran out of steam and stalked haughtily away when her sister swung to face me. "And that goes double for you, buster," then she vigorously added a few choice phrases of her own that no doubt she felt fit the situation. A dozen half running steps caught her up with her look-alike and they went off toward the office with their backs straight and heads high.

I turned an unbelieving eye to Dean who was quite literally holding his sides while he laughed. Down the green chain the other three were also in the throes of great mirth. I distinctly developed the feeling that I had been victimized, it was a show that's put on at first opportunity for every newcomer I would've bet. But I sure didn't feel like laughing. "My God man! You've got some nerve talking like that to those girls," I said to him when he finally quieted down enough to hear me again.

"Think nothing of it Byron, that's just the twins for you," he said as if that were supposed to explain everything. He shrugged, having himself under control finally. "What a pair those two are. Teamsters tongues in angels' faces. They're—like their brothers—bold, arrogant, inconsiderate and sometimes downright nasty but usually a lot of fun to have around."

"That was fun? " I asked.

"Oh, that was just to keep them in practice. Man, if I hadn't said something to cue them in we would have gotten a real raking over the coals." I shook my head in wonder as he went on, "They've got to be the worst tomboys ever turned loose in the Rocky Mountains. They grew up with the free run of the whole place including the working areas and the men's bunkhouses. No one would ever hurt them but I suppose it's not surprising that they picked up a lot of rough and ready language. When they were small, a lot of us thought it was fun to teach them the four letter alphabet. What none of us foresaw was the pleasure they would take from their new knowledge. " He paused and gazed into the distance and I felt like I was briefly forgotten before he spoke again. "But remember one thing about them as well as their brothers. They are all like their old man in one way and that is—when they call you friend, there is not enough they can do for you if you need help."

I must still have looked dazed to him for he continued to explain, "Man, I suppose that under those fancy new clothes they are still tomboys at heart. They used to run around dressed in blue jeans and men's work shirts and in the last couple of years what they did for those shirt pockets ought to be against the Compensation Board safety laws 'cause no man should be exposed to such distractions on the job."

"Fellow needn't look. Why did they come out of the mill?"

"With them you'll look or wish you had! " Then he explained, "There are family homes over the other side, I guess they've been visiting and are headed home. If the mill is in their way they go through it, not around, even if it's running."

"You must have been here quite a while."

"Man, I've been here, and I mean right here, piling lumber on this green chain since years before they were born and I guess that was at least sixteen or seventeen years ago."

"By their brothers, do you mean the Morrow boys? Are they John Morrow's daughters? "

"That's right. They are Pat and Jan Morrow. And in case you're wondering why they aren't away in town for high school, they're taking it here by correspondence. They seem to work their own hours," he added to account for the girls' appearance during what should be studying time.

"You called them the twins, are the dark haired girls in the store also twins? "

"Ah, you've met Ember and Jo have you? But sure, Ember meets the trains so you saw her last night and Jo runs the store counter part of the time. Since you have new mitts I assume you've been to the store." Finally he answered my question. "Twins? Well, yes and no. We sometimes call them the Dark Twins, mostly in jest, because of the black hair they both have and how much they look alike but actually they are sisters-in-law. Jo is married to Terry Morrow and Ember is a sister, a few years older, to those diamonds in the rough that just left us. How a man can go out in the world and find a wife who looks so much like his own sister is a mystery to me. It must have been a shock for the girls when they met, like going around a corner and coming up against a mirror. But while they may look alike they are actually quite different. Ember is like her mother—or she is now that she's grown up. They are the quiet steady ones who hold the family together while Jo is—or at least was—a wild one. She's a good match for Terry."

He winked at me then and said. "You may find it hard to believe but, man, if I hadn't said something like that or worse to the twins they really would have been disappointed in me. Especially with a new man here to impress."

Well, that gave me plenty to think about as the mill started spewing out boards again and we went back to work. I had just warmed up enough to take my coat off when a huge but very old and tired-looking logging truck lurched over from the shop and halted near us. It was high and narrow at the front and carried a trailer with a long wood-pole reach, or tongue, extending out over top the cab. This appeared to be my day for surprises because Terry Morrow leapt down from the cab and came directly to me with something very much on his mind. "Hey, kid," he yelled as he came within range, "want to be a log hauler?"

He couldn't be any older than I was so I didn't appreciate him calling me kid. There was an ornery streak, about a mile wide, in me that came out at times like this so I did my best to growl, "Not particularly," even though I must have blinked at this amazing offer. To drive log truck must certainly be easier work than piling lumber but the man simply rubbed me the wrong way so I turned my back to him and grabbed the next board.

"Aw, come on," he cajoled, still at the top of his voice, "Ember says you are a truck driver and here's a truck that needs driving. Why spend the winter freezing your feet off out here stacking boards when you can have your own heated cab to ride around in?"

Now that was a powerful argument and I felt the animosity slipping away as my lazy bone fought it out with my ornery streak. His sister Ember knew very well that I was not a real truck driver but she must have said something to him of our brief conversation last night. He in turn must have been so desperate for drivers that he was willing to scrape the bottom of the barrel.

"But I've only driven on highway and not much of that, I've never hauled logs nor even pulled a trailer."

"That's okay, I'll show you everything you need to know."

I still shook my head, "They'll be short-handed here if I leave."

"That's okay too," he said, "I'll stop at the office and square it with Allan. Lumber pilers are easy to come by—a dime a dozen."

I guess that did it. Something new and foreign in the back of my mind insisted that I wanted to be more than a dime-a-dozen lumber piler and truck driver seemed a step in the right direction. As I picked up my coat I cast a glance at Dean. He looked so crestfallen that I almost changed my mind but not quite. I followed Terry over to the waiting truck but as I walked alongside the tall front end, the smell of hot oil and leaking diesel fuel almost stopped me. 'This is not good,' a voice inside told me! But I was no longer in a mood to listen—if Terry's sister, Ember, thought I could be a truck driver then I would climb the steps to that high cab door and become one. Terry was already behind the wheel and he crunched the shift lever into gear before I could get settled or even close the door. It felt like the front wheels came off the ground as we lurched ahead, my door slamming shut of its own accord with the movement, quite indifferent as to whether I was fully inside or not.

"Clutch is a little grabby," he confided loudly over the roar of the engine. He shifted gears at least six times just going to the office and our top speed with engine screaming still wasn't over twenty miles an hour. He made a panic stop in front of the office and opened his door to jump out. "Wait here I'll be right back—just got to tell Allan that I've stolen you."

It was several minutes before he came back with his face

flushed and angry so I guess they had a row. Just as he opened his door to climb in a red metal arm with lettering on it that said LOW AIR dropped from a slot above the windshield and swung like a pendulum in front of the driver's position. At the same time a loud obnoxious buzzer started up its irritating dirge somewhere under the instrument panel. Terry punched his foot down on the accelerator and in a moment the buzzer stopped and the red arm slowly climbed back up into its hiding place.

"Got a bit of an air leak." he said. "Nothing to worry about, just have to keep the engine RPMs up to make the compressor run faster. We've only got one operational air tank left on this rig so the air pressure drops kind of fast. It's got other problems too but these air brakes always fail safe anyway as long as you keep them set up. If you lose your air while coming down the hill there are springs that will automatically set the brakes and bring you to a stop until you get your air built up again. Just keep your engine running fast and you'll have no trouble. You probably know all that anyway."

I didn't bother telling him that the truck I had driven was only a small one and air brakes were a mystery to me. The air pressure had climbed well back into the safe range by then so he pushed a knob on the dash, engaged the gears and we took off up the hill toward the railroad tracks. I knew right away that if he expected me to drive like he was doing then I was not going to make it as a log hauler. But as if he read my mind he cleared the issue right away.

"Now I'm only going to haul one load while you ride along and watch, next trip it's all yours. I'm not going to go with you and get you all uptight, I'm just taking you on this first run to show you where to go and what to do."

I nodded noncommittally.

"Don't worry too much about procedures at the log landing or the mill, the landing crew knows what to do and they will help you out. Same thing at the log dump in the mill yard, just get this old girl up and down the hill with the stakes full of logs and that's all I ask." He watched something intently in the rear-view mirror for a few seconds before returning to the issue at hand. "Actually

I want you to drive carefully and don't worry about making time until you get the feel of the machine. In other words," he grinned at me, "don't drive like I do—drive like I say!"

At that instant we rounded a corner to meet a big haystack of a load of logs bearing down on us and no room to pass. I just about put my head through the windshield as Terry slammed on the brakes, juggled the gearshift levers and began backing down the hill at a fair clip while watching in the rear-view mirror to stay on the road. In the meantime the loaded truck slowed to our speed and when we came to a wide spot, Terry swung out to let the other truck go by. Then for a moment he rattled one of the shift levers around. "Seems to be getting loose but you'll get used to it. Another thing I should mention is don't shut off the engine unless you have to because it won't always start from in here. Sometimes you have to crawl underneath and short out the starter terminals with a screwdriver. That's what that's for." He pointed to a screwdriver poked into a hole in the dash that may have been recently drilled just for the purpose.

As we started back up the hill, Terry explained the meeting and passing procedures to me. He picked up a few gears as we crossed the flat at the tracks only to drop one again as the grade steepened once more.

Up till now I felt that if he did like he said and left me alone to figure things out for myself I could handle the job okay. But now we came to a side road that turned off to the left and climbed steeply away from the main line. It was narrow, winding, and it tilts first one way and then the other. Over the long, square engine hood in front of me it looked more like a bicycle track than a truck road. I could now understand why, except for the steering axle, every wheel on both the truck and trailer was wearing tire chains. I had noticed too, back at the mill, that there were a lot of missing cross chains and even some repaired with haywire. I also remembered that they were of a smooth-link, non-ice-biting variety. Even with the weight of the trailer perched on the very tail end of the truck, we still spun and slewed in a few places.

"Once you are on this road you don't have to worry about any other logging trucks. This landing up ahead of us will be yours alone to haul from. If you can't keep up to the loggers, we may send in another truck to help you but we will tell you about it and you and the other driver can make your own arrangements to travel together or meet in certain places. On the other hand, if you run out of logs to haul from here, we may send you farther out the main line for a few loads, or you might have to do some work on the truck in the shop." He grinned, "This old girl needs lots of work but it's a good truck to learn on, she's a tough old bird and I doubt you can hurt her. A lot of drivers have learned their trade right here in this old heap including me," and he patted the steering wheel fondly. "We have newer and better trucks and once you get the hang of it you can have one of them."

We now rounded a sharp corner with a rock cut on one side and a sheer drop on the other to face the steepest grade we had encountered yet. As Terry floor boarded the throttle to gain speed he explained, "This is the only spot that might give you trouble—going up is okay—just keep her chugging and she'll chew her way up as long as you haven't lost any tire chains and there's not too much new snow. But coming down on a day like this when there's a bit of fresh snow between each trip, you will slide and there's nothing you can do about it. That fresh, wet snow is like greased ball bearings under your tires." We passed under a big, house-sized boulder that partly overhung the road and we seemed to be over the worst part of the hill. Terry continued to shout at me, "As long as you can hold your load under control to this point you're okay, you can slide or shift up from here and still make the corner below. But if you lose your traction and go into a slide above here, you've had the biscuits. Don't hesitate—jump out and let the truck go. They're building new trucks every day but you only get one shot at life. Incidentally, we haven't lost a truck yet." He grinned and patted the wheel again.

Finally we eased over the crest of the last bit of the hill and I breathed easier to see relatively flat ground around us. We were on a large bench a lot flatter than most of the mountainside and we soon came to a landing where a Cat was being unhooked from a turn of trees it had skidded in from the woods. A hard-hatted man was working on the skidded timber with a chainsaw while a rubber-tired loader moved the long logs to a pile that threatened to take up the whole landing area. Terry made a quick turn-around and backed alongside a ramp of frozen dirt that gave the loader some height advantage over the truck. The loader immediately hustled over to us and the operator expertly lifted the trailer from the back of the truck while Terry ran us ahead a few feet. Terry took me to the back and initiated me to the proper technique for hooking up the trailer brake lines and the trailer hitch with it's compensator arrangement. It turned the reach into nothing more than a steering linkage while the load itself served to pull the trailer along behind us. In no time at all we were set up for loading. It was snowing so hard I could hardly see the loader.

"That's what lets us get around these sharp corners without having to build wide, expensive roads so don't forget to throw off the towing latch on that compensator. Without slack you could find yourself in difficulty, even bound up and unable to turn a corner or straighten out after one. It's easy to accidentally be looking at the road from down in the devil club patch without stacking the cards against yourself. So remember!" He tapped the hitch significantly.

Then we climbed back into the cab and he gave me a lecture on the various controls, the trailer brake valve and so much more that I knew I wouldn't remember half of it. But I got what he said about the emergency valve, that was the one that, to use his wording, 'dynamited' the brakes and brought the truck to a halt if the air pressure fell below sixty-pounds per square-inch in the air storage tanks bolted into the frame. Tank—singular—on this truck—with problems! By the time we had reached the landing I had firmly decided that I would never dare take a load of logs down that impossibly steep and narrow road. Now, listening to him explain everything matter-of-factly in common terms, it all began to look rather simple and certainly easier than piling lumber so I decided to reserve judgment until we were unloaded down at the mill. Then I would make up my mind whether to come back up myself for a load or to ask for my old job again. Several times while the load was being put on, the 'low air' arm dropped and the buzzer sounded, spurring Terry to step down on the throttle until the air pressure was back up in the safe range. Finally the load was on, the wrappers were tightened up around it and we swayed off toward the edge of the hill Terry shifting up a few gears on the way, making new tracks in the fresh snow over the icy ruts we had chewed down to on the way up.

"Now the big secret in going downhill on slippery road," Terry resumed his monologue bellowing to be heard over the many noises of the truck, "is to keep your wheels turning. Even if you are sliding a bit, as long as your wheels are turning, they are holding you back some. But if you apply too much air and lock up your wheels you might as well be on a toboggan 'cause you are going to go down—fast. So it's best to keep watch in the mirrors to see that all the wheels are turning and if some aren't then you release the brake until they do turn and maybe even apply a little power to catch your drivers up closer to your ground speed. And don't let the engine over-rev," he added.

All this time we were approaching the drop-off where we will start down the hill and I distinctly had butterflies in my stomach. But his confident talk has reassured me that all will be well so as we broke over the crest of the hill I was leaning forward to watch our back wheels in the mirror on my side of the truck with the engine brake rattling my eardrums.

We were in trouble right away. Several things happened almost all at once that took only seconds to do their damage but it took much longer to tell about. First there was a loud explosion of escaping air somewhere under the cab, then a deadly silence behind me as the exhaust of the engine brake was stilled. It felt like something from behind has given us a mighty boost as our traction with the road broke loose. Already the low air indicator was swinging wildly but if the buzzer was doing its thing, then my senses were too busy elsewhere to hear it. All I had time to think of was that the emergency valve had set our spring brakes and we were shooting forward with all our drive wheels locked and sliding on the icy, snow-covered road.

The engine was dead—stalled! Terry grabbed the main gearshift but it flopped loose in his hand. The look on his face seemed to say this was all impossible and could't really be happening. He instantly tried to turn us into the cutbank to run up the slope and flop the truck and load onto its side in the middle of the road, normally an unthinkable circumstance but right now looking pretty good compared to our other options. At the same time he was stabbing at the engine starter button but we were already bouncing so much that he couldn't seem to find it or else it didn't work and he gave up after a few tries. With the power steering lying dead alongside the engine, he fought the wheel with all his strength but gained little. At first, when ditching might have worked, the front wheels refused to climb out of their slippery ruts. When they did leap sideways against the hillside it had become too steep and abrupt to climb. We crashed against the cutbank, rebounded to crash again and again with gut-wrenching shock. The front and side of the truck and the front log bunk tore great gouges in the nearly vertical bank and ripped out chunks of rock that were flung over and around the cab and even sent skittering on down the road ahead at great speed. Bumper, fender and sheet metal in general from steps and fuel tank melted into the shower of dirt, rock and snow. Miraculously the windshield remained unbroken. The front tire on my side blew out probably with a roar that should have been deafening but my hearing seemed to be overwhelmed and the flying chunks of rubber were what impressed me. All that should have checked our speed but it didn't. We were going faster and faster.

"Jump! " Terry yelled at me but for a second I sat frozen until his next shout jarred me into action.

"Get out, or ride with it, I'm leaving!"

So I jumped. My last memory of him was of his struggle against the nearly useless wheel, trying now to pull us away from that murderous hillside to give me a chance to jump without being ground under. Mine was the uphill side with the steep cut in dirt and rock streaking past at higher and higher speed. The bouncing, pitching motion of the runaway truck spoiled my leap and sent me cartwheeling helplessly through the air. I hit in snow but it wasn't soft, there was solid rock or frozen dirt hidden in it. Stunned beyond hurting by the impact but still conscious of the danger behind me I grabbed at anything, as I skidded and rolled, to keep from falling back to the road under those sliding wheels. It seemed to take all day for the truck and trailer to go by behind me. Though I couldn't see it with my face pressed tight against the snowy bank I could feel it if that makes any sense.

Finally it was gone with a rumble of tumbling logs and a scream of dying metal. As the roaring in my ears faded I slowly let go and slid, then rolled backward till I lay face up partly on the inside track of the road. No matter how I try I could not move. My field of vision narrowed till all I could see were a few tree tops far above leaning in over the road. They went around and around. Pretty soon I couldn't see, or hear, or feel anything.

I still break out in a cold sweat just thinking about it and I certainly have lost all ambition toward driving log truck.

Feeling a chill creeping into the cab with me I turn the heat up a bit and flick on the inside light to look at my watch. Still fifteen minutes till No. 8 is due and it will be a little late because it had to wait at a passing track a few miles to the west for No. 9 and that earlier train had been behind schedule. I roll my window down to check that the night breeze is still coming from the west. It usually does right here though it may be different down at the mill. I like to park facing it so the exhaust fumes are carried away from the front end of my truck where the heater air intake is. No use asphyxiating while I wait if it can be avoided.

By the time I woke up in the hospital it seemed that the staff were laying bets on whether I ever would come out of it or if I did, in what condition I would be. At least that's what they told me but it was probably part of the therapy. I saw no cause for alarm on one score at any rate, my mind was clear as a bell. That is, right up to the moment that the twins were reaming out Dean and I. From then until I woke up in a four-bed ward, the space of time is roughly equal to a snap of the fingers so far as I was concerned.

They told me I had a fractured skull and a broken neck besides numerous less serious injuries. A lot of healing had already occurred and as the days went by the details gradually came back to me until after awhile I had things pretty well sorted out. But it escaped me to wonder about Terry—that part was still in the blackout zone.

Somewhere along in that period the doctor told me that I was exceedingly lucky since only my legs were affected by the damage in my neck. That didn't sound like all that much good luck to me but he assured me that, although it might take a lot of hard work and time, eventually I should walk again, perhaps quite normally.

I regret to have to admit that I was a poor patient, I was so sorry for myself, so down in the dumps, that I must have been quite a trial for the nurses and the therapist. The doctor, in my opinion, didn't help any either. He wandered in once in a while, asked a few questions, prodded my legs a bit, then invariably when I asked what he thought, he would mutter something that sounded like, "hmmm," and walk away. If he was trying to make me angry he was succeeding, but if he was trying to win my vote for anything he failed on a grand scale. It took the twins to do that. They waltzed in one afternoon, all smiles and brightness.

"Hi, By," they said in perfect timing then looked at each other and grinned. One went on from there, "Boy are you the lucky one, just think, if you hadn't landed on your head you might have been badly hurt."

They stayed over an hour and most of the conversation was in that light, happy manner. I learned among other things, that they were in town with their mother on a one-day shopping trip and would be returning to Rainy Mountain on that night's train. More than once their rank talk had me blushing with embarrassment and they seemed to think that was funny to no end.

All at once out of thin air I had to ask, "How is Terry? " There was dead silence for an agonizing long pause while I looked from one stricken face to the other and wished I hadn't asked.

"Terry didn't make it," they said almost together.

That put a damper on the party and they soon left but even then their natural exuberance was reviving and they both insisted that when I was well enough I was expected to return to Rainy Mountain. But at that moment Rainy Mountain was the very last place in the world that I wanted to see. In fact, I vowed it would take nothing less than the proverbial wild horses to drag me there.

2

Wild horses came disguised as financial necessity. The Compensation Board proved unwilling to support me in even the poor manner to which I was accustomed. I had, over the years, developed a number of bad habits, such as eating at least once a day and sleeping under something for a roof at night. Now I found that the size of my disability cheque was determined by the amount of my earnings prior to my accident. Since I had always arranged to be unencumbered as much as possible by minor inconveniences, such as an occupation, my earnings had been small. Accordingly, my pension calculated out to a sum that allowed me to indulge in food, or in lodgings, but not both. My years of deliberate unemployment had caught up to me with a vengeance and I felt no better for knowing the fault was entirely my own. It was a low blow and seemed all the worse having just come from the lap of luxury in the hospital. There was a tidy little sum which had built up while I enjoyed their hospitality that got me through to spring but I was soon looking around desperately for help, even a part time job would have done. But I hadn't enough brains for anything that could be done sitting down and being on crutches ruled out the type of work I ordinarily would have been able to handle. Of course I thought hard about the chance to dispatch trucks I had once been offered. If only I could have had that job now. Just while the boss took a vacation even. Or to have the cheque I had torn up! On one particularly bad day I actually looked up my former employer's phone number and several times I dialed part or all of it before chickening out and hanging up. In theory he still owed me that last pay but it was only one of many closed doors and burned bridges on my back trail that I lacked the gumption to try to open again. No one had ever hired me back a second time.

"I can't go backward in time," I thought, "I can only go forward."

A fine resolve! It was hard to understand how I got so quickly sidetracked from it but I could think of only one place where I might be taken in and fed a bit without looking for out-and-out welfare. So on a soft June night filled with mosquitoes and the promise of gentle rain I found myself on the eastbound passenger train with a ticket to Rainy Mountain and a big lump of pride in my throat that was tough chewing.

It did more or less occur to me that Morrows might not be glad to see me, but by the time I reached the point of desperation to actually board the train I really had no alternative. A ticket stub in the window clip beside me and the princely sum of twenty-seven cents in my pocket meant that once again my back trail is closed. If Morrows didn't want me around they would have to buy my passage to town and presumably feed me a few calories in the meantime.

My second arrival at Rainy Mountain was completely different and yet just the same as the first over half a year earlier had been. It was summer and the night lasted about long enough for darkness to fall and then steal away in the early morning mists. It was warm and it was wet, there was no wind and no drifting snow but same old flatdeck truck was being loaded at the express car and the same small person in the glow of her truck's cargo light was overseeing the operation and glancing occasionally down the track to see who and how many get off from the passenger cars.

As casually as one might comment on the weather Ember Morrow said to me as I reached her truck, "So, Byron, you've come back." At least she remembered me. Before I could answer with more than a nod she added, "Climb in, I'm ready to go, we can beat the next rain so I won't bother with the tarp."

It took no small effort to hoist myself into the truck cab without letting the effort show, but I managed and we were soon on our way. Ember double-clutched and shifted gears up and down as neatly as any professional driver while we flowed downhill around corners and the switchback like quicksilver from an old clay jug. It was a lesson in driving for she never once touched the brakes but slowed when needed by shifting down and even dropped the tires a fraction into the ditch on the inside of each of the sharper corners to help pull us around. If she was trying to frighten me, she failed because her control of the truck was so precise that there was nothing to fear—only to admire. She drove like her brother Terry—extremely well but right up on the edge. All the same—I'll bet not many willingly made a second trip down with her.

This time she took me to the bunkhouse nearest the store and just across from the cookhouse. By the time I untangled myself from the cab and got moving on the ground she had my meagre luggage and was leading the way to the dark-windowed building outlined in the headlight beams. She opened a screen door then an inner door, flipped a couple of switches and we had light on the porch and in the entry. She crossed to the door on the left turning on more lights as she went. The whole building was identical to the one I occupied last fall so briefly except the room was set up for one person. A good-sized table, more like a desk, and a pair of chairs took up the space and then some where the second bed would have been.

"It's a bit damp but you can get the heater going and have things dried out soon, or just leave the door open whenever it's not raining."

"It looks good," I said, "is there no one else staying here?"

"No, this and another bunkhouse were furnished like this for our foremen so they would have a bit of privacy and a place to do their bookwork. Now all the foremen are men with families and they have houses over in the married quarters. About the only use these get is when the occasional equipment salesman or mechanic stays over or during hunting or fishing season when some of Dad's business friends from town spend a few days with us. They usually prefer the 'cabin' atmosphere out here to staying with us at the house." She sniffed, somewhat indignantly I thought. "And just as well too. They seem more intent on having a party than a hunt. I'm sure it will be good for you here where you can set your own schedule without bothering others or being bothered by them."

I don't believe she noticed my nod of agreement.

"But if you would rather have company you can make your own arrangements, just talk to the bullcook before you move. In the meantime," she added, "I'm off to the warehouse, morning comes early whether I'm ready for it or not."

As she was leaving I had a thought and hobbled to the door to call after her. "You could use some help to unload the truck," I suggested. "I may be slow but I'm not totally useless."

She stopped and turned back to me, her features visible yet at the same time blurred by the reflected glow of the truck's headlights. Surprise was what I read on her face. "Well that's fine but we don't unload until tomorrow during any breaks we have from the store and post office." She anticipated my next question. "The weather is no problem at all because we have a truck bay right inside the warehouse so I just back it in, close the door, and we unload at our convenience."

"Okay, then I'll come and help tomorrow."

She regarded me briefly in silence before lifting and dropping a shoulder, "why not?"

In a moment she and her truck were gone and I turned to survey my new home. I could scarcely believe my luck. As Ember said, the place was damp and on second look it was also shabby and dirty, but some drying out and cleaning would soon fix that.

My last thoughts, before sleep came, were of the black-haired, grey-eyed girl who has just left. Last fall when she brought me down from the train I was tongue-tied with surprise and overawed by her competence and authority. But there had been something else too, something I have refused to think about until now because there was no room in my life for complications. There had been a definite spark of some sort pass between us that wintry night—it had added to my confusion by no small amount. Someday I was going to find out if she felt it too. "Fool, I scoffed," smiling in the darkness and glad no one knew my thoughts, "every man who comes here on the night train is bound to fall a little bit in love with her. She catches the imagination—that's all it is. Should I be any different?"

And yet—while I was searching for work in town—every time I thought of Rainy Mountain it was because first I found myself thinking of Ember Morrow. I couldn't then have given a description of her and I probably couldn't yet. Tomorrow I should finally meet her in the light of day and it was not possible she could fit the image my mind had built of her. I thought that if that tricky little character who shares a back corner of my mind had lured me here because of her—well—it was not a good reason for coming. Sure—I was broke—but I'd been there before and always survived. There are people you can go to when things get bad if you can make that deal with your pride. I wondered now if there was some hidden significance in the fact that every time I counted my nickels down to 'broke' tucked away in another pocket there was enough to buy a ticket to Rainy Mountain.

Like Ember said, morning came early, but though I was guilty of many sins, sleeping in was no longer one of them. I beat everyone to the cookhouse and was casually sipping coffee when Dean sauntered in looking like an ad for physical fitness. He glanced my way but chose to ignore me; then he looked again and when he had a plate full of bacon, eggs, and pancakes he came to my table and sat down across from me.

"Now I've got you placed," he said. "It's Byron, isn't it?"

"Right first guess."

"Man! When we put you on the train last winter I didn't think I'd ever see you again."

"I'm a slow learner I guess. I couldn't think of any place else to go."

"I don't mean that, I'd say it's good you came back. Shows you retained at least a little of what I told you."

I have to admit that I stared at him blankly.

He nodded toward the crutches propped against the table beside me. "I meant it when I told you that John takes care of his friends and employees, stick here like glue and you'll be okay."

I didn't remember him telling me anything quite like that but I fervently hope what he said was true. It was belatedly occurring to me that since John's son died while trying to teach me to drive truck, my needs might command a rather low priority rating around here.

"Man!" Dean said again. "When we flagged down that highball freight to ship you off to town, the way you looked and hardly breathing, I thought you'd croak before you got halfway. Ember said later that you didn't improve any on the way in either."

I guess my ears picked up another inch in length. "Ember said what?"

"She said, in fact, that you were sinking and even the ambulance crew that met the train figured you were gone at first."

"Now how would she know that?"

He gave me a look of mild surprise before he explained. "Well somebody had to go along to keep an eye on you since the train crew had their duties to attend to. I volunteered but Ember pulled rank on me. Since she has the first aid ticket I backed off.

She stayed in town too hoping they could tell her you would recover but she came home in time for Terry's funeral. At first I couldn't see why she went off with you when her mother and Jo both needed her but then I got to remembering how close her and Terry were. They always were each other's best friend. It could be he was her only real friend. I guess she needed you and your injuries to keep from thinking of what was going on back home"

I had never before seen events from any point of view other than my own. Now it came home to me that while it had been a hard experience for me I was quickly out of it—unconscious and uncaring. For Terry's family it would have been a complete disaster. For his wife Jo, it had likely seemed the end of her world. To cover my surprise I asked, "Just how do you flag down a fast freight?"

"Simple," he grinned, "a bunch of guys run up to the crossing as the engine approaches, two of them packing a stretcher and the rest waving their arms like crazy. All very modern and technical. It being a mile-long train the engineer gets it stopped with the caboose in about the right place. Of course someone might have phoned from the office ahead of time but I wouldn't know about that."

"Sounds logical," I admitted. "But tell me, how come were you up there? The last I saw of you was at the mill."

He spread his arms, his hands palms up. "One man dead on the hill and another maybe dying, everything around here stops right now. Just about everybody in camp went up, some to look and some to help. The rest sat around the coffee pot here and talked about it and every other fatal accident they could remember."

"Terry died right away?"

Dean nodded. "When we got the logs cut up and rolled off of him we scraped him from the rocks into cardboard boxes and empty oil pails, that's how 'right away' he died."

"Sorry," I said, pushing my plate a few inches to one side, "I didn't mean to spoil your breakfast. We'd better talk about something else."

"Oh, that's alright I was sick all that afternoon, you guys weren't found till after lunch, but it hasn't bothered me since. And of course I exaggerate but not by much. Compensation Board man sure raised hob around here when he came to investigate the accident. He grounded every logging truck in camp because of faulty brake systems even though some of the trucks simply didn't have the brakes set up as tight as he liked them to be. Some of the drivers got pretty hot under the collar but under the circumstances no one was going to argue much. He wasn't too pleased finding no radios in any of the vehicles either so now there's a two-way radio in every truck, crummy and pickup on the claim and a big base set in the office."

"But, man, once he looked at that old truck you guys piled up he was mad clear through and he picked this place over with a fine-tooth comb. He shut down most of the operation for one reason or another and left instructions saying not to start up until he came back and found everything fixed to his satisfaction." Dean chuckled. "And he wasn't in any hurry about getting back either. He left us to make changes and stew for over a week before giving the nod to start up again."

"What was so wrong with the truck that made him mad? I remember hearing an air line blow out, surely that must happen once in a while."

"I suppose so, I don't know anything more than what I've heard around camp about air brakes but there was something about a check valve that had been removed or bypassed or whatever. It seems that truck was no more than an accident rushing toward its place to happen."

"I have to agree with that and next time you tell me to stay on the green chain with you, I will."

"Well, man, I should hope so," he grinned at me, "but I suppose if your number comes up there's no escaping. At the mill a chunk of ice might have fallen from the roof and done the same thing to you."

"No I don't think so, I believe life is a series of decisions or forks in our road if you wish. Somewhere I made a wrong decision—a wrong turn."

"Man, I'll buy that. Hindsight doesn't require eyeglasses to see that going with Terry was not an overly wise choice."

"I mean it goes farther back than that," I said. "For instance, had I decided to go to some other job obviously I wouldn't have been in that truck. Someone else would have been instead, or maybe it wouldn't have happened at all. If I had put my left boot on first or had one more cup of coffee, my day might have unwound differently. And—by that token—Terry's too."

Dean eyed me curiously "Man, that's too deep for a simple-minded old fatalist like me." He glanced at his watch. "But if I don't get back to the shack and rouse my buddies they will be taking a different fork in their roads later today when Allan finds out they slept in."

"Okay Dean, see you later." I had to laugh softly at his determination to babysit us young greenhorns. It's about time, I decided, to get started at my own self-appointed job, that of unloading the supply truck. Uncharacteristically I took the bull by the horns, so to speak, and entered the office, store—whatever the place is called—by the main office door.

I found John Morrow alone, writing at a desk. "Ah yes, Byron, Ember said you had returned."

He was cool. I could feel no welcome as he examined me with a sour intentness that I hadn't expected. He seemed to be wondering almost out loud why he had been blessed with my presence. For a moment I hesitated, wondering which way the wind blew. He lifted and dropped one shoulder in the same 'what does it matter' way his daughter had the night before, took off his glasses, rubbed his eyes and all at once he was friendly the way I remembered him.

"I'm sorry to see you on those things," he said, indicating my crutches. "How serious is it?"

"I'll be able to throw them away someday, in fact I can get

around well enough without them now. It's just that I can move a lot faster with them yet than without."

"I'm glad to hear that. We'll find things for you to do as you improve, in the meantime, feel at home."

"Oh, I already have a job," I answered him. "I'm here to unload the supply truck. I imagine there is a way into the warehouse from here?"

I've got to give him credit for coolness, only the faintest shadow of surprise crossed his face before he gave me his tight grin. "Why yes, just around the corner here and then to your right, you'll find Nightrider in the truck bay."

"Nightrider?"

He laughed, "It's Ember. You see she has her own pet name for everything, the truck is Nightrider." As I followed his directions he called after me, "Take your time, I don't think there's a rush for any items on last night's load."

I found myself in a T-shaped hallway, quite wide, the right hand long branch leading to the store end of the building and the shorter branch going straight ahead to a back entrance with a couple of doors to the left along the way. I took the route toward the store. There are several doors on the right hand side, one I soon found to be a washroom, but the largest is the first aid room. The door was open so I went in and looked around. Directly in front of me, as I stood in the doorway, is a neatly made-up cot with a big window right behind it that let in lots of light. A little to one side of the bed is an outside entrance to the yard between here and the cookhouse. Along the wall to my right there are shelves, cabinets, oxygen tanks and things of which I had no knowledge, and wanted none.

The left one-third of the room is of a different nature altogether. It contains a huge oil furnace, almost totally silent, as it sends out warm air through overhead ducting, probably to every room in the building. The morning chill won't stand a chance against that monster. But there is also a wood heater alongside the oil burner connected to its own separate chimney. Near the head of the cot, at the opposite end from the door to the yard, is a large woodbox half-filled with trimmer ends of rough lumber from the mill. I now remembered noticing from outside that just about every slope of the roof has at least one chimney protruding so it would seem that each major room has its own standby wood heat. Probably the furnace is of recent installation and not yet trusted to the point of removing the wood heaters. It didn't take much thought to understand the motive though—it would be a fair-sized disaster if the store and warehouse were to suffer freezing temperatures and it could happen quickly in the thirty to fifty below of a winter night if the oil burner failed. The furnace end of the room has no door to the hallway so access to the furnace will always be by way of the first aid room.

With my inspection of the first aid/furnace room done, I crossed the hallway to a wide doorless opening to the warehouse, a huge, unfinished looking cavern of a place. Right in the middle, parked in a recessed well, was the supply truck, pardon me, Nightrider, her flatdeck exactly on a level with the warehouse floor. One can walk right out on the deck at any point across the width of the truck bed. There is even a hinged iron flap to flip over to the truck that will allow running one of the rubber-tired handcarts right onto the truck for transferring the freight. It only took a few minutes of looking around to get the lay of the land. Then I tipped the iron flap onto Nightrider's deck, commandeered a four-wheeled cart, and proceeded to unload the groceries and other freight. I stacked the goodies in what appeared to be their allotted places along the storage rows. Actually there was not much in the line of groceries stored here, it seemed to be a catchall place and most of the goods stacked about you would expect to find in a furniture or appliance store or sports shop or a home entertainment centre. A lot of it looked used—a second-hand store too?

When the eight o'clock whistle blew to signify start-up at the mill and planer, I had been at it in my own clumsy way for nearly an hour and was about half finished with the small items on the truck. There were also two crates of machinery at the front of the deck, one looked like an engine block and the other a big gearbox of some type. I doubted they were to be unloaded here and I couldn't handle them anyway because there was no overhead lifting device to be seen in the place.

"Well! What's going on here?" came sharply from the hall doorway behind me. I turned to find the dark-haired girl who works in the store watching and plainly wondering what I was up to. "Have we finally gotten the help we've been requesting for ages?"

"Yes," I said quickly. "Yes, it would seem so."

"Well in that case you might as well learn to do it right," she said brusquely. "We need most of these things up front in the store to restock the shelves. I can't imagine why you were sent in here without our knowledge." I sensed that she had more to say on the subject but for whatever reason of her own, she held those thoughts to herself. "You had better come up front with me and we'll go over the stock, making a list of what's needed. Then you can bring it up and put it on the shelves."

If nothing else she is certainly an opportunist, I decided as I hobbled to where my crutches leaned against the wall.

"Lead on, MacDuff," I quipped foolishly.

Now she really did give me a perplexed look. "My name is Jo," she said stiffly, "Jo Morrow." Then in a slightly easier tone, "Can you really do the lifting needed here? You don't look very strong."

"I can do it in my own time and way. I have no other duties so don't worry about me.

"Okay." Her decision made. "Come on."

In the store she led me to the front near the checkout counter and post office where she halted. "Hey, Em, look out here a moment will you. We seem to have the helper we've been needing but he's kind of stove up. Probably no good for anything else so they've pawned him off on us."

Besides being an opportunist she is also dismayingly blunt. A trait that I soon found is shared to varying degrees by the whole family, including the in-laws. Ember leaned over the post office counter, smiled and winked encouragement at me. "Hi, Byron, you're around early this morning." I wish she hadn't done that! I meant the wink. She is the boss's daughter and seems to be a principle in the business so I need not fear there will be a place for me in her thoughts. But this was my first chance to see her clearly in daylight and all I could think of is the need to have a protective wall between us. Just one wink left me frantically scrambling to rebuild its crumbled wreckage.

"You know him?" Jo asked.

"He came on the train last night, Jo, and I hired him for us before the front office got hold of him." She gave me one more conspiratorial wink then turned serious. "Jo, he's the one who was with Terry in the accident on the hill and has just come out of hospital."

That was not strictly true, I had been out of the hospital far longer now than I was in it, but it sounded good so I said nothing.

"Oh!" was all that Jo said, but she looked at me with keener interest—more than I would have expected—a glance at Ember then back to me. Then she said it again, "Oh! In that case, welcome to this club of misfits, now come on and I'll show you what to do." She got a pencil and a slip of paper from the counter and led me along the aisles of store goods examining the quantity of each stocked item.

"When I first started helping Em here, I invented my own system of stocking, I'll show you how it works and you can use it or invent your own style." Right away she showed to me a hyphenated number penciled very small on the shelf under each section. "For instance, under these shirts you see the lettering 6-12 under each pile of small, medium, large or extra large. That means I like to keep at least six but no more than twelve of each size on display." She went into more detail, "Fewer than six means not enough choice in colour or style and more than twelve means a god-awful mess every time some yahoo goes through the pile looking for one that suits him."

I wanted to laugh but to be frank I didn't quite dare. I just hope that this outspoken young woman wouldn't prove too difficult to get along with since it appeared that I would have to work with her. We moved along, making a note here and there of what was needed and how many.

"Some of these numbers are about faded away so as I have time I'll freshen them up for you or better yet, do it yourself if you need them. After a while it will all be so familiar that you won't need reminders like that. Some of the spaces, especially the canned goods, are self-explanatory, just keep them full. All fresh produce goes on display right away."

"I don't see any prices on anything."

"No, I have all the prices at the counter, if the customer doesn't like the price they can return the item to the shelves. Since there's no competition in town there's not much of that," she smiled, a little ruefully I thought. "And since we sell at just over break-even prices, on Dad Morrow's orders, there's not much margin for competition to start up on."

"There can't be a big load every night like there was last night?"

She shook her head, a movement that showed off to advantage her luxuriant head of hair. "You will find that we have one night a week that's heavy to groceries and other than that some things sort of trickle in unpredictably. Every second week most of the order goes to the cookhouse so it's not even unloaded here." Catching my look of alarm she went on, "you're lucky today, this order is for the store so you won't have to reload it."

She left me eventually to my own devices and I spent the morning moving cases from the warehouse to the store and filling the shelves. It was notable, I thought, that Jo has failed to say anything about being glad to have help and I am sure it's because she feels I won't last on the job. I vowed to show her that in my own slow way I will get it done.

When the noon whistle announced lunchtime, I was sitting on the handcart totally exhausted, hoping that I hadn't bitten off more than I could chew. But at the same time I felt good mentally having done something useful for a change. While resting I admitted to myself that what has taken me five hours to accomplish, a fit person could probably have done in one. But no matter, if the girls have been able to cope with this and handle the store and post office at the same time then I am simply going to manage somehow. It's a place to start and I surprise myself with my own thoughts. Never before has it felt so good to have a job. Even knowing I am only accepted because I was injured while working here hasn't failed to dampen my gratitude. No one else has any use for me, I know that from my futile search for work in town. For the first time in my life I experienced a tickle of loyalty to someone other than myself.

After having lunch at the cookhouse I hung around the store until I realized that Jo can't stand to see someone idle. I appreciate her interest in me but enough is enough. So to stay out of her sight I wandered around the rest of the building satisfying my curiosity; it took a while to realize that Ember was not to be found.

"She's home sleeping," Jo said when I went to her and asked. "We keep this place open from seven a.m. to nine p.m. six days a week and on top of that Em is up half the night meeting trains. She takes enough hours off to catch a nap just as I take off the evening and sometimes part of the morning depending on what's to be done. I guess you could call our scheduling—um—flexible." Her eyes showed the first sign of humour that I'd seen in her yet, perhaps a wry humour but that's okay.

Along in the afternoon I nosed around the front office to see if there were any little chores there I could do. John and his two sons were in deep consultation over an array of papers spread out on one of the larger desks. Tom gave me a curious look as I picked up an overflowing wastebasket and made off to the furnace room to burn the refuse. When I came back with it I realized I had made an unnecessary trip; there is a wood stove in the office as well, but no one pointed that out to me.

This is to be the shape of my future I soon learned. No matter how many mistakes or errors I make as I work my way deeper into their lives never is any comment made to correct me. They just accept me the way I am, complete with imperfections, and let me learn everything the hard way—by trying it myself. Whenever I see a chore that needs doing I just go ahead and do it, and not once has anyone said that I should, or shouldn't, or for that matter—thank you. Nor did they show me an easier way to do it.

Sometimes it seems they're not even aware of my presence, such as now, as I edge closer to see what occupies them. There are blueprints and sketches that I take to be of the sawmill, and the discussion sounds to me like pretty high finance and major renovation. They must not have minded me listening because Allan even unconsciously moved a little to give me a better view. It was the beginning of what Ember soon noticed and laughingly called the 'Invisible Man Syndrome' though I learned of it from Jo.

The entire Morrow family took me under their wing. Then I evidently became a part of the background. It didn't happen exactly overnight but in time I found I could walk in on any pair, or group of them and no matter how private or personal their conversation, they simply failed to care that I was there. They would go right on without the loss of a single word or gesture. Yet if someone else came near, even an old, trusted employee and friend like Dean, they immediately stopped until he was gone. It was uncanny, I could not and still cannot explain it but being an opportunist like my new friend Jo, I took every advantage.

I quickly discovered there are even more of the family working here than I first thought. While John and his boys headquarter in what is known as the 'front office'; there is also a 'back office' where Allan's wife, Erin and Tom's wife, Jennie, do most of the paper work for the company including lumber shipments and the payroll. My estimation of the two young women went up dramatically when I learned that they also sign the company cheques. The form seems to be that they both sign each cheque, or if a cheque has to be made out while only one of them is at work, then John also had to sign. Only John's signature is good in solo yet is almost never seen on payroll cheques.

I was interested to learn that both of these women had come to Rainy Mountain as school teachers then stayed to marry into the Morrow family. Erin had come before Jennie, taught school a season, married Allan and went to work in the office. Jennie came for the next school year but after a romance—rumoured to have been both torrid and stormy—she was married to Tom the following summer. Then she too was working in the office.

There were a lot of wisecracks made about Morrows not being able to afford bookkeepers so had to marry them into the company. But actually the example had been set even before the advent of Erin and Jennie for, of the young and pretty girls coming each year to teach in the one room grade school, it was said that only one escaped still in the single state. She was to be remembered yet as a symbol of failure in the system. Many of these one-time teachers are no longer in Rainy Mountain having since moved away with their logger or millworker husbands to other places. But enough remain to lend some credence to the theory that without the children of the ex-schoolteachers, the school would no longer be needed. It is said, moreover, and I now believe it, that there is not a homely one among them.

Erin and Jennie at any rate are certainly not homely. Jennie is a tall blonde now in her mid-twenties who has deservedly won the title of Sweater Girl from Ember. Erin, while also blonde and on the tall side, is slim and willowy. She seems the true siren, catching every man's eye and always ready to flirt a little but when you get to know her you find that here is just the girl from next door who wreaks male havoc without seeming to know it. Ember's private and somewhat irreverent name for Erin is, Stinger—as in bee—for her habit of addressing nearly everyone as, 'honey.' To me, 'Stinger' and the Erin I see here don't fit—there must be more to it that I don't know about.

Both women tend to dress on the conservative side most of the time but on certain days they dress to be noticed. Especially Erin. It didn't take long for me to realize that those special days were paydays when the crew was allowed to file down the hall into and out of the back office to pick up their cheques. I'm sure they consider it a day of more than financial gain because on payday both Erin and Jennie dress as provocatively as conventions—and husbands—allow. I never did come to understand the reasoning.

The large room known as the back office, where Erin and Jennie rule, had once been the warehouse while a third room on the back of it, now the meeting room, served as the first store. In later years, as the company grew and expanded, an identically- sized building was erected paralleling the original and became combination store and warehouse. It was evidently only a few years before my arrival that the centre section was added joining the first two efforts to come up with the present arrangement. It doesn't take much thought to see that there is really only one word our nickname queen could apply to the place. When you wanted the store you said store, when one meant office or first aid room, that's what one said, but overall it is 'the Mall'.

I've always been aware that I possess an undue dose of curiosity but as long as I was whole and healthy my world had been large enough to accommodate it. Now I am surprised at the warm glow of satisfaction that came with all my afternoon discoveries. This could be as good as prospecting I marveled. Getting to know these people and their ways suddenly loomed as challenging as walking the other side of the next hill had once been. Feeling quite pleased with myself, I started back to the store to see if Ember had showed up yet but I skidded to a halt at the warehouse door when I saw that Nightrider was gone. Gone and the door shut behind her! I feel betrayed but rather than running, or perhaps I should say hobbling, to Jo once more with my ignorance I went straight outside by way of the first aid room exit to look for the missing truck. I didn't have to search far because just around the corner of the office I came upon a sleep-freshened Ember dismounting from her nocturnal GMC.

"I've just been to meet the local and then to the shop to unload the machinery parts," she explained. "The bullcook always meets the local but sometimes I do too if we have something coming for the store. Now I'll leave my truck here till it's time for tonight's trains."

So! I had forgotten about the daytime train and the crates of heavy parts. I won't again! Ember went off to start her evening shift at the store while I retreated to my room to reflect on this day and await the supper bell at the cookhouse.

Shortly after midnight I was doing my best imitation of pacing circles around Nightrider. Not knowing what time Ember goes up to the railroad I made sure I was plenty early. But despite the daytime heat, tonight is chilly enough to send me back to my quarters in search of a warmer jacket.

Eventually Nightrider's partner in crime came along and though I'm sure it's not every night that someone shows up to go along for the ride she expressed no surprise at all on finding me waiting. I am beginning to think that she is quite unflappable but if I was looking for her to be pleased that I want to help then I am only fooling myself. It became more than evident over the following weeks that I am tolerated and that is all. I told myself at first that the reason for her coolness is because of the way the train crews took to teasing her about me once they realized I am to be a permanent fixture. It's all in good natured fun, and probably speaks volumes of their respect and affection toward her but some of their little jokes get quite crude in my opinion. She takes it all with a purely innocent smile and not a hint of ruffled feathers, sometimes giving it as good as she gets. She seems even to know the families or girlfriends of some of them and uses that knowledge to her advantage at times. Actually I seem to be the one who is most embarrassed but as long as Ember takes no offence I am determined to remain quiet and exactly neutral.

I suppose if I were a gentleman I would have quit forcing my presence on her but instead I never missed a trip and it soon became routine, up the hill at night, unload the truck by day. One of the first evenings that I was at the house to eat with the family John asked if I still let Ember do the driving. Startled, I blurted, "Of course!" How else could it be? Then he kidded me about my bravery while Ember, deadpan, gave me that conspiratorial wink that said we were together on something. Seeing my face turning red, the twins grinned wickedly.

Without being told to, or not to, I started taking the truck to the shop to unload any heavy parts that had come. Sometimes at the shop I was directed to the mill or planer to deliver pieces but not once did anyone in the office or store either censure or encourage me or make any comment at all about my initiative. I am well on my way to being firmly established as 'the Invisible Man'.

Ember and I became reasonably comfortable in each other's company but it was a long time before I risked asking her for a date. I really had no intention of doing such a thing. If I had thought about it before opening my mouth, I would have shoved my head into a bucket of water until the urge passed. I'm sure it was simply the challenge she presented. I had before me, every week, the example of others more interesting than I being turned down. Nearly every man who came here to work tried his luck with her eventually only to find that—while she was pleasant enough in her refusal—he had none. It was discouraging to see her so alone and so in time I felt drawn, like all the others, to try also thinking it would be different for me yet knowing it was safe because she would say no. Besides, if I didn't she might start thinking I found her unattractive.

But instead, with a—'good idea'—sound in her voice she allowed, "hey, why not?" Then a quick glance to gauge my reaction and maybe even some regret that she had agreed so quickly. I was shocked into silence.

At other times I had wondered what people do on a date in a little place like this but I soon came to see that there are no end of possibilities. Besides the once-a-week movie at the dance hall or the Saturday night dance there is a seemingly endless network of scenic and interesting logging roads to explore in a borrowed

Company 4x4. There are places to fish or swim or ski, skate or Skidoo depending on the season; there are motor boats on the river and miles to hike on the railroad. Different than most of us are used to or maybe not so different either if you consider end results.

Admittedly a lot of these fine pastimes are physically beyond me but I had deliberately started small anyway and asked to accompany her to the show. Her acceptance came so quickly and naturally that I believe she was as surprised as I. Maybe because we are together so much it seemed no more than normal to go to the show together too. But whatever, it was an accomplished fact before either of us could think of a way out. Neither mentioned the irony that she has a truck while I am afoot or that we both live a hop and a jump from the hall. I guess we simply intended to sit together, eat Cracker Jacks and watch the show—but it didn't even come to that.

Our routine after meeting the trains saw us driving back to the mall where I got out to open the door to the truck bay. When Ember had backed Nightrider in I pressed the switch to close the door then walked away as it came down leaving her and the truck inside. The shortest way for me to reach my room was to go around the back and then forward between the buildings thus directly to the bunkhouse. But that way is over some rough, willow covered ground, poorly lit, so instead I go the long way, around the office, past the front of the store and on to my place next door. It's twice as far but good going, usually I'm in my shack by the time Ember finishes whatever she does, comes out of the front office and drives her pickup away to the Morrow home a block beyond the cookhouse. But tonight as I rounded the corner of the office I heard the telephone ringing our code inside. No one in their right mind would call an empty office in the middle of the night even though it is the only phone in camp so it has to be a wrong number.

With no late shift working this weekend night it's so utterly silent that I heard Ember's footsteps as she crossed the office. I could even hear the murmur of her voice as she answered the phone. I couldn't make out much of the conversation but Ember seemed at first surprised then wary and very, very cautious but only a moment later she sounded joyously happy and excited. Such strong emotion came into her voice that I was embarrassed and uncomfortably aware that I was eavesdropping since the call was obviously personal and for her so I moved on. But I was disturbed because it was plainly someone who meant a lot to her and instinctively I knew it was a man. One who knew what time she would be around the office after meeting the trains. I hurt my foot rather badly opening the door to my dank and chilly bunkhouse.

The next night as we drove up to meet the trains she told me flatly that she wasn't going to the show this week, no excuses, just a plain statement. I should have felt relieved but instead it hurt enough that I went to the show anyway, picked a strategic spot to sit, and watched to see if she came because she always does. But this evening she didn't.

I waited a couple of weeks before asking again but she just said no, then added that she wasn't going that week. It didn't take long to realize that the only times she didn't attend the shows and the dances too were on the occasions when I asked for her company then she was conspicuous by her absence. I can be as thickheaded as anyone but eventually I saw that I was too frequently spoiling her day so I stopped asking her to go with me and there's no doubt we got along better again. I guess in her own way she was trying to be nicer to me than just saying no, but I ended up feeling very confused and frustrated. I consoled myself by thinking that, in a way, I have a date with her every night at train time.

By this time, I had learnt a lot about both Ember and her family from other sources including Dean who is voluble and enthusiastic about the Morrows in general. But he is decidedly incommunicative when the subject comes around to the post mistress unless he can tell me something that's slanted to reduce my interest in her and then he has lots to say. Other than that minor lacking he is becoming a better friend than I am used to having. I learned more from Jo than she knew she was telling me in our many hours together at the store. I think that behind her tough facade she is a very lonely person almost desperate for a friend, besides Ember, who would ask nothing of her. And I got no little bit from the cookhouse crew where I have become a regular in the off-hours at the cookshack. They will feed me at any time of the day and ply me with questions to find out all I learn around the office and store. This works both ways for I benefit by them too. I learned, among other things, that there are two Morrow boys I haven't met yet, one of them I never will. A brother older than Allan, John's namesake, died in an accident back in the river-running days of the spring log drives. He is buried in a cemetery that is supposed to be near the switchback on the road to the railway. Later I found that wasn't quite true. His body, as well as one of two others who drowned in the same incident, was never found. There are only monuments to their memory up on the hill.

I felt it necessary to look up the cemetery because of two points. One, Terry is buried there and I feel I have an interest in him. I think he passed up his best chance to jump so that I could have mine. I believe the Morrows think this also. I will never be sure of course and I see it as best that way. It would be a heavy load to carry. The other reason, in retrospect, is almost funny. When I heard that there is a local graveyard my first panicky thought was, "My God! You mean they would have planted me here if I had died with Terry?" As if it mattered! For me, finding the cemetery lent weight and substance to what I was coming to believe must be the Morrow motto—'We take care of our own.'

The other brother, named Theodore but for reasons that remain obscure, is called Tim, comes in age between Ember and the twins. Tim is away at UBC. studying to be a professional forester—an apt vocation for a lumberman's son it seems to me.

The older brothers took high school by correspondence as the twins are doing now, but they didn't all carry through to graduation. Ember and Tim were the only ones to go away to attend a regular secondary school. Tim was nearly two years younger and two years behind Ember when he started school, but while Ember was barely average in her classes, Tim turned out to be a brain. By the eighth grade he had skipped twice and handily outshone his older sister in their final year of grade school. Ember rebelled at the prospect of four years of rivalry by correspondence with her uppity young brother and announced that she was going to her grandparents to live while she took her grades 9 to 12. But Tim also thought grandparents near Edmonton an excellent idea and insisted on going there too. Now Ember was in full flight, she about-turned at the last minute and went instead to Prince George where she was boarded with the family of a business acquaintance of John's.

True to form, Tim zipped through high school with flying colours and straight 'A's then moved on to Vancouver to take up his forestry studies. Meanwhile Ember spent four uneventful years of hard work getting to and through grade 12, then came home and threw herself fully into running the store. When Jo came on the scene as extra help, the elder Mrs. Morrow decided it was time to retire to babysitting her grandchildren so the daughters-in-law could spend more time working in the office.

When I heard about Tim I thought to myself, "Ah ha! That's who was on the phone the other night. Who else would know when to call to get her after train time?" But on the phone she had sounded much too enthusiastic and emotional and that wasn't right after hearing of all the friction between them. Time passes, I mused, people change.

But then from Dean, I learned of Peter. Poor Dean, he didn't know how to bring up the subject so just blurted it out. "Byron, I know it's none of my business but, man, I hate to see you getting in so deep with Ember. Peter will be home someday, you know."

"Who is Peter?" I asked, ignoring his insinuations.

"When Morrows first came here John's best friend Jock Patten and his wife Lily came with them. They all grew up together on neighbouring farms and they tackled this proposition here almost as partners. Pattens had only one kid, a boy about Tom's age or a little older. Now they, the parents, were all such close friends that they decided it would be great if Peter and Ember got married when they grew up. This was when Ember was just months old and Peter still a wee little guy. Peter's mother and father are both dead now but I'm sure the pact still stands."

"You're talking about an arranged marriage. Such things don't happen nowadays."

"Man, I'm sorry, but that's the way it is. I haven't heard anything to indicate it's been called off. Someday Peter will come home and that will be that! Except for you she's had no serious boyfriend for years. I don't know why she leads you on so I thought I had to warn you." He was so apologetic and embarrassed that I had to take him seriously and after all, it did explain just about everything I have wondered about. "Considering her young age she's had a lot of man-trouble," he went on, "and I hate to say it but I guess it's mostly her own fault. She's always known that she could snap her fingers and take her pick then if the guy didn't rouse Peter's attention just swat him around a bit and he's gone. I'd hate to see her treat you like that."

"What do you mean?"

"I mean that if she wanted to she could probably wipe the floor with just about any of the young fellows in camp." My look of skeptic disbelief led him to explain. "When Terry was taking high school by correspondence, he decided to use boxing as part of his physical education. After he got tired of hitting a punching bag that never hit back he asked me to be his sparring partner since he knew I used to box some. But I found out I was too big, too old and too slow for him. He seemed to forget it was supposed to be fun and exercise so I begged off and became just trainer and referee. Then, until Ember went away to Prince, he talked her into being his partner by convincing her that every girl should know how to take care of herself. The funny thing is she got to be better at it than he was, considering her lack of weight and reach. She took to boxing just like her sisters took to shocking people with their swearing and dressing to show off their unbelievable good figures—well—I guess Ember did some of that too. Of course Terry at that time was no bigger or heavier than her and any time he hit her too hard and got her mad she could make him wish he hadn't. She is her father's daughter for dead certain. I've never seen such determination—the same as John. She could be knocked down but she could not be beaten. Sometimes she got so intent on inflicting pain that she felt none herself. I often had to stop it before one of them got hurt beyond a thick lip or a half-closed eye and I was sure glad when the school year ended and the gloves were put away. And if that's not bad enough I understand she took some kind of a so-called self-defense course—whatever that amounted to I don't know—while she lived in town. I'm afraid she knows more ways to injure you quickly than I learned in fifteen years of boxing."

"Well, different maybe," I conceded. I'm a little shocked, no doubt about it and trying hard without much success to see the high-heeled and very feminine Ember I know in what I'm hearing. "But nothing so unusual about it," I insisted, feeling for some obscure reason that I should defend her. "I've known of sisters who played hockey with their brothers just so they could get up a team. Or even one or two who played goal so the boys could practice their hardest shots. I'm sure that would cause even worse bruises than boxing."

"I wouldn't know anything about hockey, Byron but I know it raised a lot of eyebrows around here and gave some smart alecks the biggest surprise of their lives. But I guess surprise has always been her biggest advantage because no one would ever expect the likes of her to come at them with the intent and ability to put them down and out. Temper!" He shook his head perhaps a bit in admiration.

I couldn't help but remember now how Dean had once told me that Terry was Ember's best friend—maybe her only real friend. Like Dean had before, I suddenly wondered about that day when her brother, who was also her only best friend, lay dead on the hill and she had chosen to take me to the hospital and stayed in town for several days. Another unspoken link of some sort between us. Perhaps it was true that she simply had to get away for a while—to be alone with her grief and shock—but there was one thing for sure and that was at some point on that trip she cried. I think maybe she cried a lot, probably alone at night in a hotel room. So strange it has taken me this long to realize that.

But with Ember herself, I had very little deep discussion. In all our nights of waiting for trains we sat together in Nightrider's cab a total of many hours but except on two memorable occasions we never got beyond talking about the weather, the trains, the river, the mill, the recent news on the radio or similar safe subjects.

The first was the time I said to her as casually as I could after No. 9 was gone and we waited for No. 8. "If the truck is Nightrider, then who is Nightrider's driver?"

I guess that got her attention because she looked long and hard at me by the faint glow of the instrument panel before she laughed lightly. "So you've heard of my silly habit of naming and nicknaming. I've got to stop doing that. I think someone has been telling on me because I'm sure I've been careful to not call her by name in your presence." She patted the steering wheel so exactly as Terry had done in the big truck that I was unable to suppress a shiver.

If she thinks her little idiosyncrasy is not public knowledge, then she is simply not up on camp gossip. Her private capers of the tongue are one of our daily highlights as we wonder who or what will be her next victim. I guess she lets slip to Jo or the twins what her thoughts are and that's the end of the secret. For someone who seems to be foremost in so many people's thoughts it's sometimes amazing how little she notices of what goes on around her.

"But you haven't answered me," I persisted.

"No. I was hoping you would let it alone but I should know by now that when you get something on your mind you have to see it through." She sounded a little peeved and maybe a little pleased too if such can be the case. "Long ago when I was a little child," she paused. "No, not so long ago either, perhaps I'm still a bit of a child. Anyway, I called myself M, just plain old capital letter M." Then she laughed at me again but almost self consciously this time and that should have warned me that I am prying too deep. "See, nothing mysterious or romantic at all, only a short form of my real name—sort of. When I was small a lot of people called me Ema or worse yet, Emmy. I didn't like that so somewhere along between my ears and my mind I changed it to M and that somehow made it alright. Your next question will be—why call a truck Nightrider."

"No, I thought that rather self explanatory given the nature of the job."

"Not so at all, though it does fit as you say, the nature of the job. But until I went away to high school I always had a cat and the cat was always black and always named Nightrider because he went outdoors at night and slept in the house all day. The hardest part about going away was leaving Nightrider behind. When I finished school and came home to stay, there was no Nightrider and I no longer wanted one. I have my truck instead."

She stopped and I thought she was quitting on me. There was a sadness, quite bitter, in her voice that sent my imagination into wild overdrive. Something had touched her young life deeply at that time and it had to be more than the loss of a pet cat. Graduation is, I admit, a time of great change for many of us. Finish school at eighteen or nineteen and suddenly it's time to grow up, get out from family ties and earn a living. But Ember hadn't done that—quite the opposite—she had tucked herself firmly into the nest and become a cog in the family business. My speculation will have to wait though for she picked up the conversation in a suddenly stronger voice.

"I got involved in the store and post office which Mom had run practically alone till then, and I soon saw problems in our train meeting arrangements. At that time my brothers Tom and Allan were sharing the job but it was a constant headache, each of them claiming after the fact, 'I thought it was your turn.' Terry was no help at all if it meant getting up during the night. We reluctantly tried a succession of hired men with spectacular lack of satisfaction—you know—trains not met, outgoing mail not on-board, incoming mail lying in the rain, groceries wet because the trainmen got tired of doing our job for us and stopped moving it into the station—all kinds of fun. I could go on for hours about it but the upshot of the matter was that I got mad and took the job myself. My truck soon became my Nightrider. Satisfied, Mr. Curiosity?"

"Well, some," I admitted, torn between wanting to ask her more questions while she was once again in a good mood and a fear of overstepping and antagonizing her so I switched the subject a little. "A job with working hours like you keep would run you straight into the ground if you didn't have Jo's help."

"You're a hundred and ten percent right there, Byron. When Terry brought her home Jo was a total surprise to us because it took him just two weeks to take delivery of a new truck and in his spare time, find Jo, court her, marry her and bring her home. That has to be some kind of a record even for a Morrow." At the time I didn't know what she meant by that but eventually I found out.

"She seemed a bit standoffish at first and none of us knew what to think of her but it's worked out okay." Ember smiled a little, "I've been told there should have been pictures taken of our meeting because as Dad likes to say, we both fell right out of our socks with surprise. It's said that everyone has a double somewhere in the world but mostly they never ever meet. I know, we're nowhere near identical like Pat and Jan but still, it's too close for comfort and we can and have passed ourselves off as twins. When Jo and I took our industrial first aid courses—her first, my upgrade—we stayed with the same couple that I lived with while I went to high school. They met us at the train and they were floored to discover that there were two, not one, sets of twins in the family. It would have been easier to let them go on thinking that than it was to convince them that Jo was actually a sister-in-law.

"It could easily have gone bad between us but it didn't and she's become the very best friend I've got. Dad liked her right away but Mom didn't. All she could see was this hussy who led darling son astray and had the nerve to look like number one daughter. But that's all changed—now Mom thinks the sun rises and sets on Jo's house and her only regret is that there was no grandchild." Then she almost giggled and added, "but I still wish I could have been in disguise and travelling one step behind Terry on that trip because there must be a marvelous story in there somewhere. A short one though."

Ember was definitely sounding more relaxed so I decided to press my luck after all. "You sounded sad about coming home...." That's as far as I got. Back suddenly stiffened, hands clenched on the steering wheel, she clammed up and refused to talk to me about anything for the rest of the night. I don't think she was exactly angry at me, if I read signals correctly, it was more like I had touched a taboo subject and she didn't trust herself to speak. The one glance she gave my way seemed almost to beg me to not ask her more.

The other time we had a conversation was a couple of weeks later, after the trains had been met and we were coasting down the hill to camp. I had this bee in my bonnet. "You know by now that I can get up without fail in the middle of the night and you also know that I am completely familiar with the job. So why don't you sleep on through starting tomorrow night and turn this chore over to me?" Then I settled back to weather out her storm of protest.

"Sure, why not?" One shoulder—lifted and dropped.

She didn't come right out and say "I thought you'd never ask," but she might as well have.

3

So that's how I happen to be sitting here three years later, in a newer Nightrider, waiting for a train that is definitely late. The crew on No. 9 would have said something if the other train were going to be drastically off schedule so I guess it's just a matter of waiting it out a little longer. I have developed something of a sixth sense about train arrivals but I don't know what causes it. Perhaps a vibration in the air or the ground when a train gets so close. But if that's so then it's strange because while it works to the west as well as the east if, for example, the first train is late and the normally second train comes first—it only works on the passenger trains. And it's a sense that does me no good now because it's a feeling I have to either wake up with or gradually become aware of—I can't go looking for it. But when the feeling does come there is just enough time with little to spare, to dress, get my truck and drive to the station.

I may have given the impression that I am alone here every night but that's not so. On a probable average of two nights a week there are others too, from one or two to a dozen or more despite the lateness of the hour. If there's a family going out or expected in there might be another truck or two as well. Mostly though they use the trail and they come for one train or the other and don't stay between trains so for the most part I am alone. Once I've figured out what they're up to I don't usually pay them much attention.

If I had realized how much I was going to miss Ember's company I think I would have continued just riding along to help, but that's all water past the log boom now. Perhaps it's just as well for tongues had started wagging about us, unavoidable I suppose, with us together so much in the wee hours. About half the people in camp figure Ember and I are like—that! But the other half, the old timers and the romantics, shake their heads and say she is waiting for Peter. The one thing for sure is that no one knows better than I do that there is nothing more than a mutual wariness of each other between her and I. Like two magnets constantly maneuvering to be neither drawn nor repelled. Of course there has become a friendship too but at times it is stretched mighty thin if I read the signs right. My curiosity seems to rile her at times. Or maybe she understands that I like her more than is good for either of us.

The sadness that came as she talked of her high school years could be only one thing. I know the family well enough by now to know there had been no tragedy or scandal about that time so logic indicates it must have been a young love affair gone sour. Over and done with I hope though plainly not forgotten.

But it seems she must miss her night time work as much as I miss her because I soon discovered she is coming some nights to the office in the extreme a.m. and working till near breakfast time. Breakfast over at Morrows' that is. They are early risers and Lora's table is set even earlier than the ones in the cookshack.

When I go to bed after meeting the trains I sleep soundly for an hour or two but then lighter toward morning so any unusual sounds will wake me then. The mill and planer crews have their own small offices and first aid rooms on-site and almost never come to the main office except in daytime when the boss is there. So a truck starting up and driving away from out front has to be considered unusual when it has become a regular event. One morning when I was awake enough to be curious as an engine started outside I jumped up and rushed to the window in time to see a pickup that must have been parked wrong way to the office, make a U-turn in front of my place then swing around the corner onto the main drag. It could be going anyplace but I wasted no time wondering because I knew exactly where it was going and even who was driving. Every vehicle in camp carries a unit number painted half a foot high on each door to help the shop crew with their service records. There are only two exceptions—because she refuses to be pigeonholed in any way, shape or form—any truck that becomes Ember's and the current Nightrider have the number removed or never put on.

So, definitely curious now, I spied on her. That means I set my most comfortable chair by the window and spent some very dull hours watching not much of anything after train time for the next while. But eventually nearly a week later it paid off for soon after I could be expected to be asleep, Ember came drifting around the corner and coasted to a quiet stop in front of the office. Actually she overshot a bit and came to a stop almost in front of my shack but she didn't back up. She climbed out, reached back inside for a briefcase, shut the door soundlessly by pushing on it while holding the latch button then went to the office entrance and inside.

I still wondered about it for a while because I simply could not imagine what might need working on through the night. But from my time spent around the Morrow house I know that away from work Ember is a voracious reader of about anything in print. Historical novels are her favourite but she reads fiction or nonfiction on just about any subject and John's newspapers and trade journals too. If she has a good story going she will stay up all night or until she finishes it.

There have been some hot and heavy clashes between mother

and daughter lately, something about late night hours but I didn't get much of it because for some reason I seemed to be on Lora's hit list about then too—showing up right at mealtime too often I guess—or it could be because I declined her invitation to move in with them. The invitation was given obliquely a few times as though she wanted me to ask. When I didn't, she delivered it in front of the whole family pointing out that with all her boys gone on their own there were a lot of perfectly good rooms going to waste. And wouldn't I appreciate having my laundry done instead of taking it to the wash and dry room when I ran out of clean clothes? About then Ember left the room choking on something—laughter I think—but the twins were all eyes and ears. The top half of John's face over his paper gave no hint of what was on the lower half. So I went back to eating mostly at the cookhouse again.

Ember showing up here in the night will be the reason for her mother's anger or more likely the result of it—sending daughter looking for a quiet reading retreat. I have no doubt that her current bit of fiction is in the briefcase and she is closing herself away in the back office with its heavy blinds and door that locks.

And the telephone!

She could always catch a nap on the cot in the first aid room if needed. So having it all figured out I was happy and put it out of mind. It was years before I learned how wrong I was.

I got to know Tim somewhat too. He manages to drag himself home every year at Christmas but not often or for very long at any other time. He's a friendly sort, easygoing and not much like any of his older brothers, a notable lack of temper for a Morrow. But the first time I saw him climb off the train I sure did a double take wondering if Terry had come back to haunt me. There's not really such a striking resemblance in features, it's more general than that, it's mostly the way his clothes fit him to such absolute perfection. He's about the right size too, easily the smallest of the Morrow men.

Ember is the only other one of them to share that knack of their mother's for always being impeccably dressed though with her I have never decided whether it's the clothes or the girl in them. She could probably make flour sacks look comfortable and chic—it's at least partly in her confident attitude. Where the twins are concerned, they possess such striking good looks that I doubt anyone dwells overlong on how they are dressed. Just as well too because despite spending a fair bundle on wardrobe, they always manage to fall short of the standard set by their sister.

But that minor detail didn't stop me, along with a lot of others, from being an avid 'Twin Watcher.' And it paid off with an unexpected dividend—I learned to tell them apart. One day while they were walking by, a little distance from where I sat, I noticed that for a few paces they were in step, then out of step, then back in step. Their movements are just different enough that I was soon able to know one from the other as long as they were active. About the same time I discovered that Jan's cheekbones are slightly more prominent than Pat's and one of the dark streaks in her hair looked wider so now I know which is which at almost any given time.

That in turn brought on two more discoveries—the first being that, aside from Lora, I was evidently the only one in camp who could tell them apart—or bothered to try. And the second was that the little devils love to switch their identity colours—broaches, plastic flowers, hair ribbons, or whatever, and take fiendish delight in fooling us all. Mostly there's no point in it but it seems to amuse them. I don't think I've ever seen them so genuinely angry as when they found out that I was on to them. We went through a spell of time when they went all out to trip me up and only quit in disgust after having to admit that they couldn't. Naturally I didn't explain to them what I found different for I knew they would then work long and hard to cover up and become even more alike.

This family never ceases to amaze me with the offspring resembling in appearance either their yellow-haired, light-skinned mother or their black-haired (grey now) darker father. All the children have inherited the amazing good looks and intelligence of both their father and mother but unfortunately they have also inherited John's fearful temper. Unlike most families of light and dark complicated parentage the offspring show no shades of compromise in between unless you count the twins with those odd streaks of black on their otherwise blonde heads. The only common thread is that quick and fearful temper. They are, however, equally quick to cool down though I've yet to hear one of them apologize to anyone. Ember is the obvious exception. I've only seen her come close to being angry that one time and what she did was to shut her mouth and say nothing so I can't even be certain that anger was one of the emotions involved. But I distinctly get the message that she could hold a grudge long enough to more than make up for her lack of theatrics.

At last No. 8's headlight beam dragged its reluctant train in from the west, whistle blowing for the crossing and bell ringing. While I was busy exchanging information with the train crew as they produced a load of supplies for me, I noticed a man carrying two duffel bags get off the lead passenger car. I am mildly surprised because it's too early for logging crew to be coming for the winter work and I can't think of anyone who should be arriving tonight. As the train accelerated away leaving us in the shimmer of the northern lights he came along the track looking closely at me as though I might be someone he knew. But then he said, "Hi, friend, guess I'll hitch a ride down the hill with you."

That tells me he has been here before or, I amended my thoughts, he's been clued in by someone on the train to the fact that the town is "down the hill."

I've learned my lines well over the years so as we coasted down around the corners to camp I asked, "What's your contract?" There was good reason for asking because we like to keep men with similar jobs together in the bunkhouses. That way their lights-out and getting-up times are more likely to be similar and they will have more to talk about. We don't mix five a.m. arising loggers with mill crew who might not want to get up till seven.

For the mill and planer there were often two or sometimes three separate shifts to be accommodated as well. My passenger was unimpressed.

"I haven't one."

"You mean you've just come on speculation hoping to find a job?" That happens now and then, in fact some of the best men like to do their own negotiating in person and demonstrate their financial independence by being able to come and go at will.

"Guess you might say that," he allowed after some hesitation. At the switchback the sweep of our headlights highlighted the trunks of tall spruce trees standing almost like a picket fence along the road. "This must be the only sawmill town in the country hidden away in mature standing timber."

"Yes," I agreed, pleased that he had noticed because a lot of newcomers don't see that. I'm as proud as any of the Morrows of the tall timber that surrounds the town. There are reasons of course but what you can't see at night are the old rotted down stumps scattered all through the woods here. It's all been logged once already but has come back maybe as good as it was in the first place. He wasn't interested beyond his first comment so I didn't explain to him that this was all second growth timber and in my opinion there was no good reason why more of the logged-off country couldn't look like this. I realize I start sounding like a lecturer when I get wound up on the subject of logging methods past and present so I let it drop. I have to be careful who I talk to about this. Besides, the old-time horse loggers didn't always do it right either.

Well, all that didn't help me out too much as I still don't know where to put him. I quickly decided against bunking him with any of the present crew since he would almost certainly have to be moved again tomorrow. I could put him in an empty shack, but for tonight, as I sometimes do when I have a square peg and nothing but round holes, I dropped him at my own place and directed him to the vacant half. He seems a decent sort, if a bit secretive, and is sober which is something in itself. He looks to be a few years older than I am, about the same height but a lot heavier. Actually, he is so well proportioned that it's hard to say for sure just how big he is. As he disappeared into the shack lugging his baggage I shrugged and pulled Nightrider away toward the warehouse. "I'll sort him out in the morning." Then I promptly forgot the new man.

But there are a lot of things that can't be forgotten. I have allowed my mind to wander too much tonight and now I know I will pay the price in restless tossing about until morning. Things have certainly changed in the last few years I reflected and not much of it for the better. The Morrows are in a real bind financially, I know that just as I know every thing else about them both company-wise and personally. My years as the Invisible Man, accepted as one of them, leave no secrets untold. Or so I thought.

John and his two older sons are the darndest trio I could ever imagine existing, they are all so much alike that at times it seems there is no possibility of them getting along. I can't begin to remember how many times I have found them discussing an issue, all three at the top of their voice, all three shouting and no one listening. The odd part is they might all have the same general idea but are each wording it in a slightly different way. Since none of them would stop to really listen these sessions sometimes went on almost to the point of a free-for-all brawl.

Somewhere along the way I found that if I listened to them long enough to get the drift of their talk, I had only to wait for the inevitable breathless pause then feed back to them a slightly modified version of what they have just been saying. Invariably they are astounded at the simplicity of the matter and all will go off happy, each one sure in his own mind that it was his idea that I supported.

It isn't all a case of familiarity breeding contempt, I really want so much to help that I am willing to try most anything. These awful but wonderful people have been so good to me that I can never feel less-than-the-deepest gratitude toward them. Even though it's become all too apparent that it will be a long time before I walk well enough to hold a proper job again not once has a one of them so much as hinted that I might not be worth the price of my keep.

These thoughts take me back to when I first started helping in the mall and was so careful to spend as little as possible on myself in the store, sure that I would have to pay the bill from my Compensation pension. I also worried about my board which I hoped would come to a lot less than it had been in town. The months rolled by and no bill showed up for my purchases or board either. I was afraid to ask Jo why—sometimes she can make me feel my ignorance—so I went to Erin who is always nice to everyone. She was confused that I was confused. "But none of us get a bill from the store," she explained. "Nor do any of us get a paycheque for our work as you must have noticed by now. It's all taken care of." She waved a hand toward the file cabinets as though by some magic I should understand what she is telling me. As I turned to leave I wondered—irrelevantly perhaps—if the taxation department understands it any better than I. Before I got to the door she called to me and I turned back to find her looking concerned. "If you feel you are getting behind in benefits," she said, "then spend more. You've been awfully frugal." She dropped her eyes to the papers on her desk then as if with an afterthought flashed me an impish grin. "Do like the rest of us, buy yourself some good furniture and clothes or like Tom, get a Ski-doo, a boat or a rifle or two. Ember or Jo will order whatever you want through the store but if you want a trip to town, Jennie or I can give you some cash from the safe."

I left Erin with my head swimming because I know who she means when she says "us." When used the way she meant it 'us' means family. 'Morrows plus in-laws.' I know that all the employees get a statement and paycheque twice a month. I know too that I haven't been getting one but I hadn't expected to. What little help I've been giving can hardly be worth the effort to write one out. What caused my head to swim was realizing from the way she spoke that the interpretation of 'us' has evidently been broadened to read, 'Morrows plus in-laws and one outlaw.' In the past this would be my cue to throw a tantrum, stuff my gear into a bag and if the train was too long coming, start walking toward town. This is just the sort of attachment I have scrupulously avoided for years. Startling now to find how good it feels.

No, the real problem here has been building for years and it's possible that it takes an outsider like me to see it clearly. But seeing it doesn't rank with curing it. The Morrows themselves will have to do that, hopefully while there is still time. If there is still time! The Morrows, despite their reputation, personality and temperament, are actually quite ordinary people who now find themselves in a most extraordinary situation caught quite firmly between their dreams of how it should be and the harsh reality of the business world. John in his younger years had obviously been an able administrator or the company would have failed before I came to hear of it. But times are changing and John isn't, he has resisted improvements like the plague. And to make matters more difficult he is, in his own strange way, trying to turn management over to the boys. But in this he is his own worst enemy for he just cannot let go. There were a few bad decisions made, a couple years of low lumber prices and suddenly we are on thin ice.

Looking back it appears to me that the worst single mistake was Allan's—not in his decision but in his failure to carry it through. He wanted to build a dry kiln to speed up the lumber drying process. "We are," he pointed out loudly, "the only sizable sawmill left in the area still one hundred percent air drying our lumber." I had no idea if that was true or not partly because I don't know what 'sizable' means. I doubt if he knew either but it made a good argument so I backed him up by pointing out how expensive it was becoming to air dry our lumber in our short wet summer with interest rates rising as if to compete with the humidity reading and us depending more and more on bank money to keep operating.

John blew hot and cold on it till the building was actually

completed but not much hardware for it bought or installed. And that's where it died for lack of a bit more funding because now, with tens of thousands of borrowed money tied up in it, John dug in his heels and could not be budged toward finishing it. Allan and John couldn't even stand the sight of each other for weeks at a time.

Then overnight John was gone, leaving us in a void. He and Lora were in town where John was attending an association meeting when he was stricken with a heart attack. He survived, but while he was hospitalized and later recuperating at a friend's home in town, we were in limbo, unable to do any more than carry on with basics.

And just like the others I've been skating all around the main issue. None of us like to talk about it because there are no solutions in sight. But at the same time it's not hurting us yet. It's like a mountain range in our path but still off in the distance. We know we will have to climb it but for now the going is flat and easy so we ignore it pretending it isn't there.

It has been Morrow's practice for many years before my time, and maybe Allan and Tom's too, to put on logging crews each winter far out of proportion for the size of their sawmill and sell the excess log production to buyers on down the river. Just another way to keep them from coming and doing it themselves. Through the winter and in the springtime as much as 75% of the season's cut of timber goes on rail cars to various other sawmills. It used to go into the river to float down to them but the end result is the same either way, it's logs sold that don't go through our sawmill.

All this extra logging activity meant that when the government brought in the quota system to timber supply management and based it on past production, Morrows suddenly found themselves the uneasy possessors of a huge quota. On the ledger these trees on paper showed up as wealth at the stroke of a pen or—'Paper Trees'—to Ember. To me it looks more like trouble because it's not real money. Maybe not even real trees. It's actually nothing more than collateral on which to borrow our way farther into debt. But it seems to add to the sale value of the place—were it ever to be sold—for the quota alone is now valued, by some slight of hand that I don't quite understand, in the millions of dollars and the people downstream who bought our logs want what they see as their share of it. Sounds fair enough only they don't want to pay for it even though the value of quotas has been well established around the province by now.

But there is far more at stake here than mere dollars. Control is the name of the game! Those who control the timber sales and tree farm licences will control the future. And the dream comes in here too. No one has said it in so many words but a little here, a small story told casually there and now I see it all. John came here as a young idealist intent on farming the forest as his father and grandfather had farmed the land. He saw no reason that, treated right, the forest would not support him and his descendants for all time. Along came reality in the form of competitors eyeing the vast expanse of timberland around Rainy Mountain. Expansion to show that Morrows needed all that forest was the only way to hold them at bay and keep some breath of life in the dream. Compromise was next because expansion of that magnitude required money in amounts that not even Morrows dreamt of. An army of fallers to work in the short daylight hours of winter—floodlights on the landings and skidding—bucking crews on shifts around the clock to get the maximum from a small fleet of machinery. Trucks that never cooled down till spring breakup and logs sold to those same competitors who made this all necessary.

All the same, differences of opinion or not, it was business as usual and for a while it looked as if things might go on indefinitely as long as John didn't overcharge for the logs. Then the complications started rearing their ugly heads. Several of the downstreamers were old family owned companies like Rainy Mountain and their era seems to be ending with deaths or retirements among the old guard. A lot of companies changed hands, new money came into the country and all at once there is one lean and mean competitor looking up-river at us. They don't yet have the clout that the big integrated forest corporations enjoy but from our viewpoint the new TL&NY Timber Co. Ltd., or, to us, simply L&N, is sufficiently large and solvent to be a real danger to us. Unlike Rainy Mountain, L&N is managed by young aggressive executive types who see no reason to be generous unless it will show a profit on the balance sheet. They see us as an uncooperative anachronism and are eager to pick at our bones.

I think that John might have sold to them if they would have allowed him to keep some quota and continue to log just enough for his own mill and the dream. But that is not their style, they now want it all including the townsite land and Morrows are all to sign a contract to stay out of any forest-based business for a minimum of ten years. John was tired—the sum of money dangled before them might well have swayed him and the boys but the prospect of seeing 'her' town razed to the ground and left to return to nature brought Ember out of her cocoon with a vengeance. She banged her fist on the table in the best fashion even if it was a small fist on a big table and talked tough turkey to her father and brothers until John's resolve was bolstered and he declined to sell.

Ember is not an emotional person but still it seemed an emotional decision, not based too firmly in reality, as the next year's lumber market soon showed. Every board sold went out at a loss but had to go just to keep some cash flowing. I guess everyone else with older, less efficient mills like ours and no market for wood chips suffered to some degree along with us, but some found ways to cut their losses. L&N cut theirs dramatically simply by not buying logs, they managed quite nicely on what quota they did have.

When L&N got a salvage sale in a large fire-killed stand and needed no logs from us for a second year in a row, we were plainly caught between a rock and a hard place. We are now so far behind in our timber-cutting requirements that the Forest Service are making nasty noises. For the quota is of a 'use or lose' nature and we have been issued an ultimatum—we now have just this one winter, one logging season, to show that we can handle our commitments. If we cannot log our quota this winter and also make a gain on past shortages then the quota becomes forfeit and all Ember's 'Paper Trees' will be gone just as they came—at the stroke of a pen. Any thoughts of controlling the forest that is our future will vanish with them.

So here we sit, leaderless, aimless, and deep in debt while the first skiffs of snow brush the mountain tops warning of winter's southward march.

The night that John and Lora had unexpectedly come home my hopes were raised. But only until John explained to me, on the way down the hill, that he is leaving for good. I still wonder at being the first to be told of it. "Byron," he said to me, "I've never acted the coward before in my life, but I'm going to now. Years ago when we bought this land, there was nothing here but a passing track in the wilderness. Starting from scratch was part of the challenge but it was also cheaper, money was a stranger to us then just as it is now."

I stole a glance at him, something has changed a good deal since I last saw him and I didn't have to wonder long what it was. I've never known his exact age except that I know from things he talks of that he is a lot older than he looks. When he left for town a few weeks ago if asked to guess judging by appearance I would have said he might be pushing sixty—not an old man. Tonight, illness and worry lines make him look deep into his seventies. The age difference between him and Lora shows now making her look more like his daughter than his wife. She must have been very young when they first came here. Premonition nibbled at the back of my mind as he went on.

"We had just a small crew, working mostly for their board, times were hard then too but different than now. Jock and Lily Patten, our closest friends, came with us to share our fate. If only we could back up and do things differently maybe they would be with us yet. We cut down timber, learning how as we did it, cleared land, built roads and made a mill and a town out of next to nothing. Lily died suddenly while she was still young—it was a terrible shock to us then only months later Jock was killed in the first serious accident we had in the mill. There have been others too." He let that thought dangle between us and I knew they were both thinking of their own two sons whose graves we are passing close to right now. "Quite a few people have died in the making of Rainy Mountain and now it seems to be my turn."

He shouldn't say things like that! I came very close to driving us into the ditch I was so startled at the morbid tone in his voice. "Only, unlike the others, I have been given a choice. The doctor says it's quite simple—I can stay in business and die rather promptly—or I can get away from it and possibly beat the odds for a while longer. It depends on how well I can clear my mind of your troubles here and make myself a new but simple life."

He wasn't making much sense to my way of thinking because I have no troubles that I admit out loud. Fortunately I didn't say so, because with a second thought I realized he has already made a fair start on clearing his mind and now implies that while I am a part of troubled Rainy Mountain—he is not.

"I don't feel ready to die yet, but then, who ever does?" He managed his usual tight little smile. "So tomorrow night we are leaving for good, we are only stopping over a day to pick up a few personal things and to tie up these loose ends. You, the boys and Ember will have to carry on the best you can till Peter gets here."

"Peter?" I asked stupidly, as though refusing to admit his existence would keep him away.

"Yes, Jock's boy, he grew up here, we raised him as one of our own. He has all the abilities that we need and I believe he is the only one of us who can help find a way out of this mess. I know now that I can't. I hope you and he will get along, and I ask you to back him all you can. He will need you because both Allan and Tom are sure to resent him coming. They were always at each other's throats as boys but I hope that's all behind them now."

Lora Morrow has not yet said a word since "hi," and that tells me who has worked the hardest to bring about this amazing development. Now that she is getting her way she will remain mostly quiet rather than risk saying the wrong thing. About the same as I would expect from her oldest daughter who manipulates, motivates and activates then steps aside as if she were an innocent bystander. I probably shouldn't think of Ember like this but I still hold her responsible for getting me into that truck with Terry. An uneasy silence, as thick as the early morning mixture of grey rain mist and burner smoke at the bottom of the hill is riding with us in Nightrider's cab. But when I stop at the house to let them out John has more to tell me.

"I can't afford to get into an argument with anyone about anything," he tapped his chest over his weakened heart, "and you know perfectly well how easily my temper gets the best of me so we are telling no one but you of our plans. Tomorrow night we leave and the next day you can tell the others what I am telling you now. One more thing—I have arranged at the bank for cheques, other than payroll, to be signed by Ember. That will be temporary, just until Peter gets here then it will all be handed over to him."

"When is he coming?" I asked, still trying to get a handle on what I'm being told.

"I don't know. I don't know where he is, but I've put advertisements in all the papers and my friends are passing the word and looking for him. Soon as he hears he is needed at home I know he will come right away." It occurred to me that his daughter could probably tell him of Peter's location but I didn't say so.

I pulled their suitcases to the edge of the truck deck but before I got any farther John opened one of them right there. From it he produced a cardboard folder that he handed to me. "Take this with you, look the contents over carefully then put it in a safe place. Everything you need is there and I've already signed before a witness wherever necessary. It's plain and simple enough as you will see once you have read through it. Ember will have to go to the bank to leave them a sample of her signature and

MacKenzie, the manager, wants to talk to her. I think it would be a good idea if you went too, I know you won't appreciate being loaded up like this but she will need help till Peter comes and you are the only one I can count on."

As I helped carry their luggage to the back door he continued, but more quietly to avoid awakening the girls sleeping upstairs. "Once Peter is here you will have to take him to the bank and the lawyer's as well. At that time give him those forms so he can fill in his name where needed, sign accordingly, and leave a copy with the lawyer. The bank may want one too."

Later, in my room, I looked hard at the outside of that slim, brown folder that represents the turning of a big, big page for Rainy Mountain. I am not going to open it tonight, nor tomorrow unless John insists. I'm sure no one would ever suspect that I might have something of value in my shack so I put it in the drawer of my writing desk where it will share space with paper, a ruler, envelopes and pens. For one of the few times in my life I am not the least bit curious, actually I am apprehensive and saddened. The way John has pulled me into his personal troubles is certainly the last thing in this world that I would have expected and my old feeling of panic is there as it always is when someone expects too much of me—but this time I am determined to conquer it. Whatever his faults, and mine, whatever my relations with the rest of his family, it was his nod of acceptance that allowed me to stay when really I was too useless to bother telling about. Through all his rough talk and temper blow-ups he has treated me fairly and with respect so by the request of John Morrow as for no other man, I will carry out the required deception at the office to keep his secret through the coming day. Once he is gone though, my loyalty to his children may be up for review since it seems unlikely that they will need me as much as he thinks.

John didn't come near the office at all the next day, nor did anyone mention him in my presence and that made matters a lot easier for me. In my heart I know I still didn't really believe he would leave. For all the time I have known him he has been such a stubborn authoritarian presence in the office that I cannot imagine the place without him running the show in his own unique way.

Without him we shall be, though, because the two of them were ready and waiting at the mall when I collected Nightrider to go to meet the trains. "You got away without anyone knowing?" I asked.

"Yes."

That was almost the full extent of our conversation except I did learn that they were going back to Prince George to pick up the car they own. It was only used on the occasions when they were in town so though it is several years old, it has seen very little mileage. With the car they intend to find their way eventually, by roundabout roads, to his youngest brother's farm near Edmonton. The old home place on which John grew up then tired of and left behind years ago.

So the man who stopped here many years ago with not much more than his bare hands, a wife and some friends—who built a town and a business in the wilderness—got on the train and left without looking back. It's a good thing his wife is still with him because he has very little else.

Now we are breathlessly awaiting Peter's arrival and if I sound sarcastic I guess it's because I have come to like things the way they are. It's obvious that I have fallen into the same apathy as the others. None of us have the faintest idea what might be done to avoid the approaching crunch, so we do nothing at all other than the daily chores that have been daily chores for so long that they are done automatically.

The morning after John and Lora caught the train I broke the news to Ember when she came to open the Post Office. As far as she knew, her folks were still at home sleeping late as they did the day before so she accused me of trying to play a nasty joke on her. She glared at me, hands on hips and was not to be convinced by any means. Then Jo arrived. An indignant Ember swung about and promptly informed her that Mom and Dad have flown the coop!

The store was left locked and the mail unsorted while we held a brief council of war. Then in case either Erin or Jennie were planning to stay home today, Ember sent Jo to make sure both found babysitters and came to the office with their husbands. The more heads in on this the better seemed to be the theory. Jo was hardly out of sight when Ember decided we had to have the twins too. "They are old enough, and then some, to start taking a part in our meetings," she said.

I don't know why she sent me to get them when she could have gone herself. It could be a hazardous undertaking for any man to roust those two out of bed so early in the morning for with their parents gone they have been shifting their hours to later than Mom would have allowed. But against high odds the twins and I all survived and soon we were gathered in the meeting room where Ember explained, for those who hadn't heard yet, the reason for us being there.

To my surprise they accepted the matter so easily you would think we were discussing no more than a summer rain shower. I had almost expected to face a firing squad once my role of complicity the day before was revealed. But the only comment on that came from Tom and he sounded no more than idly curious.

"How come Byron gets the inside track here?"

"Because Dad knew he could count on Byron to keep the rest of us in line. There will be no bulldozing him to suit our individual whims."

With that ill-considered statement or maybe too well-considered instructions given to me by answering Tom, Ember changed the whole complexion of the meeting. Especially for me. After years of being in the background—unseen, unheard, and liking it that way—suddenly every eye in the room is on me. There's not a thing I can do about it either except to sit there with a straight face and take it. It was probably only a matter of seconds but it seemed more like hours that I was under the intense scrutiny of the group.

Sweat was starting to trickle down my spine before Allan ended it. "That makes good sense, we can't all run off in our own direction, we need someone in overall authority alright. Byron has been Dad's shadow and right-hand man for so long that I guess by now he has a broader understanding of the operation than any of us."

Now this was not in my script at all. I wanted to jump up and shout "No! Not me!" But, because it was Ember's idea and she must be counting on me, I sat there like a conk on a log and was given no choice in the matter. It may not have been the most democratic election in the world but from then on I was the closest thing we had to a general manager, like it or lump it.

And actually nothing changed at all except my high and mighty concerns about my loyalty to these people went out the window, like birdshot from a twelve gauge as soon as I realized I was still as welcome as I had been while John was here. I soon saw that the arrangement was to the liking of all the family because it let them carry on exactly as they always have without the complications of having to reorganize themselves. What opportunists they all are! When I finally decided it wasn't likely to kill me then we were all happy.

Ember refused to go to Prince, to the bank. She said, right or wrong I don't know but she got away with it, that the bank already has her signature from the personal account she opened when she went to school. In her opinion if they need more they can mail her a form. As for meeting with the bank manager, she said it will be nothing more than a lecture on the use of the bank's money and only one of us was needed to listen to that. Another free, fair, and democratic election! But I did refrain from calling her a coward in case she should notice that I am a bigger one.

I left for town that very night feeling much like I was climbing onto a handcar to outrun a freight train. Ember drove Nightrider and saw me off with an altogether too cheery wave to suit my frame of mind. I should have had my camera because it must be the first time she has smiled when someone was leaving her town. As I found a seat and settled in for the trip to Prince I couldn't help but marvel at her knack for turning my world upside down. Every time she puts her paddle in the stream to steer my canoe I wind up wrecked on a rock.

When Ember first told me I was going on the bank errand alone I was tempted to take along my crutches though I haven't used them in years. It was purely defensive thinking; "you wouldn't hit a man with glasses, would you? You wouldn't kick a man on crutches, would you?" It sounds better now to remember that I discarded that idea than to admit I simply forgot to take them along. The bank encounter wasn't all that bad anyway.

H. M. MacKenzie was the manager and when I entered his office, wearing my best jeans and cleanest work shirt, Ember's nickname for him was front and foremost in my mind. She had never met the man but his initials were all she needed to come up with—what else—"His Majesty." At first glance it seemed to fit but despite that handicap, I liked the man almost on sight and came to have a high regard for him in short order. But he surely had some difficulty with his first impressions of me. He eyed me with considerable interest but it was that kind of arms-length interest usually reserved for things found unexpectedly in rotten logs that got bumped by accident. Contrarily, his obvious skepticism set me at ease, because that left me nowhere to go but up, and after that shaky start we actually got on reasonably well.

"I am completely in the dark as to why you have been selected as spokesman for Rainy Mountain Lumber but at the same time I am gratified—first that John Morrow understands the situation well enough to have removed himself from it, and secondly that he has excluded his sons from financial management. They, I must say, possess distressingly naive ideas on finance and business."

I didn't have to say much but I listened plenty as he settled in for what I feared would be a long session.

"Our arrangements will be very simple, you and Miss Morrow should have no difficulty comprehending that there shall be no further use of bank funds. You will have to live and work on what is presently in your operating account and your month-by-month receivables. According to inventory reports that I have here, you appear to be in a strong marketing position going into the autumn so you should experience no difficulty doing this and," here he raised his voice, "reducing your outstanding notes with us by at least fifty percent before the winter's logging expenses start coming in. At that time, if good management is in evidence, you will be able to draw on bank funds to an amount to be determined after viewing your plans."

I nodded in as wise a manner as I could manage after absorbing all that but he didn't even notice. He went on to ask a lot of questions about our business and here I was on firm ground. My years as the Invisible Man in the organization paid off now and I sat back with my confidence rising and answered without hesitation everything he threw at me. Eventually he was satisfied.

"As you are aware this is merely an interim solution, you and Miss Morrow will hand over all authority to—," he glanced at the papers on his desk, "Mr. Peter Patten as soon as he arrives. We shall all hope that Mr. Patten is as competent in business and management as John seems to think he is. I have never met Mr. Patten so I want you or Miss Morrow to bring him to me personally, I'll need to go over this in much greater detail with him."

Back at home events seemed to go well enough, lumber is moving, receivable accounts are coming in, some less promptly than others. For the first time in a long while our badly battered chequing account is showing enough on the plus side to start thinking about making some substantial payments to our long suffering creditors, the people who sell us fuel, parts and supplies. On paper our prospects are looking better every day as the price of lumber inched upward for a change, instead of the long downward slide we have helplessly watched over the last couple of years. So over the short-term things are just fine.

For the life of me though, I can't see any way to come up with half of that monstrous debt that has built up over the years. I apply a lot of time to thinking while I'm waiting for trains but I haven't come up with any practical ideas for that. Or for handling the glut of logs we are supposed to produce this coming winter. We have the mechanical capacity to do the necessary logging, but at the sawmill end we fall far short. We will wind up with a pile of logs that have to be paid for and no way to get them through the sawmill before they rot away on us since more yet must be logged next year—and so on. I guess we need Peter alright, we certainly need someone with a brain in his head to think us out of this tight corner we're in.

There was one other unpleasant little chore that I attended to that probably cost me some marks with Ember. Tom and Allan were both in the office one Friday afternoon bringing their paperwork up to date. As usual they were both a few days behind and the women needed it for the payroll at quitting time tonight. It must have been a slack time in the store because Ember wandered in, like she often does, even though she likes to say the office is not her territory. She censors our company mail now and sometimes even prepares an answer for it before bringing it to us but that doesn't count because she does it in the store. No one was talking much until Jennie came from the back room.

"I thought I heard you come in, Em. Here's Tim's cheque, or should I just mail it off to him?"

"No, I'll take it Jennie, I'll write to him tonight and put it in with the letter."

Tom was always in a foul mood while doing bookwork, and today is no exception. "What in ham sill is that useless pup doing now?" Irritation was written large all over his face, but then Tom's emotions are usually the large economy size.

"He's still in university."

"He finished his forestry studies, didn't he?"

"Yes, but he's studying other things now." Ember was starting to sound a bit defensive.

"Well the way I see it, he is the only one of us with a decent education, and a degree or whatever in forestry, at that. I need him here to help me in our woods operation. Besides, he's costing us plenty."

"I don't think he has any intention of ever coming home, Tom. I think he plans to stay at the Coast."

"What's he studying now?" Allan asked.

She hesitated as though she didn't want to tell us, then when she did, she sort of spit the words out like they had a bad taste. "Political Science—and—" she stopped there confronted with dropped jaws and wide eyes.

"My god!" Someone finally surfaced through the shocked silence. A Morrow studying something other than trees, sawdust and boards and how to arrive at the latter when starting with the former was clearly unthinkable.

Tom tends to speak slower than normal when his ire is rising but not really outraged yet, and he did that now, "Tell him to get right home!"

"I've been more or less telling him that all along but I don't see any way of forcing him."

When no one had an answer to that I put in my penny's worth. "There's one sure way to either bring him home or be rid of him, and that's to cut off the money supply."

"Sounds good," Tom agreed. "He'll have to come home or find a job."

"I don't think we should do that," Ember objected, "his studies are important to him."

"I don't know why you stand up for him the way you two used to fight. Or maybe he's big enough now that you can't beat up on him any more?"

Ember laughed uneasily with a sidewise glance my way, "Oh, that's all over with now that I don't have to listen to him tell me where I went wrong in my algebra. We get along quite well now that we're six hundred miles apart."

"Well I also think it's a good idea," Allan said. "Jennie, you tell Erin too, that there will be no more cheques to Tim."

Caught between Ember and the brothers, Jennie looked to me. "That's how it is, Jennie." Then to Ember I said, "Send him that cheque you have there but tell him it's the last one and we really do need him." Then I added to the room in general, and only half joking, "I don't know how he will fit in around here, though, with all that education."

Sometimes when I am alone and have time to think about it, I can only shake my head at the way they have come to take my pronouncements as law. Even the independent-minded Ember had reluctantly accepted my verdict concerning Tim. While John was here I merely refereed their arguments but that has changed now in some elusive manner that I had not expected. I suppose the hopelessness of our position is becoming so firmly fixed in all our minds that they are casting about desperately for advice from any quarter.

4

Eventually the lights came on across at the cookhouse and I soon heard the flunkies preparing for breakfast and setting up the lunchroom where everyone who works away from camp through the day will make and pack their own lunches. I was in the cookshack well before they rang their bell and out again before most of the crew were even getting up. By the time Ember came in to sort the mail, I was seated on the four-wheel cart mostly just thinking of this and that. I was also quietly stacking cans of vegetable soup one on top another along a lower shelf at the back of the store trying to be as silent as possible. I am aware that this sounds like a novel pastime for the general manager but no one else seems to see anything untoward about it. Nor does anyone else appear inclined to do the job, so here I am and happy enough about it too—not so many headaches back here. Besides, Erin and Jennie are perfectly capable of running the office without anyone's help. Ember didn't see me as she came in and Jo hasn't arrived yet so the outside door is still locked.

Footsteps came in a hesitating manner from the direction of the office and I paused to listen, wondering who it was. It certainly wasn't Jo and it isn't the nature of Allan or Tom to be hesitant about anything. As I waited and watched, the sound of a mail bag being dumped came from the post office. Then a man walked slowly into the store from the hallway and darned if it isn't the stranger who came on the train last night, I had totally forgotten about him. And he isn't really hesitating, it's more that he is looking with keen interest at everything as he advances slowly toward the checkout counter.

There was a rip of paper in the post office then total silence for about ten seconds before Ember, thinking those quiet footsteps had been mine, called out with a strange urgency in her voice. "Byron, did someone come on the train last night?"

The stranger, knowing whose footsteps she was hearing, answered before I could.

"Yes, Em—I did."

The door to the post office flew open and Ember, a sheet of yellow paper clutched in one hand and holding the doorknob as if for support with the other, stood there wide-eyed and scared. A wild young animal cornered and undecided whether to fight or flee. For two or three blinks of the eye the tableau held then broke.

"Peter!" She cried, and flung herself into his arms.

Even after what seemed to me an unnecessarily long and ardent embrace she continued to cling to him as though afraid he might disappear. I am distressed to see that she is crying as she presses her face against him. My unflappable girl is certainly undone this morning.

"Well, Em, I thought a telegram message would be phoned out from town. I see now that someone has goofed and my telegram and I have come on the same train."

While their attention was still on each other, I made my escape down the hall and after kicking and banging things around for a while I got down to the business of unloading Nightrider. I am surprised and dismayed at my reaction to the scene in the store and there is no ready explanation that I am willing to admit to. I have to think back a few years to remember the last time I so completely lost my composure. Now I have to remind myself that Ember is old enough to choose her own friends and may kiss whoever she pleases. She is no concern of mine—never has been and never will be. With that off my chest I still feel no better but at least it has been said.

I heard them in the hall before they came in sight and had, I hope, the right look of casual interest on my face as they came into the warehouse.

"Byron," Ember said with an anxious little catch in her voice that immediately caught my attention, "this is an old and very dear friend of mine, Peter Patten. And Peter, I want you to meet Byron Smith."

We shook hands rather mushily, I'm afraid, neither of us too impressed with the other. Ember, as she stood by, was actually wringing her hands. I don't know why she should feel such intense strain but I will hazard a guess—she wants me to like him. So I made the effort to smile warmly as I told him that I hope he has had a pleasant trip. I can see that he is puzzled too and impatient as Ember tells him that whatever he wants to know he can find out from me.

I wondered if he too can see that she has the fidgets. He made a little barely polite small talk then said he wanted to see if Tom and Allan have arrived in the office yet. As he led the way back to the hallway Ember threw me a look over her shoulder as she passed out of the room that quite frankly I didn't understand. I would almost swear that she was scared silly and was trying to warn me of something. What on earth is going on around here anyway? I actually found I was scratching my head in wonderment.

"Well," I shrugged, muttering under my breath, "five minutes ago you had yourself convinced they were none of your affair and I reckon that notion still holds water."

But I poked my head out the door to watch them go and I guess

I shouldn't have done that because Ember is talking about me and with far too much intensity. Due to some strange acoustic quirk of the hallway I heard every word.

"Byron," she was saying, "is our local odd character, he has ears a foot long and a nose to match. He knows absolutely everything that happens in camp. He's up to his neck in everyone's business and if you don't look out he will soon be winding your watch for you."

I hope she is smiling as she tells him that I thought while gently exploring one ear with a finger tip.

There was nothing on Nightrider for the shop or any of the woods operations so when I finished unloading the few goods intended for the store I took the rest of the load over to the cookhouse which, after all, is our best customer. Then I slunk off to my room to get a bit of much needed shuteye and of course, to think about Ember's revealing remark that obviously I wasn't supposed to hear. She is right, no doubt about it, I live and breathe on curiosity and satisfying that thirst for knowledge is what keeps me ticking. Sure, I'm meddling in their business but I thought they wanted me to. My many chores around camp put me in close personal touch not only with the Morrows but with the many other families living in the married quarters as well. But, really! Winding their watches? It's embarrassing in the extreme and all the more so because the tone of her voice leads me to wonder if she was making an apology for me.

I was able to sleep this time and it was way past noon when I awakened. The cookhouse crew are used to me prowling around on a different shift than everyone else, so getting lunch was no problem. They piled ten times what I could eat in front of me and then proceeded to pick my brains for all the latest news around camp. Anyone who thinks the ladies at their afternoon tea party have the monopoly on gossip just hasn't checked us out at the cookshack yet. The crew there seem to think that what I don't know isn't worth knowing and I do my best to keep from disappointing them.

That's where Peter found me, working on my fourth coffee. He filled a cup and joined me without any particular greeting. "Just who and what are you anyway?" His words were rough edged with suspicion and there was a hard glint of anger in his eyes.

I gave him my most innocent smile. "Why, don't you remember? I'm Byron Smith, the assistant bullcook." I confess it was on the tip of my tongue to say local watch winder, but I resisted.

"Baloney!" He snapped. "I've come home against my better judgment to try to do what appears to be the impossible because I owe it to John to at least try. I need to know everything about anything that's been going on here and every time I start asking pertinent questions all I get is lifted shoulders and the suggestion to 'ask Byron about that.'"

"Well," I said reasonably, "Ember told you."

"I know, but I didn't understand, I didn't realize then that the flunky ran the outfit."

"Assistant bullcook," I corrected.

"Whatever. But you weren't here when I left five or six," he paused, looked a little startled, "or more, years ago and I've never heard so much as boo about you. And yet I come home to find Allan and Tom happily doing their own thing and you—a total stranger—seem to have stepped straight into John's shoes. Now I'd like an explanation, something simple and logical that I can understand." Signs of suspicion and distrust fairly oozed from him as he waited for my answer.

I sighed without intending to. "That could be a tall order because I don't understand it myself."

"Well, I'd like to hear you give it a try!"

So I tried to tell him about being the Invisible Man only I didn't use that silly phrase. I gave him a sketchy rundown starting back when I was in the wreck with Terry and coming right up to the present. I can understand his distrust easily enough but as I finished my story I saw no lessening of hostility. I wound up lamely, "Sometimes I wonder if because I was with Terry when he died, his family think either that they owe me or I owe them, I'm not sure which. There have been times I've almost thought that they,

John in particular, see me as Terry in a different form and by a different name."

I could just about hear the click in his head as the light of understanding came on behind his eyes. Instantly he relaxed and even smiled. "Of course! I should have thought of that. To a Morrow mind that would be right as rain and twice as beneficial."

Just like that! I can see and feel that I am now accepted by him as completely as only a moment ago I was unacceptable. To myself I said he's been around the Morrows too long and thinks just like them, in fact he's worse, it took four years to work my way into their lives and only four minutes with him.

"Know what, Byron?"

I looked up cautiously to find him grinning widely. "What?"

"I like your style."

And there you are! This man, who is here to steal Ember away from us, who is right now stealing my job and will make sure I remain no more than assistant bullcook, has the unmitigated gall to tell me he likes my style! Would he like my thoughts if he could read them? I hope he cannot sense the amazement and turmoil that swirl in my mind—I do not wish him success—yet I want Rainy Mountain to survive and prosper. I said he was stealing Ember but it's plain enough she has been waiting for him all along. As for my job, it's only the management part he wants, that much he can have and good riddance to it. He won't want Nightrider and all the associated follow-up work that goes with my self-appointed title of assistant bullcook. To me that's the part that counts so why should I be unhappy? I guess because demotion is still demotion, and no matter how welcome it may be it's still disturbing and demeaning. I would gladly have given the job away but I do not like it being taken just like that. I know there will be some hard mental adjustments for me to make.

I had lowered my eyes to examine my coffee cup more fully, but try as I might, I couldn't stop the smile that came sneaking across my face nor the chuckle that was with it. So I guess there will be a truce for a while. Just for you Ember, I promised to myself, not sure why I call it truce when there has been no war.

I began to learn right away that Peter is one of those rare people who it is impossible to dislike completely. It doesn't matter what shocking things he does or says, all he has to do is to smile in his special, charming, crinkle-eyed way, and you know that all is well in the world yet. He has a magnetism that unknown to me has already been at work on my subconscious causing me to feel relief that he now understands my position, even though ten minutes ago I hadn't given a hoot whether he understood or cared, or not.

We went to the mall where we took over the meeting room at the back of the office wing. It's a halfway room—halfway comfortable, halfway private, and also only halfway illuminated. There is a fine old hardwood desk at the far end of the room as you enter at the doorway, set so the person seated at it faces the room like a teacher faces her pupils. Scattered between it and the door are a dozen or so leather-seated wooden chairs, all fugitives from discarded dining room suites. Most have seen a better day and are just barely halfway easy to sit on. Three of the four walls of this room that used to be the store, in older days, are still covered with shelves that go right to the ceiling. They are stacked with an endless variety of office supplies and even some of the more valuable or fragile parts for the shop such as spare fuel injection pumps and nozzles for diesel engines. So it's also halfway a storage room.

We spent the rest of the afternoon just talking but I realize that he is getting the information he wants in the process. At one point he got up and went to the back office where Erin and Jennie work. Neither of them were in at the moment so Peter helped himself to the timebook in which the hours worked each day by each member of the crew are entered as reported by the various foremen. He wanted to know exactly how large the crew is right now and the best way seems to be to count up the names listed in the book.

But when he finished he just set the book amid the clutter on the desk instead of returning it.

About an hour later Erin came in looking a bit puzzled. "I seem to have misplaced the timebook, it's not in here, is it?"

Peter casually rearranged a couple of trade magazines to hide the volume in question. "Of course not. Why should it be here?"

He took it for granted that I would say nothing and against my natural urge I did remain silent. Half an hour later, well past quitting time, she was back, really upset now. "That timebook is just not around and I can't imagine what could have become of it."

"Maybe it went into the garbage with the junk mail," Peter suggested darkly. This is something totally foreign to me and I don't care for it, but I already like and admire him enough that I want to make excuses for him. I want to think it's just a lighthearted prank but Erin is frantic and in no mood for a joke. Peter must be able to see that too, but instead of producing the book and us all having a laugh, he turned the thumbscrews tighter.

"If you've lost that book, Erin, there will be a real shmozzle trying to make up the time on payday."

Erin turned to go and as she did her eyes caught mine, she is more than worried, she is overwhelmed at the prospect of having to dredge up all that information again from scratch—literally—in the foremen's notes. It's a book that has to be available for inspection any time any of several branches of government decide they want a look at it. It carries their most recently dated stamp of audit. Time books do not go missing!

Enough is enough I thought. "Have a look through those lumber magazines on the desk, Erin, I know it shouldn't be there but I can see the edge of book that looks like it."

She was so relieved to find the time book that she didn't even question how it got there but just took it, hugged it and left.

"You're a bit of a spoilsport, Byron. But at that, Erin is slipping, she used to catch on to me quicker than that. She's out of practice, you must not cause her the trouble that I used to."

I can't tell if he is peeved with me or not and strangely I now find myself wishing I hadn't broken up his game. But at the same time I know that he not only had his joke at Erin's expense but also has tested to see how far I would go along with him. Well, he now knows that is not very far.

After a break for supper, we were back there again, though now it's more a case of him just needing someone to listen to him think out loud. For someone who has been away for nearly six years he strikes me as being remarkably well-informed. When I commented on that to him he admitted that John had left a long letter, almost a report, for him with the lawyer. The main point in the letter, Peter told me, was that every effort is to be made to salvage the company in its entirety and not allow bits to be sold to save the rest. Peter's interpretation of that sounds to me exactly as if John were sitting there talking to me. It almost seems as though Peter is more like the old man than John's own sons are and I'm not sure if that's good or bad. But at first impression at least his temperament appears vastly different than any of the others. I soon learned that he has a sufficiency of temper but seldom allows it to show. In fact he can be exceedingly angry and if you don't know him well, his anger will be past and gone before you have an inkling that it existed. Even now, after only a few hours acquaintance, I am marveling at his mercurial personality. Never before have I known someone who could sit silently and run through every emotion in the book in five to ten seconds and finish up calm again and ready to carry on. Not only can Peter do that, but three out of four people in the room with him will fail to notice anything amiss.

Along about eight-thirty Ember interrupted by surprising us with a tray loaded with coffee and cookies. For me the surprise comes because it is not her way to be either thoughtful of others or to be caught in a serving role. She is so openly relieved to see us getting along reasonably well that after she left to put in the last half hour at the store I commented on it to Peter. "Ember has gone quite hyper on us since you showed up and here I have always said she is unflappable. She is, I've always thought, the most even-tempered person I have ever known, totally unlike the others."

Peter choked at that moment on the cookie he was eating but when he got it cleared he chuckled and said, "Ember? Even-tempered? She has changed some since I last knew her then." Seeing my disbelief he added, "I think you will find, my friend, that she has her full share of the famous Morrow temper. You can only push her so far then look out! When she blows her top she starts with a big loud bang and climbs from there."

Ember came back to us after closing the store for the night and she is in an exuberant, almost giddy mood. Peter decided to tease her a little, "You still lock the store door at night?"

"Of course, we always have."

"But you leave all the other doors in the place unlocked, so anyone who wants to can get in by way of the office, first aid room or the back door."

She was too pleased with life in general tonight to be concerned with where his odd humour might be leading. "You know as well as I do that no one will ever come in to steal from us. It's just my way to say that we are closed, otherwise there would be customers coming till traintime and starting again at four in the morning."

He smiled and dangled a different bait. "Do you call Rainy Mountain 'town' yet? Or have you joined the majority who say 'camp'?"

She grinned right back at him. "I've slipped shockingly. Nearly everyone says 'camp' so gradually I've conformed. Mom and Dad are the only ones who persist in saying 'town'. To me, and I suspect all the rest of us, we live in 'camp', and 'town' means Prince."

Peter wasn't satisfied yet but if he was trying to demonstrate Ember's temper quotient for me, then he was not having much luck. "And by 'Prince' do you mean Prince George or Prince Rupert? Or by chance, Prince Albert?"

"Oh get off it, Peter," but she was still smiling, "all along the line every one knows 'Prince' is Prince George and 'Rupert' is a long ways away. Prince Albert, indeed!"

He stared her down but couldn't remove her smile, then he laughed. "I've worked in many places along what you so loosely term 'the line' and if you mean the seven hundred-odd miles of rail from Jasper to—ah—'Rupert' then I have to inform you that there are wide variations of opinion on that matter."

"Well, I know what I'm talking about and if you've wandered around so much that you've become confused, then that's your tough luck." They both laughed with an easy pleasure, quite friendly, and on the surface at least, seeming to thoroughly understand each other. Not behaving like long separated lovers, not at all like their emotional meeting this morning.

Peter may have known Ember longer than I, but not in recent times. Over the last four years no one has been closer to her than I have, unless perhaps the twins, for the three of them live together. I'm not implying that we are close in any manner other than that we are thrown together in our work because we are not. I appreciate her attractive presence and no-nonsense manner but it seems we are forever on opposite sides of fences. And it's my opinion right now that—despite her smiles and banter—we are entertaining one nervous lady who is doing her best to hide it. I'd give a pocketful of loot to know what is bothering her.

Ember got us back to the business at hand, briefly that is. "Did I hear you two talking about an ice bridge when I came in?"

"We were just tossing around whether to go for an ice bridge this winter and get some close and easy timber from across the river. Byron seems to think we should concentrate on this side and leave the uncertainties of ice and weather to another, less demanding, year."

Actually I hadn't said much of anything, it's plain to see that hogging credit is not one of Peter's vices. He is almost a non-stop talker but still manages to invite the opinions of others. If a decision comes from that one-sided conversation then it seems to be his way to heap praise all out of proportion on his listener.

Having just nicely gotten us back on track, Ember now derailed us completely with a story about another winter. "It seems like every time we depend on the ice we get a mild winter, like two years ago when we were counting on logs from the other side. It stayed warm so late, Peter," she said, "that we couldn't get the ice bridge hardened up enough for hauling right into the first week in January. The small vehicles could cross but not the trucks so the piles of logs grew but couldn't be hauled. With all our road and trail work already done over there and not much on this side, we were getting into a bind alright. Then suddenly it dropped from above freezing to forty below in only a couple of days—it was a shocker the way the temperature went down."

"At about seven-thirty that first real cold morning, I took the Company mail in to the office and found Dad and Allan trying to make sense of what Tom was raging about. He was so mad I could hardly understand him at first." Ember laughed at the memory of that scene. "What he was saying was that the men were claiming it was too cold to go to work. We all scratched holes in the frost on the windows so we could look out into the marshalling yard in front of the office. There was a line of busses, I mean crummies, waiting with most of the crews milling around refusing to get in but trying to keep active enough to stay warm."

"Dad was fit to be tied but to his credit he had enough sense to not go out himself to face the loggers—a good thing too because he is even hotter-tempered than Tom and would probably have provoked an insurrection. He has always considered Allan as cool and level-headed so he sent Allan out to talk reason to them."

"But Allan was soon back, and positively livid, to report that not only were the men refusing to go to work, but they also wanted call time for showing up at the marshalling yard. They were planning to demonstrate and to intercept the mill and planer crews until the call time was entered into the timebook."

I knew now what she was leading up to and I almost got up to leave, I'm not sure if she was out to embarrass me again or if she had it in mind to show Peter that sometimes I accidentally manage to do something useful. Either way, I don't like it but I decided to stay and see what damage she can do to me this time.

She lifted a hand toward me. "Byron was there in the office, keeping out of everyone's way but missing nothing as usual. Now he suggested that we all just sit tight and within ten minutes or so he would have the crews on their way to work, then he disappeared into the hallway to the store.

"Well, it sounded so preposterous that we did just as he said all the time watching out the window. It seemed like a long time went by then Byron came strolling idly along, as only Byron can, with that hop-and-shuffle gait of his. He carried a big wrench in each hand, both hands bare, no coat, no hat, a big long flashlight sticking out of a hip pocket and whistling as if he were in his right mind. He didn't even seem to notice anything unusual about the crowd of men standing around under the yard lights but they sure halted everything to watch him in disbelief." She stopped for a moment as though to get her story straight in her mind and Peter was just starting to say something when she went on.

"He had almost walked right on by them before someone shouted, 'Hey, By, what are you doing?'

And Byron hauled up short like he had finally just noticed the gathering. 'Oh, got a few chores out along the water line, nothing much really.' Now he faced them squarely and plainly he was puzzled. 'Something wrong? How come you guys haven't been taken to work?'

Well, they looked around at each other for a few seconds before someone said sheepishly 'It's too cold to work.'

Byron carefully rubbed first one ear and then the other with one of the wrenches. 'Oh! Yeah,' he agreed, 'it's a bit chilly alright, and just in time too! We would all be out of a job soon if it had stayed warm.' Then he turned and walked away from them into the darkness as if they were the last thing on his mind while they watched every step he took as he faded then vanished.

"Pretty soon the muttering started, I heard someone say loudly, 'if he can take it, I can too.' Then Tom slipped out the door to join them and in five minutes all we could see of them was a cloud of snow settling on the road.

"As soon as they were gone Byron came back in to the office but neither Dad nor Allan had anything to say to him. They were still plenty peeved and Dad growled, 'Now how are we going to stop that from happening every cold morning?' Again Byron supplied the answer.

" 'Smash every thermometer in town,' he said.

"There was no reaction to that suggestion so after a while I said to Dad, 'Byron said to break all the thermometers in town.'

" 'I heard him daughter, I heard him, I was just thinking about it. It's a good idea but I don't think we can do that.'"

Ember laughed. "For all Dad's faults he is too honest to tamper with other people's property, even such a minor thing as an offending thermometer. So that night, unknown to anyone, Byron took it on himself to go around and steal or break every thermometer in camp, including ours and all the new ones in stock in the store. There was a lot of speculation a good deal hotter than the weather over the next few days as to who had done it but there were no more 'too cold' problems all the rest of the winter. A pretty good black market developed for thermometers though."

"Very neat," Peter observed, "but tell me, how did you manage to carry an iron wrench in each bare hand at forty below without freezing to them?"

No one has ever asked me this before and not surprisingly I am reluctant to tell because the truth is a whole lot less impressive than the deed had appeared at the time. I wasn't sure how Ember had guessed so quickly who the guilty party was either. She had confronted me the moment she heard that all thermometers were missing and I fumbled my denial so thoroughly that she knew it was me. Of course she knew the idea was mine to start with but I thought I lived so low on the totem pole that no one would connect me with it. Reluctantly I answered his question. "While I was in the first aid room pulling on an extra pair of 100% wool long johns from the store stock, the wrenches were on top of the furnace getting hot—they kept my hands nice and warm. Other than that I was only outside a few minutes and didn't have time to get really cold."

Peter tipped back his chair, laughing loudly with appreciation. "I finally begin to understand why the flunky is giving the orders and the boss's sons obey them."

I didn't like this turn of words, especially in Ember's presence so I tried to set the record straight. "No. You have that wrong, I don't give orders to anyone, I've just tried to keep things a little bit organized till you got here. The most I've done has been to make a few suggestions when it seemed needed."

"He's right Peter, but he's being overly modest because while Tom and Allan and all the various foremen used to consult with Dad, now they come to Byron and they don't argue with his suggestions either."

"But what has become of Allan and Tom? I remember both of them as completely capable, and qualified to take over at any time." He grinned. "It's partly why I left when I did."

Ember was shaking her head but I answered before she could. "They both have fully demanding positions that would be even harder to get replacements for than finding a manager. Managers have only to supply the control needed so the people who know what they are doing can get out and accomplish something. A manager can be hired any time, doesn't have to be overly brilliant, except at covering his own tracks, can be fired whenever he gets out of line and won't be missed much"

"I'll take that as fair warning," Peter said testily. "I had you figured as a nice guy but now I find you have diesel engine antifreeze in your veins and steel in your heart."

"And rocks in my head." I added, disgusted with the way I have let the tone of the conversation get away from me.

Peter pushed back his chair, ready to rise. "Yeah. Well, friends, I've had all I can take tonight, I've got to get some sleep. And you have trains to meet yet! I don't know how you take these cruel hours, Byron. When I go to bed I like to stay there till morning."

Ember was leaving too, she was passing behind me as he said this and now she paused to lay a hand lightly on my shoulder. "He is Owl, Peter. He sleeps by day. My great snowy owl. I named him one winter night in a blizzard." Then she laughed at me. "You didn't know you had picked up your very own nickname, did you? Curious Owl, always asking—who? I don't often tell people what I have named them but I like yours too much to keep it secret."

Peter was scowling. "So do I, Em, a devil of a lot better than what you've inflicted upon me."

"Raven." She smiled. "I like that too, it suits you, Peter."

"Black scavenger," he snorted.

"Bird of legend, mystery, and adventure," she countered, "and, as it happens, black feathered just as you are black haired."

I don't know about Peter, but I am feeling more uncomfortable with each exchange of words between them. Ember has obviously had too long and exciting a day, and has fallen off the deep end. I can only hope that a good night's sleep will bring her back to her senses. All this foolish talk of owl and raven makes me uneasy and I wish I didn't have to listen to it.

But all at once Peter has come alert and does not look the least bit tired—or embarrassed either—the way I'm sure I do. Suddenly he is the cat with the canary cornered. Just as suddenly Ember's hand is lifted from my shoulder and with a small, sharp intake of breath, she is gone from behind me to the doorway where she turned to face Peter. They stare at each other for long seconds then Ember moves her head in an almost imperceptible motion of no'. After a few more seconds Peter relaxes into a slouch and Ember immediately leaves.

Something that I don't understand has passed between them.

Something that I'm afraid concerns me as well if the acutely inquisitive stare that Peter has now turned my way means anything.

"What is it? What's happened?" I ask. Not who but what!

By the time he answered his face was smooth and blank but his eyes still glittered strangely. "Not a thing. I've just discovered something is all. Sometimes it affects me that way."

Ember, with her 'head in the clouds' mood of today has been kinder to me tonight, with her words, than I had any reason to expect, perhaps too kind in Peter's view. Maybe he's the jealous type and Ember shouldn't have been so friendly. But he should show signs of anger in that case, and all I see now is a tired man who has been travelling a lot, thinking too much and missing his sleep. It's the first time she has ever deliberately reached out to touch me and warmth lingers yet where her hand had rested—where her hand had flexed gently while it touched.

I got up to head for home, not caring a great deal what Peter might have in mind but he tagged right along and I wondered if he intends to remain at the bunkhouse with me. "You'll be moving to the house, I suppose?"

"Why no. I like it here just fine. Why would I move out?"

My normal style is to beat around the bush and try to learn as much from what is not said as from what is. When I do throw caution to the wind, I pick hurricane weather to do it in. "Well," I said, not even trying to sound casual, "it's your home isn't it? And I've been told that you and Ember have an understanding—."

"Oh! So you too have heard that old yarn." He was quiet for a moment. "A lot of parents have dreams for their children—" he was going to say more but shrugged instead. "That's life. Aside from that, Em and I have had our ups and downs, sometimes it's hard to tell where I stand with her."

Amazing, I thought how much that last statement sounds like some of my own uncertain experiences with Ember. I like to call her the quiet reliable one of her family. And she is. Until every so often when she tosses the rule book in the waste bin and all bets are off.

"If you want to get right down to hard facts," he said, "the twins are my favourites. I've always had a real soft spot for them even way back in the days when they used to put salt in the sugar for me and—well—you get the drift."

He has evaded the issue, perhaps he's not so keen on the arrangement as he might be. Maybe Ember's not either. How much easier to face the future if only I could believe that but in the face of her performance today I can't. And already I have learned that to Peter, truth is a tool, and if fiction is a better tool for the moment then, truth takes a beating. The big question mark though is why was Ember first so concerned, then so pleased and relieved that I should get along with Peter? Compared to him I am nobody at all, it shouldn't matter whether I like him or not. It just happens that I do like him, maybe with a few reservations. I am already convinced that John was right in sending for him, he is intelligent, knowledgeable and seems decisive, all qualities that are not really overflowing in my own personal makeup. He is just the man we have been needing though twelve short hours ago I would have been hard to convince. That's how much he has charmed me already. But that contrary little devil who lives in the dark side of my mind still wants to see him stumble enough that Ember loses interest in him.

Once home in my own room I went straight to bed and wound my alarm clock, it's seldom allowed to ring—but—just in case. If I could either sleep until traintime or sleep late in the morning I wouldn't have to steal nap time during the day but I often read until time to go up the hill. Then in the morning nothing seems so important as being the first one to the coffee pot. After all, fresh coffee is the best coffee.

Ember is not the only one who has put in a long and exciting day. I too feel like a wound-up spring with nowhere to go because I'm connected to jammed wheels. Her intent tonight, I think, was to improve my image in Peter's eyes, but her story of the thermometer incident raked up old coals in my mind that I would sooner were left to die. There had been a sequel to that story, one that I hope Ember has not heard of.

On that cold evening two winters ago, the streets were completely deserted as one would expect with the mercury sliding ominously past forty below zero. It was so cold that not even a dog barked at me as I went from house to house stealing every thermometer in sight. Those too well-fastened received a firm squeeze over the bulb from a pair of pliers that I carried in a pocket.

The snow squeaked loudly at every step and the sound must have carried well but I encountered no one and I'm sure I was not seen. It was early enough that nearly everyone was up yet but there was ample racket from radios and such to cover the noise I made on walks and porches.

As I got closer to Jo's house she came more and more to mind. A pretty girl, perhaps as pretty as Ember, for when they wish to they can be incredibly alike. She would be steady and true, a good person. Almost as dedicated to her work as her sister-in-law but one can sense a difference for with her the work is not a be all end all but is used as a time filler, to help keep thoughts of a lost husband down to a size she can handle. It's like she is afraid to fall hard for someone again in case she should lose him too. Someday she will decide it's time to look around and some lucky man will be there. More than two years at this point since Terry died, perhaps one should let her know that one is interested—my life is messed up too.

At one time or another, in the face of Ember's studied indifference, I have half-heartedly tried my luck with every girl in camp who is single and old enough to date. There aren't many, but because she still ranks in my mind as Terry's wife and I am still uncertain about my possible part in his death, I have never included Jo on that list. Our contacts are all strictly business but I'm sure she likes me in part of the comfortable background sort of way. We talk a lot as good friends do. Each of the others in their own style let me know that while I might be cheerful conversational company in the store, I am not to be considered for anything more serious.

Jo looks enough like Ember that when they wish it so, they can be taken as sisters, or maybe even twins, though Ember is at least a year older. But I think Jo is lucky to be living in her shadow because while she tries to copy her sister-in-law's confident manner she lacks the steel trap mind and determination to carry it off. Perhaps I should give her more credit, perhaps she still has the cold hardness in her eyes when she needs it—I only know it's not there for me anymore. I sometimes fear she could easily fall for the wrong guy who has the right line. But there seems to be a natural safety screen for her as long as she's with Ember when the dozens of men pour into the store at shift change or in the evening with little on their minds but to spend a bit and visit a lot. They must see the equal attractiveness but it's Ember who draws them like bees to a pail of honey—and she can handle it. Ember makes me think of the word enigma. To be near her draws you to look her way, she makes you think, she causes you to wonder, to wish and dream and then to wonder again only this time—why?

Then there are the twins, bless the twins, they have a happy way about them that would help anyone forget their troubles. The problem is how to separate them. I can now tell them apart without fail much to their dismay. But separate them? It doesn't seem to be possible, try to date either one and you wind up with both—every time. In other words, they too, have no intention of letting anything develop. Anyway, I can't take the steady diet of four-letter words, it stopped being cute somewhere along the way.

So, unlikely as it seems, here I am in a crowd of friends and lonely for close company. Rumours of her life 'before Terry' have followed Jo from—somewhere—but if anything they only make her more interesting. It does bother me though when I hear snatches of conversation in the bunkhouses between young guys with more ego than sense, "You don't have to be lonely here, not with Jo around."

"There's a path beaten wide and deep from Bunkhouse Row to her back door."

"How can you tell if you'll be welcome?—Don't worry she'll let you know."

One moment I was at her back porch dropping another thermometer into my collection bag and the next thing I know I have tossed them all into the snow and am knocking on the door. The pleasure that lit up her face when she saw me and the way she hurried me in so she could shut the door against the cold told me it was good that I had come. But I quickly had to revise my line of thought because I sensed instantly that she was not welcoming me as material for a possible romantic adventure but as a trusted friend come to help pass a lonely evening. Now that I am here I can see it simply is not the time or place to let her know I like her as I had fooled myself into thinking it might be. She probably knows that already and isn't planning to go anywhere with it.

As she put water on to boil for coffee I struggled out of my heavy coat, a lighter jacket and a sweater under it then sat and sweltered, still dressed too warm for indoors. After she poured the coffee we talked a little about everything except her and I but then somehow we got on the subject of the Morrow family and the conversation became more lively.

"They surely are a strange lot," Jo said. "Sometimes I wonder why I stay and other times I think I will never leave."

"I know just what you mean, you've put my own thoughts exactly into words."

She nodded then went on, "I have everything I need and I can have most anything I want within reason. That's more than I ever had in life before I met Terry. But at the same time I have nothing I can really call my own. The house is only mine because I live in it, if I leave it will soon become someone else's. Like you and all the Morrows I work nearly every day but, like all of you, have never seen a paycheque to hold in my hands and say, 'I have earned this.'"

"But still—like me—you don't suffer for the lack of anything."

"No. Anything I want I just order through the store." She

smiled. "Anything from nylons to a refrigerator. Why I'll bet I could even go over to the shop and lay claim to the newest pickup in the lineup, drive it home, park it out front, and it would automatically become Jo's truck. No one would take it away or say I shouldn't have done that. But sometimes I would simply like to have a little cash in my hand, and my own bank account."

I had to laugh for I could visualize it happening just as she said. "Why don't you do that, Jo? I mean go get yourself a truck. Every one else in the family has one—except the Twins who would rather walk and be seen. And I have Nightrider and the use of a pickup whenever I need one."

"No, I just can't bring myself to wanting one. But," she added with a sparkle in her eyes, "if there was a neat little red Corvette Stingray in the lineup, I would have it so fast they would think it had evaporated. Maybe I'll try ordering one of them through the store." We both laughed at that. "But seriously I'm not complaining, I feel safe here and I like that—it's worth a lot to me. And I think to you too," she said with a bold glance suggesting secrets of mine that she had guessed at but still wondered about.

Jo can be a blunt-speaking person so I decided to be the same and shift the topic away from myself at the same time—curiosity cannot be denied. "How did you come to meet Terry? I've heard it was something of a fairy tale romance."

"Fairy tale?" Her eyes slowly lighted with the shine of good memories as she considered my wording. "I've never thought of it like that. For me more of the whirlwind variety I think. Certainly it was the best thing that ever happened in my life."

"You don't mind me being curious?"

"Not a bit, I've made no secret of my past, it's just that no one ever asks. The Morrows all seem to like their in-laws to remain a bit of a mystery. Either that or they are the least curious people I have ever encountered. You must have noticed that by now too."

"Well, I have but then I'm not an in-law like you, more of an adopted orphan or maybe a charity case." To myself I added, or replacement for a lost son but this is not the place to say that.

"Where did you live? In Prince?"

"No, I was waitressing at a truckstop near a little town in the Fraser Canyon. I was doing other things too, but Terry fixed all that." She was quiet for a long moment then added gently, "Terry fixed everything for me." She tossed her head a bit and gave me such a smile I could have cried for her. Plainly there is no pain in the telling, maybe even the opposite.

"Terry, who I had never seen before, drove in with a big new truck he had gotten in Vancouver, fueled it up, parked it then came inside. When I handed him the menu he took one shocked look at me then jumped up and demanded, 'Ember! What in hell are you doing here?' Well, of course I thought he was crazy so I backed away and told him my name was not Ember. He stared at me a moment then he sat down and smiled the most devastating smile I had ever seen. With that smile he won my heart but not yet my head because what I thought was that if he liked me so much maybe he would stay till I was off work and maybe he would even pay me for the night. Do I shock you, Byron?"

"Aw—You're trying to but no, nothing that turned out so obviously right could ever shock me—uh—much. I know what you mean about the smile too—all the Morrows, even Ember—can give that marvelous, that truly genuine, 'I like you' smile. But it's so rare. And it's not really a 'Morrow' smile because it comes from Lora. If John had to smile like that it would break his face."

"Yes. I knew you would understand but then you have to, don't you. Or you wouldn't be here."

I'm not at all sure what she meant by that so I just let it go by.

"Anyway, he said that, yes, he could see now that I was not who he had thought but then he explained that I was such an almost perfect double for his sister that he had been fooled for an instant. He said it had been a long tiring day for him driving in traffic that he wasn't used to or he wouldn't have made the mistake. I thought it was just a cute line to get my interest. I thought he simply didn't realize that someone as good-looking as he needed no line, just another smile might do."—Then, more like she was asking rather than telling—"there was no warning came that he spoke of a woman who would cry with me someday. Or that it would be him we cried about.

"Anyway, he did stay—the next day and night too and then I went with him. But he wanted to get married and I was too young, so we had to get a form and go back for my mother's signature. Mom was doing pretty good for herself running a convenience store and she got real excited when this strange guy came along wanting her only daughter. We let her think we had been friends for quite a while but even so she figured he would only want me about as long as my father had wanted her. Mom can be quite hyper, hard for anyone to keep up to. She likes quiet men but she won't be quiet herself, so they move on. But somehow Terry managed to convince her, the smile I think, and we were off north again. I was becoming a problem for her about then anyway so she might have thought, 'good riddance' but I hope not.

"We were a few days in Prince while Terry got a flatcar and loaded the truck on it to ship out to here. Then we got married and caught the next train. Poor Ember, I thought she was going to faint when she first saw me and then found out I was married to her favourite brother. I guess I wasn't much better but at least I had been forewarned. It's just that I didn't believe it till I actually saw her. It was pretty scary meeting his family—so many of them and so intimidating that I just put on a stiff upper lip and pretended to be unimpressed. And you know—now that I've been around this bunch a while—I think that was accidentally the best possible thing to do. Dad Morrow saw right through me and knew I was scared silly but he was good to me then and still is. Mom, though, thought she saw me for what I really was and I swore I would never forgive her. What she saw was this slinky little teenage minx with the pointy blouse and no brains who had probably seduced her son—true—then gotten him drunk enough to marry me. Also true but only on love and I was drunk on it too.

"I wouldn't call you slinky, Jo, definitely not a no brainer and you're not even hyper like you say your mother is."

"Well I guess that's true though you didn't know me when I still lived with Mom and her succession of men friends. I visited my mother and her new husband last year, as you know, and for the first time ever I looked at her hard and critical and discovered that, despite what I used to think, I now like her a lot. She gives me hope for my future because even at her age she is a trim and attractive woman who is on top of her business and quite satisfied at last with the way her life is going. I was surprised to find that in many ways we think the same, only I'm turning out quiet and easygoing like my father. After watching Mom again, I'm glad that's so. I saw Dad too but his wife wanted to control the meeting so it got a bit stiff."

"You said you were an only daughter. Do you have brothers?"

"Two, quite a bit older than I. Well, half-brothers actually." Then she grinned. "And they are half-brothers to each other so I guess I came by it honest."

"Did you ever forgive Lora?"

"Oh yes! Right away because she asked me the one question that let me understand her perfectly—she asked what my mother had thought of Terry. It was just mother's protective instincts at work. If she had feelings about me she quickly did away with them and it was her that arranged for us to have this house. She made sure too that I had everything in it that I could possibly need although you will notice that I use the word 'need' not 'want.'

"You're right, I've made it all sound like a fairy tale and yet—who can say—if Terry had lived maybe by now we would be fighting or even divorced. But I don't think so. I choose to think not."

"Not likely," I agreed, "I've never heard of a failed marriage among the Morrows, either the bunch here or the relatives across the mountains. All the Morrows seem to be blessed with the knack of knowing when they have found the right one for spouse or maybe they have the good luck of being picked by the right person"

"Yes, that's true, just look at Erin and Allan, married umpteen years now and obviously still in love like a pair of newlyweds. Worse luck for me that and too bad I like Erin so much or I'd sure take a flyer at Allan."

The twinkle in her eye and the slight upturn of one corner of her mouth told me she is having fun and trying to shock me again. She must think, as the twins always have, that I am so hopelessly naive and bashful that I must be jolted every opportunity with bits of real life so I gave it right back to her.

"I'm on the loose, Jo, you can take a flyer at me any time you like," The flash of panic that swept over her face surprised me as much as I had surprised her.

Then she decided I was joking—just teasing and she arched her brows and teased also. "Oh, I couldn't do that, after all, Em is even more a friend than Erin." Before I could wonder or form a question about that comment she hurried on.

"Now if ever there was a marriage that could use up all the adjectives under the word 'stormy' it's Tom and Jennie. I'm sure they both take liberties that few other couples would allow and yet they are a pair—a pair that I simply cannot imagine coming apart. Anyway, Jennie is safe because Tom is just too big and tall for the likes of me. I mean my ambition runs higher than making love to a shirt pocket, I get a crick in my neck just talking to him." She giggled and I had to laugh with her.

But then she took advantage of having been too frank with me and asked too many questions of her own and some too personal. So reluctantly at first then more freely, I found myself telling her things I had never told anyone before. When I saw her looking puzzled and much too interested I stopped and changed direction for I had almost told her of my problems and frustrations with Ember. But I think I managed to hold back on my discovery of how unwanted I was everywhere else, and how Morrows must never learn that I needed them so much more than they needed me. Because a thought that has never before entered my mind is now struggling up from somewhere and waving a red flag at me.

Jo, as Terry's widow, is now a full partner in Rainy Mountain. She is one of those who are collectively my employer and she, like the others, must not learn too much about me.

Soon after that I pulled on my sweater, jacket and heavy coat and left as I had come—by the back way. As I picked my bag of contraband out of the snow bank I looked around and saw what I must have seen but failed to take note of when I came—the only tracks coming to her back door are mine. There is no path at all in that sparkling scene of snow.

It left me smiling at the thought of young adventurers coming cross-country from the bunkhouses, halted in consternation at the last of the tracks going their way.

5

With Peter staying in the same building my circle of friends has enlarged considerably as his many acquaintances come to pass the time with him. They nearly always see to it that I am included in the gatherings, which is nice of them but sometimes hard on my resting time. They like to stay up late and I like to get up early.

I have known Alec Hanson for about as long as I have been in Rainy Mountain. He has worked himself up to be Tom's second-in-command in the woods operation and that in itself has to be something of a miracle considering the way they get along, which is to say—they don't. But on the job they complement each other as do a right and a left in a pair of gloves. I've always thought the arrangement said volumes about Alec's skills with the combination of men and machines and Tom's honesty in acknowledging them.

Alec doesn't live in camp like most of us do, he stays at his parents' home on their farm a half mile down the river from the mill and townsite so he's not to be seen around camp as much as might be expected. His father owns the only real farm in our area. Wherever men gather to work and live there will always be a few who want to till the soil no matter what it costs them in time and money. Rainy Mountain is no exception and we have our full quota of weekend horse ranchers, chicken farmers, stump growers, or what have you. They work their forty hours a week for the Company and another forty if they can find it, for no pay on their own properties. What sets Thomas Hanson apart is the fact that he has never worked for another man in his life. He and his wife earn their entire livelihood for themselves and their large family from the land and the country. In my opinion that makes them real farmers. They have a few sidelines for cash such as guiding, trapping and horse training but nothing that even remotely compromises their independence. It all fits in with their agricultural base anyway.

Alec is truly his father's son, as hard a worker as ever came down the line but his fancy took him to the woods instead of the farm. Had it been Morrows practice to hire logging contractors Alec would have been one of them. As it is he has had to either work for wages like everyone else or look for greener pastures and he has done some of that too. He has never managed to stay away for very long though, always being drawn home like an old horse to a familiar field. Ember smiles knowingly and says it's the twins that bring him home. She says he's had his eye on them since they turned to teenagers and has been waiting years for them to grow up and now that they have, he doesn't know what to do about it. Ember might think that Alec doesn't know what to do about the twins but my guess is that he is getting ideas. There's no denying the three of them have been making waves, gale-force style, at recent dances and parties. But even if Ember is only partly right I can well understand his dilemma. My own frustrating experiences with the lovely Jan and Pat suggest to me that what Alec needs most of all is a cooperative twin brother. Now he does have a younger brother, in fact two of them, but one is already married and living in town while the other is still in school. I am also fully aware that he has two good-looking sisters, one taking grade twelve by correspondence and the older one working as a secretary in town. Miss Secretary comes home as often as she can manage and I have driven her from the train to the farm many times but indications there lead me to believe that either she plans to be a spinster or her special interests are all in the city we call town.

So up until recently there hasn't been much reason for Alec and I to become well acquainted. But that's all changed now because he and Peter are best friends from away back and some of it now spills over to include me. They are both here in my room tonight, Alec sprawled in my one and only easy chair and Peter in his favourite position, perched on a backwards ladder-back chair, his arms crossed on its top edge and his chin often sinking to rest on his wrists.

I've been stretched out on my bed watching them and trying hard to keep from laughing at their antics as they play the game Peter likes best. They are, in other words, arguing. Peter will argue with anyone on just about any subject. He has opinions on everything and is willing to share generously at any time. Strangely though, his opinions vary depending on who he is talking to and when. I've seen him take one side of an issue and only hours later uphold the opposite view with no less determination.

Alec owns a 30-06 rifle and swears by it but Peter is scornful of such a cannon and says that a .270 is better. It's an argument that's been around for as long as both calibres have and better informed debaters than these two have failed to arrive at a satisfactory conclusion. They have been at it now for half an hour, quoting bullet weights, muzzle velocities, foot-pounds of energy and fabulous hunting tales till I'm quite addled from listening to them. But what makes me smile is remembering that only last night Peter came noisily into our shack packing a couple of rifles and a shotgun. He leaned in at my door to proudly show me his collection. "Been over to the house to pick up my artillery."

"What have you got?" I was interested because I do my share of target practicing and maybe I've got a partner here.

"Oh, just an old twelve gauge, a Cooey .22 and my pride and joy, my moose medicine."

He had the guns all bundled together under one arm so I couldn't tell for sure what he had. "A Winchester?" I guessed.

"Husqvarna 30-06, the only rifle and calibre worth taking into the bush."

And here he is tonight ridiculing Alec for preferring the same thing. All in the name of sport I suppose. The smile fades slowly from my face as a new thought presses for attention, why now I can't say, it's something I should have seen much sooner. It would seem that Erin and Alec are not the only ones who have been victimized by Peter's weird sense of humour. I've been had too, perhaps biggest and best of all. Peter says he has a letter, a long letter from John and I believe him because it's the only way to explain him knowing certain things that he does know, things that have come about recently. But the point that hits home with a jar now is that I cannot believe for a minute that John could write a letter in such detail without mentioning me. After all, he told me about Peter and requested that I support him so I can't see him failing to tell Peter to look to me for assistance. That means the confrontation in the cookhouse and the mushy handshake in the warehouse, Peter's first day here, was all a hoax—a put-on show to intimidate me and establish my inferior standing. He will not ask for my help—he will allow me to offer my assistance. I can see it as typical of him. Lord help me if he ever senses my insecurities, my need to be needed because with my uncooperative legs, there is nowhere else to go.

Alec is his victim tonight but at least it's all in fun and no harm is being done. Alec is so casual and comfortable in my easy chair, totally unaware of the storm front that he is playing around the edges of. How I wish I could talk to him. But not about Peter! I would say to him, "Alec, these Morrow girls are nothing but bad news for simple boys like you and I. They are bright, pretty candles in the darkness while you and I are grey moths that found a tear in the screen door and flutter in, drawn to their brilliant firelight." But of course I can say no such thing to him, perhaps if he were my brother, and then again maybe not. I am confused, I don't know where this strange thought has come from. Or why. If Alec wants to risk singeing his wings that's his affair. As for me, I'm smart enough to stand back from the flame. Or perhaps I should be honest and admit that the flame has been wise enough to bend away from me.

Their friendly disagreement has ended and I didn't even notice, my own thoughts were so far away.

"I see that you and Tom haven't mellowed too much toward each other yet," Peter said to his friend.

"Well, we get along fine on the job but he has always had an attitude toward me that I just can't tolerate. I can't explain it any better than that but you're wrong, we have mellowed, age perhaps."

"No more fights?"

"Fights? Be serious Pete, we've never more than kept each other in tune, he wins one, I win one and we can't even do that any more—Byron won't let us." Alec stood up and stretched luxuriously pressing the fingertips of both hands to our low ceiling, bringing creaks of protest from the attic. "Well, the old man wants some help on something or other tonight so I'd best toddle off home."

As Alec went out I made myself more comfortable on the bed, hoping Peter would take the hint and leave so I could get to sleep or if that won't work then into a book. But Alec was no more than off our step when Peter spoke to me with an odd tone in his voice.

"Byron?" Somehow he put an entire paragraph into that one word.

"Yeah?"

"Tell me a story."

"What's that?" I must have missed something.

"I said, tell me a story."

I looked sleepily at the light bulb overhead and smiled a little bit. "Okay. Once upon a time there were three bears, Poppa bear, —"

"Whoa boy! Not that one. Alec says you won't let him and Tom fight anymore. That has to be one of the most fascinating statements I have ever heard. Tell me about it."

"Oh, that! That was nothing at all, not when compared to the incident that made them want to exterminate each other."

"Okay, tell me about that first then."

I shifted position a bit, took a deep breath and wished I could get out of this. But from the glint in his eye I can see that he is going to have this story one way or another so there's likely nothing to gain by evasion. "It was during my first full winter here, actually it was along towards spring breakup time. The logging road was in really good driving condition as it sometimes is when the days are warm and clear but the nights still cool. It had melted down so that some dirt showed on the road, then before turning to mud and ruts it froze smooth again so you could make fast time on it, and everyone did, especially the log truck drivers.

"Alec was hauling logs then, and even though he liked to quit once in a while and come back when it suited him, he was always hired again and treated as if he had never left.

"I had been out to a landing with a load of parts for a D7 that was being worked on and not long after I started back to camp I heard Alec on the radio calling out the mile posts as he came off the mountain behind me. I was in no hurry and first thing I knew he was catching up to me so I pulled in on a wide corner to let him pass. I took off after him but not really trying to keep up as we entered a big open area made even bigger by a lake along my left side. I could see the road for more than a mile ahead where it lay out before us on a gentle downgrade and a long sweeping arc to the left. It was the sort of a place where the loaded trucks could get out and roll and Alec was doing just that."

"But out ahead of him there was a short spur road that turned off the main line just far enough to allow for a log landing out of the main flow of traffic. There was a loader working there sorting logs but it was stopped and someone stood on its cab steps, head and shoulders inside the open door, talking to the operator and out on the main line Tom's 4x4 was parked smack in the middle of the road.

"You probably know Tom as well as I do and are familiar with his habit of driving in the middle of the road, through every pothole and over all the bumps as if they didn't exist."

Peter nodded. "Yes and I know what you mean when you say his truck is parked in the middle of the road, it's his way of saying 'I'm the boss and if you can't find a way around my truck, you can wait till I feel like moving it.' He has always done that and gotten away with it simply because, in the woods, he is the boss."

"But he didn't get away with it this time, suddenly Alec's voice came over the radio loud and angry, 'Morrow! If you don't get that bloody truck of yours out of my way I'm going to run right over top of it.' Then to show that he meant what he said he floorboarded the throttle sending the black exhaust smoke rolling over his load. That big P16 Pacific seemed to lean forward eagerly just like Alec must have been doing over the steering wheel, the pair of them hungry for a pickup snack.

"Alec could see Tom as well as I could and knew he would get the message over the radio in the loader. And he did too, he leapt to the ground without using the lower step and sprinted for his pickup.

"I knew there was going to be one godawful smash-up so I speeded up to be there sooner to help pick up the pieces. I was watching the road with about half of one eye but otherwise concentrating on the converging courses of those two idiots. From my angle of vision it looked impossible for Tom to get to his 4x4 before Alec creamed it. But his size is deceiving, he moves faster than it looks and he reached his truck, flung himself inside, and then while my heart stopped beating, just sat there. At least that's the way it looked—my mind was calling out for action but with enough logs to keep a king size bonfire going all winter bearing down on him at close to fifty miles an hour, he sits there as if there were no other traffic on the road."

"At what looked to me like the last possible instant, snow, dirt and ice flew from all four wheels of the pickup and it slewed forward leaving a great cloud of blue-black smoke where it had stood. Alec sliced through that smoke puff scattering it to extinction faster than an eye wink.

"There was one burst of disdainful laughter over the radio—I've no idea which one of them it was—then Alec simply drove on and Tom swerved back onto the main line and came tearing toward me. It's always a good idea to give Tom lots of room when meeting him so even though the road was wide I pulled right over to the edge and practically stopped. You may believe me or not—as you choose—but when Tom went by he was grinning like a coyote at a rabbit convention and gave me a big friendly wave."

Peter was grinning too, with what I am coming to think of as his hungry wolf-about-to-eat grin. "By all! I wish I could have been riding with you that day, I'd give a lot to have seen that." He was all admiration and approval, it was just the sort of a nervy prank that really appealed to him. I thought for a moment he had forgotten about the fight that followed, but no such luck.

"I take it that they fought over this later?" He didn't wait for an answer. "Not too surprising, Tom was still riding a high and just glad to be alive when you met him and saw him grinning, later he would get angry, very angry. Alec doesn't start many fights but he finishes quite a few, that's what happened, is it?"

"I suppose so. All I know is that this was on a Saturday and even though the truckers and some of the woods crews were working again the next day, not many of them missed going to the dance that night. I was sitting on the bench along the wall near the kitchen, staying close to where the goodies come from, just watching the dancers and the crowd in general.

"I wasn't aware of anything out of the ordinary until Dean

came in looking worried and made his way straight to me. He sat down beside me but on the edge of the bench like he might want to make a quick getaway again. 'Man, I think you better come out and have a look at this, I don't like the look of it.' I had to ask him to explain because on dance nights when some of the boys get into their bottles there are a lot of things happening that Dean doesn't like."

"It's the father hen in him."

"Turns out that Tom and Alec are fighting and for some reason Dean thinks I should stop them. How he has come up with a winning idea like that is beyond me. Maybe he figured I should wallop them each over the head with a crutch since I was still using them at that time whenever I had to go any distance. But there was something ominous about this battle alright, it struck me as soon as I got near—the silence of it. Even the ever-present ring of volunteer referees were so quiet that I could hear every blow land and every gasping breath for air. They must have been at it for some time because they both looked about done in, they just sort of leaned into each other and slugged away without much thought for strategy and none at all for defense.

"'Stop them, Byron, they won't listen to anyone else,' Dean said.

"I tried to ignore him but he kept pushing me forward. The footing was treacherous, the snow had been packed down hard but the warm afternoon down here in the lowland had turned it soft so that one step was fine but the next you were halfway to your boot top in slush. The crutches worked okay, they went to the ground every time, no problem there but I never knew how deep my feet would sink so I was still having a rough go of it to stay upright and Tom and Alec were having their troubles too. In fact that's what gave me a chance when Alec knocked Tom down but at the same time lost his footing and had to stagger off to one side to regain his balance as one foot sank in the snow. That's when this fool on crutches swung in between them as they got up and I maneuvered to stay there as they tried to get at each other again. Then I quoted ancient words of wisdom to them:

'Knock it off, you dough heads!'

"I guess they were ready to quit because within twenty seconds they were each making tracks to their respective homes. Alec, holding one arm tight to his side with the other, off on the long walk to the farm and Tom staggering to his pickup pretending he was okay—both of them were bleeding about the face. That's all there was to it except that Tom was broken and bent bad enough that he had to go to town for repairs at the hospital.

"The best of it was that when I took him and Jennie to the train a few nights later, after he finally admitted he needed patching up, he told me to put Alec on as temporary woods boss until he could return to work. 'That'll teach him,' he said with considerable satisfaction."

Peter looked quizzically at me for so long that I started feeling as though I simply must change my position or fidget in some manner. But I refused to give him that satisfaction and remained quite still trying to appear unconcerned. "I suppose you realize that had anyone else, including me, stepped between them they both would have attacked and trampled right over top to get back at each other?"

"It's because I was on crutches, that's why they left me alone."

"No, I don't think so. I think there's something really weird about the way you've taken over here. You've come out of nowhere and the whole family leans on you like you are a tower of strength. But I can see for myself that you're not. If anything you are the epitome of the 97-pound weakling, and yet I find that I too am driven by some inner desire to have your approval on everything of importance. What's up, Byron? Have you got some spell cast over us? Or are you just the perfect patsy, looking out for our best interests, steering us clear of trouble and willing to accept responsibility for us all? A younger Dean in the making but aiming at management level?"

Lord no! Just the thought of it screeched through my brain with the sound of a worn and dragging brake. Accept responsibility for this reckless bunch? Not a chance! I must have flinched but at least I kept my mouth shut.

He seems to have it in for me tonight because he now began the oddest interrogation I have ever been subjected to. He started by changing the subject and almost causing me to jump again.

"You're older than Ember."

"What's that got to do with the price of huckleberries?"

"Maybe quite a bit. She is certainly on her best behaviour with you around and I find that most remarkable because she's never bothered to clean up her act for anyone else." Then for whatever reason of his own he nodded and let that one drop. "No one seems to know anything about your past—before you showed up here. Care to tell me where you came from?" The way he said it was more like a command than a question.

"From town—Prince." He didn't need to know anything from before that.

"I'll bet! What did you do for a living?"

"As little as possible," I admitted, never dreaming he might refuse to believe me.

"You had to do something unless you are either independently wealthy or a welfare case."

"Oh, I worked when I had to—at whatever was easiest—but only during the winter." Lesson number one; never volunteer more information than requested.

"So what did you do in the summer?"

"Nothing."

"What do you mean 'nothing'? You didn't reverse hibernate, you had to be doing something."

"I prospected some."

"Well, that's a respectable trade. Why call it nothing?"

"Because the way I prospect it is nothing. Nothing but a nice word for wandering over the hills and being lazy."

"Yes, I've noticed how lazy you are," he said sarcastically. "You're into everything around here, I'll bet if you were laid up sick for a week this whole show would whimper to a standstill."

He is getting too close to things I would sooner not talk about. I want desperately to explain to him my fear that if the Morrows ever decide they don't need me, I will soon be out in the cold with no place to go. But he is the boss now and I can't allow him any more than the others to entertain thoughts of my dispensability. He is waiting for an answer but I have none.

"When even an oldtimer like Dean goes running to you with his troubles after you've been here just a year or so I can come to only one conclusion."

"What's that?"

"You are the eye of our storm."

I'm afraid I laughed at him.

"It's true, we swirl about you with our tempests in our teacups and when they are about to overwhelm us we can reach out, touch you, and share your calm. There's something about the way you are so willing to listen that makes everyone want to confide in you. When I'm with you, like tonight, all I want to do is to run off at the mouth." He smiled, showing there was no sting intended in his words. I'm sure he doesn't need me to start his mouth flapping, I have already noticed that talking comes as naturally to him as breathing does to me. It seems his second favourite game, after arguing, is flattery, complimenting his victim of the moment in a sly way, enjoying himself tremendously while inflating the other's ego. That must be what he's trying to do to me now and there's no telling for sure if he will be satisfied when I puff up with my own importance or if he will deflate me with one final knife sharp comment.

His mention of Ember must be a red herring of some sort, I can think of no logical reason for his observation that I am older than her. I'm younger than he is, I know that because he is said to be between Allan and Tom in age and I know how old they are. If he wants to learn my age so badly he could try a simple question. Had he asked outright I would have told him—this way all he will get is obstinate silence.

"Ember would give a bundle to be taller than she is. She looks at her tall brothers and sisters-in-law and wonders why she can't be like them."

"What's that?" I heard him alright but I couldn't shift gears fast enough to keep up with him.

"Have you ever seen her wearing low-heeled shoes?"

"Not often, now that you mention it." When she met the trains she wore serviceable shoes for whatever the weather but that was in the darkness and is now a past era. A time that I remember as a shared experience that I will not be talking about with anyone—Peter least of all.

"No and you're not likely to either except maybe in the privacy of her own home. Back when she turned seventeen and finally knew she wasn't going to grow any more she started wearing high heels. Then higher and higher till soon she had the highest, sharpest spikes she could find." He grimaced almost painfully as though it were a thought that hurt him physically. "Not really suitable footwear for the mud of Rainy Mountain, I suppose that's why she drives everywhere she goes no matter how short the distance."

"She's as tall as her sisters and being a tad on the small side of average doesn't seem to shake them up too badly."

"Nothing less dramatic than running out of fingernail paint or eyeshadow would shake them up. They are such a happy pair that sometimes I hold my breath for them." Whether or not the twins are really his favourites, his thoughtful pause suggests to me that he does think a great deal of them.

"And her hair," he continued, evidently back to the older girl, "that precisely arranged disarray that she piles on top her head is nothing less than a bid for the impression of extra height. The heels and the hair put her up there with Erin and Jennie."

All the time he talks of Ember I feel he is watching me like a hawk for my reactions so I allow him none at all. I am sure that he is not so much telling me these things for my information as he is searching out my feelings toward Ember. If he is unsure of her faithfulness and my possible part in the matter, then he is lost in the wilderness and I have no sympathy to spare for him.

Uncannily he almost understands my thoughts again, a grey

veil of disappointment drops within his eyes and he turns a little defensive. "I was just trying to sound you out a bit, I have to know where I stand and you don't seem to be coming forward to tell me. I need, somehow, to get you talking."

I could only stare blankly at him. "There's nothing I can tell you."

"I think, my friend, you could tell me a lot of things if only you weren't so close-mouthed."

"What do you mean? What is it you think I should be telling you?"

"I need ideas—I need the benefit of your experience over the years you have been here. I'm told that your influence has been considerable even before John left and I find that quite amazing because no one else has ever been able to influence him."

"I've done nothing but to go with the flow. I just pick the easiest ways of avoiding problems, no secrets about that."

"But you've done miracles in holding this unpredictable family together this long. I need your help to take us the rest of the way."

"Peter, I hate to disillusion you but I have never come up with an original idea in my life! I've spent all my grown-up years avoiding anything that smelled the least bit like work and I've done nothing constructive that I wasn't coerced, tricked or otherwise led into." There! One unguarded answer and the secret is out and to the very person I wanted to keep it from. But amazingly it seems to be okay because I can see that he still does not believe me.

"But things keep happening around you, my friend, the right sort of things. If it's been good management I want it. If it's good luck like you insinuate then that's better yet."

All I could do was to shake my head in awe at his warped reasoning.

He rose reluctantly to leave. "Okay, I can see you've got to think it over. I hope you realize I'm sincere in my efforts to live up to John's expectations, it's just that I have nothing to work on."

It took a while after he left for the truth to dawn on me—either he is pulling my leg again or he has mistaken my silence and reluctance for wisdom. I think that leaves us both in a pretty deep hole without a ladder. Then I thought about last Sunday when Peter had spent several hours moving things about in the office. By the time he finished not a chair, desk or file remained in its original location in either front or back office. Most of Monday was an uproar as he argued with everyone about efficient office arrangement. It seems we all must dance to Peter's fiddle and if he can't push us around one way, then he will have our attention by another. Perhaps tonight has been his way to get my attention. If nothing else, he has set me to thinking hard.

I am more than mildly shocked at how close he has come a couple of times to reading my mind tonight. He was just wrong enough to confuse himself but any closer and he would have been inside my skull. Up until this evening only Ember has done this to me, she operates on the same wavelength as I do for sure, and now it seems Peter is only a millihertz off. To Ember I am an open book whenever I forget to send out jamming signals. So many times when I have been doing something and hoping she will notice or more likely hoping she will not notice, I will hear footsteps and here she comes. Often I start to ask a question and she answers before I've said enough to disclose my line of thought. At the family gatherings, birthdays, holidays—whatever—from across the table or across the room either of us will suddenly look up and catch the other looking too. Even when involved in separate conversations we frequently raise our coffee cups at the same instant, sip together, and set the cups down simultaneously. It was the twins who brought it to my attention—they think it's hilarious but I find it downright scary.

Because there are secrets that I want to keep from her, among them the foolish incident after Tom and Alec's fight. It seems I am forever getting into trouble and seldom able to find my own way out.

After Alec limped away and Tom struggled into his truck, I

stood there in indecision, worrying about Tom who appeared to be badly injured. When he drove erratically away I made up my mind and went into the hall looking for Jennie, besides, she was afoot now and didn't know it yet. When I found her and explained, she stared at me a moment like she couldn't absorb a word I was telling her. Then she snapped out of it and said, "Okay, I'll get my coat and you can drive me home." The hall is located in Bunkhouse Row, not far from my own shack, for the simple reason that it was convenient to build it on the foundation of a large two-story bunkhouse that had burned to the ground long ago. That earlier building was less than a year old when it burned and the only good things to come of it are the new hall built with 100% volunteer labour from material donated by Morrows and smaller, more home-like bunkhouses.

The hall lot was hardly behind us when Jennie slid over against me as we were approaching my cabin, reached out turned off the ignition and pulled the key from the switch. We coasted to a halt almost in front of the store but when I held out my hand for the key she laughed and shook her head. "Not so fast, let's go look at your place for a while first." That's when I smelled the whiskey on her breath, it's the first inkling I've had that Tom doesn't always drink alone.

"Sure, Jennie, that sounds nice, but I think we'd better check on Tom first and if we find he's already dead, then we can come back."

She slapped the key into my hand and zipped to the far side of the cab so quickly that if I didn't still feel the shape of her against me I could have believed she'd never been near. "What kind of double talk is that?" she demanded indignantly as I started the engine again.

"Well, if he's still alive and ever finds out we stopped at my place there will soon be a nice, economical two-for-the-price-of-one funeral, featuring just you and I. I'd as soon pass on it." When I pulled over at their home she was gone without a word before the truck fully stopped.

It was an hour till traintime but, heavy-hearted, I picked up the outgoing mail and went up anyway. I've made an enemy, I thought sadly, one I can't afford to have because we have to work in the same building. I can avoid her some of the time but it won't work for long. I wish we could back up the clock and try again so I could tell her 'no' in a nicer way instead of being so panic-strickenly blunt. Sometimes I simply feel unable to cope with these people, it might be best if I just get on the train along with the mail and don't look back. Ember can find Nightrider abandoned at the station in the morning and shaking her head say, "I knew he'd fail us sooner or later. Just like all the others."

But I simply don't have the courage to leave.

I got through Sunday okay but Monday morning found me in the warehouse sitting morosely on a carton with the invoices for last night's load on my knees. My attention wasn't on the papers though, it was fully occupied with desperate plans on how to avoid not only Jennie, but Ember as well. She will need only one look at me when Jennie is around to smell a packrat even though none exists. The invoices are going to be my first test because they have to go to the back office now that I have finished checking them against the contents of the shipment. It's too late to expect the office to be empty, either one or both Jennie and Erin will be at work and if I forget to deliver the invoices one or the other will be along looking for them. I considered leaving them where they would be obvious and making myself scarce but that won't help for tomorrow or the next day. I even thought of getting sick for a week and taking to my shack till this sorts itself out. What a situation! I've done nothing but as I see it I'm in trouble right up to my ears.

The only warning I had was one creak of a floorboard then hands came from behind to cover my eyes and a throaty voice breathed, "Guess who."

Well, I knew who all right and I sat dead still.

"May I sue for peace, Monsieur?"

I swung around to face her as she removed her hands. "Of

course," I said, hoping I had heard correctly. She was laughing at me and not a trace of worry or anger in her eyes. As if I could read it in headlines I just know she's already told Tom all about Saturday night and they have laughed their fool heads off at my expense.

"I had you worried the other night, didn't I? I guess I had more to drink than I realized. Wow! did I ever have a hangover yesterday." She must have thought she saw disapproval because she laughed again. "You can add my name to that long list of people who have sworn to you 'never again.' Only I mean it! It will be that good old frosty Friday in July before you find me tipsy again."

I'm not the least bit interested in just how drunk she was or wasn't, but I recognize an honourable easy way out when I hear it so I kidded her. "We do get the odd bit of frost in July you know, so watch out."

"In that case I'm on safe ground aren't I?" Then she turned serious. "Tom has a hand and wrist that's swollen to twice its normal size so there must be something broken in there. He's fighting the issue but I've talked him into going to a doctor, so stop for us on your way up to the train tonight." She took the invoice from my hand without bothering to ask if I was finished with it. "As long as I'm here I'll take this along with me."

About ten tons of worry jumped off my shoulders and slunk away looking for a new home as Jennie left. How light and free I felt! The sun shone again! With just the application of a little sense of humour the world is right once more.

That was only one of many little jolts the various members of this strange family dropped in my lap. I guess the one that churned me up the worst and for the longest was when I learned it was to be my duty to enforce the 'dry' edict. Rainy Mountain was declared a dry camp long ago when John and Lora—teatotallers both—became appalled at the number of injuries among men coming half-drunk to work. I'm sure the situation is different now with so many families and proportionally fewer bunkhouse dwellers and so many recreational opportunities. Aside from the ethics of the matter, it's quite unenforceable anyway. Just the same, somewhere along the way John decided that as 'meeter of trains' and 'hauler of supplies and people,' I was in the best position to confiscate the incoming booze. I resented it because I know Ember was never charged with the job when she met the trains. I suppose the situation is different—easier for me than it would have been for her but it took me a long time to admit it.

I'm a small deterrent though to serious drinkers who have devised a multitude of ways to get their bottled goods in. I believe they actually enjoyed the game of outwitting me and had no end of fun with their smuggling. Even if I worked full time at it, it would have been a constant running gun battle with the importing loggers and millworkers whose collective inventiveness far exceeded my detective abilities. I often wondered if John knew that some of his own family were among the worst violators.

Early on I decided to grab only what liquor was blatantly obvious and not go looking for carefully smuggled goods. If I suspected someone of bootlegging for a profit, I would turn the matter over to John or Allan and they proceeded from there. It was a method that left us all in a reasonable frame of mind and I'm sure many bottles were left in sight for me to find easily so I could feel I was doing my job. I didn't go to Tom with any problems like this because his solution would have been to sit down with the owner of the goods in question and help him dispose of the evidence in a more conventional manner.

But when a grinning Tom told me it was becoming common knowledge that my inaction could be bought with the gift of that easily found bottle for myself I was mortified. Here I've been dutifully dumping the stuff down the sink and they thought I was drinking it! But rather than disrupt a system that was keeping the drinking under some control and out of sight I made just one minor change. From then on I labeled each seized flask with the owner's name and returned it to him when he took the train out again. They in turn mostly tried to be discreet with their drinking.

At the Saturday night dances they sometimes forgot about that but at least most of them had Sunday to sober up. There were a minimum of dangerous hangovers on the job and that, after all, was the main point of the whole issue. But it leaves me thinking that there must be a better and easier way to get the same results.

Now I find we have a trip to town coming up and it sounds like a real winner. I've known all along that Peter and I would have to go to the bank to get him tuned in by H. M. Mackenzie but I had thought there was no hurry.

"I'm afraid, my friend, there is a great hurry," Peter straightened me out. "I must get in to see our banker before he learns how long I've been here now. That way I can have my talk with him while he still thinks I haven't had time to get acquainted with the situation. I don't want him asking me for solutions, I've got to see him while I can still afford to be dumb." It wasn't the first time he has expressed doubts about our chances and I didn't like the sound of it. It didn't fit my somewhat elevated opinion of him.

Besides Peter and I we had the addition of another old acquaintance of Peter's in the form of a tire salesman from town. Ron had come two nights before to see how many tires he could sell us for the coming winter's logging. He had put in some long hours in coveralls at the shop checking our used tires for those worth sending to town for repair or retread. Then the twins who said they were past due for a shopping spree announced they were going also. When Alec heard that he took time off to go along as well. As we waited for the train Ron and Peter related for us, with much laughter, their various escapades during the time they both lived and worked in town. That was back when Peter had first broken away from Rainy Mountain in an early display of independence.

Alec got off to a quick start with a bottle he brought out of hiding and by traintime when Ember waved us off, he was already feeling pretty good. The twins must have been getting a few nips at his bottle too because they also seemed to be enduring very little pain.

We climbed on the front coach and while the train swayed away from Rainy Mountain around the first of many curves we barged our way back through its entire length—a noisy, boisterous crew looking for whatever suited us. On our way through the cars many of the people awakened by the stop, especially the men, stared in awe as the twins passed by. They can't believe their eyes—that such mirror images of bold, tantalizing beauty could materialize from the endless dark forest as if by magic in the night. It gave me an unexpected and perverse satisfaction to see their wide-eyed surprise and to know that the legend of Rainy Mountain would grow that night. As the last one along the aisle of our group, I could hear some already asking others what the name was of that place the train just pulled away from.

Alec led our flying wedge along the aisles, around the varnished smoking parlours, past the newsy's stand and across the bucking steel plates between the cars. Finally he opened a vestibule door to find there is no more train, just a little railed-in platform with the song of steel wheels and iron rails beneath it.

He shut the door carefully against the swirling tendrils of fog that chased our marker lights along the track and turned to face us. "We are on the tail end—of Number Nine," he announced slowly and solemnly. For some reason it was the signal for a lot of laughter with even Peter and I, who were stone cold sober, being caught up in the mood of the moment.

This tail end car was mostly empty of other passengers so we settled in right there. The twins and Alec took a double seat near the middle and Peter and I sat facing forward in another double seat across the aisle and one space ahead of them. Ron looked wistfully at the twins wishing, I suppose, that he could make it a foursome. But very pointedly there were no invitations so he reluctantly slumped into the vacant seat facing us.

Alec was getting louder in direct proportion to the diminishing level of liquid in his bottle and the twins were not to be outshone. As a few people got up and left, presumably for quieter surroundings on forward, our rank-mouthed threesome became derisive and louder yet. Soon all that was left other than our own group were two young men so soundly asleep that they remained that way. A few minutes later the conductor came in looking suspiciously stern but he caught our wild bunch in an uncharacteristic mild spell so after selling us tickets to town he left and we saw no more of him until we got off his train.

We hadn't gone far before Ron was grinning and pointing, Peter and I both turned to look and we were treated to a rare sight. Jan was snug on Alec's lap and her already well-filled blouse has taken on grotesque proportions with the addition of Alec's big hands inside it. Pat seemed to be cheering them on. Peter snorted his disgust and determinedly faced front.

It couldn't have been more than five minutes later Pat went flouncing past us. "This party is getting too rough for me," she said indignantly. That's what she said but she said it a whole lot more thoroughly than I ever could. But, what I have always thought impossible has been accomplished—the twins had finally been separated!

Pat went to the very front of the coach and sat facing away from us. Ron kept giving a running commentary on proceedings across the aisle and Peter was going deeper and deeper into a slow burn. I didn't blame him either remembering his claim to affection for these girls. Their conduct tonight was certainly not calculated to make him proud. Had Alec not been a close friend of lifelong standing I'm sure there would have been fireworks, I have only to watch Peter's fists clenching and flexing to come up with that idea.

We had a diversion then as the newsy came clanking into our car with wire baskets containing pop, candy, sandwiches and magazines. He also managed to carry a blanket and a pillow under one arm. After selling a sandwich and renting the pillow to Pat he came on with his eyes on us, already sizing us up as small spenders.

"Nothing for me," I said as he reached us. Peter echoed me but Ron bought pop and a chocolate bar, offered to treat all around but found no takers. The old boy who is newsy has, I guess, seen about everything at least twice that can happen on a train. The couple across the way didn't faze him a bit. He just chuckled and murmured, "I don't think they need anything from me."

"Hold on a minute," Peter called as the man was leaving us to return up train, "how much for the blanket?"

Peter dug out his wallet and paid the requested rental, accepted the dark grey blanket then as the newsy left, dumped it in my lap. "Here, go throw this over those lovebirds."

"Heck no," I answered, startled, "If you want them covered go do it yourself!"

"Byron, don't get finicky on me," he snarled in a choked up voice, "If I go over there I'll kill somebody, maybe both of them. You've got to!"

I had already committed to tossing the blanket back to him but one look at his face as he surged to his feet and I knew I had made a bad mistake. There really is murder in his eyes maybe starting with me!

I think that if I was walking in the woods and saw a tree falling on me that was impossible to evade I would put up a hand to ward it off and be crushed in that one-arm raised position. That's what I did now, I reached out to ward him off and somehow my hand closed over his wrist. He stopped.

"Okay, Peter, I'll do it." I took the blanket once again and used about the same tone of voice as when telling Jo that we are low on size 11 Dayton Light Cruiser boots so would she please order some. "You just sit down and take it easy." To my surprise and relief he sat down.

Glad that Peter has controlled himself but still with great reluctance, I stood up, shook out the blanket, and with it held out before me, I advanced on the offending pair and sort of tossed it in their general direction. Alec was turned away from me by now and too busy to notice anything anyway but a disheveled Jan gave me a crooked grin and clutched at the blanket, pulling it around her and Alec as I hastily retreated to my own seat. I felt it quite in character that Peter, with the crisis over, failed to express even the slightest gratitude.

Our salesman friend was shocked into silence by Peter's near violence and he tried to ignore the action on the far side of the car but finally he just had to make a comment. "What they are doing now would work a lot better in a bed."

"Well! If that wouldn't frost you!" Peter exclaimed, "I'm sure glad I'm only here to run John's haywire business and tattered finances, I wouldn't want a really tough job like taking care of his daughters."

Things did quiet down after that, Peter cruised the length of the car turning off all the lights he could find switches for. Alec was sleeping fitfully while Jan and Pat, who has carried her rented pillow back to her original seat, whispered loudly and giggled intermittently. Fifteen or twenty minutes before we slowed for the bridge at the outskirts of town Peter fell into a heavy sleep so that everyone else was off ahead of us and fanning out in various directions. Our salesman friend seemed in a great hurry to leave us in his dust now that we are on his home turf. One of the twins has vanished but the other was leading an unsteady Alec across the street and along to one of the first hotels they came to.

"Would you look at that!" Peter said in awe. "They haven't had enough of each other yet."

I was still intrigued at seeing the twins willingly splitting up but I noticed something that Peter didn't. "That's the other twin that's with him now," I told him.

"Are you saying to me that you can tell which is which at that distance?" He looked at me skeptically.

"That's right and I'm also telling you that it was Jan with him on the train but it's Pat leading him into that hotel."

He shrugged with an effort. "I guess it's none of my business and the sooner I can accept that fact the better. Maybe she is just seeing that he has a room to sleep it off in and then she will go to wherever Jan is." But there wasn't a lot of conviction in his voice. It's plain that he is deeply disturbed but doesn't know what to do about it. I was uncomfortably reminded of my own surprised and hurt feelings the day I saw him holding Ember in the store. Only I don't think he is jealous, I'm sure it isn't that he wants one of the twins for himself, worse luck. He just doesn't approve of the way they are carrying on and is confused and frustrated to find they are too grown-up to spank and scold. Perhaps it's unkind of me but I expect he would be quite satisfied if someone else's daughters or sisters showered such attention on him but his own stepsisters are supposed to be more decorous.

No matter how you look at it, it's still early a.m. following a nearly sleepless night so we stopped at the Keller House where Morrows always stay when not at a friend's home, got a room and crashed till around noon. Then we had a late lunch and called at the bank but the meeting didn't live up to it's billing at all. I introduced Peter to H. M. as I had been instructed to do and started to leave.

Peter said softly, "Byron."

I looked at him.

"Sit," he said, pointing to a chair, so I sat. But all I learned was that bankers too have their funny ways, for right off the bat Mackenzie told us that regretfully he had to leave in just a few minutes for a very important meeting. Probably his coffee break I thought uncharitably. He was pleased, he said, to meet Peter, too cordial for comfort to me and totally unconcerned about any conversation that he might once have wanted with Peter.

"I hope you haven't come all the way to town just to see me," he sounded genuinely concerned, "but if there is any business you wish to discuss perhaps you could stay over until tomorrow."

"No, no! It's nothing at all," Peter quickly assured him trying not to sound relieved. "It's only that having just come to take over my duties at Rainy Mountain I thought I should drop in and get acquainted."

"And I'm glad you did but I'm sure Mr. Smith can tell you all you need to know of your company's arrangements with us.

Nothing has changed," he added more or less to me, "in fact it will take close to a miracle to change this bank's outlook where Rainy Mountain Lumber is concerned. Now I really must leave, be sure to stop in any time you are in town, perhaps we can find a not-so-busy day and have lunch together."

So he shook hands again with us in a thoroughly friendly manner, not at all like he was planning to put us into receivership at any moment. We next found ourselves wandering aimlessly along the sidewalk each wondering what has gone wrong.

"Now, my friend, can you tell me what that was all about?"

"All I can think of is that either he has already written us off and is just waiting for the opportune time to lower the boom—or," I hesitated, "he knows something that is causing him to wait and see for a while longer."

"I hope your second guess is the right one and what he knows is that the price of lumber will be going up."

"It has been rising," I ventured, "and that's not strictly normal for this time of the year."

"Normal or otherwise we'll take it. But in the meantime we've wasted a day coming in here and there's still a few hours to kill before catching our train home."

"What about the lawyer?"

"Nix on the lawyer, those papers he drew up for John are as simple and straightforward as can be, we don't need him to watch me sign them and add more to his bill."

So we each went our own way for the rest of the afternoon after agreeing to meet for supper and then catch the train. I just shopped for a few small items while Peter went looking for Alec and the twins. But we went home without them for they simply were not to be found. We both carried packages onto the train.

Ember met us and as we went down the hill in Nightrider Peter told her about the trip. Now that the ordeal was safely behind he found an uncommon lot to tell her. After a while I began to wonder if he were talking about the same trip I had just made with him.

Ember was not concerned about her sisters. "They know the

town and they will take care of each other," she said. Neither Peter nor I were brave enough to tell her what had happened on the train nor what we presumed to continue later. It wouldn't surprise me if she has a pretty good idea of the situation anyway since she has more or less predicted a matchup of some sort involving Alec.

The next night I managed to get to bed early but my head had hardly hit the pillow when Peter burst in slamming the outer door behind him. He thrust his head into my doorway. "Cal and Arnie are after me," he said breathlessly. "I've locked the door and I'm going to pretend I'm sleeping, you had better do the same."

I sat up like an alarmed gopher wondering—hawk or coyote? "What's up?"

"I brought some whiskey from town for them, they've gotten drunk on the first bottle and now they want the rest of it."

He must have jumped into bed with his clothes on because he no more than vanished from my doorway when I heard his bed crunch against the wall then all was silent until a whirlwind hit our door. Calvin and Arnie are loggers, they've been here longer than I, their bunkhouse in Rainy Mountain is the only home they have and I suppose Peter knows them from years ago. When they hit our porch and found the door locked I thought at first they were going to beat it off its hinges. They pounded and kicked and they shouted and pleaded. When that brought no results they bitterly cursed Peter almost as well as the twins could have done. Eventually they went around the side of the building to peer in his window.

"Look at that! Pretending he's asleep. He's got our booze in there some place, let's bust in."

"Naw," his slightly more cautious companion counseled, "We'll just get fired and I like my job here. Maybe Byron will let us in, let's see if he's home."

I snuggled deeper into my blankets as they tramped around to my window.

"Yeah, he's there," one said and tapped on the window. "Mr. Smith?" He called softly and tapped lightly again, "Mr. Smith?"

"Hold on," his friend said, "he's sleeping, don't wake him up, he's just had a couple of nights on the train."

They went back to the door and pounded some more while cursing Peter out royally. Then they went back and forth between the door and his window a few times but you could hear them running out of steam and winding down. Eventually they wandered off muttering something almost indecipherable about extract from the cookhouse. I wish them luck! If our cantankerous old cook finds them raiding his pantry they had best be fleet of foot. It's probably an old contest since the cook has been here a long time too.

A few minutes later Peter was in my doorway again quietly and thoughtfully watching me. When he saw that I knew he was there he said in a half puzzled, half scoffing tone, "So! It's 'Mr. Smith', is it?"

"You just got what you deserved for bringing in liquor for them. I'm supposed to control the alcohol coming into camp but when the boss bootlegs it in under my nose I haven't much of a chance. Have I?"

"Maybe so," he conceded, "but working nearly every day and living in the bunkhouses isn't much of a life without a drink now and then. But those silly so-and-so's have been sober for so long they don't know how to handle it any more. I gave them a bottle and they, maybe with a few friends, have killed it in one sitting and now they want the rest. I can't let them have any more until they sober up or they will cause no end of trouble."

"You have a problem."

He smiled. "If all my problems were as simple as this I'd be well away." Then the puzzled tone returned to his voice. "I had you figured as too pantywaist to mix with the rough crew we have here. Lord knows you look and act it sometimes. But it seems I was wrong—so wrong that I can't quite grasp it because it's coming to me gradually that they are all in cahoots to protect and care for you."

"It's called respect." He's had plenty of fun at my expense so I couldn't resist evening it up a little.

"Yeah," he paused uncertainly, "well—good night—Mr. Smith."

It was nearly two weeks later that the twins and Alec came home, even Ember had started worrying. At least they did check in once by phone. The twins were sober—viciously so—but Alec was still on a tear or at least he thought he was though it has degenerated to no more than a crawl. He had lost most of his coordination and had to be helped off the train and along the track to my truck. He didn't know me, he didn't know where he was and I was sure he planned to lose no sleep over either detail. As soon as he was left to stand on his own, he went nose down in the cinders and showed no desire to upgrade his situation.

"Put him on the back," Jan said. "He's been train sick all the way home."

"He nearly got us thrown off," Pat added.

I looked at big Alec. I looked at the height of the truck deck then at the unlikely-to-be-helpful girls already climbing into the cab and wondered how I'm going to pull this one off without a winch and a plank. The train was just starting to pull out when one of the trainmen recognized my problem. He stepped out of my sight to where he must have sent a signal to the engine crew because the train stopped after moving only a few yards. Two of the crew jumped down from the passenger car to lend a hand. Then with Alec unceremoniously sprawled on the back of the truck, they returned to their train and I waved good night and thank you to them.

"Someone had better ride with him to see that he doesn't fall off," I suggested.

"The Devil may have him! If he falls off it's good riddance," was Pat's assessment but mild at that compared to Jan's. So I wedged him between crates and hoped for the best. I left the cargo light on the back turned on as we went down the hill to camp, so that I could check on him from time to time through the back window. All I could see of him, between and around my load, was one shoulder but I reasoned that as long as that much stayed in place the rest of him would too.

When I stopped at the house to let Jan and Pat off I asked, "What should I do with him? I can't take him to his Dad's place the shape he's in."

"Dump him in an empty bunkhouse and let him freeze," Pat said.

"Or dump him in the river," contributed Jan. "I've seen enough of his ugly face to last me a while."

"You wouldn't really mean that, would you?" The answer I got fairly sizzled.

With my ears still burning I considered the immediate fate of my comatose companion. Since he was in no condition to complain I got a mattress from storage and plopped it on the floor of my own room. Then, almost gleefully, remembering all the times Peter has interrupted or prevented my sleep I woke him and with his grumbling assistance got Alec flopped on the mattress.

He was still there when I went to breakfast in the morning but before I finished eating, Peter literally herded him into the dining room and proceeded to pour coffee into him. Other than looking pale and shaky Alec appeared much improved from the night before, at least he was walking and in a straight even line at that. They might be the best of friends but I could see by the grim set of Peter's jaw that Alec had a debt to pay.

That much I understand but their outlook on life in an instance like this is totally alien to mine. To these two, and Tom as well, any serious difference of opinion, or conflict of just about any type, can be settled only by physical force. A fist fight is their usual vehicle of peace, strange as it sounds. But for reasons that elude me, Peter has evidently ruled out that course of action for today. I'll have to give him the benefit of the doubt. Perhaps he's less a roughhouser than I have been led to believe by all I have heard second hand about him. Or maybe he knows Alec is a dangerous opponent even now while in a half-befuddled condition but the occasion cries to Peter for a physical satisfaction and that is what he will have.

"Byron, you know that big gully that runs south from the Six Mile Creek crossing?"

I knew where he meant.

"I've never had a look at the lay of the land in the Six Mile Creek drainage and since there are no roads in there it will be a walking job. I want you to drop us off at the Six Mile Bridge, Alec and I will hike up the creek and over the summit into Case Creek. You can pick us up at the top log landing on the Case Creek road," he looked at his watch, "say about four this afternoon."

Alec groaned and I don't blame him, he's certainly in no fit shape to keep up to Peter on a walk like that. The pass between Six Mile and Case Valleys is almost five thousand feet in elevation and they would be starting from not much over three thousand feet at Six Mile Bridge. Not really much of a climb and not many miles across but from what I've heard there isn't even a game trail up that narrow valley. It's so thick and dark that nothing useful grows at ground level, no moose or bear would be caught near the place except in passing through. In there, big game means squirrel. I was in there a ways once because there are fish in the creek up to a waterfall but it's not a pleasant place. Among all those big old trees, many dead, others in various stages of death I wasn't comfortable breathing the possibly flawed oxygen put out by them. This, according to John, is the sort of place that should be logged right away and let some healthy young plants and trees take over to put out some good smelling, disease-free air. In time nature will do the job with fire but the process could be devastating to the soil if it burned as deep and hot as the amount of half dry fuel standing on it suggests it might. With all the summer lightning storms we get, only luck and timely rains have let it last this long.

John might talk about logging such places first but it doesn't always happen because of the way logging costs skyrocket in old stands like this. It can only be done when there is top dollar for the end product and we have not been getting much of that. I hope that on his way through today, Peter doesn't let the impressive look of the timber fool him into thinking this would be a good area to get set up with a logging plan.

I knew they had a day's work cut out and Alec knew it too but he also knew that this is punishment that has to be endured to put Peter into a more gracious frame of mind. Had the circumstances been reversed, I'm sure Alec's treatment of Peter would have been as harsh if not worse. I'm sure glad they are good friends!

In general terms I wasn't too pleased about it either because it looks to me like just one more way for Peter to get out of a day of work. He's been getting altogether too good at that lately, leaving it for the rest of us at the office to guess at what he wants done.

It's just as well I went early because it wasn't much after three o'clock when they came down an old skid trail to the log landing where I was waiting for them. Peter was feeling great and striding right along but Alec was almost tripping over his tongue as he staggered the last steps to my truck. He was well past the end of his endurance and only habit put each foot forward in its turn.

They climbed in with me and as he feebly pulled the door shut Alec croaked, "I'm dead, boys, just see that I have a nice funeral." With that he curled up as much as a large man can in one third of a truck cab and for all appearances went to sleep.

We hadn't gone far when we passed Tom's 4x4 parked on a wide spot along the road. We could see Tom down in the creek bottom at a log jam in the stream intently fishing for trout. Nearby, his constant companion, the big wolf-like dog Lupe, watched us go by. "I think he's been here all afternoon," I commented. "He was here when I came up two hours ago and there were no fresh tracks on the road so he must have come before the frost thawed out."

To my surprise Peter was irritated. "Out goofing off on company time again, is he?"

I found myself rising to Tom's defense. "He gets his job done and well done at that, if he finds time to relax now and then, why, more power to him."

Peter growled dissent but dropped the subject talking instead of the timbered valley they had walked through and then about anything that came to mind as his mood improved again.

Alec woke up with cramps in his legs and when he got them settled he stayed awake but had nothing at all to say until we neared camp. Then he told us quietly, "I'm in trouble, boys, and I'm going to have to ask one of you for some help."

"You're in trouble?" Peter sneered sarcastically. "Has it taken you this long to figure that out?"

"Aw, Pete! It's worse than you think."

"I don't know how it could possibly be worse."

"I got married to one of the girls while we were in town."

"You what?" I'm sure the roof of the cab bulged a few inches in fear of Peter's anger then lowered again as he relaxed and even smiled a little. "Well! Maybe that wasn't such a bad idea after all but I'm sure glad it's you and not me. Which one is the lucky girl?"

Alec stared straight ahead as he answered. "Aw, that's the whole trouble—I don't know!"

Peter and I were both speechless for about ten turns of the truck wheels. Then while I tried to choke back my laughter Peter found his voice. "You married Jan or Pat"—up goes the roof of the cab again—"and you have the witless nerve to sit there and tell me you don't know which?"

"Aw, Pete, I can't tell one from the other when I'm sober. What chance did I have while I was drunk?"

I think by now the funny side of it has occurred to Peter but he's not going to admit it too quickly. "So who did you have for your best man?

"Uh—your friend Ron. The girls found him and brought him along."

"Hmf! Now why the devil? And what's this help that you want?" he asked grudgingly.

"I thought you could drop me off at your shack and you go over to the house and sort of find out which one of the girls is married to me then I'll go over after you tell me."

"Not a chance! You threw your own horseshoes in the forge so you can fish them out yourself."

We were in camp now and I was wondering where to let these guys off. I know that I would want the cookhouse but I wasn't sure how much lunch they had packed on their hike or what plans they might have now.

"Take him to the house," Peter answered my question, "he's brought it on himself, let him face the music."

Well, it looked like a hot old showdown coming up because the twins were sitting in lounge chairs on the glassed-in verandah as we drove up and stopped. I have never seen a man in more misery, both mental and physical, than Alec was as he slowly straightened his cramping legs and climbed out of the truck then started step by agonized step to the yard gate.

Pat and Jan, straightening in their chairs, watched his painful progress until he was inside the yard. Then both girls jumped up. Jan stalked indignantly off into the house while Pat threw open the screen door, unmindful of its overtaxed spring, and simply flew down the steps. Alec, being no dummy, wrapped his arms around her, lifted her off the ground and swung her around giving us a big, toothy grin over her shoulder about the time the screen door recovered and banged shut.

I let out the clutch and stepped on the throttle. We were almost to the cookhouse before Peter spoke.

"My friend?"

"Hmm?"

"You've heard of the luck of the Irish?"

"Yeah."

"Well, let me assure you that it pales to insignificance compared to the luck of the drunken Canadian logger."

"I can't argue with that statement," I admitted, still marveling at the change in Pat's demeanour toward Alec in less than twenty-four hours. That marriage would need some luck I thought.

6

Whether I liked it or not Peter dragged me even more into the social whirl of camp for he is not a man to enjoy going anywhere alone if he can help it. And quite frankly I find it hard to say no to him though I would be hard-pressed to explain why.

Of course I'm using the term 'social whirl' rather loosely here. There is a movie every Friday night but because there is only one projector, each show is made up of three or four segments with intermissions in between while Allan rewinds the film and changes reels. Every so often he tries to palm the job off on me, saying that since I do everything else around camp I might as well be projectionist too. So far I have resisted. There is a fellow in camp who says he will buy a second projector and run the show more professionally if we let him charge admission. Allan is balking at that one. I think what will happen is that Allan will buy the second projector, turn it all over to the guy and tell him a wage or flat rate but no admission fees. Then there is a dance every

Saturday night and these Rainy Mountain dances are real humdingers, starting early and running late. Usually they last far on into the night until the last people capable of playing a bit of music are exhausted and can't be bribed, blackmailed or beaten into continuing. It's not at all unusual to see groups and individuals making their way home in the chill light of the Sunday dawn except maybe during the very shortest days of winter. Then by the time some ambitious group gets back to the hall to clean up the mess it's time for church for those interested, seeing as the hall is still warm. There is seldom a minister of any type to be found so for years John Morrow did most of the sermonizing. When he left the services faltered for a time until one of the men from the married quarters took over and got things back on track. Church is one of the few activities to have no call on Peter's time, nor do I feel inclined to go. But Ember always does. Peter jarred me with a wry comment on that. "Atoning for past sins."

Then there are always extra do's such as the Easter party, First of July, all the usual holidays and the occasional box, pie or cake social. But the highlight of the year is the Christmas/New Year's bash starting with the kids' Christmas concert. The kids get to show off for their parents and the teacher gets to show off for everyone. Our teacher this year is something special too. But of course the school board in town doesn't dare send us any but the very prettiest and most accomplished since by now they have a reputation to live up to. The best of it is that Gabrielle shouldn't even be here. She is a mid-term replacement who was working part-time, filling in for other teachers in town when the job became open in our school. Someone else's loss was very definitely our gain though it didn't look that way at first.

There hadn't been a new teacher in camp for several years because the present incumbent while running true to tradition by getting married—in this case to one of our millwrights—also broke tradition by continuing to teach. She and her husband were ardent followers of just about every outdoor sport imaginable and that was her downfall. The very first early snow on the mountain tops lured them and another couple up the high-level logging roads with their skis. Something went wrong and she wrapped herself around a spruce tree. As one would expect, the tree was lightly injured but the teacher wound up in hospital after the rescue operation. We waited a few days, hoping for good news from town but eventually had to settle for assurances that, while she would recover, she was not going to be teaching again this term.

It's a problem we haven't faced before during my time here and I didn't know what to do so I dumped it in Ember's lap. She called on all of the ex-school teachers in camp who evidently all cried in unison, or something like that, "Not me! No way!" That's when Ember handed the hot potato back to me with the suggestion that I call the school board office in town.

The boondoggle in the affairs of Gabrielle McEvoy didn't end with her missing a job at the beginning of the term because for some reason no one phoned us to say that she was coming or when. Otherwise I would have had Ember come along with her truck to meet the train the night Gabrielle came to Rainy Mountain.

As it was she got off the train in the worst of a cold, middle of the night rain shower, clearly wishing she were elsewhere. A trainman gallantly carried her luggage to my truck and tucked it under a corner of the tarp on the back. Then before going back to his warm dry rail car, he handed her up into the passenger's side of Nightrider's cab and closed the door on her. All this time I was busy covering my small load of mail and miscellaneous with the rest of the canvas tarp. Then I jumped off on the right-hand side of the truck and stumbled around the front end checking on my way that the passenger's door is fully closed. Somehow it registered on my mind as I tucked in the last folds of the tarp that the door closing didn't sound right. Sure enough, the passenger's door was only on the half latch so I opened it a little and slammed it firmly.

The end of the train was whisking by at a good clip when I

opened the driver's door and started to climb in. My passenger, having had time to watch my strange movements, opened her own door apparently quite prepared to run off into the night. I stopped and even backed out a little.

"I—I'm supposed—I—I mean—I'm expected at Rainy Mountain," she managed.

"This is Rainy Mountain," I assured her. It has never occurred to me that I might be a figure to inspire terror in young women and it was a shock and disappointment to find this seemed to be so.

"Where is the town?" There was more in her voice than just fear of me. She simply was not prepared to be dropped in a black and wet wilderness with no one in sight but this hobbling stranger who might be anything. She was frightened out of her wits and because she was frightened and maybe thinking of the people who have sent her here she is also getting angry. I took that as a good sign.

"It's just down the hill, only a few minutes drive." I now slid in under the steering wheel and started Nightrider moving slowly, I heaved a silent sigh of relief when she pulled her door shut—half latch will do just fine after all. I apologized for not knowing she was coming and for not having someone suitable here to meet her. Then, working on the theory that the more I talked and the less she had to the better, I went on telling her about the pleasant teacherage that was waiting for her and anything I could think of about the school.

At least I hope the teacherage is ready! But the more I think about it the more I wonder who might have gotten it so. I know I hadn't! I mean things like turning up the heat and getting the water working and arranging for someone to clean up in a building that hasn't had a tenant for several years because the last teacher and her husband have one of the larger houses.

I told her my name and learned hers. I also told her that I was the one to call on when something didn't work right around her house or the school. That while I might or might not fix it myself I would at least detail the appropriate repairman to do so.

She seemed a little reassured but not much and when we got to the teacherage, I had only to open the door to know I am in trouble. The place is cold, with the oil heat turned down and the damp crowding in. It's dusty—it doesn't smell right—one quick glance into the bedroom shows a bare, mouse-chewed mattress only half on the bed and one glance at Gabrielle's white face tells me I have to get her to some place more hospitable in a hurry.

In the harsh light of bare electric bulbs she looks so small and so young that I can scarcely believe she is a teacher. Likely no more than a student herself judging by appearances. I have been assuming she is the teacher simply because no one else is expected to arrive. A few seconds of furious thought convinces me that I have to be right though because she accepted all my talk about the teacherage and the school without surprise or comment. I must be getting old for the teacher to look so young.

"I'm sorry, this is no good at all." Then I finally got my brain in gear. "I'll take you to Ember's house, she will put you up till this is ready." Then I had to explain who Ember was.

"Yes," she agreed weakly, "I think that would be much better."

On the way to Ember's I asked where she was from because she has a way of speech that intrigues me. She places a delightful sounding emphasis on the last syllable in her sentences that has me wishing she would say more. Her name—McEvoy—says one thing, but everything else about her says otherwise.

"I am from Vancouver."

That didn't quench my curiosity because Vancouver has accents from everywhere in the world. But it did tell me that she is a city girl, accustomed to lots of people and lights. To her way of thinking Prince George is probably no more than an outpost in the wilderness. No wonder she was mentally staggered when the train pulled out leaving her worse than alone in our dark woods.

At Ember's I pounded on the door, then walked in calling loudly until I heard her answer from upstairs and start down to us. Gabrielle, who had gasped and fallen back a step when I barged through the unlocked door, now followed so closely in my wake that I can only conclude she has decided I am the lesser of many imminent evils. At last relieved of my nervous passenger I finished up my night's errands and got to bed just like the normal people in camp.

The next day I saw nothing of our new teacher until late afternoon when she came in to the store. Long before that I had been able to report to Ember that the teacher's house was now warm and boasteds working water and electrical systems. From there I felt it was up to her to see that it was made in other respects ready to be lived in.

I thought Ember was cooler toward Gabrielle than necessary. In fact she'd been uncommonly snippy all day. Since Jo was busy in her accounts, from which she is always difficult to distract, Gabrielle seized on me as the friendliest and most familiar face around. I'd never been 'clung to' before but that's what she did as she thanked me profusely for my help the night before and told anyone listening what a help I had been and how foolish she had acted. It was, she said, only because she was so tired and disoriented.

"It's his job to be helpful to anyone coming on the train—that's what he's here for," Ember said crossly then tried to ignore it all. But the glances she did allow our way grew dark as any approaching storm. I was puzzled because I'd never known her to take an instant dislike to anyone before and I was also disappointed because I didn't think Gabrielle deserveed this treatment. It was no way to treat a new teacher who couldn't be held at fault either for being young and inexperienced or for arriving unannounced. It became altogether too clear that the two had not found soulmates in each other. By the time Jo relented and came smiling out of her books it was too late, Ember was smouldering and unfit company. She suggested acidly that I show Gabrielle that her lodgings were presentable and see to moving her over from the house. So I did that and wondered if it was Gabrielle's young blonde good looks making Ember feel her ripe old age of twenty-three going on twenty-four that was the problem.

At first Gabrielle was a bit scornful of our town, like some of the Morrows, town is the word she used, but it wasn't long before the strange chemistry of the place began its work on her. The more she learned of Rainy Mountain the more she wanted to hear of it and its founders. She soon idolized the entire Morrow family, including the unappreciative Ember, but she was shy and overawed in the presence of any of them.

I took Gabrielle to her first Rainy Mountain dance and turned her loose among the wolves where she had an immensely good time. But she had insisted earlier that I take her home before I went to meet the trains, so in due time I collected the teacher from the dance floor and delivered her to her house. The only sour note of the evening was Ember snapping at me as I took Gabrielle toward the door, "For pity sake, Byron, quit dragging that foot! Pick it up and put it down right."

Gabrielle blushed with embarrassment for me but I reassured her, "It's nothing, pay no attention, Ember has chosen me as her social works program is all. I have no idea why but I don't mind."

Then Gabrielle said the dumbest thing. "Maybe it's because she cares"

Sometimes I wish I could know what makes Ember tick but in moments of sanity I think it's better léft a mystery. I guess she will always be number one in my book, no matter what comes between us but the better I get to know her the gladder I am that she has kept me at a distance. At times she is not nearly so nice a person as she is easy to look at. Sometimes the sparkle in her eyes turns to a hard glitter.

And the little lady has a past, one that somehow makes her more believable, more in tune with her brothers and sisters. I've been hearing hints of it ever since I came but for me it's one of a very few things I cannot bring myself to ask about so other than the unfavourable snippets from Dean occasional chance remarks that I've had to piece together are ab,out all I've gotten. Like one night at a dance when the twins were cutting a loud, wide swath and I overheard part of a conversation among several ladies. One said something to the effect that those girls are 'undisciplined, unfeeling, uncouth, and there is simply no hope for them,' end of quote. That is an opinion shared by a lot of people but it was the other lady's answer that perked up my ears. "Oh, they'll grow out of it, their brothers were all wild too but they left it behind with time. For that matter their older sister was even worse than they are with her boy chasing and, if you can imagine it, even fighting with them. But look at her now—the very model of prim and proper. Except for," she noticed me too close then and lowered her voice so I couldn't hear the rest. Another side of Dean's warning.

One night at a recent dance I sat with Dean when he was in a reminiscent mood and not as close-mouthed, as always. As Ember and Peter danced by our position on the bench he said to me, "Man, she sure led him a merry chase when they were kids." I was surprised he would bring up the subject because he still liked to avoid talking about Ember except to demonstrate that she belongs to Peter and is much too volatile for the likes of me anyway. But with Peter here at last Dean probably thinks the situation is well in hand so now it can be talked about.

"You wouldn't believe," he told me with feeling, "that anyone so small and innocent-looking could cause so much trouble."

He will get no argument from me on that because, small and innocent or no, she has caused me plenty of trouble.

"Starting back when she was only fourteen or fifteen, but could make herself look eighteen or nineteen, whenever she was bored she would cruise Bunkhouse Row in the evening just as if the crew was only there for her amusement. She would come dressed in a miniskirt and a skimpy top despite mosquitoes or chilly weather just to see how much of a bother she could stir up. And believe-you-me that was sometimes a great plenty. The young bucks would follow her in droves to the store if that's where she was going or to the show or dance if it was a night for that. Then she could take her pick of the survivors after the fights she instigated ended. She knew all too well that she had the looks to twist men around her fingers so she was always pulling some wild prank just to get Peter stirred up to do battle for her. Anything in long pants she went after and if he swayed a lot to music or had too much hair and a beard, all the better. Always the exact opposite type as Peter."

"What did her parents have to say about that?"

He laughed, "No one ever knows what Lora thinks, kind of like Ember is now, but John loved it. She always was his favourite, the first girl after four boys so she was spoiled rotten. She could do no wrong that he couldn't right by firing the guy when things got too serious and making sure he caught the next train out. A little hard on Peter though. He usually figured John moved too slow and often had to see to it himself just to protect his own interests. He was old enough by then to take care of himself and she made sure he was well tested."

"You mean he would run off her boyfriends?"

"Man, dozens of them! He ran off more than her father did and that pleased John no end too. As for Ember," he shrugged, "a few hysterics, a good cry, maybe a try at punching Peter out then another jaunt past the bunkhouses and she was back in business. There was some good came of it though because she kept the crew culled of deadwood."

"How so?"

His eyes twinkled. "Man, she always did have the darndest knack for attracting and falling for the most shiftless, useless sort so they were the ones to get fired. Young Nick is a step up but he won't get anywhere either now that Peter is home"

Here I've always thought Dean was my friend. I've never denied being exactly the type he has described only my taste hasn't run to music, or beards. I've been caught with one a few times when I was too broke to shave, like when I first came here but that's all. Nor have I ever been ashamed of my style until now. Hearing it out loud from Dean it sounds like something best not talked about. If he weren't still smiling I would get up and walk away from him but I'm sure he is not just having fun with me, that's not his way, he is telling me something and maybe I had better listen. I know there has been a powerful attraction of some sort between Ember and I, one that she fights and I skate warily around. Now he's telling me it's because I was just another hungry, unshaven drifter needing guidance and I had better leave her alone or I might be on a train out too. Fair enough! I've known all along it could never be. She is a workaholic and worse—a perfectionist—one who demands the fullest commitment from those around her. While—to say it kindly— I am different. But just for kicks maybe I'll try a beard.

The young Nick Dean referred to is Nick Martin, the latest of Ember's many admirers, but he's smarter than most because he doesn't just lean on the counter and brag about himself. If I hadn't been the one to take his job application I wouldn't have believed he is barely over twenty. He's the quiet serious type and has figured out the girl's shift arrangement and comes a lot when Ember is alone in the store. He makes out that he is there to help her if she will let him and hasn't yet admitted to seeing that he's not welcome. I can tell that his presence bothers her since her usual tactic of simply saying a blunt 'no' to any suggestions or invitations then ignoring the guy hasn't worked. He just keeps coming and she has been polite so far in not telling him to get lost so I try to show up accidentally when he's there—just for the entertainment. I don't think Peter has anything to worry about.

When I started working around the store I thought it was Jo who was the hard one to please. It seemed she couldn't stand to see someone idle but I soon realized she was positively sugar and spice compared to Ember. At first, I now see, Jo was just trying to help me avoid Ember's ire—only after I learned to read the danger signals was I really able to shift for myself. I believe that Ember works at something every minute she is awake. She keeps a typewriter in the store and between customers does most of the more serious company correspondence such as soothing creditors. The trade magazines that come in the mail are carefully read before being passed on to the rest of us leaving her with only the late hours of each day for her fiction or adventure stories. Erin and Jennie are the bookkeepers but Ember is personal secretary and business consultant to whoever she decides needs one. If she's not working physically then she is mentally reviewing possible implications of potential problems the rest of us are as yet unaware of. It didn't take long to see that for some reason she expected me to be the same, and when I fell short of the mark, I knew that there was trouble by the way her own work speeded up until her fingers fairly flew through whatever she was doing. Her mouth line straightened and firmed while her eyes came close to squinting if the provocation continued. You could almost feel the pressure rising. It never occurred to her to say simply that this or that needed doing, I was supposed to see that myself. Instead she would snap personal gibes at me—my hair was uncombed or my clothes not suitable, but mostly she was intent on curing me quickly of my injuries. First it was the crutches that offended her sensibilities, "throw them away and you'll get back to normal that much sooner." So, being at least as ornery as she, naturally I used them long after I could have done without. At some point Jo stopped defending me and settled back to enjoy the show.

It became almost a game between us as I tested to see how much I could get away with before she started simmering. This wasn't normal temper in the way of her relatives. I've never been able to goad her into flying off the handle the way her brothers and sisters do at the drop of a misunderstanding. It's something I've never understood because she doesn't pick on others this way—only me. I didn't panic, I just learned when to retaliate, when to initiate and when to become scarce. But the fun has gone out of it lately, it doesn't seem to be a game anymore, maybe to her it hasn't ever been a game. I never know now whether I'm in favour or out until she opens her mouth. If it's just family around okay, we usually get along fine, but if there are newcomers present, such as Gabrielle, she wants them to know that—while I might not stack up to snuff—she is working on the matter.

As I implied before, now that Peter is here to make up my mind for me I never miss at least the early part of the dances. But

Gabrielle may have some influence in that department too. She is certainly a pleasant young lady to be with, not at all like Ember who has become so difficult lately that I now plan my day to be as little as possible in her vicinity.

Peter is an accomplished dancer but oddly enough he spends more time back near the entrance with the fellows who hang out in the smoky shadows swapping yarns and colourful bottles. It never fails to amaze me how much liquor slips past my half-hearted surveillance to find its way into this supposedly dry camp. There is always the glitter of glass being passed around in this group who have no women of their own to bring and are, for whatever reason, reluctant to step forward into the light and mix with the crowd. There's often a disagreement among them that erupts into a fist fight just outside. But except for the shouts and hollers of the onlookers in the doorway, the sounds of battle are never heard inside where the music and stomping drown out all competing noises.

All this time I have been waiting for Peter to come up with a plan of action that would show us that John's trust was not misplaced. But time is flowing by and hope is beginning to freeze and slow as is the water in the river where the shore ice is forming on our colder nights. After initially showing great interest in everything Peter has become quiet and evasive during working hours. At quitting time each day he shows a rare ability to throw off his cares and be his old self. While this may be an admirable trait it is certainly not helping us any with our troubles.

Then one chilly afternoon he burst into my room while I was trying to get some sleep and straddled a chair backwards after positioning it near my bed.

He minced no words. "Okay, Byron, here we are just muddling along. Not a one of us has the faintest notion how to make some money and get out of this mess."

"That's not my problem, you're here to take care of that particular chore."

"Baloney!" he snorted. "We all know I'm here as a last resort, a last ditch effort because John knew he was beat, and Tom and Allan are beat and he wouldn't wish it on Ember for anything. If John was counting on me he was truly whistling in the wind. I'm no magician, you know that as well as I do by now. I need your help and I need it desperately."

"Don't look at me like that! I'm just a dreamer, not a doer."

"So? Dream up something and I'll take care of the doing. Thinking ahead and planning are not my cup of tea but action is. You know the ins and outs here better than anyone so if you can't figure a way out then no one can. All that time you spend waiting for trains, you must do a lot of thinking so let's hear your ideas."

"Well, mostly while I'm waiting for trains, I just turn on the truck radio and everyone upstairs," I tapped my forehead, "sits down for the concert. If I'm lucky I get Wilf Carter singing about the tears and heartaches of the Midnight Train. But, ideas? Pretty wild and disjointed."

"Okay, We'll join 'em up and wild we need."

I can think while lying down but talking adds an extra complication so I delayed a bit while I sat up and pulled on some clothes. "You remember not so many years ago how the woods were full of portable sawmills in some areas?"

"Yeah. So what? They've been legislated out of business by the Forest Service and changing times."

"Maybe, but they've got to be around somewhere yet. I'll bet there's places where there's an old portable sawmill stashed away in every second or third back yard."

"You've lost me Byron, I don't see any connection with reality here."

I was lost myself so I had to back up a ways to get a hold on him again. "As I see it, if you start your figuring with the amount of our yearly cut requirement, add 50% for catch up on our past shortfalls, then subtract the maximum that we can get through our own mill we could have work for 10 to 20 portables for the winter to handle the logs that we can't. I know that's pretty vague but there's a lot of variables when you start talking about portables. Maybe beginning with how many shifts they are willing or able to work."

"It doesn't take a whiz kid to see that. What I want from you is a way of handling, selling, or avoiding that big bulge of logs."

"You aren't listening close enough, Peter, that's where the portables come in."

"All you've done is transfer the bulge from the log yard to the lumber yard where it costs more. The interest on the money to do that would break us while we waited for the lumber to dry enough to plane and ship. And that's assuming we can get enough credit to go that far in the first place."

"I'm not thinking straight, Peter, that's what you get for waking me up in the middle of my nap. I forgot to mention that we need Allan's pet project finished and operating—it's close to completion you know, all it needs is some dollars."

"The dry kiln," he supplied.

I nodded. "I know John figured mother nature did a cheaper and better job of drying lumber but in this day and age that's only true if you have an unlimited supply of low-interest money and longer, dryer summers than we have. With a dry kiln working for us, we would have dry lumber to plane and sell within a few days or weeks of sawing it. At least that's the theory of it."

"The money, Byron! What about the money to do all this?"

"Well, yeah, I'm getting ahead of myself again. We've got to convince the bank to go along because it will take a big line of credit to carry us through."

"Unless we can sell some logs again. With the market perking up like it is somebody should be buying logs this winter."

"No, you are forgetting a couple of things. First, all that cheap fire and bug kill salvage that's available west of here. A lot of it is low grade wood but logs are likely to be a glut on the market this year and maybe for a few more years as well. Also, remember that the big boys are playing politics with us. It isn't only L&N—any of the outfits big enough to help us would sooner see us go under. Less competition for timber that way. They've been wanting in here for years but Morrows have been keeping them out so far. It's a plain, hard fact of life that we are in no position to make deals without getting skinned in the process."

"The Forest Service won't even allow portables in the woods anymore. How would you get around that?"

"I'm not sure that's written in stone, Peter. It's mostly because they want slabs made into chips for the pulp mills instead of being pushed into a pile and burned. But for various reasons, some economic, some more elusive, we haven't sold so much as a jam jar full of chips yet despite having spent a bundle putting in a chipper so we burn our slabs anyway—in the burner. I expect that to change when we can get a better freight rate or a higher price but that won't be this year. In the meantime, what's the difference whether we burn them in the burner or in a pile in the woods. But if pinch comes to crunch we can always set the portables here on Morrows private land and haul the logs to them."

Peter got up slowly and headed for the door. "It just won't wash, Byron. I thought you could come up with something better than that." It's the first time I have seen him looking truly dejected.

After he was gone I looked around at my empty room and mentally shrugged, saying to myself, "well, here you are, all dressed up and no place to go." So I flung back the top blanket on my bed, crawled in fully dressed and went to sleep again.

The next thing I knew Peter was kicking a leg of my bed jarring me awake. "Come on Byron, wake up. We have a meeting at the office in twenty minu,tes. I want you there to explain that plan of yours to the others." The door banged shut as he trotted off the porch leaving me to wonder about his sudden change of opinion.

When I got to the meeting room I found Allan, Tom and Jo were the only ones there. Lupe was curled up comfortably near Tom and already dreaming of fresh rabbit tracks. "The twins will be here in a few minutes," Peter said as he arrived. Then he looked to Jo. "What about Ember?"

"Some ladies are shopping and buying money orders to send out, she'll lock up and join us when they leave. She said to go ahead and start without her."

When Pat and Jan came in I noticed that for a change they were wearing their identification colours correctly today. They've been running a neat little sandy on us, trading identification and taking turns living with Alec. I don't know why they bother with the deception, often as not both of them stay quite openly at the house one block over from Morrow Street where they will live until a new home is built for them near the rest of the family. It seems impossible to me that no one else has noticed but there have been no comments.

Jan complained cheerfully. "My god, Peter, another meeting? If you keep this up I'm going to resign my directorship."

That got a chuckle all around and Peter answered, "You can't, Jan, you were born into it and the only way out is to die."

She scowled at him in mock anger and told him what he could do, where to do it, and even how to get there.

"Okay, Byron," Peter said, anxious to get on with the business at hand and maybe equally eager to shut Jan up, "let's have it just as you told it to me."

"Wait a minute," Allan interrupted. "How come is Byron putting forth plans for us? Is his name Morrow all of a sudden?"

For the second time, and that's twice too often, I am all at once the centre of everyone's attention. One at a time I can handle these people, but in a group they make me nervous when they pull together. I don't know what Allan's problem is, an attempt at humour maybe, after all it was on his say-so that I was once installed as reluctant temporary manager of this outfit. 'Just don't have any ideas' I suppose was an unwritten rule of appointment.

"Never mind, Allan, Ember will take care of that little detail first opportunity," Jo answered him softly while watching Peter as though testing to see if he would say otherwise. It's easier to pretend ignorance of what she means than to explain how wrong she is but the twins laughed delightedly, Tom chuckled, and even Allan smiled. Peter remained expressionless but the tension was broken and I seized the moment to start.

Having talked it out once with Peter and then being allowed time to organize it in my mind, I got things in the right order this time. Unlike Peter earlier, no one interrupted except that Allan grunted his satisfaction when I mentioned the need to finish the dry kiln. At one point I felt a new presence and looking around I saw that Ember had come almost into the room and was leaning against the door frame, arms crossed in front of her.

When I finished there was a long thoughtful silence until Tom exclaimed, "I can't believe it, Byron, you're more a gambler than all the rest of us put together! What happens if the price of lumber drops twenty or thirty dollars over the winter? It's happened before."

"The same thing that will happen anyway if we continue the way we are," and I motioned downward with one hand to indicate a plane crashing. "Down the tube! I don't see it as a gamble, Tom, actually it's even more desperate than that. It's simply too late for any less drastic options. If anyone else has a better idea it's time to speak up."

This time the silence was long and thick until Peter cleared his throat. "Okay, we don't even have to vote on it, I can see that everyone is in favour except Tom. Am I right?

There was a chorus of agreement, some of it reluctant, and even Tom shifted about in his chair and spoke slowly. "I'm not entirely in disagreement, but I would be a lot happier with something safer. Really I think we should approach L&N or somebody else and negotiate a sale."

"No!" Peter said, sounding a lot more confident than he had just an hour ago when he came to me in the shack. "We are in a position of weakness and we must never deal under such a handicap. They would just laugh and then pick up the pieces at the receiver's auction."

That brought on yet another silence, a shocked one this time. Ember's face was turning white even as I watched. Amazing how her complexion swings with her mood—she is like Peter in a way only slower and more readable. It was, I suppose, the first open mention of bankruptcy and plainly it was a chill prospect to these people who, except for Jo and I, had all been born and raised here expecting the good times to last forever.

"I just want out, the sooner the better," Tom grumbled. "This could go on for years before we get something out of it. I don't know if I can take it that long."

A surprising statement from a man like Tom. I have always seen him as such a strong, commanding figure that it never occurred to me he might suffer frustrations the same as any lesser person. "If we succeed this winter, Tom, by next fall or even summer, we will have moved to the driver's seat. We will have regained the confidence of both the bank and the Forest Service. I'm sure that if this group's intention at that time is to sell, then a serious buyer can be found."

"Okay," Tom gave in. "I suppose the first step is to send a delegation to talk to MacKenzie and also the Forest Service."

Ember, still at the door, shook her head. "Not a delegation, Tom, we are all too long on temper and too short on persuasion to talk under duress with that kind of people. It's one thing to deal with them when your account shows a healthy balance but a different matter altogether when you are dipping deeply into minus balances. And it's worse yet when you are firmly in their black books as we are. There's only one person here who has any hope of pulling this off and that's Byron."

"Right you are, Em, it will have to be Byron," Peter agreed and Allan echoed him altogether too quickly.

Yet another democratic election! But at least I know now that I haven't lost favour in Allan's eyes, his strange remark at the start of the meeting meant nothing after all. I think Allan is the only person I have ever known who can tell—with a straight face and even tones—a perfectly funny joke and no one laughs until they are very sure he meant it as a joke. Except when his anger is in command he is so serious looking, so dignified, so punctual and proper, one forgets that along with his temper, there is a sense of humour lurking. There is one other thing too—Allan would rather I took the lead in our efforts to survive because even if I attain some glory by succeeding I will never be a threat to his position as senior son and resident head of the family. But if Peter were to engineer a financial turn around then he would be the big frog in our puddle and not of a temperament to let anyone forget it. Allan and Tom have, to my surprise, gracefully accepted Peter as manager but there are evidently limits to what they will allow him to achieve. Aside from that they are both so bound up in their work that they have no time for frivolous niceties such as talking to bankers. They need someone with less on his mind to do it for them.

Undercurrents run in every direction in this room. Tom seems to have knuckled under but I know better, I can almost hear the machinery clicking in his head. I don't know what he might be working on in there but if he keeps grinding away at it he may be the one to come up with that better idea I asked for.

Peter is less a mystery to me now that I am getting to know him. His quick agreement is pure relief that it isn't going to be him facing the people of authority in town. It would take a D6 Cat to drag him there knowing what he now knows of our position. He is only here because of a debt of gratitude to John. I think when he feels that bill is paid he will be a different, more difficult, sort to deal with.

The women had all been uncommonly quiet during this meeting. Jo, I am sure, is completely open-minded and ready to wholeheartedly follow whatever seems our best route. She strikes me as that sort, uncomplicated and always ready for anything. Anything from an unwanted proposition to—um—well, maybe a wanted one. She has been in mourning an uncommonly long time—it's with a bit of a shock that I suddenly sensed that it's finally all over with.

Ember, though, seemed to be strung tight as a fiddle and I wish I knew why. The one thing I do know about her is that she is absolutely fanatical in her feelings of family pride. If her cherished Rainy Mountain were to go under, she would be the most devastated of all. I'm not certain she would want to survive and I suppose that's ample reason to be tense and jumpy the way she is lately. There would be little to gain in talking to her of her father's dream of a managed forest and sustainable yield from it. To her the town has become all that the whole operation was to John. Rainy Mountain is the heart of her only reason for living and the lumber flowing outward is the blood of life that must never stop or the town will die. In her view any cutback in production would be a threat to her town and therefore to herself. Anyone supporting said cutbacks would be her enemy. In my mind's eye I can see the flow of timber slowing; people leaving as their jobs dried up. I can see the mill dismantled; the houses leveled but the Mall would always be here. In it an ageless Ember would sweep away cobwebs from the store shelves in case someone should happen by and need something. Finally, she would be dragged, kicking and screaming—by whom I'm not sure—and put on the very last train to ever stop here.

But I guess that picture is just my own personal rambling of the imagination and doesn't really fit. She is one who cannot see what is under her nose but her vision goes far down the road instead. As the only one in this room with a clear head for the business side of the operation she is probably way ahead of me and I am witnessing her kicking and screaming right now. When, if, the time comes to go, she will climb on the train with her head up and no looking back—just as her father did. But at this moment I'm sure she feels very much alone and frightened. Obviously, anything I can do to help her—and at the same time help myself—must be done no matter how unwelcome a chore it is. A daytime nightmare! I had to shake my head hard to rid myself of the image and come back to the present.

Where the twins are concerned, I doubt they have an idea in their pretty heads beyond getting back to Alec.

I was shipped off to town that very night, wondering what I have done to deserve this. It's a tangled trail that stretches out behind me and somewhere I have strayed over a ridge I shouldn't have crossed. In my dogged effort to make myself indispensable to the Morrows I seem to have overdone it. They are always in need of, and receptive to, help and ideas from me. That's good, it suits me to be useful, but these trips to town representing them are a different matter. I don't mind talking to MacKenzie or anyone else necessary. They hold no terror for me and shouldn't since, unlike the bunch at home, I have nothing material to lose. That alone should disqualify me as their representative because I might take 'no' too easily, but there's more to it yet. The chain of circumstance that has led Rainy Mountain to its present brink of disaster was set in motion years ago, even before I came here. I suffer no feelings of guilt for the way things are, but I feel a deathly fear of failure on this present venture I've been conscripted into. Either MacKenzie or the Forest Service can put finish to us if they don't like the shine of my smile—one by shutting off the money—the other by shutting off the timber supply. Either one would be fatal and the blame would be mine. There's not a hole in the country deep enough to hide in if I have to return home and report failure. It's just the sort of corner Ember is always painting me into.

Tom went to town on the same train as I to attend a two-day industrial equipment demonstration and we sat together. But we had next to nothing to talk about so I slept most of the way waking briefly at every stop. We went our separate ways from the depot and I did the same as Peter and I had done last trip in. I got a room at the Keller House and, after tea and toast with Mr. and Mrs. Keller, went to bed. I was up again at noon and by one-thirty I had finished my breakfast and was sitting in MacKenzie's office only half as nervous as I should be.

This is my third visit here and MacKenzie welcomed me like an old friend, indeed I feel at ease in his presence. I find the more I see of this elderly banker the more highly I think of him. This man is no stuffed shirt as I had thought when I first met him. His clothes are of a quality and type I have no desire to ever be seen in but that is the only jarring note about him. Probably a lot less jarring to me than my manner of dress is to him at that. If we were neighbours I think I would be mowing his lawn—free—with pleasure. Our discussion on present matters of business were no more tense or difficult than any other subject we could have pulled out of thin air. All my apprehension of the previous night melted away and I was almost too relaxed as we talked. By some great good fortune he was in a fully receptive mood for he heard me out and asked only a few questions.

"Well, this is all quite irrelevant anyway unless you can get Forest Service approval so why don't you run over there and talk to them. You can come back to see me again later this afternoon." He rummaged around in a drawer of his desk and handed me a card with his name, address, and phone number printed on it. "In case you are late, give me a call at this number and I'll see you this evening at my home."

I didn't say so to him but I had every intention of being on the train heading for my own home by evening time. I was greatly encouraged though, for surely he wouldn't send me off to see the Forest Service if he planned to refuse us the money to work on. If permission is not to be had for the mill sites, that will be a snag but not insurmountable. I will then have to convince H.M. that we can still do the job but at a slightly higher cost by putting all the portables on the private land around the Rainy Mountain townsite and hauling logs to them. Or, better yet, simply don't tell him.

For some reason, in all the years I have spent in and around town, I had never learned where the Ranger Station was, so I took a taxi. Probably would have anyway.

At first my luck didn't seem too good because the man I

wanted to see was tied up in a meeting with officials from one of the big forest companies. I had to settle for the assistant ranger who is in charge of logging inspections for the area that included Rainy Mountain and even that was accidental. He walked in from outside while I was still wondering what to do, recognized me and stopped to find out what I was up to. When I started to tell him, he interrupted with a suggestion that we go back to his desk and chew the fat for awhile. I didn't think he had the authority to give me a yes or a no but I had to start somewhere. I knew him well enough from his visits to check our logging show but his name escaped me until someone called him Walter, then I was all set.

He too heard me out patiently. We discussed at length our logging plan for the coming winter and a few times I wished Tom was with me. At my request for mill sites in the woods he tapped a pen on the desk briefly, started to speak, stopped, then said very carefully, "Your plans seem to conform quite well with what we would like to see happen out there. Except for the mill sites! As you know it's now policy that all slabs be chipped for pulp and from your portables you won't find it practical to do that so they will wind up being burned. Then too, portables are not very efficient—thick kerf saws, and all that." He held up a hand to stop my protest. "Yes, I know. You, and some others too, haven't been able to negotiate a sale for chips yet, but in our opinion that is largely your own fault. The market is there and we don't care if you have to get your chips to it at a financial loss. The official view is still that slabs be chipped and because of that I think you are wasting your time asking for mill sites, even one, let alone ten of them. Also, there are more people to see than us where mill sites are concerned these days. Pollution Control—the Regional District—seem to have a lot to say on them now but I haven't a clue what their criteria might be. Come to think of it, I'm not even sure if their authority extends out as far as your area. Probably does." Pen tapping the table again. "You could find out though by setting up and then if necessary arguing with them all winter.

After spring breakup you won't care if they win or not. As for us—as I said, we're not likely to be issuing permits for mill sites—not in writing—but we're not likely to be out to shut you down either. Despite what you probably think it does make sense to restrict portables—too much hurry for volume and not enough technology for recovery. In most cases the new policy is good and leads to less waste. But way out there in your circumstance, I see nothing to gain and maybe a lot to lose. It might be interesting to go ahead and give it a try—we could all learn something. Just so long as you keep everything tidy, burn your refuse promptly, and do a good job generally I doubt anyone will object. At least the objections aren't going to come to a head before spring breakup does, if you understand what I'm saying."

I did indeed understand him but he stopped me when I started to thank him. "You didn't hear a word of this from me. I haven't told you a thing and you might find out the truth of that over the next six months. But I think you'll be okay. Remember, if anyone jumps you about your mills, even me, drag it out in argument till it doesn't matter anymore. Throw up a big enough smokescreen and you may not even be fined. When you come down to the bottom truth of the matter, we would rather see Morrows in business out there than some new bunch taking over. At least with Morrows we know there are good and responsible people in charge."

I left with the feeling that Walter is basically on our side. One of the old school of forestry men perhaps not fully in tune with this new age of regulations and still able to see a compromise now and then. Possibly even with an axe of his own to grind and us the willing stone. Now I'm glad I didn't get to see the head man for he undoubtedly would not have given me the 'maybe' that Walter has.

I am under no illusion about our position. As Walter implied, it could turn out to be interesting and educational. The education might prove to be painful but that appears to be a chance we will have to take. I know very well that if there are complaints or if firm instructions are issued from Victoria to adhere to the rules, then we are going to find ourselves far out on a very thin limb. We have been in this shady grey area with the Forest Service before when sometimes just a change in personnel would bring about a different interpretation of regulations. It leads to a more interesting life is the only way I see to look at it. At least the man who comes once in a while to inspect our logging show won't be running into sudden surprises when he finds us with portables operating in the woods.

Back to the bank and a very slight misrepresentation of facts because I told H.M. only that we have a green light from the Forest Service. I didn't go into detail and I don't think he wanted me to. "I'm very relieved that you appear to have found a route back to profitability though I must warn you that in large measure my apparent change of opinion is due to the way lumber prices are rising. In effect you are a much better risk now than just a few months ago. Nonetheless you will have to perform minor miracles of cost-efficient production or any little slip in the market will have you in trouble again."

He sighed and admitted something he may not have intended to. "Besides, I'm afraid I let John get rather too heavily financed, considering there now seems to be some doubt as to whether the quota would be ours, the bank's, to sell if we took over. With the harvested volume so far in arrears, the Government might cancel it before we could recover our investment. We might find ourselves with nothing but a lot of used machinery and a plot of land and buildings good to no one. We could take a fearful loss." While he was saying this he was getting together a bundle of papers which he now pushed toward me. "Take these back with you, they are nothing more than copies of last year's report on inventory, receivables, and so on. Get this year's made out in the same way right up-to-date and signed by the right people. Mail them back to me, then get yourselves to work and make some money for us all. We'll review your situation again in the spring and make whatever decisions are necessary then."

Just to satisfy my curiosity I asked who were the right people to have sign and he smiled. "Let's play it safe; have them all sign the main document—Miss Morrow alone need sign the notes." I wondered but didn't ask if he had forgotten about Peter. Of course he hasn't yet been given anything on paper to show that Peter has taken over. Whatever he wants is how we will do it. Then as I rose and turned to leave he added in a different tone, "Byron?" I paused. "And you sign too."

I have heard of bankers being described as 'flint eyed' but until this moment it hadn't occurred to me that such a description could be so accurate. My friend, H.M.! Talk about chilled to the bone! That's me right now and no reflection on the weather! Outside on the street and feeling both safer and braver, I reflected on the change in attitude a few dollars rise in lumber prices could make. Lord help us if the market starts downward again. Just a year ago being told I should sign too would have had me hunting for a Greyhound headed south—or north—or somewhere—but recent events have led me to consider my position more carefully and I see nothing really to worry about. Even if we go bust and somehow they manage to tie me in with Morrows as responsible, I have very little to lose. Just a few dollars in a bank where my pension has been accumulating because I have no way to spend it. So what? It's just money—it came easy—who cares? My old reaction was there for a few minutes but I'm okay now. He can't scare me like he could have one time but just the same I think his lawn will have to do without me.

The only other chore I have to take care of right now is to place Peter's ads in the paper for operators with portable mills.

I felt pretty good about my day's work as I caught the train for home. When we started moving I looked around enough to see that Tom is not here. At least he's not on this forward passenger car where the trainmen like to keep us locals who get off at the bush stops. I didn't really expect him to be going home tonight anyway since the trade show runs another day yet. But the youngest Morrow son, Tim, was on board and it tells how preoccupied I was with my own thoughts when he saw me first. I only became aware of him as he slipped into the seat beside me.

"Well, Byron, been to see the bright city lights have you?"

"Tim! I didn't know you were coming home!" It's a wonder he didn't read on my face that I am responsible for his change in fortune. Tim is now twenty-two years old, the same age Terry had been when he died and every time I see Tim he reminds me even more of his late older brother. Class! That's how I would describe him if I had to in one word.

"Yes, I've been hearing disturbing news about troubles at home from Ember. She's the only one who writes other than mother and mother never says a word about business. Thought I would come home to see if I could help."

That, I thought, was a moderately nice way of explaining that he was broke and hadn't found a job to his liking. "Well, I guess we can use a professionally trained forester alright." I'm afraid I said it doubtfully for I was still wondering how he would fit into our rough-edged crowd. Because, while he may look like Terry, he seems so mild-mannered that it's hard to think of him holding his own with his rough-and-tumble brothers and sisters. He gave me a sharp curious look and I mentally kicked myself for my wrong tone of voice. After all, he's one of a bunch who can claim to be my boss—he's not a new employee. Hastily I rearranged my line of thought. "I'm sure Peter will be glad of all the help he can get."

"Are Pete and Ember married yet?"

"No!"

"That's good. I wouldn't want to miss the wedding and they're both such impulsive people that it wouldn't surprise me to hear they had run off to the courthouse and tied the knot."

Ember? Impulsive? Here is another person who should know her better than I describing her with words I would never think to use in the same sentence with her name. "What makes you think they would be getting married?"

"Oh, they always were nuts about each other. When she fought with me or anyone else she fought to win and always did but when she fought with Pete she fought to be won. But then he's so quick he could make her look like a rank amateur and as you probably know she's far from that. He has actually put her over his knee and spanked her—the fact that he's still alive can only mean that she's in love with him yet. I know Pete is home again—and so—something's bound to come about."

I won't pretend that I enjoyed his company the rest of the way. Here is another who knows it all just like the folks in Rainy Mountain. Oddly enough it was with a great and growing sense of letdown that I rode that eastbound train for home. I know that really I haven't accomplished a thing I can be proud of. Oh sure, we are set to go now for the winter but ironically it has been too easy. I don't mean that an easy victory is not worthwhile but I had come, however reluctantly, filled with the importance of my mission and fully expecting to meet resistance that I would have to overcome. Instead, by way of nothing more than luck that lumber prices are rising and Morrows' reputation as good and responsible people, it was all handed to me on a platter. That makes me feel like no more than an errand boy. Sharing the trip with this man who is Ember's brother and can see only Peter in her future didn't help matters any either. I worked myself into quite a discouraged state of mind by the time the train slowed for home. This might be another way of saying that I was very tired.

Ember met the train and in her quiet way threw a happy fit over Tim's unexpected arrival. She never had much to say when anyone took a train out but always greeted her people with comparative exuberance when they returned home. Except for me! For me there is always that carefully maintained distance kept between us. She's like a cautious animal of the wild with its safety zone around it—I'm allowed no closer than just so. She said no more than "Hi," to me until the three of us were in the truck cab with Tim in the middle. Then she asked, "Well, By, how did it go with you in town?"

"All signs are go." And darned if I didn't hear bitterness in my voice.

"Well! You don't sound too happy about it!" She gave me a quick, wondering look then turned her attention back to her driving which as usual would scare you silly if you weren't used to it.

"I'm sorry. I seem to have been wound up tighter than I realized over this and now I'm just plain thrashed out." That must have accidentally been the right answer because she almost made it all worthwhile just by reaching across Tim and touching my hand.

"We put you in a rough spot but you are the only one of us who could pull this off."

Knowing that had we been alone she wouldn't have touched me cancelled out the encouragement she intended to convey and I wound up feeling even worse. So then we argued halfway down the hill about who should have gone to town instead of me and why and why not.

"Say! What's this all about?" Tim asked when we finally allowed him the chance to say something.

Ember slowed the truck and actually dropped one gear as she very briefly outlined the circumstances for him and as she talked Tim looked first at one of us and then the other. I can tell that he believes he is discovering new and uncharted territory but I really couldn't care less what he thinks. By tomorrow morning—late tomorrow morning—I will probably be in love with the world again but for right now they can all go fly a kite. I slouched into my corner and ignored the both of them.

Habit is so strong that I woke at my usual getting up time next morning but I cured that in a hurry by turning over and going back to sleep for a couple hours more. When I awoke the next time I still felt no better than I had last night but at least now I know why. It had been such a close thing there in town and blithe idiot that I am I hadn't even noticed until later. I can see now from the vantage point of time and distance that MacKenzie's mind had been made up about us before I walked into his office. Rising lumber prices had done that along with the fear of losing money on our bankruptcy. All he needed to know was that we were still trying. That last frozen steel look when he insisted I sign the papers too told me that had his mind been set against us or had he taken a dislike to me, then Ember's Rainy Mountain, paper trees and all, would right now be sliding into the sticky realm of receivership. The full blame for that would rest squarely on my inadequate shoulders. It staggered me to think how close I had come to losing it all for them. Even if the fault were not mine the blame would have been. The old saying 'fools rush in where wise men fear to tread' could have no better illustration than me and my expedition to town. How could Morrows trust me with such a vital matter? More to the point! How could I have let them?

While I was mulling this over Peter breezed in and set a chair backwards by my bed. "Well, friend, thought you'd still be sleeping."

"How can I with you barging in and stomping all over the place?"

"Ah yes, Em said you were in a bit of a snit."

"She did not!" I flared unreasonably, "she's too polite to say that."

"So? Shows how much you know about it."

I tried to stare him down but had to give up and change the subject instead. "Well, you've got some breathing space now." I meant with the bank and he knew what I meant.

"So Em tells me. Through the night I looked over the stuff you left on my desk and as far as I can see it's just the usual sort of thing that one has to put up with when you operate on someone else's money. Judging by the bundle of blank promissory notes included for signing he must be turning us loose again, creditwise."

"That's how I interpret it," I agreed. "There will still be that day of reckoning but it's been put off a few months."

"Yes, that's to be worried about but not for a while now." Then he smiled so blissfully that I knew he was about to tell me a lie.

"We're all very grateful for your help on this. I guess—," he paused. "No, I don't guess. I know and admit that we all lack courage when it comes to something like you just did for us. The only way you could have gotten me in on that errand would be in my coffin with six strong men struggling to get me through the door."

"Peter, it was a piece of cake!"

"What?"

"I mean exactly that. I wasn't more than half an hour in either the bank or the ranger station. All I did was tell them your plans and they quite literally said, 'sounds great, see you next spring.'"

He stared at me blankly for about five seconds then on came his slow smile and he shook his head in mock sorrow. "Oh no! False modesty will get you out of nothing around here. Ever since John left you've been trying to take his place. Now you have proven that you can so from here on you are going to find yourself cast in the role of front man for Rainy Mountain Lumber."

"Now I know you're putting me on," I sneered.

"Not a bit of it," he assured me. "Actually you seem to have been that for some time already only no one fully realized it. You have been leading from the rear and they didn't even know they were being led."

I shrugged. "I listen to them and I make a few suggestions, that's all."

"Suggestions! Yes, I've heard about your suggestions. I just hope I'll be favoured with some of them from time to time." He gently scratched his jaw and added, "Come to think of it I guess I already have been." When I made no answer he went on, "It really is an odd setup here, isn't it? I mean John Morrow himself was one thing but his kids are something else. John was the complete entrepreneur, he was equally at ease doing anything from falling a dangerous tree that some over-careful faller was afraid of, to skidding it to the landing, hauling it to the mill or filling any position around the mill or planer. I can remember seeing him piling lumber on the green chain when it was necessary. Then he dresses up like he just stepped from the fashion pages of Eaton's catalogue, zips off to town to mix with a bunch of executive types and comes away president of their association."

No getting around it, I had to laugh. "That lets me out if you're thinking I'm going to take his place. I couldn't do any of that."

"Oh sure, you're different. But still, in a way you're the same, you see the big view while the rest of us are scrabbling around all tangled up in our own shoelaces. You are a jack of all trades and if you don't know how to do something that needs doing you just go ahead and slash away at it anyhow. But what I was getting at is that none of his kids have inherited his tackle-anything outlook on life. They are all specialists, even experts maybe, in their own field but don't ask any of them to cope with the whole show. And I've found out that I'm no different except I have no field of my own in which to be an expert. Unless it's troublemaking." He grinned that pleased grin that would make you forgive him for most anything. "I was raised as just another Morrow, you know, I can hardly remember my own parents though I have pictures of them."

I've seen pictures of both his mother and father, they are prominently displayed in the living room of John's house where Ember has of late been the sole occupant. That is, she was until Tim came home. I presume he will live there too now. I want to tell Peter the only big view I can see is that if Rainy Mountain goes under then I too am out of a home. But of course I can't admit such a thing. It might lead to avenues of discussion where I would rather not go. Besides, that seems to be no longer strictly the full story. For one who likes things kept simple I seem to be running into an uncommon lot of complications lately and this fellow holding down my chair right now is certainly a major one of them.

Peter loves to talk, especially when he has a captive audience like now. "Anyway, John gave us each a job as we finished or quit school and we were supposed to get good enough at those jobs to eventually rise to be superintendent of our sector or division.

Rainy Mountain was a pretty small operation in those days, I suppose it still is by industry standards but John always thought big. He put Allan in the mill, Tom in the woods, Terry in a truck, and me in the shop. Each of us was to rise to the top like cream on milk and I guess we did except for me. I was to become shop foreman or master mechanic, however you want to say it, but I had a distinct aversion to dirty oil and greasy coveralls so I never did come up to expectations. The others though all turned into first class managers in their own small way. If John had switched us around once a year or sent us off to work for someone else maybe one or two of us would have developed some leadership skills. But John himself was all the leader he needed, or even wanted, so he left us each in our own rut. Now suddenly he's gone and we're a nervous bunch of chickens facing Friday dinner—a disaster partly but not entirely of our own making. And make no mistake, it will be a total disaster if we go under. No doubt you have noticed the absence of the word 'limited' after Rainy Mountain Lumber?"

I had and admitted it.

"This venture is a private family proprietorship so if we go bust it's not only all gone but we could each be facing personal bankruptcy as well. Like it or not we will all leave here with no more than the clothes on our backs and whatever we can cram into a suitcase or two." He paused a moment to let that sink in. "Can you imagine Ember without her store and post office?"

I could not! Nor could I imagine myself without Nightrider and trains to meet.

"But with your help and the good luck that seems to follow you if we all chip in and work hard, hopefully we can bring about some good times again. Just think, someday years down the road, some old fellow might say to his friends, 'You know, I can remember when Byron himself used to meet the trains every night.'"

"Don't be ridiculous! The sooner we get off this subject the better I will feel," I told him.

"Me too," he said, rising. "Incidentally, my friend, I could use some help at the office this afternoon. We have a lot of fine-tuning to do, equipment and supplies to order and etcetera on to no end."

He left me alone with the knowledge that my snit is all gone. I can see though that I will have a problem convincing these people that what I did in town could just as well have been accomplished by any of them. Even the twins could have handled it as long as they minded their tongues. For Ember it would have been a breeze compared to steering her store and town through all their many problems. But it no longer troubles me in the least—if they want to give me more credit than I am due then without any loss to them that will be my gain—I think! I hope!

I also hope I can be with her when the time finally comes that Ember must visit H.M. at the bank. Knowing all too well his general opinion of us Rainy Mountaineers I want to see his reaction when she sails regally into his office with her high heels, coifed hair and clothing that seems personally tailored for her. If he liked John as it seems he must have then he is going to be bowled over by the daughter. And then—when he discovers that where the lumber business is concerned her mind is sharper than his!

What does concern me at this moment is how much of Peter's gratitude on behalf of the family I can believe. Never before has anyone here said thank you to me for anything, it's simply not in their vocabulary beyond basic table manners. I have to judge that this outpouring today is Peter's own idea and there will be some good reason for it. More than likely he was watching me closely the whole time for reactions to his praise so he could gauge just how high my ambitions run. He is a terrible tease, I charitably call him that for the lack of a better word. If he were to decide that I entertained thoughts of grandeur I would never hear the end of it. He would worry and badger me at every turn, all very innocently of course, it's the way his humour runs. The message is clear—I must never allow him any insights to my personal thoughts.

Late in the afternoon Ember marched into the office where I

was keeping Peter company while he listed our winter needs. She was followed closely by an uncomfortable-looking Gabrielle. "Here he is," Ember said. Then, to me, "Gabby wants to bend your ear, Byron." She wheeled and left.

I winced. I suppose it was inevitable that a name like Gabrielle's should become Gabby to our Queen of the Shorter Form but she didn't have to be so crude about it, almost insulting.

"It's the hot water at the teacherage," Gabrielle explained half-turning to watch Ember vanish. "I'm sorry to bother you but there isn't any. I mean it all runs cold and you did tell me to see you if I had any problems. So?"

"Oh sure, that's no bother. Probably just needs a new fuse or something simple like that." Then I turned to Peter, "You don't need me now and I'll see you after supper anyway."

"Yeah, that's fine." But as I turned away to go with Gabrielle he added, "Have fun, kids." I shot a quick suspicious look back at him but all I learned was that he was hugely enjoying some line of thought.

I took the pickup that was sitting in front of the office waiting for Peter to want to go some place and drove Gabrielle to her home. Despite several years of vacancy, now that it has an occupant, the building is no longer the teacherage. To most of us it's already Gabrielle's place—and about to be amended to Gabby's I thought ruefully. As I drove I apologized for Ember's treatment of her name.

"Oh heavens, I'm used to being called Gabby. My father says it's because I talk too much but having the name Gabrielle is really begging for it. It's quite natural and okay but I am wondering though why Miss Morrow doesn't like me?"

"Ember?" I stalled for time while I wondered too. "Ember likes everyone but she is moody and rather an odd character. She seems to think the future and well being of this place and all of us rest squarely in her hands and she takes it much too seriously at times. She is unofficial mayor, councillor, treasurer and civic works boss besides running the store and post office when she isn't guiding the rest of us in the right direction so she hasn't much time for being nice. If you are addressing her as Miss Morrow, that might be the problem. Around here everyone is just what their name says. There's almost no use of Mr. Mrs. or Miss. It's something you will get used to."

As I expected there was no big panic with the hot water, it was easily fixed. Then either I asked her to go to the movie with me Friday night or she suggested that I ask her to go, I'm still not clear on how that happened. But, whatever, it turned out to be another pleasant outing together for us. I refuse to call them dates because I wasn't thinking that way—she seems too young—I was just helping her get used to our lumber camp ways.

Tom came home that night, three sheets to the wind. Two trainmen helped him off the passenger car and I reckon they were glad to be rid of him. He was in an abusive mood and an independent one, he wanted no help but couldn't navigate by himself. At his house when I tried to help him he cursed and took a wild swing at me that, had it connected, would have had me looking back from next week. But he missed and the momentum of his swing sent him sprawling through his gateway to land heavily on the lawn. As I left him there struggling—and failing—to get to his feet I figuratively brushed my hands of him just as the trainmen had done and promptly forgot about him.

7

We were all so busy that we hardly noticed the last of autumn sneak by as winter bullied it southward. Peter, now that he has his teeth in it is a whirlwind of activity. He's been going to town to meet with people who are answering the ads for operators with portable mills and for a full week set up office in his hotel room. As I had suspected there are still a lot of them around. Made obsolete by changing times and maybe not too successful in the first place, they are rusting away in backyards and behind shops that now cater to logging trucks and rubber-tired skidders. The independent sawmill operation having evolved into a logging contract with one of the big companies now emerging above the thicket of smaller shows. Many of the portables were piles of junk with owners who would never dare rub two quarters together for fear the finance company might hear the sound of money. They muck about on the fringe of poverty defying the odds and living quite well and happily while they look for a better next year. Like farming, logging often seems to be a 'next year' occupation. But they are self-reliant men who given a box of wrenches, a roll of haywire, a cutting torch and a welder can fix anything in any kind of weather. They are an independent lot that smart under the new type of management that comes down the pipeline from distant boardrooms.

This was the group that Peter chose from. He got along well with these men for he spoke their language and would certainly never be an absentee boss. He knew a couple of them personally and had skidded logs for one of them some years ago.

Peter made them the standard deal that we had worked out among ourselves at another meeting in the back of the office. Each operator was to supply himself, his sawmill and bring his own crew. We would provide him with a place to stay, transportation and fuel besides putting logs to one end of his mill and hauling lumber away from the other. With that in mind we have had a crew of carpenters hammering together a lot of skid shacks as large as can be easily transported, they are well insulated but simple. Each contractor has the option of setting his men up in skid shacks at or near his mill or adding them to our camp area and utilizing our cookhouse facilities. This is the route they all chose so our Bunkhouse Row is now nearly an extra block long.

Since we have enough of our own logging equipment and trucks to handle the full quota, and then some, we discouraged the sawmill contractors from doing their own logging. But Peter made one large exception when he shook hands to seal a contract with George Schultz who is not your average logger. George has three modern high-production portable mills that have not been allowed to rust away. On the contrary, he has used a lot of time and money to automate and improve them with hydraulics and electric controls. These mills have already earned a small fortune for George so when the time came that he no longer had profitable work for them the switch to contract logging was easy enough but not fully welcome. But he also has two sons who have done their best to put him out to pasture and he saw this as a golden opportunity to show the boys he still has the old touch. He wouldn't come unless he also had the contract to log to his own mills. He drove a hard bargain with Peter and was the only contractor shipping in his own bulldozers, skidders and loaders.

"He's worth it," claimed Peter, defending his decision. "George's three mills are worth the best five of the others and let's face it, if we are to move an extra fifty percent of wood over the quota our own equipment will be stretched pretty thin. This gives us some backup capacity." There's no way he could have convinced me how much we would need that later on.

One other detail was being taken care of in the shop. Since a large proportion of the timber to be hauled this winter would be in the form of rough lumber from the portables instead of logs, several of the log trucks were being converted to flatdecks to work as lumber haulers.

Peter had several interesting confrontations along the way. The first with me when he began insisting that I resume the post of acting manager so he could be free to supervise the portables and all their necessary support structure. For some reason all the activity, shipping in, unloading, hauling out and setting up of the portables had caught his fancy. I flatly refused on several counts. "In the first place, Peter, you have Tom to oversee the woods, that's his department and you will be horning in on him."

"I see the mills as separate from our normal logging show and Tom is as busy as he needs to be now."

"You must have noticed," I told him, "that Tom has been sober ever since we started getting busy now that freeze-up is on us. Don't go and crowd him at this stage. Besides, he has both Alec and Tim to help him. I imagine Tim is less help than hindrance yet but that will change and we both know that Alec is capable of running the whole woods show alone in a pinch."

"That may all be true enough but there is still room for me in there. In fact I believe we need a direct liaison between the office here and the portable operators."

"Alright, but let Tom work that out and if he asks for help then we'll discuss it again."

"Say, my onetime friend! Just who's running this outfit anyway?"

While I tried to shrug that off he pretended to be irked with me. "Okay, so you had to drag the real reason out of me after all. I simply need you to handle all the day-to-day drudgery so I can be free to tackle whatever I'm needed at."

If Peter is trying to aggravate our working relations to a breaking point, he is certainly finding all the right ways today. I actually saw red at the prospect of him meddling at the operational level. "If you go around tackling everything you think you are needed at we will be in trouble from day one with foremen quitting right and left. It's taken Morrows many long years to accumulate the men who are the nucleus of our supervisory staff. They work as common loggers on our small summer crews and gravitate to foreman status as the winter workers come in. The whole setup is too delicately balanced to have you rooting around looking for trouble where none exists."

He stared speculatively at me for a few long seconds while I hoped I hadn't overdone it. I don't want to anger him, I just want him to understand the error of his notions. "My! You are prickly this morning aren't you? What's the matter? Too much devil's club for breakfast?"

I ignored his sarcasm. "What's more to the point is that you are making the same mistake the Morrows insist on making. You are all somehow deluded into thinking I can be a manager. I want you to understand that I have no management skills at all, nor inclinations either. My one brief spell when I was shanghaied into it has cured me completely." As if a cure was needed! "I haven't the right disposition, knowledge, or education let alone initiative or desire to be successful as a manager."

"But you can't deny that, no matter how you stumble along, the right things get done around you."

"Once again all pure luck," I insisted. "There have been times I've been aghast the way some frivolous suggestion on my part has been taken seriously and acted upon. It's a wonder I've survived the results."

"If I could choose between skill and luck, friend Byron, I would take luck without having to think twice."

I clamped my jaws shut and refused comment.

"Very well," he accepted it reluctantly, "I'll take this an example of your good judgment. I'll try to stay out of Tom's department but he had better run it right."

"Peter, Tom doesn't have to lift a finger for those portables other than to put logs to their landings. This is something you and Morrows don't seem to understand with your history of hiring only day-wage crews. The mills will run themselves or go broke themselves. Each already has its own owner-operator, all have a radio equipped pickup and crummy so if any of them need you they can find you quick enough. Most of them will be living right here in camp so you can talk to them almost any time you like."

He also had a minor problem with Ember.

Since we have to supply all the sawmills with pickups and crummies we had a lot shipped in. It sounds like quite an investment for an outfit already on the rocks but really it's only a drop in the bucket, looking ahead to the end gains if the winter pans out as planned. And then, in simple language, we had to have them.

The morning after the new pickups had been unloaded from the flatcars Peter drove one up to the office and parked it alongside Ember's older 4x4 where that truck stood hitched to the mall by its block heater cord. He held the office door open for Jo as she came in to go to work in the store. "Tell Em to come out here a moment, will you Jo," he called after her as she started down the hallway.

In a few minutes Ember appeared, taking the opportunity to bring along the company mail—already opened and no doubt well read. Maybe even answers ready to go.

"What's up, Peter?"

He gestured to the window with a flourish. "Your new truck. If you have anything in the old one best move it over right away. Someone from the shop will be along very soon now to collect it. It's going to work in the woods."

"Now why on earth would I need a new truck? My own is quite satisfactory." The fact that her truck had already been retired from the woods before she got it didn't reduce its value to her.

"I need your old truck to give to a woods crew so you get a new one."

"Then give them the new one, Peter. They're more likely to need it than me. I only drive between here and home and sometimes up to the railroad or out to Hansons'. For heaven's sake I can walk and you can give both trucks to the woods crews if we are short."

"We might be short but you're missing the point. As the only Morrow living in the big house, other than Tim who doesn't count yet, you have to keep up a good appearance. We have a lot of people here for the winter and there are more coming. Can you imagine their thoughts if we let them see the number one visible Morrow driving around in an old clunker? The first conclusion they will come to is that our cheques will soon be bouncing."

"Well! I never heard anything so stupid. If you want to talk that way Allan is the number one visible Morrow. Not me. Then comes Tom. Still not me."

"Nope! In the eyes of the public you are number one. No one is going to give Allan or Tom a second look but they will all see as much of you as they can arrange. Besides, Allan and Tom get new trucks too."

Outside a truck door slammed saving him from Ember's reply for she wheeled to look out the window then with a short angry cry that I may have heard wrong, darted outside. She was just in time to reach her old truck and jerk the passenger side door open before it was backed away by a mechanic who had already unplugged it from the electrical outlet. Quickly she rummaged through the glove compartment, along the dash and behind the seat forcing the mechanic to climb out for a moment. Then, standing there in the cold with both arms full, she watched her old 4x4 being driven away.

I suddenly had a feeling for her that I know Peter is not tuned to. I expect she came within an eyelash of putting the run on that young mechanic but she hesitated because that's not her style and now it's too late. She is like her brothers and has fallen in love with her machinery. For someone who feels it necessary to name her truck, that truck is important—an extension of herself. She is now watching, if not the funeral, then the beginning of the terminal illness of an old friend. Our older 4x4's don't last long between shop calls once the loggers get them.

Finally she went to the new truck and yarded open a door losing her grip on a few things she held onto in the process. She dumped the whole works helter-skelter inside, picked up the strays, then threw the door shut and beelined back to the office. Peter had won but only by default and he was wise enough to retreat out the back way grinning as he went leaving dummy me caught in the crossfire as she came in the front. She stopped abruptly and glared. "If you think that silly beard you're trying to grow becomes you—think again!" Before I could begin to wonder how we had jumped from old trucks to new beards, she was on her way to the store.

I got in on the act the very next morning without having the slightest intention of doing so. The words that popped out of my mouth were formed without conscious thought as I watched Ember drive up in her swanky new truck. A light, cold snowfall so diffused the outdoor yard and street lights that she drove up with her headlights off as though it were day. She hopped out and stood back to survey its rakish lines, a smile spreading over her face, plainly she is tickled pink with it. Today she is wearing high, shiny, black leather boots, a voluminous but sharply tailored overcoat, and a fur hat I haven't seen before. To go with the new truck maybe? In fact it's rare to see her wear a hat.

Now, Ember is an indoor girl. Her idea of fun is hiding away in a private place to read a fiction story. High adventure is found with Mowat or Berton. Unlike her younger sisters she does not keep a saddle horse at the farm. She has in all likelihood never been on a horse in her life. Yet as I watch she is transformed to a ghostly dark shadow by a swirl of wind driven snow that gusts across the rooftop and settles in racing eddies about her. The image I get is of flowing mane, clattering hooves and a flash of steel. Then the snow whirl trails off letting the outside lights turn morning darkness brighter than the coming day may be.

"Named the new truck?" I asked as she closed the office door.

"Not yet," she answered gaily, definitely in a good mood but no comment on a clean-shaven assistant.

"How come you're so slow?"

"Oh, I guess the right moment of inspiration hasn't struck."

"May I name it for you?"

She stopped so quick that she skidded a little in her snowy boots and nearly turned an ankle. Suspicion is loud and clear all over her. She trusts me exactly as much as I trust her. "Why?"

"Because that right moment of inspiration has struck for me."

"I guess you could give it a try," she said doubtfully. "What have you got in mind?"

"Cossack."

Her eyes opened wider for an instant and she almost smiled. "Hmm, not bad," she allowed, turning for another look out the window. A lift of a shoulder. "Why not? —But—there's just one thing."

"What's that?"

"You will have to think of her as a lady Cossack."

"That's fine Ember, a lady Cossack is exactly what I had in mind."

Peter's next problem was more serious and for this he called another of his, by now, infamous board meetings. He has a rebellion building around him and he needs to get the air cleared. Our own logging crews are in high gear and the log trucks are hauling around the clock. Some of the portables are operating, some are setting up, and a couple haven't arrived yet. It's no time to trip over our own shoelaces.

Peter had warned us all there would be a critical decision to vote on and urged everyone to attend. We were all informed that the question would amount to a confidence vote for him—attempt to sell out now for whatever can be gotten—or let him carry on.

Tom and Tim came together and I guess there is nothing strange in that since Tim now lives at Tom's place. When Ember told Tim she wouldn't housekeep for him, nor cook either unless he kept the same mealtimes as she did, he didn't believe her. Once he saw that she meant it he moved out and into a basement room at Tom's where "Jennie fusses over him as is deserved by a husband's younger brother"—Ember's sarcastic comment. I heard no harsh words between Ember and Tim other than their normal abrasiveness with each other. It was just a matter of convenience for both.

Alec was the next to arrive, looking around belligerently, challenging anyone to say he shouldn't have come. He knows everyone here too well to be intimidated so when there were no objections he tossed a piece of paper onto the desk in front of Peter and sat down. Peter looked at it then, expressionless, turned it upside down in front of him. Ember and Jo came together and that left us waiting only for Allan and the twins. There were smiles as we caught each other checking the time. It's still ten minutes to the hour and we all know Allan won't show until exactly then so we passed some time in idle talk until Tom caught the attention of everyone.

"I see the road construction survey crews are still working though I'll bet the snow and cold soon stops them."

"Are they still pouring money down that old rathole?" Ember scoffed. "They've been working off and on at that since back in the Depression. We've all seen the old right-of-way west of here that they cut by hand labour back in the '30s. Are they surveying it yet again?"

Alec had seen the surveyors too, "No, they've got a new line altogether, nowhere near the old one. It crosses our Chicken Falls main road about three miles out from the railroad crossing. It's going to make some big changes when we can drive to town."

"It will never come to be anything useful. It will always be so much faster and easier to go on the train."

"I don't know, Ember, the busses might put the passenger trains out of business like they have in some other places. You might have to drive to town for your groceries and mail."

"Tom! Be serious! Greyhound through the Yellowhead Pass and down the Fraser? With 4x4s and riverboats maybe. Tell us another tall one. They would need a good road to compete with the trains."

"It will be a good road. We're not talking about a winter road nor about two muddy ruts winding around the trees. The surveyors tell me it will be two-lane blacktop with a shoulder on the sides. There's already construction at both ends and since we are somewhere in the middle they will reach us someday. We are going to leap from the dark ages straight into the future in one dizzy instant the day the ribbon is cut."

Ember is not the only one disturbed at the prospect of the highway, I feel chills up and down my spine every time I hear talk of it. I'm not fussy about change, I tend to like things the way they are.

Allan had arrived by now but we were too deep into highway speculation to give him any notice till he spoke up. "Maybe we can put some of our equipment to work on it. They'll work mainly in the summer and most of our equipment sits idle at that time."

Trust an opportunistic Morrow to think of that. But Alec threw cold water on the idea. "They use a lot bigger equipment than we have, I don't think we'll get much out of it."

"Trucks, Alec, they will use lots of dump trucks. Our log trucks are as big as anything on wheels in the country, all we need is a bunch of dump boxes."

"Troubles and problems! We've got our share of both without worrying about the highway. And that's why I've called you all here tonight." Peter is evidently going to start without Jan and Pat but he soon put us straight on that. "We have a landmark meeting on our hands tonight in that the twins have sent Alec to represent both of them." He waved the piece of paper in the air. "They have signed a statement saying so. Any comments?"

Tom protested immediately and loudly. "Not a chance! I will reluctantly put up with him voting for his wife but not for Jan."

"It does seem a bit irregular," Allan agreed. "One man shouldn't be allowed to cast two votes. I say that if the girls want their vote they had better be here." There was a babble of discussion in which Peter took no part but instead stared impassively at whoever happened to be talking loudest.

I could easily understand the objections from Tom and Allan. Salt in a wound would hurt less than seeing Tom's assistant come up with double-voting power. When the talk finally died down with no consensus reached Peter said, "Byron? Any thoughts on the subject?"

Instead of answering him with an opinion of my own I just stated some facts for the gathered company. "Well, we all know that the twins have never voted against each other and probably never will. So however it's done their votes will always be a block of two. As for sending Alec in their place, it's nothing new, both Allan and Tom have sent their wives to represent them on at least one occasion each over the last month."

"In fact, Peter, if you want a shortcut just multiply Ember's vote by three because they always vote the same as her." That was from Jo. Allan and Tom both nodded, having noticed the same thing.

Peter looked to each of them in turn. "Okay, that's settled then."

But it wasn't. I could see that Tim was greatly agitated but for some reason was trying to stay quiet. Now with no one else saying what he wanted to hear, he pointed at Alec and blurted it out himself. "He can't vote, not even for Pat, and he shouldn't be here at all. He's not one of us."

That remarkable statement brought on a long pause that in any other group would probably be described as an embarrassed silence. Only I have never known a Morrow to be embarrassed under any circumstance. No one seemed inclined to either answer him or change the subject so I said in as neutral a tone as I could, "If you are going to exclude everyone who is not a bloodline Morrow, then you will have to do without half of us here tonight, including Peter, Jo, and myself as well as Alec.

"We might get things settled in a hurry if it was left to Tom and Allan and I."

But Allan shook his head. "Kid, you don't know beans of what you're talking about. This jam we're in now is at least partly Tom's and my doings. If Byron and Peter have a way out then more power to us all and I couldn't care less if their names are Smith and Patten. If you want to get right down to basics I'm not sure you deserve any voting rights here. You're hardly more than a visitor. About all we've seen of you over the years is your endorsement on our cheques."

Peter grinned about the way I imagine a wolf would after bringing down a deer. "Alright, now that we've settled matters of protocol let's get on with the issue at hand, and on that line I have a few things to say." Satisfied that he had our attention he went on, "I started these meetings because when I came home I was totally out of touch. I couldn't get a feel for the situation. I was, in other words, like Tim is now—uninformed, dumb and ignorant—only difference is, I knew it while Tim doesn't. So, I figured if I got everyone together and talking I would learn something and I did too. I learned that all I had to do was to get Byron talking and I would soon hear all I needed to know."

There were a few chuckles around the room that eased the

tension, but I don't know why because in my opinion Peter's idea of humour is completely lacking in taste. He's not the one who started these meetings either, this room has been called the meeting room for as many years as I have been here and has always gotten its share of use too. Though he has refined the process considerably.

"Somehow we got into this voting system, I suppose because I was unwilling to make decisions on matters I didn't understand without some help from the rest of you. Anyway, we seem to be stuck with it now so yes, Tim, you will have your vote just as Alec will cast his double one. But the point I'm coming to is that while I plan to go by the wishes of the majority, I don't really have to. I have a piece of paper, signed by your father and witnessed at the lawyer's office, that says I am in complete control here. I don't have to listen to any of you but I have as you well know. I can take full and sole control of the bank account just by presenting myself and my authorization at the bank. I haven't done that and I would rather not. So you see, you can't get rid of me any more than I can get rid of you. And that's why we are here tonight because some of you are trying to go around me and make a deal with the opposition." Peter looked directly at Tom as he said this.

"That's pretty strong talk for all I've been doing. I've only sounded them out a few times and I haven't made any secret of it."

I knew there had been rumblings among the brothers, even Allan but I hadn't heard this.

"They are definitely interested and are open to offers. They want us to name a price."

"Have they given you any idea as to the price range they have in mind?"

Tom named a sum that sounded like a lot of dollars if you didn't know what it was being offered for.

Peter let that sink in to us for a while before he commented. "And what do they want to buy? Half the quota?"

"Be reasonable, Pete. They would expect to get the whole quota, all the logging equipment, trucks, skidders, crawlers, and loaders." His voice was getting noticeably defensive as the silence around him grew more shocked. "And also the private land that is the townsite but the sawmill, planer and all other improvements would be ours to auction off under a complete removal clause."

It took a while for us to get the implications and surprisingly, Allan, not Ember, was the first to respond. Plainly his rumbling hadn't meant the same as Tom's because he simply reached out for his larger brother's throat and the two of them crashed to the floor amid the splintered wreckage of Tom's chair. The timbers of the mall hadn't shaken so since the night my foot slipped off the clutch pedal as I was backing Nightrider to the unloading dock.

It was all one-sided because Tom had no chance for more than a token effort to fight back or to protect himself. He was weakening before he could find a way to break Allan's grip on his windpipe. I may be speaking only for myself but I think we were all absolutely dumbfounded. Fortunately Peter and Tim came out of it in time to leap in and haul Allan away from his expiring victim before the throttling became fatal. It was an incident that should have had a different outcome because Tom is a bare-knuckle brawler of some local reputation. Allan, on the other hand, also has a reputation—that of never having been in a fight in his life. His hair-trigger temper leads him only to verbal blasts and emotional tirades. But he is fighting mad now.

"Believe me, Tom! I'll kill you or any one else who tries to sell us down the river." Peter and Tim had their hands full struggling to pull him farther back while he snorted and snuffed like a mad bear trying to get close enough to a fleet-footed lunch for one more good swipe.

Tom was impressed and subdued. Despite his size advantage he has always shown great respect for his older brother. Disagree with him? Sure. Argue and be uncooperative? You bet but that's about it. He would never ridicule or pick a fight with Allan. When he had his breathing back to normal and Allan had quieted some, he said, croaking a little in the process, "It's okay, Allan. All

I did was talk to them, I can't sell anything out any more than you can. It's not mine to sell."

"He's right, Allan, I'm the only one here who can do any selling and that's not in my plans." Almost as quickly as he had flared Allan now cooled and when released he returned to his chair but his eyes remained warily angry. Tom got to his feet, absently kicked aside the remains of his chair, selected another from the back of the room and also sat down but this time with the full width of the room between him and Allan.

But he wasn't out of trouble yet for now Ember lashed out at him. "Tom! You couldn't possibly think of selling out, could you?"

"I not only think of it," he answered bitterly, "but I long for and dream of the day I can kick the mud of this place off my boots and make a new start somewhere else." He looked around at us. "Oh, I know, you keep saying the quota, these 'Paper Trees', is worth millions if only we do this and do that and hang tough for a while. But I've had it clear up to here." With one hand he slashed an imaginary line above his head. "I don't want millions or any part of it years down the road. I'd be satisfied, even pleased, with only thousands now as long as it's soon."

"But what would we do then? Where would we work? What would become of our town and our people? Just look around a bit at what's happening. Put your finger on the map at McBride and trace out the line to Prince George. Call out the place names along the way and think about the fact that most of them are ghost towns. In fact few of them are even on the newer maps. For instance— Bend; not far from here—mill gone, town gone! Guilford; gone, no one there! Penny, once as big an operation as ours—gone—swallowed, a few people still there who have to go somewhere else for work. And so on and so on—all grabbed by the giants in town. That must not be allowed to happen to Rainy Mountain. No, Tom, we have a tradition to live up to."

What I've heard since coming here is that Bend burned to the ground during a windstorm back in the 1940s and I think Guilford might have closed down before the day of quotas. Nobody grabbed either one but who am I to quibble over details? Penny went broke and that's not a good thought right now—one is so vulnerable when short of money.

"Ember, Dad grew up as a farmer's son in Alberta. He didn't know a spruce from a balsam until he came here with a little money, mostly borrowed, and hacked this place out of the bush. You and I and the others are the first generation born into the lumber business. That does not make it tradition."

"Well, it does to me!" She shot back at him. "And what about your children? Don't you want the best for them?"

"Yes, that's just it, I do want the best for them and I think that's to be found in town with me bringing home a proper paycheque for a change."

Now that was a point that stung, for of the lot gathered here, the only one who has ever received a paycheque from Rainy Mountain Lumber is Alec. And I happen to know that he is no longer on the payroll since his marriage to Pat. It's a policy that may need change.

"But it just isn't fair to have to fold up because one or two want to quit. What about the rest of us who want to keep going?"

"Okay, okay!" Peter broke in. "Maybe once we are on our feet we can see our way to buying Tom out, and any others too, then everyone will be happy. In the meantime this is exactly why we are here tonight. In as few words as possible do we struggle on for millions in Ember's Paper Trees or do we call it quits and sell for the best poor deal we can make now? It's voting time! You all knew this issue was coming so you should have your minds made up. Tom! We start with you. We all know your opinion but say it for me."

"Sell."

"Tim?"

"I say the same as Tom, I want out too."

Ember laid some nasty and insulting words on Tim, then

added, "Out? You've never been in! You just want to cash in and hang out your shingle down in Vancouver even if it means wrecking the lives of some others." It's the first time I've heard her demonstrate such an easy mastery of lumber camp lingo, but when I looked at her I could see she is wishing she could call back some of it and is working hard at calming herself. In fact, now that we are down to the nitty-gritty, everyone seems calm, the 'carry-ons' confident of a majority and the 'sells' knowing from the start they can't win.

"Cool it, Em, it's your turn."

"Don't sell!" Back straight, chin up, dander too.

"Jo?"

"I'm with Em all the way on this one. Our net worth is zilch the way we are, let's have a whirl at building it up."

"Allan?"

"Let's keep trying." But he sounded tired.

"Alec, your double vote please."

Alec's eyes were downcast, studying the piece of paper he had handed to Peter earlier and I knew instantly there was more trouble brewing. He slowly raised his head to meet Peter's suddenly alert gaze. "Well Pete, it's against my advice but Pat and Jan both say sell."

And here we all thought the twins wishes would be an automatic rubber stamping of Ember's vote like they always have been—till now. You could have knocked me down with a chickadee feather and Peter too by the look of him. First his face registered shock but he struggled to keep it from showing, then a wild anger flashed briefly before his eyes settled to acceptance. Finally he was amused, or made out that he was.

Ember had leapt to her feet then without saying anything sat down again, white-cheeked and angry but puzzled too. "Why, Alec," she got out almost gently after a moment, "do you think they understand what their decision means? Do they know what they are saying?"

"Yes, they do. They see their father as a broken man forced to literally run for his life and they see others they love going the same way." Perhaps it was accidental that his eyes turned toward Allan and Tom. "They see the business as the reason. They see it as a killer. They've already lost two brothers to it and almost their father. They want it ended and all of us settled in to simple jobs for someone else. They know it means the end of our town and way of life and they are prepared to leave."

We were a surprised bunch of people but none more so than me. With a guilty twinge I remember just recently assuming the twins had no more serious thought in their heads than getting back to Alec. I expect each of us felt differently but I know that at this moment I could walk under any table on the claim without ducking.

Ember is perfectly seething with pent-up fury and hasn't a clue what to do about it. What a ruckus we would have on our hands if the twins had come in person. I now see the wisdom of them sending Alec in their place— pugnacious, unhindered soul that he is—he is a cool head in a bind and no one chose to tackle him over the girls' views.

"That means we sell!" Tim whooped.

Tom was as stunned as anyone, unable to believe what he now took to be his impending good fortune.

"Hold on, Tim, what it means is we have a tie because I vote no sale."

"It means you are beat, Peter, because you haven't a majority behind you."

"Not so quick, there's one man hasn't voted yet. What will it be Byron? You will have to break the tie." At the corner of my vision Ember gave a thumbs up sign to Jo.

"Oh no, you don't!" Tom shouted. Seeing his unexpected victory evaporating lent power to his voice but I noticed he was no longer objecting to Alec's double vote. "Let either Byron or Ember vote but not both of them."

So! There it is again! That open insinuation that Ember and I travel in tandem. I know my face is slowly turning red and I looked her way to see how she is taking it.

She winked at me! The same sly way she did four years ago in the store when she told Jo that she had hired me for them before the front office could get me. Bless me but even in this moment of stress she seems to think it's funny! Isn't that great! For four years I've been doing everything I could to show I wanted to court her and all I've gotten is the proverbial cold shoulder and hot tongue. So now she's winking at me again! At this rate we should be holding hands by the turn of the century!

Jo broke my dismal line of thought with an answer to Tom. "Byron has more than earned the right to a vote along with the rest of us. If it wasn't for his efforts and self sacrifice there probably wouldn't be anything left to vote about. Ever since he came here he has lived and breathed for Rainy Mountain and like every one else has never drawn a paycheque for it. If nothing else he should have inherited Dad Morrow's voting rights."

"You're joking!" That was from Tim who seems to set a lot of store in paycheques but I'm not sure if it was in awe, or in scorn.

"I don't think anyone has forgotten Byron's contributions or would seriously argue against him having a vote. But what about you, Jo? Terry has been gone a long time."

"I own a full share, Allan, equal to yours in whatever comes of this venture. Any time you want to test that statement in court I'm as ready as you are. Besides, I'm voting the same as you so you should be a little more respectful."

Allan nodded, already looking ahead and totally unconcerned that his ill-thought challenge had been met. Maybe it was just his way of testing—or demonstrating for others—her resolve. With Allan you just never know. Then he grinned at Tom and said, "Well, we all know how Byron will vote so that's that."

Tom lumbered to his feet. "Coming, Tim? I'm sure we can find something better to do than waste our time here." Neither of them seem too cut up over the way things have turned out. But I am! I'm cut all to ribbons with rebellious impulses over the way they use me and take me for granted. What a jolt I could give them if I stood up and shouted, 'Sell'! I'll bet I'd be disenfranchised so fast I'd be left gasping. But as usual I sat quiet.

As soon as the others were all gone and Peter and I were alone, he laughed, "See what I mean about luck? I dumped you between a rock and a hard place and without opening your mouth to say one word you settled the issue or at least it was settled because of you."

"If you think I'm so all fired lucky how do you explain my wreck four years ago and what about Terry?"

"Terry's luck was bad but it was all his own. Jumping to the high side against a cutbank on a narrow road carries poor odds but your luck kept you alive and has been rubbing off on us ever since. Stop and think a moment—where would you be now if that spill hadn't happened?"

"A long way from here, I guarantee and that might represent better luck yet."

"Not for us, and I think not for you either. Has it been so bad for you here?"

"No!"

No, it hasn't, I have to admit that life has been good to me here—enough work to keep my conscience clear and my wits sharp avoiding more of it. I've learned to enjoy having friends and a lot of other things I would one time have considered impossible.

"I thought not. But if it was up to me we would have a collar and chain on you to keep you from getting away. Or maybe there is one that just doesn't show?"

This sounds like a good time to change the subject. "What would you have done if the vote had gone against you?"

"Like Krushchev, my friend, I'd have vetoed them."

"Then why bother with this whole charade we just went through? Why not just ignore them?"

Because none of them are people who will stand being ignored. Now, whether they won or lost, whether satisfied or not, they all feel they gave it their best shot. Now they'll tag along—at least for a while."

"Too bad Tim is so antagonistic."

"Yeah, he's worse than Tom who is after all just being his normal old self while Tim is trying to copy him."

"I don't know how useful he is to Tom but I think that given a better chance he could be a lot of help. We've shoved him into a corner at the side desk in the front office where he is right in the flow of traffic. I notice he spends very little time there but he has dozens of air photos, maps, and also plans that he has drawn up, probably at home in his basement room."

Peter nodded noncommittaly knowing I am leading up to something he might not like. "He's touchy enough to resent the way we've put him on display. We've all said at one time or another that we need him with his forestry training. Now we have him but we don't listen to him because we think his inexperience shows too plainly when actually it might be our inexperience with proper procedure that is the difficulty. We set him up in a public corner and then pretend he's not around. Not good."

"So what are you suggesting? That we add yet another room to the mall?"

"Well, maybe in time but I'm sure a good housecleaning could find other places for two-thirds of the stuff in this room." I waved a hand vaguely at the unattractive racks of miscellaneous junk around us. "Remove the shelves from a couple of walls to give him room for his maps and let him add whatever working furniture it is that he needs. The place could still serve for meetings. Then there will be only one thing missing."

"Yes? And what will that be?" He mocked me with a grin that shows altogether too much tooth. He knows very well what I am getting at but is going to make me say it out loud.

"Then we have to start looking at what he is trying to show us."

The grin snapped off and storm clouds swept across his eyes. "Okay," he said crossly trying to sound tough, "see to it then. But it's Tom who has to work with him, not me. Tom and Alec."

"You're both right and wrong. You will have to lead the way, show them it's desirable to consult Tim, that it will save time and money in the long run. Another thing; Tim will appreciate it more if you set him up instead of me. If everyone thinks it's your idea they'll be more receptive."

He made a face of disgust to cover his returning good humour. "That's not my way of doing it, I'm more likely to grab Tom and Alec by the scruff of the neck and shove them nose down to one of Tim's plans and tell them this is the way we do it now."

I shrugged. "Maybe that's the language they understand." Peter's antagonism toward Tim seems so similar to Ember's that at first I thought he was merely taking her side but now I think his is a separate problem. Ember's dislike is based on a past inability to compete with this very brainy younger brother. Brains don't worry Peter because he can't see any 'smart' along with them but I think that education does. Tim has such wide training and schooling in the forest industry that should he gain a measure of control here sweeping changes would be sure to follow. Right now Tim is green as grass in practical experience, unsure of himself and for a Morrow, easily intimidated. He looks to be a slow learner now that he is out of the classroom. Peter would like matters to stay that way. His dislike has more to do with fear of what the future might bring from an older and wiser Tim.

Odd, how much like John, Peter has turned out to be, not only in his outlook and style but physically too, though on a larger scale. More than once I've looked up as he approached, but still at some distance, to be shocked to see not Peter but John in every movement. The likeness is broken though as he draws near and starts waving his arms for my benefit and talking full bore ahead even before he is close enough for me to make out what he is saying with all the background mill noises. Peter has a lot to talk about and wastes no time getting it off his chest. The big problem for me, is deciding how much of it to believe.

"As long as we are discussing plans do you have any for getting us back on track toward sustained-yield logging?" I might well be a long, off-colour worm in his salad to deserve the look he gave me now.

"Have a heart will you! I've got enough problems already without you digging out old skeletons." Then, his curiosity winning out, "I thought this was something that went under the rug long ago. Don't tell me John got you hooked on it too? —He must have."

"Enough to have a pretty fair appreciation of what he tried to do."

"It wasn't a very practical idea, was it."

"I thought it all sounded reasonable. Expansion and increasing production has to stop somewhere otherwise where is the timber for the younger generations?"

"Who cares? Least of all those younger generations you sound so worried about! They will find their own ways to make money, probably with a lot less strain and risk. As far as the forest is concerned it will grow back and no one could stop it from doing so. In most of this country trees come like weeds—slow growing but useful weeds."

He almost had me fooled! And angry! Until I realized that he is into his special trick of deliberately taking the opposite side in order to get and keep an argument going. That's alright then, maybe we can both learn in the process. He has anticipated my next point and already countered it but I had to make it anyway. "The most noticeable skeleton will be our rocky, bony ridges stripped of timber. At the present rate of production our guys will be sharing noon break with loggers from Quesnel and Prince George in a few years. Northeast of the river we will be knocking on the Alberta border. That's all to be expected eventually but there hasn't been time yet for the second growth to come up to size on enough of the old cut blocks. Our outfit here won't be worth much without wood to saw."

"That's the way it is in the real world, my innocent young friend. You take your profits as long as they last then you pick up your marbles and look for a new game."

"Not when your marbles are people! And their lives and homes."

"Now you're trying to sound like Ember but it won't work because the words don't roll off your tongue with the proper fervor. But she looks at it under yet a different light. If I have your meaning right I believe you are talking about cutting production to where the timber is growing faster than we are cutting it. If she heard you talking like this she would yank the rug out from under you so fast you would land on your head again and much harder than last time! Cut production? You might better make plans to cut her throat. It would be a lot safer and healthier for you."

"Seriously though, Peter, don't you think it would be better to have a reasonable supply of wood lasting forever to plan your operation around? You could get by with a lot less guesswork and high interest financing as compared to this never-ending buying of equipment and machinery to cut more and more but with fewer and fewer men on the crew."

"Our quota is good anywhere in the Prince George supply area. When we run out here we just reach out farther or move to where there is still timber. The Forest Service is committed to finding wood for us, if not here then somewhere else. Right now they say we must cut. So we cut—all we can! Besides, who says we are cutting too fast now? Do you know something all the experts don't?"

"That's part of the problem, we don't know enough and we are too poor to get out there and find out. If we were wealthy enough to command some respect in higher circles we might be able to negotiate our quota downward and still keep others out of our territory. If we could prove the quota is too big for the area we would have a strong bargaining point. Or maybe we should be trying to buy more timberland instead of the short-term leases that timber sales amount to. As far as Forest Service commitment is concerned, I'm not sure that's the way it reads. Besides, 'commitment' is worth the same as old sawmills and bush towns if there is no timber to be had."

"You make me laugh, Byron. Rainy Mountain has been in business for nearly forty years without becoming overly encumbered with wealth. Nor can I see much change in the forecast for the next forty so I don't see your—'wealthy enough'—amounting to much."

"Hasn't it occurred to you that we are right now in the best possible position imaginable to make a lot of money in short order? That all that's happened over all those years every decision—right or wrong—has contributed to the fact that we are finally poised to make it really big? Why else do you think the outfits in town want us so badly?"

And that brought him to full alert!

"Now, my fine-feathered friend, if I have learned anything at all since coming home it is that when you start talking in circles it's because you are herding your listener up to a very specific point. Let's just cut out all this beating around the bush and you can tell me exactly what you have in mind."

Actually, I had very little in mind at the start of this conversation. I just wanted to needle him, like he does to me, to let him know that while John might not be here in person to watch his progress I fully intend to do so on John's behalf. But now, arguing with him has loosened a lot of sawdust that's been clogging my thinking process. Like the others I'm so used to a hardscrabble existence that I can't quite believe what seems to be coming just around the corner. I've been watching the gradual improvement in the market, a price climb that has moved us from a loss on every shipment to the break-even point, to making a small profit and now to profits that are no longer small. Our rate of production is certainly at an all-time high as well, but just in case the trend should turn out a flash in the pan I have discussed it with no one till now. "In this business there are really only three things that determine the make-or-break factor—timber supply, cost of production and price of the end product. Each of those three have a million little variables that offset or enhance each other so that usually you make it but not big. Or you don't make it but not so bad as to go bust. To put it plainly, when production is up—price is down. When price is up, for one of many possible reasons logs are in tight supply or too expensive. See what I mean?"

"Sure. It's called Murphy's Law. It takes care of every situation and leaves a fellow just enough hope to keep on trying."

"Never mind Murphy, we've got him beat every way from Sunday this time."

"Say, I'm glad you told me! I'm sure no one else has noticed. Not even Ember."

He's right. Ember, with her far vision should have seen this long before me. But it's also true that sales and pricing are one of the few areas where she is not involved. To her that is 'after the fact' stuff. "Well, take timber supply for example, we certainly have no problem there as long as our loggers come through. We're so far behind on cutting that we are, as we all know, vastly oversupplied. Many others in the country have already overcut their quota and are depending on low quality salvage timber. But not us. And, the nice thing about it is that, thanks to your arrangement with the portables, we now have the means of handling all those logs. Then there's price. It's still inching upward. As you are quite aware, the price of lumber runs in cycles. There has been a long spell at the bottom but now it looks like we are heading into the top-end of the swing. And all this at the exact same time as we will have a lot to sell. The timing couldn't be better! Cost of production can always stand improvement and portables aren't the best long-term route to that. But we are actually making a profit on every board sold now and there are so many boards to sell that I'll bet the numbers are going to boggle your mind next spring when you tally up. And the buyers are out there eager for every car load."

"Yeah? Well, I hope so. I could stand a little of that." He didn't sound too impressed. "What would you have us do with this windfall that you see coming? Bribe the Minister of Forests into waving his magic wand in some manner to our advantage?"

"No, I don't think Ray bribes well. Mostly the money would help us feel, look and sound confident in our dealings with him. And it would buy ammunition for us. Do you think a quota could be negotiated downward?"

"How would I know? No one has ever tried that. Everyone wants more, not less, so maybe you could surprise them into falling for it—once. What kind of ammunition?"

"Information! I think we need to know everything there is to know about our territory. We can hire professionals to work under Tim to go out and learn for us—first of all—exactly how much timber is out there so that we can plan to cut accordingly. Not even the Forest Service can tell us that with any accuracy. Our territory is no more than a pinhead on their map and they are too short of staff to do the surveys we need. In the meantime it would be better to undercut than overcut—we really don't need that last tree from the last alpine basin out there. We can keep our job numbers steady from less timber by getting into more finished products and getting a higher price for them. Or, there might be mineral possibilities that in some way might allow us to set aside some timberland. It might lead to the town supplying two industries instead of one. There are things of a different sort too," I hesitated, knowing I am on unfamiliar and uncertain ground. "Hydro potential for starters. Not on the main river, that's for the big boys, but on some of the tributaries, 'run of the stream' stuff. To cut our fuel bills. And also, just for instance, one of those tributary valleys north of the river, in the Rockies, should be selected, one with no logging in it so far and a fly-in lodge built on a lake at the upper end."

"You mean a hunting lodge? For us?"

"Not for us! Maybe some hunting. Certainly some fishing. But the lodge should be built with every modern luxury money can buy and be staffed with the right people to give the best service in every sense. Combine that with a natural, secluded setting out of this world and it could attract a clientele all its own. Show people, politicians, sports stars, playboys and artists. Who knows, it might even make money but that wouldn't matter. What counts is that valley would become so valuable to so many important people that only the most careful selective logging would ever be allowed in it. Not the virtual clearcut that we are forced into now. So the quota might have to be reduced to make up for the timber that would have to be left standing. And I've been hearing a lot about tree farm licences lately, maybe we can trade some quota for longer term farming opportunities."

"You are a devious so and so aren't you! I guarantee most of that won't fly, you're dreaming again but just the same remind me to appoint you to handle my affairs when I write out my will."

I can't tell if I've gotten through to him or not but I've certainly opened up some new thoughts to delve into for myself. Sure—I know most of what I said won't fly but it made for a good argument where I held up my side for a change.

"Now that you've solved all my troubles for tonight I'd be interested to know, my friend, how you're going to handle your own."

"My own? I have trouble?"

"Looks to me like you are in pretty deep water with our cute little school teacher. Pleasant trouble though, I suppose." His smile was almost predatory.

"You'll have to explain that a bit farther, I don't know what you're talking about."

"She has plans for you, my boy, and I'm thinking that it takes two to have tangoed into that position."

"I still don't know what you're talking about," I said, all too aware that I am sounding like a broken record.

"Well, I can give you some clues to refresh your memory. Remember you took her to a dance when she first came?"

"Sure, and she had a good time too but not with me."

"No, when she found out that you couldn't, or wouldn't, dance she danced with a lot of others including me and she used the whole time to ask questions about you."

"So what? She had a guilty conscience over the way she acted at the train and has just been nice to me since to make up for it."

"My! She must be awfully contrite."

"Now what are you getting at?" I asked suspiciously.

"Just the way you grabbed her off the dance floor in front of us all that night and took her along when you met the trains," he paused, "then neither of you came back afterwards. Right or wrong, draw your own conclusions."

"Ouch! That wasn't too tactful was it? But give her some credit if not me. I took her home—to her home, then I met the trains after which I went home—to my home."

"So you say, now I'll tell you something else. But first; we do agree don't we that she danced quite well that night and seemed to enjoy the evening?"

I nodded. "She seemed to have fun dancing if that's what you mean."

"Precisely! Now, when is the last time you saw her dancing with anyone?"

With a sinking heart I saw what he was driving at. "That first time was also the last time, the only time, I've seen her dance. Since then she works in the kitchen, serves, helps with the music, entertains by singing or just visits around but no dancing."

"Precisely again! Erin's been reading between the lines again and pointed this out to some of us at the office the other day. So last week when I thought Gabby might be getting tired of being a wallflower I asked her to go to the dance with me. She declined and when I persisted—politely and with humour of course—she told me that dancing is not for her. That, in fact, she doesn't dance and so would prefer not to go with someone who would expect that she would. So if you can see the same story Erin is reading to the rest of us you should now know what I'm talking about."

"She's not dancing anymore because I can't?"

"In some ways you are amazingly slow-witted but you got that one first try."

"This doesn't look to me like any of your business."

"Oh, I agree, just thought I'd mention it." He walked out on me with his grin firmly in place and I knew he was coming closer to laughing outright with every step.

Only now that he's gone does it dawn on me to wonder why he is asking someone other than Ember to go dancing with him. Or, for that matter, what concern of his it is that I squire the teacher about? He's not the only one who has been giving me flak over this either, almost the entire family has been frowning every time I show up some place with Gabrielle. It makes me wonder if their royal assent is required to go near the teacher. Tim is the most agitated about it but him I understand he—like Jo—and the others too I guess, is laboring under a delusion and thinks I belong to Ember. They see her as abandoned to entertain an unwelcome Nick at the store. Thinking of Nick—it's strange she hasn't put the run on him properly by now and I guess it has to be because he is making himself into a key man at the mill. Certainly no one can accuse Ember of being impractical where lumber production is concerned.

Tim came home asking if Peter and Ember were married yet. Then he witnessed Ember and I verbally sparring all the way down to camp and he comes up with an idea like that! Incredible but that's what he has done. He had stared in amazement first at one of us then the other, tossed out his preconceptions and came up with all the wrong assumptions just as some others have done.

But that's his problem, mine is how to get out of this without hurting Gabrielle. There's no denying I've been playing with dynamite and hadn't even given it a thought. She is the first new teacher in the time I have been here so I have never witnessed the phenomena of the teacher stalking a potential husband. If I had I surely would have been friendly from a greater distance.

I expect that's not the way it really happens, it's more likely that the local young unmarried men, starved by the lack of eligible girls, give the teacher such a rush that she has to choose one in self defense. That hasn't happened to Gabrielle because she has been hanging so close to me—Good God! What am I saying? I've been so blind, it's no wonder I'm in trouble. I sat down at the desk that is soon to be Tim's in hope my brain might function better at a lower altitude. Even so, think as I may, I can only see my relationship with Gabrielle as casual, very casual. But history indicates that Rainy Mountain has a strange effect on young school teachers—they start thinking of marriage about as soon as they are off the train.

But not to me! Not if I can help it!

Until I came to Rainy Mountain I scrupulously steered clear of having a girlfriend. Friends who happened to be girls were not unheard of but since coming here the eligible girls have been equally determined to steer clear of me. To my careful way of thinking a girlfriend is potentially a wife and a wife soon means a family. All very nice to think but a family means lots of hard work to pay the bills. And that's where the bubble bursts.

So what about Ember?

I just don't know about Ember or the trouble she causes but it looks like Peter will be taking care of that one for me. That's what luck is for isn't it?

I am already 'Uncle' to Allan's and Tom's kids and for now that's about as close to marriage as I expect to get. I suppose I'll be 'Uncle' to Ember's children some day too—like Dean.

Really! Am I to be responsible for only the second breakdown in the 'system'? What's wrong with Gabrielle? Life with her could be very pleasant. She is intelligent, good-humoured company, an accomplished pianist who can play acceptably well on just about any other instrument and a singer of almost professional ability. A remarkably talented young lady. It could also be pointed out in her favour that she has a sizable independent income. Independent of Rainy Mountain Lumber that is. Peter called her our cute little school teacher. Cute is the understatement of the year and little is a relative matter. Beside tall women like Erin or Jennie she is inarguably short but really no smaller than Ember who, thanks to her high heels and hairdo, actually manages to give the impression of taller than average.

Strange new thought! Maybe I don't want out of this. Maybe I'm so used to a girl who wants no part of me that I can't quite cope with the idea there's one who possibly does.

Gabby, Gabby, could I love you? In the corridors of my mind I hear no echoes for guidance so in my usual fashion I will have to sort it out tomorrow. Or whenever.

8

Winter is now fully upon us but at least the weather has been good for our purposes, cold enough to freeze the roads but not bitterly cold. Enough snow to smooth the bumps and help make skid trails but again, not too much. The new skid shacks are filled with workers for the portable mills and the regular bunkhouse row is overflowing with our own winter logging crews and men for the mill and planer. Allan's newly completed dry kiln is going twenty-four hours a day but unfortunately, with our stepped-up production, it's less than half the size it should be. But it helps, in fact without it I think we would be lost.

The cookhouse too is a busy place and a very good customer of the store with all those loggers to feed as well as two shifts on the portables and on our planer and three on the sawmill. Actually they are serving four shifts because I still eat at odd hours half the time just to keep them tuned in.

With all these new men arriving from the wheat fields, forests and ocean inlets of western Canada, Ember had to take over Nightrider again some nights while I and sometimes others drove crummies to haul everyone down to camp. Tim is always willing to come out in the night for chores like this and I think that has been a surprise to many, maybe including Tim.

Once as we waited for a train Tim confessed his gratitude for his new office and higher profile. Peter, he said, had been about as gracious as a grizzly hunched over a two-week-old moose carcass and in case anyone should think he was turning soft in the head had told Tim gruffly that the whole kibosh had been my idea. So much for my effort to improve Peter's image.

Several times a week strings of boxcars are being snaked up the long, steep grade to the mainline and fresh empties left for us. But, best of all, cheques are rolling in from our lumber brokers. The money all goes out again to meet expenses but there will come a time next spring when most of the expenses cease while the incoming payments continue. That's when we find out for sure if we have accomplished anything. In the meantime it all looks good on paper, we're not borrowing as much as we expected to, it looks as though Peter has actually gotten the operation organized and on the right road.

But we have a problem. It almost seems that Murphy is about to get his law into the act after all. To be exact, someone doesn't like us because all kinds of nasty things have started happening to our logging equipment. Oil plugs mostly, being loosened so they fall out while the machine is working. Engine crankcase plugs, transmission and differential drain plugs were falling out all over the woods. We were spreading more oil on the ground than Esso was pumping out of it until we browbeat every operator into checking all drain plugs and fluid levels before every start-up. Amazingly, not that much damage was done as the operator or some nearby worker usually spotted the oil trail on the snow or ice before parts started seizing up. But diesel engines don't last long without oil so the shop got a few to overhaul despite our relative good luck.

Tom was alternately frantic or indifferent about it and quite useless while on his drinking binges which seem to have returned. Perhaps he couldn't be blamed under the circumstances, it was maddening to us all. The inevitable result of Tom's alcoholic setback was that more and more the load of running the woods operation fell to Alec whether he wanted it or not.

The sabotage was costing us in both time and money but it tailed off as we increased vigilance and machine inspections. Now we really needed that extra equipment of George Shultz's and I blessed Peter's deal with him though at first I hadn't appreciated it.

With so many strangers in camp for the winter logging, it looked an impossible task to single out the culprit. My first thought was it could be anyone with access to a vehicle and that made a long list. We would simply have to catch them in the act but as time went by it became apparent that was not so easily done as said. The only other thing that struck me as obvious was it had to be someone in the pay of L&N.

Since Peter's warning, or whatever it was that he intended, I have paid more attention while with Gabrielle and I have to admit he could be right. When we are together she displays a definite proprietary air that now sets my teeth on edge. It doesn't take much thought to remember that every time I have driven over to pick her up it's because, one way or another, she has let me know that she expected it.

It's not very far from my place to hers or from there back to the hall so we could very well walk but I'm still touchy about walking any more than necessary in her company so we drive. The only pain involved when I walk is for the people who have to watch me go through the necessary contortions. Even so, the whole process is getting smoother as time passes and I have to admit that it often depends on who is watching as to how I go about it. Actually I can, and often do, hike for miles without great effort but the style is a bit unorthodox. That never did bother me in the least, not until Gabrielle stepped off the train. Now I'm suddenly self-conscious and also suspicious that her solicitude for me stems at least partly from sympathy. I had to chew on that for a while but I can finally admit that sympathy is not the best base for any long-lasting friendship.

I'm not being honest on my part either. The only reason I'm not running from this girl is because I hope she will help me forget another. I'm torn in half, one saying 'go man go' and the other 'whoa man whoa.' If only time could stand still. I would be quite satisfied with things just as they are now. But it seems that cannot be, since others will not allow it so.

Having come to these weighty conclusions I am probably no farther ahead but at least I feel, like Peter's victims, that I have given it my best shot.

Predictably tomorrow has come as it always does but this one is Sunday and that means some of us have at least part of the day off. I hadn't yet begun to wonder what to do with the day when Alec settled it for me with an invitation to go along on a Ski-doo party. "Tim and I have three of Tom's Ski-doos tuned up and ready. Pat and Jan have a lunch fixed and I've got everything we need to do a little ice fishing so I thought we could all whistle up to Second Lake and try our luck."

It was a suggestion that I was slow warming up to, but Alec doesn't often make offers like this so it deserved careful consideration. He added the clincher even before it was needed. "Why not get Gabby to come along? Each machine will carry two of us. We can show her that we do more than work and semi-hibernate during the winter."

"Sounds good to me." And it did too all of a sudden.

"Okay, pick Gabby up and meet us in Tom's backyard as soon as you can and we'll head right out from there. We'll take the old road past the garbage dump, the cat trail up across the railroad and then go cross-country a bit to avoid the logging road seeing as some of the trucks are hauling today."

Twenty minutes later Gabrielle and I joined the others but not in Tom's backyard because by then they had all three machines on the main street in front of the house and the air was smoky from idling Rotax engines. Tom buys a new Ski-doo nearly every year and the old ones get shunted to one side hardly used or are traded to some kid for a few chores. I don't know how many he has and he may not either but it looks like some of them will get some use this winter if today's gathering is any indication. Gabrielle stayed close to me as we milled about getting the food and gear loaded. Strangely she is still shy around these Morrows and here she is plunked right among a bunch of them today. "Byron, I've never been on one of these things. What's it like?"

Before I could answer we had a diversion, Ember chose that moment to drive by in her 4x4. Since we had the road mostly blocked she had to slow down and edge over to the side to creep by us. Unfortunately I looked up exactly when I shouldn't have and locked eyes with her. It was instant panic for me! I have never before experienced such a shock as I got from that brief contact. It travelled from my eyes right down to the toes of my feet and left me rooted to the spot on which I stood. I couldn't look away but since she was driving she had to so the spell was broken. As I came out of it I felt as though everyone should be staring at me but that didn't seem to be the case, only Jan was watching with mildly amused interest.

Gabrielle's voice came to me again as if from far away, "Byron, what is there to hold onto on this thing?" Once again I didn't answer for Jan moved up beside us and took over showing the other girl how it was done. Then while Gabrielle sat on the idling machine Jan stepped back closer to me and muttered toward my ear, "Got a problem, By?"

"Nothing that won't sort itself out I guess."

Jan sprang forward to Gabrielle's side again and tapped her on the arm. She spoke loudly to be heard over the combined noise of the three snow machines, "Hey, Gabby, come on over here with me, Tim is an expert on these rigs, I'll have him show you all about them."

The little schoolteacher flashed me one quick uncertain look then was hustled away by Jan. I stood there like an old spruce stump and watched while Tim, after his initial surprise, made a big fuss of showing Gabrielle there was nothing to it. In less time than it takes to tell Tim was seated on his Ski-doo and Jan was coaching Gabrielle into position behind him. Then while Tim had his unexpected passenger's attention Jan left them, spoke a few urgent words to Pat who right away swung onto the other machine with Alec and whooped, "Let's go! Last one to the lake has to build the fire."

Still in a daze and not yet understanding what has happened, I find the power of suggestion has put me on my borrowed machine and with Jan clinging tightly on behind I am trying frantically to keep up with the others.

It took me a while to find enough dry wood and then build our warm-up fire over which we would also boil some coffee and cook our treats. Meanwhile Tim has been positively vindictive in his monopolizing of Gabrielle. As he initiated her to the mysteries of ice fishing I could sense his pleasure in depriving me of the company of this girl who, in his mind at least, I have no business being near.

It was long after dark when we returned the three sleds to Tom's backyard shop and it was not me who took Gabby home. Instead, I said a carefully casual good night to Alec and the twins and went off homeward still not sure whether I should give Jan a good swift kick from behind or a kiss on the cheek. All the way home and for a long time afterward I marveled at the fickleness and the intricacies of a woman's mind.

But that look from Ember as she drove by! Her eyes were open windows to a bared soul and mine must have been the same for the contact to be so shocking. What I saw in her eyes is beyond me to understand or describe but certainly there was strong, even violent censure of me, something so close to hatred that I am shaken yet. There was pain and hurt but there was challenge too. And promise? Everything and nothing! I don't know—it was such an unguarded moment for both of us that we saw emotions better kept secret. What still raises hair on the back of my neck is—the eyes I had stared into were green—burning gunpowder fiery green! And that's just not so. I must have been hallucinating.

One thing for sure, no matter what the others had in mind, Ember's part was not planned or if it was then she is in the wrong profession with her store and post office. No, her part could not have been deliberate and without her the rest falls apart under even light examination.

But still, it had to be more than just incredibly fast and opportunistic thinking and acting on Jan's part with some ready assistance from Pat. It couldn't all have been coincidence, it must have been deliberately planned with the intention of getting Tim and Gabrielle together. They knew well enough that she was still shy and afraid of them in a group so I was rung in to get her to join the party. Somewhere, somehow I would have been dumped. Ember happening along gave them the perfect chance to alter the plan and do it quickly and neatly. I can hear, somewhere in the back of my head, an echo from the past; 'We Morrows take care of our own.' Boy oh boy! We sure do!

Sometime ago Ember warned Peter to be careful or I would be winding his watch for him. Today her younger sisters have not only wound my watch—they have also reset it to a different time zone.

But half-hidden at the bottom of it all is the reason I sit quietly licking my wounds. Instead of wanting to lash out for revenge I hang my head almost in shame at the great waves of relief that are sweeping over me. It was a close one but I feel so free again!

The next Monday morning, or to be exact, blue Monday morning, I had it in mind to avoid Ember. Usually I can do that when I want to but today I had no chance because she came looking for me. Her eyes showed nothing more dangerous than a deep-seated worry so hidden in grey smoke as to be quite indecipherable. She wanted to talk. But a serious talk with her is the very last thing I want right now. I do not, at this moment, feel up to a lecture from any of the Morrows, especially Ember, on why I must stop seeing the teacher. She sensed my mood and that was no surprise, what did surprise me is she decided—reluctantly—to respect that mood. I could see the struggle as she bit back what she had intended to say. It must have been hard because her way is to say what she thinks and if it needs to be tough talk it comes in short choppy sentences cutting directly to the point. She can be single-minded and even narrow-minded but now she came up with a subject so far from that which dominated my own thoughts that I almost had to laugh.

"Gabby wants to take the train out Wednesday night to go to her parents' home for Christmas. So the school concert will be held early that evening. Are you going to it?"

"Probably, I usually do."

"I'd love to go too but I don't care to go alone."

Only now did I realize I had stepped into a trap. I almost snorted derision! Ember not want to go out alone? The fact is that Ember goes where and when she pleases and nearly always alone—at most with her sisters or Jo. If this isn't a poorly disguised invitation for me to be useful in her game with Peter then I am even more dense than usual today. It didn't deserve an answer so I let the silence run wild between us until it was too late to say anything. She left in a considerable huff.

Since the fat was in the pan and well-fried already, I saw no reason to continue avoiding her so I followed along to the store to get on with my chores there. But I seem to be jinxed today for I was hardly started stocking shelves at the back of the room when the door bell tinkled to announce the arrival of customers. The change of shift rush was over and it was a bit early for the family trade to be starting, so I straightened up to look over the rows of merchandise to see who had come in. When I saw it was the twins I ducked back down out of sight and proceeded quietly with my work because I am still smarting severely from their treatment of me yesterday.

Once I was sure they weren't here to tell Ember about our Ski-doo adventure I didn't pay too much attention to the conversation though I couldn't help but hear some of it. I heard Pat tell Ember and Jo, who hadn't gone home for her morning break yet, that she was going to have a baby. Ember was pleased and started making suitable remarks that were cut off abruptly when Jan chimed in, "And I am too!" Just as happy as if she had a husband to go along with the bargain.

It was during the ensuing silence that I raised up to look again. The twins appeared their usual high-spirited happy selves quite unaware that they have just dropped a big bomb with a touchy fuse. Jo had turned to watch Ember, at the post office wicket, and I did too as her face went through several shades of red, each darker than the last, her mouth still open from words ended in mid-sentence. For Ember with her strong dose of family pride this was simply too much! When the last of the colour drained away from her cheeks, leaving her as white as her golden-toned skin will ever allow I knew it was time the twins should duck for cover.

The ensuing fracas was something I would sooner have not witnessed. Ember blew her stack! I thought for a moment she was going to physically attack her sisters as she came careening out of the post office like a destroyer charging from the flank, slamming the door shut on her way. Remembering rumours of her fighting ability I feared for the twins' health and well-being—mine too if I should be called upon to separate them. She bent forward to face them, like a loaded spring but with clenched fists kept at her side and I'm sure it was not the odds of two to one that kept them there. It's just that right now she had a lot to say to them. Her voice climbed to a screaming pitch as she told them in no uncertain terms what she thought of their conduct. Every little, or not so little, transgression of the past months over which Ember had swallowed her pride and taken in silence now boiled over in a poisonous stream beyond anything even the twins have dealt out in my hearing. Dean need feel no guilt about helping teach the twins the four-letter alphabet because it's clear they had an even more knowledgeable tutor closer to home. She wasn't just angry, she was right at the end of her rope, a stranger seeing this would question her very sanity.

Pat and Jan were surprised to say the least at this uncharacteristic and unexpected outburst of verbal abuse being showered upon them. They looked uncertainly at each other and edged cautiously toward the outer door with Ember pressing closer at every step.

But it's simply not in the twins' makeup to yield gracefully to anything less than a log truck, loaded at that, so I was not surprised to see them slow, then stop their retreat and try to join in the fray. But their effort was pale by comparison to Ember's vicious outburst for she simply gave them no good chance to get started so they attempted instead to save face with a grand and haughty exit.

Ember, straightening up to her full if less than impressive height, got in the last word. "Why don't one of you have the decency to go drown yourself in the river? Like the pregnant cats that get tied in a gunny sack along with a big rock and tossed in!" Then louder yet and so high-pitched that her voice is breaking, "I'll even give you some help if it's needed!" The door crashed shut in her face at this point and I thought she was going to rip it open to follow after her sisters but she didn't—she let it end. In the sudden silence my imagination had groceries and other goods all around the room settling back into place with great relief.

I slipped back down out of sight but too late, she saw me and called shrilly, "Byron! Come here!" I hobbled reluctantly to the front where both women were. I'm angry with myself for being caught watching and even more so for letting my limp look worse than it really is just because I'm afraid she is going to sink her fangs into me next. She is pale and smouldering with anger, her face pinched and creased—her mouth a hard, straight, bright artificial red line that clashes garishly with her waxen features. It seems impossible but I would swear there is that greenish flicker in her eyes again. It took faith to remember how pretty she is.

"Byron, take over for me the rest of the morning so Jo can leave at her usual time. I have a terrible headache coming on. I'm going home."

"Sure, don't worry about a thing."

We were all quiet while she got on her boots and coat but as she turned the doorknob to go, she stopped and faced us with tears of rage and frustration streaming down her cheeks. "You don't know the half of it—Jan hasn't been living with me at the house like everyone supposes. They've been taking turns living with Alec and the poor guy probably doesn't even know it. I wouldn't either except they have made no effort to keep it secret from me." For a moment she faced us, unmoving except for the fingers that took a tighter hold on the door knob as she struggled in her mind to make some sense of what has happened. Her eyes are still flashing a fire that frightens me—not so much now of what she might do to me as of what she might do to herself. Something in the door's works let out a click. Slowly her features relaxed as the wildness left her eyes and she seemed to be wanting me to say something or do something but I couldn't think of any way to help her. When she left us seconds later, though the tears still flowed, I knew she was once again in complete control of herself but quite sick from the effort.

I think that Ember has had her head in the sand again if she thinks that the rest of us, and most of the camp too, don't know that Jan's presence in the big house has been purely token in nature. As for Alec not knowing they were sharing him, I can't go along with that, surely by now he has learned to tell them apart as I have done. It's not possible they could fool him this long. Even their voices sound different to me now.

The next day, Tuesday, Peter had a conversation with Ted Jonas, the shop foreman, that upset him mightily. The upshot being that he called for a meeting in Tim's office at 8:00 p.m. It wasn't necessary, he said, for the women to attend as it was not a policy meeting but purely operational and there would be no vote taken on any matter. Having overheard his talk with Ted I knew what was coming but not how we would cope with it. A couple of skidder engines have been smashed with a sledge hammer or some equally heavy tool, breaking not only the block casting but the fuel injection pump and turbo charger on both machines. A very costly matter this time. Serious steps need to be taken, the sooner the better, and Peter knows it as well as I.

Tim and I were the first to show for the meeting, Allan coming promptly on the dotted hour as usual. Tim informed us that Tom was going to be a little late but would be along as soon as he took care of a couple of chores that he couldn't avoid. This we understand because Tom's duties, like for all of us, are seldom done just because night has come. We made small talk while waiting for the others to show up.

Alec came about ten past the hour and Peter was less than a minute behind him. He delayed only until quarter past eight then decided to start without Tom who, like me, would already know all about the issue at hand anyway. But only a couple minutes later Tom arrived and we all knew something was wrong by the pound of his footsteps along the hall. He almost forgot to open the door before crashing through and sent it banging against the inside wall. Then he stood there in the doorway staring at us with a rare mixture of anger, exhaustion and fear written over his face. His whole body shook as he tore off his mitts and threw them at the pile of mitts and coats in the corner. I'm sure I have never seen a man in such a state of emotional shock before. Allan jumped up and caught him by an arm to steer him to a chair where he slumped like a grain bag not quite full. A scene quite different from the last time these two made contact in this room. Tim reached them in a couple of big strides, fumbled into Tom's own coat pocket and came out with a small flat flask of whiskey that he opened and applied liberally into Tom's mouth tipping his head back at the same time. It was cruel medicine because Tom didn't swallow when he should have but did breathe in when he shouldn't have. Once again he nearly choked to death on our hands but eventually Tim and Allan got him talking coherently.

"It's Lupe," he managed, "someone has shot Lupe!"

The other five of us looked around at each other in mutual amazement, we had all expected some earth-shaking statement from him. Though the shooting of dogs is uncommon around our community it does happen once in a while, but a dog as well-known and as well-behaved as Lupe should have been exempt from anything like that. All in all it seems quite a letdown after a big buildup, I should have known there was more coming.

"What happened, Tom? Who shot him?" Allan asked.

"I don't know, it was just a rifle shot from somewhere in the mill. I was working in the shop on the engine of one of the little light plants we use for light and power around machines that are being repaired or serviced during the night. I needed some small tools of about the same type as I use on my outboards so I started down to the boathouse to get them. Before I got past the engine room at the mill there was a shot and Lupe went down. I heard the bullet hit him." Tom's eyes showed he was reliving what for him was a moment of horror. To Allan it's just another annoyance while to Peter it must be nothing at all because, as is often the case during out-of-the-ordinary discussions, he is totally expressionless. Alec and Tim seemed more concerned that the shooting had been done after dark and within the camp area than with the primary fact that it had been done—period.

Tom took another pull at his bottle, coughed, then looked at it in surprise as if wondering where it had come from, capped it and shoved it back in his pocket. We all asked questions but he had no satisfactory answers for us. He still looks uncommonly disturbed but has at least recovered his composure to the point that he now speculated on the source of the shot.

"I had my ears covered because of the cold so the report was no more than a pop somewhere nearby. At first I assumed it came from the sawmill building but now I think it could have come from the engine room or near it. A lot of the lights are turned off tonight so there is plenty of shadow around there to hide in. For that matter it could have come from the engine-room doorway as long as the inside lights were off. That would fit because Lupe was out in front of me, trotting along looking forward when he was hit."

That statement jarred all my notions of Tom and his dog because it's a long time since Lupe was a pup and he has become careful of energy expenditure the last year or so. I can see him following behind but not leading the way. However, I was not there and Tom was and it couldn't be relevant anyway. I guess he is just referring to obvious frontal damage to Lupe from the bullet. "Did you stop to examine him, Tom?"

"No! I knew he was dead from the way he folded and went down. I was afraid the next one might be for me so I crouched down beside him for a while to make a smaller target. When there were no more shots I ran for Allan's place to tell him but when I was almost there I remembered all you guys, including Allan, would be here so I turned around and came back. I guess I wasn't doing any thinking because I ran it all on foot even though I must have run right by several pickups at the shop including my own."

Unless he angled through the log yard he must also have run past the four or five 4x4s parked outside the office too. All of us gathered here tonight either too lazy like me, or too busy like the others, to walk. Even though I live right next door I also arrived by truck because I came from elsewhere. I like my wheels nearby except on those rare occasions when I want to prove that I can so walk.

I can see that Peter assumes the emergency is over and is about to get down to the business at hand but before he did so Tom beckoned me closer. "I can't stand to see Lupe again the way he is and I couldn't touch him anyway now that he's dead so would you take care of him for me?"

"Sure, Tom. Don't give it another thought." Funny how the strongest men turn out to be the queasy ones. I doubt there will be anything discussed here tonight that I don't already know more about than they do so I'm going to go for the dog right away. I have to admit that curiosity is eating me up. I got up and picked my coat, hat and mitts out of the jumble near the door—no coat hooks in this room for some reason. "What do you want done with him, Tom?"

He looked for a moment as though details were too much for him then said, "I guess the ground is too hard frozen to dig a grave so put him in the river."

"In the river?" I know my surprise was showing.

"Yeah, I don't want him just thrown in the dump or tossed over a cutbank along the logging road, he's been too good a friend for that. But the river would be okay. You'll find open water yet at the boat dock where that bit of turbulence and the warm creek entering the river there keep it open till it gets real cold."

I know where he means, that boil of current stays ice-free all winter some years, it's probably open yet—just getting smaller. I thought it over as I drove past the shop with the snow shrieking a continuous rolling squeal at all four tires on this, our coldest night yet. I doubt that anyone downstream on a river as large as this drinks the water without boiling it first so I can't see where one dog more or less will do much to all those millions of gallons of water. It's not unusual to see dead animals floating past, so the river it will be, though I'm sure the ground is not frozen under the snow's insulating layers. Tom knows that as well as anyone because his crews are building roads and trails in snow and dirt every day. But it's his dog!

For some reason, probably because Tom orders it done, the road to the boathouse and dock is always kept snowplowed so I will be able to haul Lupe right to the river's edge. In days past the boathouse was winter shelter for the long home-built riverboats used to keep the log drive moving from the upstream logging camps to the boom at the mill. The log boom is still largely intact despite the ravages of the annual high water but nothing ever gets caught in it anymore. The top end is closed by a swinging length of boom that also opens the main channel steering all the debris of the river on past us. The log pond nowadays is the kids' winter skating rink and the boom nothing more than a distant encircling border. The jack ladder that used to lift the logs from the water up into the mill is also still in place. It's no longer operational except for the upper end that has been remodeled with a deck of side delivery chains to feed and process tree length timber from a dry-land sorting yard. This, along with changes in sawmill technology, has turned the sawmill into a year-round operation compared to a daylong before my time here when the sawing was done in the summer and the logging in the winter. Now the riverboats are gone, the rivermen too and who knows where? At least two of them that I know of to watery graves!

Today the building houses only Tom's pleasure craft ranging from a canoe with a square stern to a small cabin cruiser. As impressive as the assortment sounds there hasn't been much money spent on it because the canoe is the only one he bought. The others he built himself. Everyone else had heaved a sigh of relief when the river-running days ended but not Tom. He loves boats and he loves the river and he is an expert in about any type of craft you can put him in. As well as boats and Ski-doos Tom has what is probably one of the largest collections of rifles, shotguns and handguns to be found within several hundred miles as long as you exclude the city of Prince George.

There is Lupe, just as Tom said, but as I looked at him in the glare of my truck headlights I found a scene completely different than I expected. I've seen a few animals shot, I've reluctantly shot a few myself when it was needed and even when hard and fatally hit they often thrash around and bleed some. That's what I expected to see—a spoonful of blood makes a lot of stain on packed snow and ice, but here is Lupe looking as if he just got tired and settled down for a nap. There's not a sign of blood or struggle to be seen.

The fur of a northern breed of dog who lives mostly outdoors is wonderful insulation against the cold, even his ears are still limber and unfrozen. But that same fur is so dense that it becomes very difficult to do a close examination when looking for an injury that evidently hasn't bled. I rolled him this way and that, used my flashlight close in to eliminate shadows that the headlights caused, but all to no avail.

I shut off the flashlight and knelt beside Lupe trying to puzzle this out. Absently I ran my bare hand from the top of his nose over his head in one last gesture of friendship for this fine old dog and that's how I found it. There was a spot with a sharp feel to the finger tips on his forehead, the tiniest seepage of blood, only enough to soak a small patch of under fur and just a few longer hairs. The very tips of these longer hairs have now frozen together making the hard sharp projection that I felt in his otherwise smooth coat. Using the flashlight again to make sure I missed nothing I carefully parted the fur and found a tiny blood clotted hole. Only a small bullet such as a .22 could have made that wound but still it had killed so instantly that there was almost no bleeding. The bullet is in there yet because I can find no exit hole.

After I got Tom's dog loaded I drove ahead to where the millyard ends in a steep slope to the river ice at a thirty-foot lower level. The road to the dock starts here and angles downward passing under the skeleton of the old jack ladder. I don't know for sure if there is room enough snowplowed to turn around at the bottom so I elected to back down rather than maybe having to back up later. Once I have dropped below the level of the mill yard, it's like entering a different world, all silver-lit by the moon with none of the harshness of electricity. I can sense that it's more quiet and I feel the cold penetrating in a more determined way into the truck cab as I get closer to the ice level. The river is King down here, its presence is overwhelming in its power even if it is covered with ice. I shut off my truck lights and backed down by moonlight and mirrors.

There is a bee churning around in my bonnet but I can't quite catch it to match it up with words that I can understand. At the bottom of the hill I left the truck parked with the engine idling while I used the shovel that always rides along in the back to clean the snow from the connecting ramp out to the dock. The dock itself is no more than a plank-covered lograft nailed to the river's surface by an arrangement of wire ropes and propped with a stiff leg of logs to maintain its position in the current but able to rise and fall with the whims of the river. The pilings and other structures at the bottom end of the log boom protect it from driftwood and flowing ice. The walk, or ramp, is just a few planks spiked to the stiff leg.

Because the bee is still churning I killed some time by shoveling the entire dock free of snow. Right now it's frozen in on three sides but the last of the snow goes direct from my shovel into the open water at the downstream edge. The creek that enters here, right near where my truck is parked, is a large one. Up on top it's lazy—more deep ponds and slough than stream and somewhere there must be a hot spring entering from under all that muskeg because the water is warmer than you would expect. The last fifty yards of its existence is more like its beginnings on the mountain side for it plunges down a rocky chute and meets the river almost head-on causing the fluke of current that keeps ice from forming. I returned the shovel to the truck then walked to that open edge. Someone must have seen some advantage in this spot for the boats but it does nothing for me. One close look into the blackness of that sucking, swirling current and a shudder overcame me. It's no fit place for man or beast to my notion, I backed away wondering why I'd gone so close in the first place.

Back on solid ground leaning over the truck tailgate feels much better. I have finally corralled the elusive bee that's been causing all the fuss in my bonnet. The bullet is what I'm thinking about. It's still there in Lupe where it could be recovered for evidence. Evidence of what, I'm not sure, it can't be much of a crime to shoot a dog but the bee has its stinger deeply embedded. Maybe it's just another way to say that my curiosity is fired up and once Lupe is gone into the river so is the best chance to track down his killer.

Looking around I am satisfied with what I see. It hasn't snowed since the road was last plowed but there are several inches of fluffy frost crystals over everything, a little of it coming each night. So what I see are truck tracks on the road and walking tracks out onto the dock. My snow removal job is imperfect enough that the cold powder snow remaining on both the ramp and the dock shows good recognizable footprints going to the open water. I couldn't have done a better job of laying a false trail to indicate that I had thrown Lupe into the river if I had planned every step.

Back on top, in the mill yard, I slowed to a stop not quite certain why I am doing this or for that matter what comes next. What to do with the dog!

It's so quiet that it's eerie. After more than a month of running three shifts, everything is silent. Yet something seems to be afoot here that causes my neck hair to rise—something is happening that I can't get a handle on. I can hear only the murmur of the diesel electric unit supplying power to the camp and that small rumble seems to accentuate the complete stillness of everything else. It's been this way since the beginning of the weekend when our extra crews started knocking off and heading for their own homes for the Christmas/New Year's holiday. This is our one big break of the winter, after this it will be full bore ahead until spring breakup stops the logging. Just about the only crew left in camp now are regular year-round home-guard employees who either live here with their families or call their quarters in Bunkhouse Row home. Aside from a very few logging crews still working there are only enough men left to run one shift each on the mill and the planer and that's done on the day shift. The mill ran today but may be shut down for the rest of the holiday because I overheard Allan and Peter weighing the advantages of putting all available hands at the planer to keep it going extra shifts as there is still a good supply of dry, rough lumber on hand.

All that is no help to me in deciding what to do with Lupe so while I let that requirement percolate through the back of my mind I looked around trying to visualize how it might have happened. We speak of paths from the mill to the shop or the shop to the mall but the term is misleading because the whole area is kept clear of snow. It's either packed down by the traffic of forklifts, straddle carriers and trucks or snowplowed away. So you can walk anywhere although there are several definite routes between the shop and the mill. The shortest and most used is from a back door of the shop directly to a ground level doorway at the closest end of the mill building. But if you are going to the engine room you can avoid the sawdusty corridors of the nether mill by ducking under the inside end of the greenchain where it drops from the second floor of the mill to the ground level of the lumber piles. Or you can avoid the mill and its machinery altogether by swinging around the outer end of the greenchain. This is what Tom had been doing since he was going, not to any part of the mill but to the boathouse though judging by the dead Lupe's position he had veered slightly toward the engine room.

What it amounts to is the shooter could have been anywhere, could have gone anywhere and who can say which tracks are his. The only limitations would depend on his choice of target. If he intended to shoot Lupe then only one place of concealment is close enough for that kind of accuracy with a .22 and that is the engine room. Either from the shadows under the roof overhang or the open doorway if the lights inside were turned off so as to not backlight whoever it was. Whatever the case earlier had been, the lights inside are on now. From where I am parked in my indecision I can see the rooftop of the engine room. Snow never stays on that roof because of the heat from the engines underneath and the slope of the tin roofing so I can also see light leaking around the diesel exhaust stacks where they emerge through generously fitted holes in the tin.

If, on the other hand, the shot was intended to hit or scare off Tom, hitting Lupe accidentally then the field is much larger extending even to some of the equipment and vehicles parked this side of the shop. By Tom's account, his ears were covered and the shot no more than a pop, so his sense of direction can't be trusted. One need only to visualize Lupe hearing or sensing movement and turning his head to face it just as the shot was fired. But still, the engine room looks to be the most likely answer. I can feel myself warming to the theory that the culprit was preparing to do damage to some of the mill equipment when Tom's passage was mistaken for approach that seemed to indicate discovery. The shot then would have been in panic to buy time for retreat. A silly thing to do though with retreat to the other side wide open.

In the meantime a light has finally come on in the recesses of my mind so I drove to the back door of the cookhouse. It's late enough that the evening mug-up is long over and the few still in camp of the cookhouse crew should be in their sleeping quarters. I backed right up to the door where I usually go to unload groceries and walked in as though I had nothing more than snack in mind. But the whole building was empty except, presumably, the head cook's private room and I didn't go near there. I made my way to a supply room where I looked up one of those huge garbage bags, the size that fits a forty-five gallon drum.

Outside I dropped the tailgate and pulled Lupe carefully over the edge working him into the garbage bag head first. When I had him in but still had a hold on his hind legs amid the folds of black plastic I dragged him bodily into the cookhouse. From a high shelf alongside the freezer room door, I got a length of heavy twine and fashioned a slip knot around legs and bag, leaving enough loose plastic to hide the feet. From the same shelf I got a tag from a box of hundreds like it and a felt pen kept there for this purpose and wrote my name boldly on the tag. I tied the tag to a bottom corner of the bag and dragged the whole arrangement into the back section of the freezer that is separate and strictly reserved for the Morrows' private use. It's where they hang the moose they or their friends from town shoot while out for a hunting visit during the open season. There are half a dozen quarters hanging there now including the one farthest back with Peter's name on it. I know that he has given most of his away to Ember and Jo and other friends who don't hunt. It's unlikely he will be back for the rest right away so it can help to hide my handiwork. I know too that Tom has nothing in here just now. With the help of a piece of rope for block and tackle, without the block, I got Lupe hoisted into place and securely fastened behind the moose quarters. They are not in garbage bags like Lupe is but I can't let that worry me. With my name on it the chance of anyone looking to see what's in that bag is, I'm sure, next to nil. But still not quite satisfied I got the pen again and added 'Wolf—for mounting' on the name tag. Hope there's no health inspection due.

It all took time so when I returned my truck to the office I found the others had all left and the building was empty. How time flies when you're having fun! It's only a couple of hours till traintime.

I didn't want to run the risk of talking to Peter just now in case the story of my night's work is too easily read on my face so I curled up on the first aid cot knowing I would awaken in time to meet the trains. If I could have foreseen the events of the next thirty hours I wouldn't have gone near that bed for all the Paper Trees in British Columbia.

9

I didn't count them but there must have been between twenty and thirty of our loggers and truck drivers who caught the westbound train out to town as the wind-down to the long holiday continued. They must be about the last that will be leaving. None rode up the hill with me, instead they waited in the comfort of camp until the train was due then raced up the steep trail to the track like the work-hardened youngsters they are. That's when they started learning that they should have checked on the phone as I did because the trains were both running a little late. By the time I drove up to the track they were a cold and impatient lot with a fire going in the station stove. But that little stove stands no chance at all when the door is being fanned open every time they think they hear something so there was a lot of foot stomping and running on the spot going on for warmth. I could hear all that happening as I climbed out of my truck and the station door was wide open with half a dozen of them pouring out to see what had arrived. "Hey, Byron's here," one shouted to those still inside. "Now the train can come." And of course, it did. I made myself a bet they won't be so energetic on their return in a little over a week. Good thing it's downhill to camp.

My surprises weren't over yet for this day. On my way down the hill, as I swept around the last corner approaching the camp houses a figure made a sudden sprint into a side street, just barely ahead of being caught full in my headlights. Curious and nosy as usual I gunned Nightrider forward, swinging into the same street and sure enough I came up to a man struggling to climb over the fence into Ember's spacious yard. Once over the fence there are any number of trees for good hiding places but he ended his flight when I slewed sideways to a stop with him nailed in my light beams. The snow is just deep and soft enough to be a difficulty or I would have missed him. When he saw that he was caught he untangled himself, made a couple of disgusted gestures and tramped back to the road. It's Peter and he is some angry I can tell as I roll down my window.

"You are one curious, meddling nuisance aren't you!" His voice was so tight that he seemed to be hissing. "Why don't you mind your own business and leave me alone?"

Words failed me so I rolled up my window and drove away looping the block to get around to the mall warehouse. Later, when I got home I could hear him thrashing around in the dark of his room going to bed. I did the same.

The next day the planer was still working as were a very few woods crews and Peter showed absolutely no resentment for me catching him prowling last night. I felt it right that he shouldn't, if he hadn't acted so suspiciously I wouldn't have run him down with my headlights. If he wants to visit Ember late at night that's their business though it leaves a bitter taste.

Wednesday was a big day for Gabrielle and her students as they prepare for the concert tonight. I have decided I'm not going after all on the vague excuse that I lose enough sleep as it is. But to myself I have to admit that I simply don't want to see any more of the teacher right now than I can help. I don't want anyone to think me guilty of trying to lure her back but beyond there my thoughts are typically unclear. I'm not sure if I fear that she won't be lured or if the greater danger is that she might be.

But planning is one thing and reality quite another because Peter breezed in bursting with enthusiasm that probably has more to do with holiday spirit and a coming break in his workload than any desire to watch the kids' plays. He bent my ear and my arm until I agreed to go along with him for the moral support that he professes to need. He needs my support about as much as the Rocky Mountains along the northeast side of our valley do but when Peter is in a good mood he holds a magic key that twists others to his will—it's like being absorbed and carried along. By the time we reached the hall I was having second thoughts but it was too late then. The place is already well filled considering the numbers that have left for the holiday, but Peter spotted Ember and Jo sitting near the front with extra space on the bench to each side of them. He threaded his way toward them but stopped and looked back when he realized I wasn't following. Maybe I'm wrong but the moment I saw those two up front holding extra places I smelled a rat. There's nothing but trouble up there for me. "Go ahead, I like it better back here." He expressed his exasperation with me, lamenting having to stand when we could be sitting, but to my surprise he stayed with me.

Seeing Ember has forcibly reminded me that earlier in the day she had once again suggested, more pointedly this time and with a nasty undertone in her voice, that I go to the concert with her. I had declined almost rudely telling her straight out I wasn't going to attend. Now that I am here it seems a good plan to stay out of her sight since she has been hard enough to get along with since the scrap with her sisters—no use adding fuel to the fire.

I would be willing to play games with Ember anytime but only for keeps and on my own terms—a strange thought that! I wonder if I really mean it? Over the years I have made a sufficient fool of myself trying to prove that I mean more to her than do all the other amorous jokers flocking after her. I know by now where I stand in her scheme of things, it's bad enough having to watch from the sidelines, I'm not about to help by being bait in her trap for Peter.

And Peter has not helped matters any either because he has taken to teasing Ember about Nick. "You better marry him first chance, Em," he once said, "and we'll have another key man nailed down." She ignored him. Then he had glanced my way to be sure I was listening and added, "or at least shack up with the guy and keep him around for the winter."

"Peter," she looked at him level and cool, "shut up!" He did too but with a satisfied grin.

He is on fairly safe ground here despite the fact that he has a sense of humour while she doesn't because the only people I have known her to show or express admiration for have always been men older, sometimes much older, than herself. Ember is simply not attracted to anyone younger probably because of the way she sees her own younger brother and sisters—utter nuisances—pains to be endured since they are family. Pain from outside the family does not have to be endured except that she would not want Nick to quit and go away so the situation does leave one to smile a bit at her predicament. Despite his youth Nick is not inexperienced—he has been sawmilling since he turned fifteen and he's here not as labourer but as head sawyer on the graveyard shift. He is a top hand—a natural—he has talked a couple of other key top hands into switching to his shift and they have boosted the graveyard shift from its traditional role of low producer to the pace setter for the other shifts to try to keep up to. So it's lucky for us that in Ember's mind Peter is imprinted as an older man.'

As the kids started their show we maneuvered for the best position and I soon found myself between Peter and Tim. It lightened my heart and improved my mood to see them on the best of terms tonight, just like the good friends I would like them to be.

Before we knew it the concert was over and the teacher was on stage to thank everyone for coming and to remind us that as soon as the floor was cleared of benches there would be a dance, the last until New Year's Eve. Somebody suggested she sing for us while the benches were being moved and just about everyone else called out seconding the motion until a little embarrassed but as always pleased and willing to share her talent, she sat at the piano and played while she sang. But she sang a popular song so well that not a bench was moved and now the crowd wanted an encore and clapped and carried on until she agreed. "But," she said, "I am going to sing this song in French, the language it is meant to be sung in. I'm sorry many of you won't understand the words but I'm sure you will like it anyway and to translate it is to spoil it."

So she sang, but this is different, it is I suppose, some sort of a culture shock to us backwood folk to hear words sung that we don't understand. But language barrier or no, there is no mistaking that she sings of love and passion and inside of twenty seconds she has every man in the place on edge. It's not just her singing, which is better than good, it's Gabrielle herself, the way she gets right into her song and becomes the words she sings. We are all used to a singer just standing there and flapping their jaw but that's not what is happening now. She plays the piano so is kept to one place but she sways to some rhythm coming from the song or from herself. Head thrown forward, hair hiding her face then back, or to one side, singing softly, then sharp and imperious, then so gently and seductively that I think I blushed for her. I felt people in the audience looking at me whether they really were or not. Worse—I felt Ember looking at me, whether she really was or not and I wished I had stayed at home. I broke into a sweat, what on earth has come over my shy little school teacher? I have always thought her so young that I could never come up with any word stronger than cute to describe her. I see now that she is old as time and twice as beautiful. She is a woman in love and at this moment, like half the men in the building, I would give anything if it could be with me. The song ends on a high note of triumph and suddenly she is herself again. Shy, startled at her own boldness, she bowed then fled to the dressing room. The hall is so silent that I can hear a tap running in the kitchen. They may do it like this in Vancouver, or even Prince George, but Rainy Mountain is not prepared—we are thunderstruck. With just herself and her voice she has transported this whole crowd to somewhere filled with love and happiness and we are all richer for the experience. The hard part is that as she sang she seemed to single out one of us three to sing to, there were many glances our way but at that distance it was impossible to know which of us it was.

"My God! She's a good singer." Peter shouted to me over the applause that is now quite deafening.

"Never mind, she wasn't singing to you," I told him bluntly, getting his full attention right away.

"Oh? I suppose to you?"

"Oh, no! If she were I'd be backstage by now."

"Well? Tell me who then if you know it all."

"Our friend, Tim."

"Tim?" He looked around, surprised that Tim was no longer with us. "Where's he gotten to anyway?"

I pointed, "Just disappearing backstage," which is another way of saying, into one of the small rooms that double as entry to the kitchen.

Slowly, a big smile spread over Peter's face. "I wonder if Tim understands French? What do you think?"

"With all his education he must have picked up some."

"Why, that's great!" He said, looking as pleased as I have seen him in a while. "I'll bet there's going to be another teacher in the family —I like it."

I guess I do too.

But there are a few things that I don't like. I see now that Peter has had one of his tremendous good jokes at my expense again. She has plans for you my boy is what he told me, etc. etc., until the tinder that is the wild imagination I have been inflicted with flamed into wildfire and I convinced myself that Gabrielle had fallen for me. Now it seems I am only a friend, one that she needed and may need again. But had she been in love with me it would not have been necessary for Peter to tell me. She would have let me know.

An orchestra was soon chosen and whipped into shape and the dancing got started. Peter danced first with Jo, then with Ember and I couldn't help but notice that as they danced they were in deep and serious conversation. In fact, at one point, they stopped still and just stood there talking. A strange place to talk it seemed to me but with all the noise and movement probably the most private place in camp at the moment. Mostly it was Ember talking intently and Peter listening but once in a while looking around as though trying to find someone. Or an escape route! At one point it seemed she was bawling him out about something—another of his little jokes that she has caught on to probably as he just smiled. That's when I left to get a little sleep before traintime.

Later, while I waited at the tracks, a pickup came up the hill shortly before No. 9 from the East was due. They parked beside the station but no one got out. I didn't need to be told that it was Tim and Gabrielle reluctantly parting for the holidays. Tomorrow she will take a plane from Prince to Vancouver.

When I drove down from the railroad the dance was still in progress, I'd have been surprised if it wasn't. There will be some bleary eyes on the job in the morning but no one will worry about that. Tomorrow may be rough but the next day is Christmas, with a long weekend to rest up.

Nightrider's dash lights went out coming down the hill and it bothered me not being able to see the gauges. At first I couldn't think what to do about it so after parking in the unloading bay and closing the big door I snapped out the lights and started for home. The only lights I leave on at night are in the front office so there is just enough reflection down the hall to find my way. Then I suddenly had an idea what might be wrong with the truck so I returned to the warehouse and using my flashlight was soon upside down in the truck cab fiddling with the wiring I had added under the dash for extra backup and cargo lights. The overhead lights would have been more hindrance than help so I left them off. Once I heard voices and stopped my scrabbling to listen but there was nothing other than a distant dull roar from the dance hall. Someone going past on their way home from the dance I reasoned and went back to my chore. Then I heard a door close so near it could have been right in this building. Once again listening brought out no further sounds, I dismissed it as just more noise from homeward bound revelers.

A few more minutes and I had the problem solved, everything working again. Feeling like I have accomplished something I started once more through the hall intending to leave by way of the front office. At the closed door of the first aid room I halted in alarm, arrested in mid stride by a noise I have never heard before. I suffer an obsessive fear of freezing temperatures in this building that's full of groceries and laced with plumbing that's prone to hardening of cold arteries. The furnace is in there—it's a cold night. I have instant and vivid visions of a burned-out bearing on the blower and all those hungry wood heaters to be fired up and fed till the thing is fixed.

I stiff armed the door open and charged in, bound straight for the furnace with every nasty breakdown possibility flashing through one side of my mind while the other side reviewed our stock of furnace repair parts. Do we have the right part? Can I fix it myself right now and avoid the trouble of the wood stoves? If not, will fires in the warehouse and the store be enough for tonight? Probably not. Then lastly, which of the mechanics do I look for and is he home sleeping or off to the dance?

This room has large windows opposite the door. The moon is low enough in the sky to send its pale light across the floor almost to my feet. What it shows freezes my hand just in time as I reached for the wall switch. My mind went totally blank momentarily. I could neither move nor think. I simply could not make the mental leap from impending furnace trouble to lovers on the cot, their bodies glistening, molten silver.

It could have been no more than mere seconds before I backed out pulling the door shut as quietly as I know how but it was long enough to sear the image of that room so deeply into my brain that when I pressed my forehead against the wall and closed my eyes it was all there before me again. In one flash it is the most beautiful thing I ever expect to see and also the loneliest, most terrible moment of my life. The trail of clothing, a man's and a woman's, from the door to the bed starting with coats and ending with a tangle of the last garments off. The straining forms twined together testing the cot's strength and endurance—the girl's long, black-as-night hair fanned out over the shining white pillow.

Even stunned as I am I soon realized this is not a good place to be but my feet take me, not to the office and out but the other way to the darkness of the store. My heart is a tightly squeezed lump of ice in an iron-bound cage and my thoughts are just as cold. It's her! No one has hair like that but Ember. But though I saw them, I really didn't see them, and now I must find out who is with her. It has to be Peter but I've got to know for sure—even through the numbness it matters that it not be Nick.

In the store, with windows only at the front, back here between the rows of displayed merchandise it's dark enough for my purpose. I upended a case of canned milk to sit on while I waited where I could look down the hallway. I waited a long time. Long enough to thaw out a little inside and to know what a fool I am being. They are grown-up adults intending to be married soon. What should I expect them to do in the late hours of a moonlit night? Hold hands in a shadowed corner? Yes. Yes, I'm afraid that is exactly what I did expect even though I know better. To know better is to know nothing but to stumble into being their unwilling witness is too brutal for words.

As I wait, my feelings gradually shift to defensive anger. What right do they have to come here to be discovered by me as I go about my work? Are they so impatient, in such a hurry they cannot take the time to go the short distance to the house? I can understand them not going to Peter's room because his place is not private but Ember has a large house, as far as I know all to herself, with so many bedrooms they could spin a bottle to make their choice.

Unless Jan is home tonight.

And then at last a calmer thought—people do tend to forget that my duties keep me out and around at odd hours of the night and I've seen many strange and interesting things because of it.

I have almost reached the point of acceptance or resignation by the time a door clicked open and muted voices floated along to me. If they come this way I am discovered and until a moment ago I didn't even care but they turned toward the office. I studied the man closely in the poor light that came around the corner from the other end. It's Peter alright, then they are quickly out of sight.

In the morning I was the first one to the mall, I have no idea how I am going to face Ember and Peter today but I know that I want to be established at work and let them come to me. My world has changed and it seems to me that theirs must have too. I'm sure neither of them saw me last night so at least I have that advantage but my face has betrayed me many times before. Especially to Ember.

I needn't have worried though because when Peter came in there was no trace of last night's happiness about him, he was upset and anxious. "Em around?"

"Not yet." His expression sent alarm through me overshadowing my own worries. "What's happened to her?"

"Nothing to her. It's Jan! She's disappeared! I thought Em might have been here to tell you by now."

"What do you mean, disappeared? No one disappears around here, there's no place to disappear to."

"I know, that's what makes it so bad. If she's not holed up with someone then she's dead because no one could survive long outdoors in this weather without making plans ahead."

"I take it there's no sign that she made preparations? You know, bedding, clothes and food missing."

"I don't think so but there's so many places she could have stocked up from that it's hard to say."

I shook my head with a certainty that I couldn't have explained on a bet. "She's not one to go camping out in the winter, hardships are not her style. If she's around then she's in a building somewhere. A warm building preferably with other people."

"I tend to agree with you but if that's the case then at least she's safe, in the meantime, while she's missing we have to cover all bases. When did you last see her?"

"I'm not sure," I said slowly. "Yes I am. In the store Monday morning, her and Pat were in together."

"You're no help, that's the last time Ember or Jo remember seeing her too." Then he caught the look on my face. "What's the matter? Remember something?"

"No! No, it's nothing, you're just getting me worried too." But I had remembered something. Something that I'll not be telling Peter or anyone else about. There's no reason why the thought should have jumped into my mind. It's not good to think about those last words Ember screamed at her sisters, "why don't one of you have the decency to go drown in the river?" finishing with, "I'll give you some help if it's needed."

"When did you find out she was missing?"

"Last night at the concert," he answered. "Evidently the girls had a spat with Em and weren't talking to her but when Pat didn't see anything of Jan after Tuesday afternoon she just assumed Jan had gone back to the house. Pat said their plan was to walk up to Em as if nothing had happened and see if she was ready to be civil. They felt it was all Ember's fault but they expected she would be reasonable if they gave her the chance. So Pat wasn't worried, she just thought Jan was back with Ember because that's what she herself would have done." We both had to smile at this Morrow way of testing the settlement of a difference. A clenched fist in a velvet glove—not a one of the three would think of saying anything remotely like—'I'm sorry.'

"When Em showed up, at the concert and no Jan then they

started comparing notes and found that no one had seen Jan for over twenty-four hours. Ember told me about it while we were dancing and you can make that over thirty hours now because I've been to both places early this morning and still no Jan. I wasn't too concerned last night but now I've got to admit it looks serious."

So, I thought, that's what they were talking about so intently that they forgot to dance. Peter was looking around hoping for a glimpse of Jan while Ember talked to him. "When was she seen last?"

"The last time Pat saw her was Tuesday afternoon when Jan left for the farm to visit Alec's mother and check on the horses. Ann Hanson says she left after supper, she's not sure about the time. Ann says it was Ember's place that Jan was going to so Pat was right about that much. It puts Jan heading home after dark."

"That's no problem, she could find her way blindfolded but it must have seemed strange to her being alone as she walked."

It is to my notion an oddity how well the twins get along with Alec's parents. Better than with their own. They always have and I suspect it's largely because Ann's main business now that her family is grown up is training horses and Pat and Jan would like to do the same. People ship horses in to her from many places for her special style of handling. What that good woman thinks of their arrangement with her son I wouldn't hazard to guess. Maybe she doesn't know but the way the twins run off at the mouth I wouldn't bet on it. "We've got to organize a search!"

"I'm way ahead of you, Byron. I intercepted both Alec and Tom before they got away to the woods with their dozen or so remaining loggers. Alec is going to be a buckerman today if you can picture that and Tom will be running a skidder while they try to clean up the last of the fallen wood before the long shutdown. But first they will do a search of all the areas where the roads have still been in use the last couple of days."

"That's a big job."

"Maybe not as big as you think. We haven't had a snowfall for nearly a week here in camp but just gain a little elevation out the main road and there's been a light dusting every day lately. So each road with at least two days accumulation of snow and no tracks won't have to be checked. Since most of the woods crews went home before that most roads will be eliminated automatically."

"Okay, I don't see her going that route anyway but you're right, it has to be checked before we lose the opportunity to a heavy snow."

"Yeah. And Allan, with his planer and yard crew, is doing a search of all their working areas. That shouldn't take long with lots of men involved and really not much ground to cover. In a few minutes I'm going to get some men from Allan's bunch and do a perimeter check of every snowplowed road around the camp, mill site and farm areas. That might take us awhile."

"What do you want me to do?"

"Monitor the radio until Erin or Jennie get here then when Jo comes in send her around house-to-house in the married quarters—she'll figure out what questions to ask. Then you can search this building. Between the crawl spaces underneath, the attic above and all the stored junk, it's a rabbit warren and you know the way around it better than anyone. Also, see the bullcook and if he hasn't already done it, have him check all the bunkhouses that have been empty the last couple of days. The cookhouse crew are searching their own building, it's another rabbit warren but not as bad as this one. We'll do a quick once over of everything we can think of, then as time permits we'll do it in more detail. Just five minutes of heavy snowfall and we are whistling in the dark."

"If you have us searching attics and crawl spaces does that mean we are looking for a body?"

"Well? What else would you have us do? I can't think of anything better."

"We'll have to call the police too."

He looked pained as he protested, "We don't need them unless we find a crime has been committed."

"A girl is missing, if we don't find her, say for a week and then find that a crime was committed after all, I think we would not only be in difficulty, but by not getting help we might goof up the search job and cause a lot of problems for everyone." I could see the struggle in his mind between the desire to do it ourselves and the advantages of calling in the police.

"Give me till noon, if we haven't got something to go on by then, you can call the RCMP."

"Okay."

He started out but stopped and turned back to me. "Is there any chance she could have caught a train out?"

"Sure. I know—it seems like I should have seen her if she went on one of the passengers or the local. But if she hid in the station till the train was stopped and I was busy with express and mail she could have slipped on without me noticing. Especially on No.8—with No.9 there's not much to hold my attention."

"That means Jasper."

"And all points east," I added. "But if she really wanted she could have gone on the wayfreight when it stopped to switch cars for us. They leave the tail end of the train up on top on the mainline or in the passing track while they run down our spur. If she approached the caboose and told a tall story about having to get to a doctor they might let her on. It's not like she's a transient, the train crews mostly would know the twins by sight just like they know me and probably you too."

"That will be easy to check with CN. Same on the passenger train, someone should remember seeing her. With any kind of luck we'll find she blacked somebody's eyes and was well noticed." With that optimistic observation he left.

Ember arrived before Jo and she came looking for me first thing. She too shows no joy from last night, in fact she looks as though she has not slept at all. She came straight to me, wordless, wrapped her arms around me and pressed her face against me. Twenty-four hours ago this would have been heaven on earth for me but now I can't help glancing over my shoulder hoping to see

Peter coming to take her off my hands. She has played her game with him and evidently won to judge by the evidence of last night. But if she now thinks that makes it safe for her to embrace me then she is sadly mistaken. I cannot believe the conflict of emotions running loose within me as I discover I could still want her. And very much at that.

"You've heard?" She asked my shirt.

"About Jan? Don't worry, she'll be found, probably quite safe."

"Don't say that just to make me feel better. You heard me scream those awful things at her the other day. I even told her to go drown herself. I pray to God now that she hasn't."

The line of contact between us is becoming far too overheated for my peace of mind. Since obviously no one is coming to my rescue I gently disengaged myself from her and stepped back watching the pain grow in her eyes. And the flash of anger beginning. I feel completely rotten for failing her when she is crying out for help but really, it's Peter who is needed here, not me.

Jo and Erin came together speculating a mile a minute on what might have happened to Jan. Once Jo is sent on her errand I am freed of the office. I have no intention of searching the mall, I know very well that no one is playing hide-and-seek in here and there are no bodies underfoot either. Later I will check underneath and overhead so that I know what I am saying when Peter asks. That should take about ten minutes with a flashlight. I was still pulling my coat on as I went through the door. A few minutes spent checking the river will ease Ember's mind and that seems important to me right now.

Like I suspected the road to the river showed no tracks since my trip down with the 4x4 Tuesday night. Footprints of a search party show at the top of the hill but evidently they saw no reason to go farther. I walked on down anyway and at the bottom I got a surprise when at the end of my truck tracks a set of boot marks, at least as large as my own or bigger, continued on overtop my old tracks. They had walked down stepping carefully in the tire marks as far as they went then for want of cover went boldly onto the dock and to the water's edge. Whoever it was had tried to walk in my steps but hadn't done a very good job of it. If it was Jan wearing big boots for camouflage, then at least she didn't drown herself because the tracks also returned to the road and vanished into the tire tracks again. These strange tracks have about the same amount of frost gathered in them as my own so whoever it was must have been down later the same night as I or at latest early the next morning. The searchers had missed because no tracks show on the road except those left by the truck and Peter knew who went down there, when and why. How many other loopholes do we have in our effort?

Was it Tom? Checking to see if I had carried out his wishes with Lupe? Or someone carrying a girl's body down to take advantage of the open water? I guess I can't relieve Ember's fears after all but if Jan went into the water here then someone put her in and that's a different matter altogether. I left the river feeling rather glad I had carried out that bit of a ruse the other night.

Right after lunch I called the police only to learn they don't get very excited over young people who go missing without sign of crime or violence and we have no indication of either. They did ask a lot of questions, took a description of Jan and suggested a few things we hadn't thought of. Other than that they assured me that they would make all appropriate inquiries and inform us of any progress. For our part we were to send them a picture of the missing girl and call at any time if we came up with more information and that was it! "Goodbye, nice talking to you."

Peter was at my elbow grinning like he'd told me so. He had gotten the gist of it from hearing my end of the conversation and watching my face.

"So, we're on our own," he surmised.

"Unless we turn up a crime of some sort."

"Well, they are right, people do decide to pull up stakes and leave, you know. It's the way it should be anyway, we take care of our own here—from the cradle to the grave."

I feel too tired to get into an argument with him on this subject as I am all too aware of the independent attitude of all the Morrows and this seems to include Peter. The cemetery on the hill to the railroad is evidence of the care they give their own in the final analysis. "I suppose like you say, people do pull stakes and leave but I can see that happening only up to a point then I come up against one hard fact that makes it impossible in Jan's case." His face tightened more and more as I talked, and now he stared at me with eyes hard as ice and just as cold but his rapidly shifting moods don't bother me as much as they used to. In fact, with him, it's when you see no expression at all that you had better start worrying.

"And what hard fact are you talking about?"

"Pat! I can see that Jan might be outrageously angry with Ember though it isn't the twins' style to carry a grudge. She could be sick and tired of the rest of us boring people and by using the greatest degree of imagination I can see her running out on Alec. But neither you nor anyone else can convince me that she would leave Pat without some communication between them."

He glared at me a long time, thinking hard, before he answered. "There's two possibilities there, friend Byron. One is that you are partly right when you say they are too close to part but maybe they are so close that now when parting becomes a necessity she couldn't bear a goodbye scene. To up and vanish like that would be a typical Morrow way to do it, I should know, their ways are mine too."

There is some logic in what he says but I am not prepared to admit it. "What's the other possibility?"

"Number two is that the girls did say goodbye, maybe they even drew straws to decide who went, but Pat plans never to tell."

"They are a strange and lovely pair," I mused, talking mostly to myself, but out loud. "I don't think that ordinary people like you and I will ever even begin to understand what goes on in their heads. Nor do I think much of your ideas because I don't believe it could happen that way. And, what about Pat? She hasn't been around all day."

"She's ill and gone to bed so Alec says. He was going to stay home with her today but she told him to get out, she wanted to be alone. She sounds to be in good enough form, I think she must plan to survive the ordeal. But when her and Ember compared notes last night and realized Jan had not been with either of them she got sick right then and Alec took her home." He paused before going on with some reluctance, "She thinks, like you do, that something drastic has happened and Jan is dead. That's what you think, isn't it?"

I took my time answering because I really haven't worked up a feeling for the situation yet—but it's coming. "Yes, that's what I privately think, I can see no other alternative in this weather. But as long as there's a chance she took a train out then that's probably the line we had best take in public. It will be easier for everyone to live with."

"Right! I knew you would see it in a logical fashion eventually. I'm going to the store and tell Ember that."

His face had cleared almost magically, I hadn't noticed that he was so worried until he became so relieved. I would almost swear that he is less worried about Jan's disappearance than about my opinions on the matter. Now, should that be telling me something?

I sat in the front office alone now that Erin has gone to the back room to her own work and looked out the windows at the various activities within my view. The search has ended in failure and the planer is working again, a few loaded log trucks have come down the hill to the sorting grounds and tomorrow is Christmas day. So brief a pause then life goes on as before. It would be the same for me.

10

It wasn't a great Christmas for the Morrows but they went through the motions at any rate. Peter and I both attended the gathering held this year at Allan and Erin's place. Alec and Pat didn't come because Pat is not yet able to face a life without Jan. The rest, including Ember, seem to have adopted the theory that Jan is okay and we will hear from her in time. Ember is actually starting to make noises about it being all for the best, it will give Pat's marriage a better chance of survival. Her scenario now calls for Jan to show up at her grandparents or with one of the aunts or uncles in Alberta but not likely with her own parents. I hope she is right because if Jan is alive she is going to need help in short order. Like all the rest of the family she has never had any money of her own other than a little at a time for shopping trips to Prince. No savings account and no cash on hand except whatever was left over from her last trip to town. And very likely not one iota of financial savvy though the twins have fooled me before. Their older sister certainly has enough savvy for all of us but then her store and other involvements have been a good training ground.

After the meal while most of us sat around talking, Ember took up, in small containers, a portion of everything that had been served and put it in a roaster pan for carrying. In all innocence I watched her doing this but when she asked me to drive her to Pat and Alec's I woke up with a start to the knowledge that the holiday is over. She caught me off guard and I declined gracelessly turning ornery because she asked me right in front of Peter. She didn't ask him to take her and he didn't offer so she drove herself but only after shooting me down with a glare calculated to spoil my day if I would let it. I don't know what I've done to deserve this, seems like she should be picking on our friend Peter instead. I'll not even pretend to understand this pair, sometimes you would think they don't even like each other. As soon as she drove away I left also and went to the shack to do some reading.

Read! Not after listening to all those wild theories and suppositions passed around the table today like an extra platter of turkey. All these strange events. Are they connected? Or just coincidental happenings? When I tried to put them all in order I was surprised to find that the last incident discovered—Jan's disappearance—was possibly one of the first to happen. It was early Tuesday evening that she was last seen by Alec's family as she left their farm. Only a little later the same night Tom's dog is shot under what can be described charitably as unusual circumstances. Later yet the same night I catch Peter prowling about the townsite and he was, to say the very least, unhappy to be discovered. Maybe he had more serious business in mind than visiting Ember.

But, if I want to start adding up unusual incidents then I have to go back farther than that. First, I would say, was when the always predictable Allan unpredictably attacked his brother and loudly promised to kill anyone engineering a sellout. Just a rash statement in a moment of anger I expect though Jan did vote to sell.

The next out of the ordinary happening was when Ember chewed up the twins and suggested one go for an out-of-season swim—then thoughtfully offered her assistance if it was needed. Just another unfortunate angry outburst I'm sure.

But I'm all mixed up and rambling, I don't even know what I'm trying to figure out. There seems to be no order to it at all so I will back way up and start all over again but with two assumptions that I hope will be proven wrong. First I will assume that Jan is dead for she is either that or gone on a train and there's been no confirmation of that from anywhere—police or railroad. secondly, I will assume that someone assisted her to her death because I cannot see anyone as vibrant as she has always been taking her own life and an accident should have left us with her body at least.

Now who would want to do away with her? It's no secret that a lot of people, sometimes myself included, are uncomfortable around the twins because of their rough talk and careless ways—like Ember before them they have no real friends—except each other. I suppose there are some who actually dislike them but certainly not to the point of murder. So then, could someone profit by her death? And there I guess I've opened a lunch bucket full of green and squirming sandwiches for sure. All her own brothers and sisters could be said to profit in one way or another by her death. To be exact there are eight people who are now up a few percentage points in ownership. I ticked them off on my fingers to be sure I have the count right. They are, Jo, Ember, Tim, Allan, Tom, Peter, and the pair of Alec and Pat. No, Alec is a loser here, he is now down to one wife—and one vote. The question of the day could well be—is that loss or gain? And Peter? He may or may not stand to gain at all. So not eight, only seven or maybe six.

I can't see motive where Jo is concerned since she wasn't fanatical about the run or sell issue like Ember who could be another matter. It's possible there is motive if you can believe that averting family scandal could be that important to her. Or continuing the family business for they were on opposite sides in the vote. She has, to my surprise, demonstrated that she is capable of a raging anger but in my opinion that does not mean she is capable of killing. I have to admit though where Ember is concerned I am guilty of bias. If she were to wet down my shirt front with her tears again I'm afraid I would be willing to believe anything she wanted to tell me and any private doubts would remain unasked about.

I can't, for the life of me, see any conflict between Tim and either of the twins, they all want the business sold and the proceeds, if any, handed out. For a moment I got sidetracked wondering if the person who did her in knew which twin he or she was dealing with. Then I decided it makes no difference, end result remains the same.

Tom seems to have no motive either. I have never heard of him censuring the girls in any way, in fact, like their father, he seems to be proud and approving of their aggressive manner. He really appears to be something of a victim himself in losing his dog the same night Jan went missing. On top of that they are all three in agreement, along with Tim, on the sell issue.

But Allan didn't agree! He has shown us an uncontrollable, explosive anger, perhaps he could also show us controlled premeditated action. The twins did vote against him and even if it was through Alec, Allan can certainly see beyond the messenger boy. It is theoretically possible that he has started a program of elimination. If that is so then Tom, Pat, and Tim are in danger right now. That thought prompted me to wonder where Allan was when Lupe was shot. If I remember right though, he was among the first to arrive for the meeting that night, right on time as usual and while that might not eliminate him, it is in his favour. No, if it's Allan then he is doing a great job of playing a deep game and in my opinion not a one of that high tempered, strong-willed group could practice any long-term deception without self-destructing. I recalled again the thermometer incident in which I had figured a few winters ago. Ember commented that her father was too honest to tamper with someone else's property even such a minor property as an offending thermometer. Argue—or even fight about it with the owner—yes. Destroy or steal it—no. I feel that assessment can basically be applied without exception to the entire family.

Then there is Peter and here is a real challenge. He is not one of the family and yet he is. He seems to have every bit as volatile a temperament as the others. He has shown me on several occasions, notably on our first trip to town together, that he is acutely sensitive to the twins and their peccadilloes. That night on the train he was on the verge of launching a violent attack on Alec and Jan as they dallied across the rail car from us. He was so incensed by their conduct that he felt they had to be covered. He's obviously no saint himself but evidently young stepsisters are supposed to behave differently than girlfriends. I recognize that I am prejudiced where Peter is concerned just as with Ember only in the opposite direction. My instinct tells me to count him as a friend but if he takes Ember away from us he will be no friend of mine. If Jan has been murdered it will break my heart the least if it's Peter who is found guilty.

Alec and Pat come last and I guess that's because I dragged my heels getting to them. Here, plainly, are my prime suspects—the classic triangle, two women in love with one man, one woman is now gone. We have all about gotten used to seeing them acting as if their cozy threesome were the most normal thing in the world but in reality it must sometimes take on a nightmare quality especially for Alec saddled as he is—was—with not one but two demanding wives. Never mind that one is not by marriage, she would be no less demanding—it's simply the nature of the twins to be demanding. Always.

Has it been any less of a bad situation for Pat with her own sister horning in on her marriage? Can they really share one man and be as happy as they appear to be or is it possible for the greatest of love to turn into equally great hatred? I've heard it said that love and hate can be very close to the same thing. With hotheads like these Morrows I could believe it. If true love were being obstructed I think some very ugly emotions would almost certainly come to the surface. I have only to look at Ember and her troubles with Peter whose affection seems to evaporate with the light of day for illustration. Either Pat or Alec have cause, maybe together they have more than double cause.

I don't know what it takes to drive a person to murder but I know that Alec has skated on the thin edges of it. His past is checkered with incidents of violence including a manslaughter charge over a man who died after a drunken brawl. Alec spent a short time in prison over that but it happened while he was working elsewhere so not many people here remember it. But there has to be a chasm as wide and deep as the Fraser Canyon between accidental killing and deliberate murder.

As for the lovely Patricia, physical strength is the only limiting factor in judging what she might be capable of. I have always considered the twins as shapely kegs of powder only lacking a spark for ignition. It could be that Alec has been the flint for their steel, either her or Alec could be guilty or they could be in it together

And that's my list of suspects, all family, no outsiders. I had to give that a few minutes thought but I will let it stand because to do murder there has to be profit of some form involved. Whether it be financial, for respectability, or gain of personal freedom, every family member stands to gain by one means or more while I can think of no way that any outsider would benefit.

Any and all of the six survivors have already experienced a gain to some extent. I'm counting Jo here as Terry's beneficiary but not Alec. And because I don't know how he fits, not Peter just yet. But if this is the case then would an increase from one seventh to one sixth be enough to satisfy whoever it was? It would hardly seem so and that being the case, the remaining brothers and sisters, and Jo too, had best watch their back trails. I'm not up too much on inheritance laws but I believe that any estate goes automatically to the spouse or if the spouse dies also then it goes equally to any surviving children. Jan had no spouse and no children so that's it—final. But say in Allan's case, not only he would have to die but Erin and all three kids as well. Pretty messy for a one share gain. House fire! That's what Allan and Tom must somehow be warned to guard against.

If I'm on the right line here then Tim, Ember, and Jo would be the marks for easy gain. Who though could possibly be greedy enough to want to kill any of them, especially Ember. I have to grin wryly remembering a time or two I could cheerfully have wrung her neck myself. But all joking aside it would take a maniac to plan out and execute a mass extermination such as I have been thinking of. While all these Morrows, and maybe myself too, are crazy to some extent I'll bet my job and Nightrider to boot that none of them are that truly mad. If you were to deliberately cross purposes with just about any one of them you would be in sudden trouble. Your chances of living to old age would be vastly improved if you stepped briskly out of reach for a few seconds. But other than that they are probably as normal as I am.

Anyway, the elimination process should have started out in Alberta with John and Lora? Maybe! I still think of John as the owner even though he's absent but that may not be the case at all now. Those papers that I turned over to Peter were about the same thing as a bill of sale, a conditional one, and I wish now that I could see it again. John had told me to look it over and I did eventually do so but very fleetingly because—I hesitate to say it—I felt ghosts looking over my shoulder. Silly, but that's how it was.

This operation of Morrows has always been a one-man show, John never could relinquish the decision making to anyone else. Now I suspect he has finally faced up to that agonizing decision feared by every man with a personal business and a large family to divide it among. It seems to me that he has chosen to leave it to one of the group for the benefit of all. He has done it in a manner that resembles an outright sale—for the sum of one dollar I believe it stated which might be more than it's worth right now—and therefore is less disputable than a lopsided will might be. And of course, unlike a will which would have to wait for his death, it goes into effect right away. Then by leaving the space for the name of the recipient blank he has allowed Peter room to manoeuvre—room to negotiate—to bring some of the others onside. Because obviously, the one man he has picked is Peter Patten and we are all working our tails off for him for no pay other than our room and board. What a stunning thought! I wonder if any of the others know this? Not much chance has to be the answer to that. John gave me the papers, I looked briefly at them but otherwise kept them hidden. No one expressed interest so they were forgotten about until I dug them out to give to Peter who has waved them about and proclaimed the contents loudly but allowed no perusal. The lawyer who drew them up could tell me the meaning but he probably wouldn't, at least not over the telephone. If it comes to a point where I must know, I will just have to ask Peter outright then whatever he tells me, believe the opposite.

One thing in his favour now that I have him pegged as possibly the sole owner is that the greed motive is removed. When he already holds the key in his hand or at least has it at his disposal there is no need for him to kill off the competition. I can't find much pleasure in this thought because I was not looking for pluses on his account. But his actions of late still strike me as odd enough to keep him high on my list.

The one person in this bunch who puzzles me most is the one at the very bottom of my list as a suspect. Jo! A very exciting young lady she has become. She could just as easily be enjoying all the comforts and conveniences of town but no, she stays with us. True, it's as good a place as any for a young widow to meet single men and her work puts her where they can't miss her. She has recovered from tragedy to where she now eyes the male customers with cautious interest, very cautious and only enough interest to keep from killing theirs. She doesn't always say no to them like Ember does but then she never lets anything much develop either as I learned first-hand. But lately at a party, a dance or any gathering, with or without an escort she turns into everything you would expect Ember to be but isn't. She has fun and wants those with her to have fun too. But she's not always wise. If it were Erin who was missing instead of Jan there would be a whole different slant to this affair. Last winter Allan made a fool of himself mooning over Jo whenever his wife wasn't around and Jo had been no less a fool by showing she was pleased and flattered by his attention. It didn't go anywhere—I don't think anyone else even noticed and I wished that I hadn't. I wanted to remind her of her liking for Erin but she sensed I wanted to say something and made sure I didn't get the chance. I wasn't jealous, not much, more a case of disappointed. I thought she was too smart to flirt with a married brother-in-law—especially one she has always liked a bit too much. I was very glad when they realized it was fire they were playing with and put it out before any smoke rolled. These Morrow types seem to have her number. I wrote it off as one of the hazards of living in a tightly knit group in a small isolated community and being thrown together in our jobs. I've obviously not been totally immune myself.

But Ember—she has no fun. There is no play in her—she doesn't know how. The wheels are always spinning and clicking in her agile mind but it's a mind that works full time, even overtime, for Rainy Mountain and she misses or misinterprets a lot of the little things that make up the fabric of our everyday lives. Still, if there is a deep thinker in this Morrow tribe then it's her. Of them all I would vote her the one most likely to be able to live with a secret. She is a loner—as far as I know she always has been—at least since Terry's death. But surely, something eating at her until she reacted by killing would destroy her in the process.

Every once in a while I say something to myself that turns on an unexpected, maybe unwanted light. That's what has happened now. It has come on so gradual that it's hardly been noticeable but something has been destroying her in a way lately. My unflappable girl of the even temper is no more, her face can seem troubled and unhappy when I watch while she is unaware. Her temper is now a thing to be feared or at least avoided and she has become our resident grouch. It turns out that her command of bush camp grammar is at least equal to that of Pat and Jan who have made it a subject in which to excel. Always lighter than her curvaceous sisters she now seems thinner than ever. The motive for murder sounds weak but she is fanatical where her family is concerned. Family, tradition, and work. She has Peter fair and square but she seems to want something more, in fact she now seems to want me too. But that is so contrary to all past indications that I know I am letting my imagination run again as I did with Gabrielle. Never mind, I tell myself, I think that you will never understand that girl. She is a study in contrasts, every time I think I have her figured out she derails me altogether and it's back to square one. One thing that has become clear is that I am not on her list of general friends. It seems I am to be considered as Company Property and as such must measure up to higher standards than what seem adequate to me. Why else would she persist in trying to smooth out my rough edges and make me into something I'm not? The man who marries her will be in for a lifetime of surprises—some of them pleasant.

So, now that I have all these suspects lined out and waiting for a murder to be discovered—what next?

An answer of sorts was quick enough in coming as the electric lights dimmed, struggled, and died leaving me in the semi-darkness of a room with too little window space.

It's no big panic, this does happen once in a while so I just tried to snooze a little while waiting for them to come back on. The generating plant has automatic shutdown switches in case of overheating or low oil pressure and they have recently caused a spell of trouble so this might be more of the same. When the power still hadn't come on after fifteen minutes I stepped into my boots, grabbed a coat and headed for the engine room at the sawmill where the gen sets are. The planer has its own engine room but the one at the sawmill houses not only the two big electric sets that power everything in the mill but also the smaller one for camp lighting purposes. I was almost to the engine room when one of the big units rumbled into life and a moment later the lights came on again on the power poles all over the camp and mill area.

Inside it was comfortably warm from the heat of the engine that had been running. Albert, the head millwright, was there studying the crankcase oil dipstick of the small gen set. He was holding it at arms-length and turning it this way and that to catch different angles of light on it. "Lots of oil," he commented when he saw me, "but it doesn't look right—frothed up like there's antifreeze in it."

It looked all right to me, like black, sooty, diesel engine oil. "How about the level in the radiator?"

"It's in sight, shouldn't be any overheating problem. But the engine seems to be solid."

"What do you mean?"

In answer he punched the starter button of the silent engine but there was only a loud metallic 'clack'. "It's seized up solid and I'm wondering what on earth could have caused it. I was here just before we sat down to our dinner and checked it over. I added a gallon of oil but that's nothing unusual, it takes a gallon between low and full on the dipstick and running twenty-four hours a day like it does I have to add oil once or twice a week. Lots of hours on it now so it's burning a bit."

"When was the last time you added oil?"

"Monday. I gave it a complete oil and filter change Monday morning. I know that's almost a week ago but it lasts longer between adds when the oil is new and fresh."

He pulled the dipstick again and sniffed at the dark oil on the end then even tasted it. Looking thoughtful he fumbled at his shirt pocket producing a pair of glasses which he put on then examined the stick again. "Here it's just been changed first of the week and it appears to me that there are little flakes of something shiny in it already—tastes sweet too. The engine has aluminum bearing inserts and I think I'm seeing flakes of aluminum." He put his glasses away as though afraid of wearing them out.

"What would that mean?"

"Well, it makes me think that we've got a cracked cylinder liner or a blown gasket and some antifreeze has gotten into the crankcase and knocked out the bearings."

Even I am aware that antifreeze in the engine oil is dynamite. "Any way of telling for sure right now?"

"Doesn't matter much does it? It's out of commission and we'll find out what the trouble is when it's stripped down for repairs."

I nodded absently, my attention wandering to the barrels of oil on a rack in one corner. There were three of them and they could be rolled this way or that to turn the large bung side up or down. Two were unopened and still sealed but the other had a hand valve—a so-called 'molasses gate'—quick to open, quick to close, screwed into the large fitting. There were a pair of cans on the floor nearby. "Is this what you use to transfer oil to the engines?" I asked, picking up the largest can. It was a two-gallon, square-sided container with a screw-on cap at one top corner and a smaller vent cap on the opposite with a carrying handle between. The label said, Outboard Marine Oil and I guess that's why I picked it up. It seemed to be out of place here in the engine room and a long way from the boats.

"No," he answered, "it's that other one with the funnel and spout arrangement on it."

I put down the can I held and picked up the one he indicated. Peering into it all I saw at first was oil that had clung to the sides then drained down later, but as I tipped it to the light I could see the bright green of antifreeze settled to the bottom under the clean oil. "Better have a look at this," I told him holding the can out.

He put his glasses back on then tipped the can to the light as I had done.

"Oh oh! This doesn't look too good." He let the can drop to arms-length then stared at the rack of oil drums. It took him about thirty seconds to draw a sample of oil and find that it was well laced with a green streak of antifreeze. He looked at me help-lessly. "It's that sabotage business again, moved in out of the woods to the mill. Somebody has put antifreeze in the oil barrel so that when the engines have oil added, in goes the antifreeze too."

"What about the big engines?" I asked.

He gave a start of concern then relaxed. "They should be okay, I've not added to them since Monday. With us just running a couple of single shifts this week they've used no oil. But if we had been running our usual three shifts that stuff would be in the big engines instead and that would hurt. I don't mean that this doesn't," he waved a hand at the stricken engine, "but compared to the big units this will be cheap and easy."

"You figure the oil was okay Monday?"

"Oh, it had to be, I'm sure no engine would run five days with that much antifreeze in the oil, this trouble will be from what I put in it this morning. That stuff would go right to the bottom where the oil intake is. It must have been trying to lubricate itself on nearly straight antifreeze."

"We've got to get rid of that drum of contaminated oil before it causes more trouble," I said.

"For sure! I can see to that but what's to keep whoever is doing it from coming again and maybe dumping it straight into an engine next time?"

"Not a thing that I can think of, all we can do is keep our eyes open and hope for the best. I'll talk to Allan about it and maybe he can set up some kind of security measures here."

Albert went off then to see Ted Jonas about getting a couple of diesel mechanics to hasten their holiday and start to work on the gen set. Left to myself I wandered around the engine room wondering how any form of security could work. We can't just lock the place up because access to the engines and electrical panels is too often needed. A watchman here would mean we would be hit elsewhere and how many watchmen would be needed to guard the entire operation? More than we can afford I'm sure. We are so spread out that vulnerable is a charitable description of our situation. And who would watch the watchmen?

For some reason I was drawn once more to the two gallon can I had first picked up. Outboard Marine Oil it said. That certainly doesn't belong in here. Curious, I took off the cap and looked inside. Couldn't see a thing of course but there was the slap of liquid as I shook the can so I tipped it to spill some out and got a good-sized splash of green antifreeze on the floor.

With no conscious thought or plan guiding me I tightened the cap again and shoved the can, on its side, as far back under the bottom shelf of the workbench as it would go. The shelf is about eight inches above the floor and over two feet in width so the can is fully out of sight unless you look in just the right place from well back in the room.

I am elated! At last the saboteur has left something behind—finally we have something to start with. It's not much but there might be finger prints on it besides mine I thought hopefully. I suppose anyone carrying it from the shop, where the antifreeze is kept in forty-five gallon drums, to here in this weather would be wearing mitts. Still, it's our first break so until I can see some way to make use of it that can will stay right where it is. Out of sight, under the bench.

The next morning was another silent one all around camp. Though we still have enough crew to run a shift each at the mill and planer as well as our home guard loggers, they are all taking both today and Sunday off. But not me. The trains had rolled as usual last night and would again tonight so there is work enough to keep me on the job. Of course it doesn't take much to keep me busy. By now I am an expert at making little jobs into lengthy and impressive looking projects.

Even though it's Boxing Day the store is open because Ember would never inconvenience her people with three days running of no shopping, tomorrow being Sunday. There was sporadic activity in the office too and it was while unloading Nightrider in the warehouse that I got one of my more severe shocks of a shocking year. It started with the sound of light, quick steps coming along the hallway from the store. Ember heading for the office I expected but it's a good thing my hands were empty of anything dropable because it was none other than our missing Jan who showed up. After a quick look each way along the hall she walked right up to me, her attitude blocking out any foolish idea I might have of asking where she has been hiding out. I guess my jaw was somewhere down around my kneecaps but eventually I got my voice in gear, "Jan! My God, girl, am I ever glad to see—." But there I stopped in mid sentence for it was mighty plain that she was not glad to see me. She was impatiently motioning for me to be quiet.

"Yes, I was afraid of that," she said quite disgustedly. "You've always been the only one other than Mom who could tell us apart without fail. I don't know how you do it but it doesn't matter any more."

She was making a minimum of sense but still, I knew what she was talking about. "So! It's really Pat who's missing."

She nodded while looking apprehensively back at the doorway. "Can we get farther back in here? I don't want to be overheard." So we went back among the stacks of supplies to where we could still see the doorway with little chance of being seen or heard and she got right to the point. "I worried that you would recognize me but I can't stay in hiding forever just to avoid you so I've come to thrash this out where we can be alone."

"What's happened to Pat? Do you know?"

"No. No more than anyone else."

"You're going to ask me to keep quiet about you actually being Jan aren't you?"

"You always were an infuriating know-it-all," she snapped quite savagely but then as quickly turned it into a smile. "We might have fallen in love with you instead of Alec if you weren't such a trouble-maker for us. You always knew when we were pulling a fast one on somebody."

"But I never blew the whistle on you unless I thought you were doing damage to someone. I'm not your style anyway."

"No. Besides, Ember has had a big neon no-trespassing sign on you ever since she nursemaided you to town after your wreck. Only a dumb young teacher would fail to notice." She saw my disbelief. "You wouldn't know it but she came home from taking you to the hospital in such a state of shock and near collapse that it seemed she was only half with us just when we needed her. It was almost a case of her crying on Jo's shoulder instead of the other way around."

"That would be normal enough after losing Terry and probably getting no sleep or taking time to have a decent meal for a couple of days."

"Sure there's that, but we all felt it was excessive and too long lasting—there was more than grief—she was afraid of something too. So Erin—reading between the lines like she does—started phoning for reports on you. When she got word that you had awakened and would be fine Em came right back almost to normal practically over night. That's when we knew she had almost suffered a double loss. It's also when she told us you would be coming back and we were all to be nice to you—pretty plain I thought.

"Anyway, if you can't understand the meaning of all that I'm not going to try explaining but it's why Pat and I went to see you in the hospital. Partly to see what we were getting for a new brother and partly because Em, having declared you one of us, was just serenely assuming you knew enough to come without being told."

I let that all slide by. It's just more of the same old story easily explained by Ember suffering some guilt for putting Terry and I out on a training run in a relic truck. I'd like to believe her but I know that I can't even though it certainly would explain John's sour inspection of me that long ago day. There has to be a lot of imagination at play here because on the day I was injured Ember didn't even know me beyond having hauled me from the train to the camp. But Jan wouldn't leave it alone.

"After having such a long affair you must miss her now that

Peter is here and she's pretending to behave herself. Or have you just become more careful?"

"Jan, I haven't a glimmer of what you're talking about."

"Oh, go fly! You don't have to lie for her. She's never made a secret of it. We all knew she was spending the night with you whenever she felt like it. We couldn't help but know the way she came home at breakfast time just like it was the normal thing to be doing. Everyone on the night shift saw her truck parked at your place so the whole town knew—after all, that's being pretty open about it. That's why Mom got so mad that she tried to domesticate you and have you move in with us so it could be publicly acknowledged instead of being publicly flaunted."

"No! That's not the way it was at all! She was in the office, working or maybe reading. You know how she reads all night sometimes and how your mother gets angry about it. Actually she has never once been in my room except the night she carried my duffel bag in when I came back years ago. I did see her truck parked out front but I've no idea why she parked that way because she was in the office."

"Well, you might not know why but everyone else does!" A light of new interest—something on the edge of being funny—dawned in her eyes. "I think you've been had, old friend of mine, one way if not the other."

"She wouldn't do that!" Jan didn't answer and as fast as I defended Ember I knew I was wrong—she would do it! If the public image of her staking claim to me would cut down on the volume of nuisance visits to the store of guys just wanting to look at her and take up her time then she would do it as quick as she thought of it. Never once would she worry about what she might be doing to me in the process. She wouldn't care that it would work both ways. No wonder I'm jinxed with any of the other girls! Just one more example of the trouble she seems dedicated to make for me. And that will also be why she's always been so 'keep your distance'—in case I tumbled to it and got ideas.

"I'm not sure that I can go along with you, Jan. Or Pat, or

whoever. You see that will always be a problem for me, I'll look up, see you coming, maybe with Alec and I'll say, 'Hi Jan'." I see no way to impress on her how deeply offended my sense of right and wrong is by what she is asking so I won't even try.

"Yes, and then you can be decent enough to look confused and correct yourself. I don't see it as any problem." I must have remained visibly skeptical. "Okay, I see that you are struggling with your conscience. Try looking at it my way, By," she became very earnest, "no two people could be closer than Pat and I unless they were Siamese twins. Try to understand that." She gave me a few seconds to absorb that much. "All our lives we thought the same, looked the same, did all the same things and even wanted the same man enough to willingly share him. I know that's not supposed to happen but it did. We lived in and for each other and we always expected that if one of us died the other would too. But it just hasn't happened that way. I'm alive and Pat is dead but at the same time I can now be Pat and it's Jan who's dead." More agitated than I ever expected to see one of these girls she grasped the front of my shirt as if she could shake some sense into me. It's an unnerving experience for me to watch this strong-minded, arrogant young woman unraveling before my eyes. "I'm not saying this well, not at all like I planned, try to understand when I say that Pat is dead but Janna will be the name on the headstone. Yet I am Jan and I'm living Pat's life so we are together yet in both life and death."

What could I say? I do understand her and once again I am humbled and touched by these fascinating sisters. "Okay, J—Pat, it's a deal but do one thing for me in return. Several things really—settle some questions for me."

Her whole attitude shifted to defence so swiftly that alarm bells rang in every crevice of my mind. Perhaps it's unfair of me to say it but I think I may have been fed hook line and sinker in that fine tale of woe. I do know that this is Jan but that, I will have to remind myself, is all that I know. With a careful glint in her eyes she said noncommittally, "You could try me."

"Look me in the eyes as you answer." She nodded looking defiantly straight at me. "Did you have anything to do with Pat's disappearance?"

She blinked but held my eyes as she shook her head. "I should be insulted but I'm not. I understand that, being you, you have to know."

"Did Alec?"

This time she broke away angrily and hissed, "Don't be stupid!"

I let it hang for a moment while I wondered why I couldn't have been blessed with the ability to read the truth in people's eyes for I am sure there is more eloquence to be seen there than I am hearing from her mouth. "You seem awfully sure she is dead. Couldn't she have hopped on a train and left us all behind?"

The hair tossing shake of her head was emphatic. "No, By. Like I was just telling you we always think alike and there's nothing I can think of to explain her absence. If I can't think of it then neither could she. Something from outside her own thought process is responsible."

"You mean an accident?"

"An accident or maybe not an accident but definitely nothing that she planned herself. If any planning was involved it was by someone else." Her confidence of only a moment ago has melted away letting the ragged edges of her distress show again.

"If your thoughts are so much alike," I told her coldly, "then you should be able to mentally put yourself in her place leaving Hanson's and come up with some possibilities."

"I've tried, a dozen times a day and I just seem to get nowhere at all. I'm really dismayed," and she actually looked it. "Our minds were always in such harmony that I just can't cope with the blank wall that's there now when I try to think of her."

"If you were at the farm right now—imagine that you are—you're on your way home. Now, tell me what's happening." It didn't please me at all to goad her but if whatever she might know is not dug out of her now, while she needs my collaboration then I fear it will never be heard by anyone. For the first time ever I am seeing one of the twins twisted by indecision, she simply didn't know whether to cloud up and cry or to kick me on the shins, but wound up doing neither.

"I've been over this time and time again with Alec—but—alright, I'll play your game. What's the difference, maybe you will notice something we have missed. But it's short and it's simple because I was caught so totally unaware until way after the fact."

"It's cold," she said hesitantly. Then more firmly, "It was cold that night and if it were me I would hurry right along and I would stop in the engine room to warm up before going on home." She flung out her hands hopelessly, "but from there—nothing. I have no feeling at all and I shouldn't have told you that much because now you know how little I know. I can't help you By and it hurts to have to admit it—is something wrong?"

She asked because I had shivered violently for no reason at all. I tried to shrug it off. "No I'm just feeling that cold that you were telling me about."

"Well," she said, hauling us both up to the present, "how about it? We do have an agreement don't we?"

"Okay, Pat, it's a deal. I don't think you've told me as much as you could but I'm with you unless I find out that you've lied to me."

She was transformed, her cares seemed to fall away as she slapped her right hand into mine and we shook firmly on it. Too bad she had admitted to, 'going over it time after time with Alec because that leaves me feeling I've just been treated to a well rehearsed act. I can tell she is much relieved, too much I'm afraid.

But there was no relief for me, after she left I worried the rest of the day whether or not I had done the right thing in agreeing to go along with her. Finally I could see that it made no difference, one twin is still missing and until the details are known it can't matter the least which it is. Having put my doubts to rest on that part of the affair I allowed myself to consider the chill wind that had blown on the back of my neck when Jan, or I should say Pat, mentioned the engine room. Nothing could be more normal for a person habitually underdressed for the weather than stopping there to thaw out a bit on the way past so there should be no big reaction. It's just that the place has been altogether too popular recently. It's where our latest brush with our unknown admirer has taken place—it's where Tom's dog was shot and also where I found the can that may be a lead to unwinding this mystery. Now it's the last known connection with our lost twin—it's where she stopped to warm up on her way home Tuesday evening. I've no doubt but what that happened. I've seen enough of the twins to know that when one speaks of the other then that's how it is. The blank wall in Jan's—whoa boy, now get this straight, it's Jan who is missing. So—the blank wall in Pat's mind when she tries to follow her sister beyond the engine room is plain enough to me. When Jan left there her mind was no longer among the living. Or, I amended hopefully, merely not conscious to do any thinking.

So what is this telling me? That Pat—now known as Jan—poured the antifreeze into the oil drum and then died in some strange manner that has robbed us of her body? Really! I should be able to come up with a better theory than that in my sleep. But it's not impossible that the sabotage could have been instigated and even partly performed by the twins. They voted sell and lost. With Alec's help it would be simple for them to have pulled it off but that still doesn't account for the missing girl.

Albert is convinced that the oil was okay on Monday. Friday it's not. Tuesday evening while Jan is in or near the engine room her thought process ceases. Tom's dog is shot in the same area, also Tuesday evening, by an unknown party. Jan? Not much chance, she would just find a place to hide. More likely by someone crouched over her body desperate for time to think and panic stricken by Tom's approach. The shot that killed Lupe was a warning that may have either hit or missed its intended target but in any event bought time for body disposal and escape.

And if I keep this up the boys in white will be along soon to tote me away to a nice soft little room all my own in town. My day's work is done as long as I close my eyes to the rest of it—time for some relaxation.

So the week passed by with no more activity from our friend the enemy and only two new developments of any significance. The first is that a police officer came in on the night train and went back to town the next day on the local. After the nonchalance on their part when I phoned in, I was more than a little irked that he should suddenly arrive unannounced. I was peeved enough to point blank ask him, "How come?" He surprised me by being completely frank with me.

"There's been a development on our end that makes more information necessary. Information that is difficult to get over the poor phone connection you have here."

He probably means our party line because, mechanically, the phone usually works. I thought that was all I was going to learn but when I asked, "What sort of a development?" He wasn't reluctant at all to tell me.

"The body of a young woman, coming very close in description to your Miss Morrow, has been found near town. Now we need the photograph that you didn't send to us. Also the coroner has established the time of death so I will have to talk with all of you and determine exactly when she left here and why. Daughters of influential and wealthy men such as Mr. Morrow seldom just vanish for no known reason in mid-winter."

The coughing fit I nearly went into could have put us off the road. Wealthy man's daughter! Indeed! It seems we are to live in John's shadow even though he is long gone. And I suppose people, other than his banker, might look at Rainy Mountain and think him well off. At least they seem to have done some homework on the matter since I talked to them.

In the morning the Mountie talked to each of us one at a time in Tim's office which still serves as meeting room. We were all left with the vague and uncomfortable feeling that we have been submitted to some kind of a third degree but that smoothed out as he visited with us informally afterward. It didn't take long for him to satisfy himself—and us—that the woman in town had been dead for several days before Jan went missing. After that there was really nothing he could do that wasn't already being done, he knew it, Morrows knew it and even I can see I was expecting the impossible when I called them.

The trouble is he only got half the story. As I've said before these Morrows can be a strange lot, they will argue and bicker among themselves but let an outsider come nosing around and they close ranks on him, each one intent on protecting the others. Had he come on the local, in the daytime, he would have had us unprepared but coming at night and depending on us for room and board gave us the chance to be ready. I guess it was partly my fault too because after I found the officer an empty room for the rest of the night—as far away as I could arrange from the family area—I went the rounds awakening the entire family for an early a.m. meeting around Ember's big kitchen table. By the time the policeman got to us we had our ground rules firmly laid. He got none of the internal family squabbles nor anything about the sabotage problems though I am surprised he hasn't heard of that by other channels.

So, I, who called the police in the first place and expected miracles from them, am guilty of obstructing their investigation. At least so far as private family matters are concerned. As usual not so much as one thank you was offered. They all accepted it as entirely proper that I should warn them that the police have come and we must get our story straight.

The day after the Mountie went back to town his office phoned—Jennie took the call—to say that a commercial salesman who rode the train last week Tuesday had contacted them. He had just read of the disappearance in the paper and he remembered a pretty blonde girl travelling alone who went to the end of No. 8's run at Jasper. Unfortunately he didn't know where she got on, he thought McBride but wasn't sure because he had been sleeping as much as he could. None of the train crew remembered seeing her. "That's not our girl if only one man noticed her," I said as soon as I heard it, "anyway, most of the train crews would know her by sight if she was on their run." But the others ate it up, there was relief and glad smiles all around. Jan—now known as Pat—should know better but like me she said nothing.

The other development is ongoing. Ever since the news of Jan's disappearance, Ember has been going out of her way to be nice to me. I find it an interesting situation and if it weren't for that old stubborn streak I would let her use me in her campaign with Peter and take whatever opportunity might be offered along the way. Instead, I clammed up and pretended ignorance to her every advance. It was only after she coaxed and needled shamelessly trying to make me think that I wanted to take her to the New Year's dance that I lost patience and said sharply to her, "Lay off will you Ember! You know very well I can't dance and likely never will. Why should I want to take you to a dance?"

With a flash of anger in her eyes she snapped, "Well I guess Nick will be glad to take me!" then she flew off, back straight and head high, about the prettiest thing I have ever seen but I'm left wondering why I had to be so blunt and thoughtless. I hope she is now remembering, like me, the many times in the past when I asked her to go with me but she always refused? I know what it's like to be hurt and that does not make me feel good now. As for Nick—well—I'm not too worried. It would be such a complete turn against the grain for her that I can't see it happening. Oh, Nick would ask her alright, probably already has and been turned down but she would never go and ask him now. I'm sure.

I went to the dance anyway, partly out of spite to see if she managed to get Peter to take her. It's starting to look as though he is one of those fellows a girl should say no to until after the wedding. But there were other attractions at the dance too for someone as curious as I always am. For some reason, despite the weather, our New Year's dance always brings a lot of strangers we seldom see in camp—people we tend to forget about who are out there quietly doing their thing. They come from both east and west along the rail line and I guess, north and south out of the mountains too to a very small extent. They are from stump farms, small, one- or two-man pole- or post-cutting camps, trapper cabins and even the odd prospector breaking his winter nap. Quite a few find their way from smaller neighbouring communities that have no dance hall. Some come on the train and stay with friends here. Many of them have families as do some of the railway section men who also come. Some come on speeders or hand cars on the track, some walk for miles alongside the rails or on snowshoes out of the woods while a few manage to connect up with our logging roads and come by snowmachine and sled. By whatever means they use to get here the one thing in common is that they mingle and all seem to have a good time. I call them strangers because they only come our way a few times each year for supplies at the store or to make use of the post office. Once in a while they fall on hard times and the men or boys come in to hire on at the mill for a spell. They raise daughters too and on this long holiday week many of them are home from school or work and so they too are here at the dance. There might even be one or two who haven't heard about Ember's truck living overnight at my shack.

But our outlying neighbours suffer the same problem that we do. At high school age, while a few take correspondence, most of their girls go off to town and except for holidays like this are never seen again. Once finished school they take jobs in town and/or marry and forget about the boys back in the bush. Some of the boys go to school in town too but a lot of them come home for the mill or woods work thus compounding the problem—lots of men but just not enough women. They and their kin are all here tonight though and added to our own, thinned by the holiday, crowd they fill the hall to overflowing.

Peter is here ahead of me, holding a conversation with half a dozen other men standing in a small group nearly in the middle of the entry so that everyone arriving has to single file past them.

As I drifted by I overheard him telling about his moose hunt last fall. He's not a bragger but I was amused to notice he is improving on the truth in this instance. I moved on so as not to spoil his fun.

After I had been there watching proceedings for half an hour or so without once seeing Ember I decided to go looking for her. The crowd was thick enough to make it difficult. The benches along the walls are filled with people, some in animated conversation, others just there to watch and wait for the party due to start at midnight. Still the floor is packed with dancing pairs and the sound level is far above WCB acceptable standards. I wandered carefully down one side between the circling dancers and the feet of those sitting on the benches. I did not see Ember anywhere so I continued out into the kitchen where a few of the local ladies were loading up a coffee maker and seeing to other preparations for the feast to come. It's positively silent out here by comparison though the beat of music and dancing feet press through the wall and along the floor giving the impression that the whole building is bouncing in time to a merry tune.

I doubt they will miss the sandwich I filched on my way through and out the other door by way of the small room that passes as dressing room when a play is being done and into the hall again but on the opposite side. The kitchen was warm with its oil heat as I passed through but the rest of the place is still on the cool side. The main hall is heated by a big wood-burner in a tiny basement under one edge of the building, someone would have fired it up early this morning and fed it lavishly all day. But there was a lot of chill to thaw from a big building that has sat soaking in the cold for more than a full week. The outer wall where I sat down halfway along one side is still icy to the touch with a gob of frost on every nail head but all these warm bodies here tonight will soon have the place steaming. Small wonder the piano is forever out of tune. And lucky for us we have a man in camp who can take care of it. His latest idea is to put it on a wheeled dolly, widen one of the kitchen doors and put it in the warmth of that small room when not in use. He says it's that or get an organ instead or do without.

Peter has joined Allan and Erin just half a bench length away from me. Jo is there too and the four have their heads together laughing about some story Erin is telling. But still not a sign of Ember anywhere. Peter is obviously not the least bit concerned but I certainly am! I have been hopefully watching the dance floor but she's not to be seen there either. I am filled with feelings of guilt for the rude way I treated her when obviously she was needing my help. Maybe, like Gabrielle, she needs a friend while she sorts out a more serious relationship. But why do they have to pick on me for this role? Do they think I have no feelings? Do I look that safe to them? That's what brothers are for and I have no brotherly thoughts about her. That's a lost cause though because Allan and Tom are too caught up with their own families and business troubles, Tim might understand her but she looks on him with the same scorn that the others do. Undeserved scorn in my opinion, Tim's only failings are that—despite his age—he hasn't finished growing up and has no experience at doing anything on his own. Two of the worlds easiest solved problems. Anyway, Gabrielle will be back soon so Tim will be busy again with his own affairs of the heart. No, it would appear that, like it or not, I have been chosen as surrogate brother and that being the unpalatable case I had best go to her house and apologize. Perhaps it's not yet too late for her to come and—after all—I really should steal any march on Peter that I can.

But I sat back down with a thump that drew looks from the others on the same bench for Ember is just now coming in the outer door on the arm of Nick Martin. Now this is a surprise! This means she has gone and asked Nick or at least indicated that he should ask again! I glanced sideways to where Peter sat expecting to see the storm clouds gathering—but no such thing. He is watching but only with an indifferent sort of interest and not angry at all.

They left their coats and boots in the little rooms by the entrance and danced their way into the mainstream on the floor where I lost sight of them momentarily. In a while they were passing in front of me and Ember's cheeks are flushed as she is much too pleased with herself. Our eyes met briefly and I saw arrogant triumph in hers. She should have seen the devil himself in mine. She never looked my way again as they passed but they were always near the edge of the crowd where I could see them well. That's for Peter's benefit and I hope he is getting the message.

I can hardly wait for them to come my way each time around then I can barely stand to watch them go by. As they passed my position Ember smiled fondly at her date and he is positively dazzled with his companion. She is easily the most attractive woman in the hall and with her high heels, erect bearing and tall hairdo her smallness does not detract from that effect. In the glow of her beauty Nick has become the most handsome of the men and I am not the only one watching them. Every head in the place turns to follow them at least briefly and many turn then to Peter and some to me—wondering.

A small thing, for a long time she has ignored him, now, one date, one dance—should mean nothing. But, Tim came home describing her as impulsive, now Tim himself is dead set to marry a girl his sisters shoved at him only weeks ago. Terry went to Vancouver to take delivery of a new logging truck, took a day or two longer than expected and brought Jo home as his wife. If half the stories are half true then Allan's and Tom's marriages were classics of impulse. Allan and Erin seemed to move in different circles for the whole school year then the night Erin was taking the train out Allan was also up to the station separately and for reasons of his own. When he saw her ready to leave—maybe for ever—with her current boyfriend there to handle her suitcases he evidently said something like, "This won't do," and hauled her back down the hill before the train even came. I have to think she was willing but there seems to be no record of what the boyfriend thought.

Jennie noticed Tom alright and let him know it but he treated her for a long time just as Ember has treated Nick. Then, in the store, in front of customers and five minutes before the movie was to start, he asked her to go with him. Thoroughly miffed by then she refused. Tom blew up and loudly told her what he thought of girls who teased then shied away. When he finished she let out the breath she had been drawing in, offered her arm and said, "Let's go." The rest can be seen in the Morrow family album.

Look what one trip to town did for the twins and Alec!

Peter! What a fool you are! And, I guess, me too.

Finally the dance ended and people milled around while the musicians took a short break. Two of the ladies working the kitchen detail came along, one with a box of cups the other with coffee and tea for those who wanted to get started early on refreshments. Then, following them, a very young boy proudly bearing the cream, sugar and stirring sticks. But I couldn't face any, it would have made me sick for sure, my stolen sandwich has already turned several loops and become quite indigestible.

Ember and Nick were sitting down near the kitchen door on my side of the hall so that while I know where they are, I can't see them. They remained sitting through the next dance, thank goodness for small favours, it gave me time to settle my nerves and cool off around the collar. It was a respite that allowed me to control my emotions and return to my more familiar role of casual observer.

She danced with others and with Peter too but it was only when she waltzed past smirking at Nick that I really stewed. I should have gotten up and gone home but I was afraid I might miss something. I couldn't understand Peter's reaction for there simply wasn't any except once I caught him watching her thoughtfully and maybe even with approval. He must be supremely confident. It would serve him right if he lost her but not, I hope, to Nick.

I guess I shouldn't be surprised she could do this to Peter the way things have been on the stir between them but I am surprised to find myself so abruptly left outside in the cold. I seem to have offended her once too often and have dealt myself right out of her thinking. I know I was only a pawn in her game with Peter but even that was better than the way I feel now.

Shortly after the big bash at midnight I left to get Nightrider and meet the trains. When I came back down the hill I had no intention of returning to the dance but that's where my feet took me. Through the small sociable groups of men clustered here and there drinking stronger stuff than was being served inside. The bottles were out of sight as I passed but I knew they were there and everyone knew I knew. What a sham! But it seems to keep everyone happy except me. Now that John is not here perhaps this charade can gradually die a natural death. I stood for awhile just inside the door under the balcony, among a dozen others who also liked the shadows.

It was almost as though my return was the cue for Ember and her escort to leave. It's early yet by Rainy Mountain standards but they came along to collect their coats and boots and pushed their way through the crowd at the door. Ember brushed by without seeming to see me, her face now unnaturally pale and in very lovely contrast to her blue-black hair. It felt as though she was pushing a door closed somewhere in my mind as she passed and I didn't know how to keep it open or if I even should want to.

I stood alone, with friends and acquaintances passing by. I think I even answered their greetings but nothing much worked it's way through to me until I heard the loud cries from the steps outside.

"Fight! Fight!"

A bunch near the door rushed out en masse to see what was happening and I went along with the crowd hoping to find that Ember and Nick are well clear, but the first thing I saw was her truck still parked where it had been when I went to meet the trains. In fact the commotion seemed to centre around it. Edging through the crowd I reached a point where I could see a man on his hands and knees in the snow with blood streaming from his nose. He kept picking up a fresh handful of snow and holding it to his face but the blood still ran freely. There was a lot of derisive laughter and catcalls from the sidelines and I saw with some unkind satisfaction that it was Nick who was down in the snow.

"What happened?" I asked the fellow next to me.

"I won't guess at what started it," he chuckled, "but it was Ember did it. They got in her pickup and sat there a moment then the door flew open and she shoved him out. She had his arm up behind his back and she forced him right face down in the snow before letting go. Man, as he got up did she ever do a number on him! Went down like he was poleaxed—didn't have a hope. Guess it pays for a girl to have older brothers to teach her how to fight."

I can't begin to describe the warm thrill of pleasure and pride that went through me then. Where is she though? I pushed my way around the group toward the truck looking for her but she saw me first and called out. She was standing beside her truck hidden by a protective half-circle of men trying to look as if they stood there by accident. She seemed very small and helpless, shivering as though half frozen but her eyes burned with that now familiar blaze of anger. I fought down the most ridiculous urge to laugh. Who are they protecting? Ember or Nick! As I got closer she said, much too loudly, "By-ron! Take me home!"

I opened the driver's door of her truck and she climbed in then slid over to make room for me to get behind the steering wheel. She bumped her knees on the gearshift, lifted her skirt over the transfer case levers and sat staring straight ahead, rigid and silent, until we were away from the hall. Then she said in as small a voice as I have ever heard her use, "I'm not proud of the way I've acted tonight." I expect that is as close as anyone will ever come to hearing her offer an apology. I'm grateful she didn't accuse me of leading her into this night's devilment for she might well have done so. Her voice strengthened, "You would think I was a silly school girl who has never been alone with a man before. It wasn't his fault, he did nothing—just words, nice words but something snapped inside me and all I could see was red. I'm glad he went down so quick or I might have hurt him badly without meaning to."

"You don't have to tell me this, Ember."

"Yes I do! I don't want you thinking I'm such a ninny all the time. It could have been so much different with the right man."

The drive to her house was too short for the heater to start warming the cab but even so Ember seems to have stopped shivering. When I stepped out she maneuvered back through the levers, jumped to the ground beside me and grabbed my coat sleeve so tightly that I know she is still extremely upset. She pulled me around the house to the back porch, that is, she didn't loosen her hold on me so I had to go along or actively resist.

Inside the back porch at the kitchen door she let go and spun to face me, her back to the still closed door and the eyes I have always called grey are flashing wild, jade green messages at me. "You are supposed to carry me over the threshold—if you can!" No sympathy there! Just wicked, green eyed challenge. I swept her up, less gently maybe than I should have, shoved the door open and carried her in. Even before I had the door pressed shut she started kicking her feet violently. One boot stayed stubbornly on but the other, complete with the shoe inside, sailed a magnificent sweeping arc to and along the ceiling to score a direct hit on the light globe. Globe and boot crashed together to the floor leaving the bare bulb untouched and still working. The boot will live to see another day but not the globe.

'I will carry you right upstairs to your room, little lady, if that is the way you want it!'

If only I had said it out loud and followed words with action the rest of the night might have turned out more pleasant but—fatal flaw—I started wondering. Why is this happening? Why me? First Peter, thoughts of Nick, now me. What is she doing? Collecting us all as the twins have collected Alec? Sisters after all! As I lowered her to the floor, much more carefully than I had picked her up, I thought of a moonlit scene. Do I even want her? Dumb question, easily answered. But she is too fine-tuned to me at this moment and has read my hesitation, the light in her eyes dulled to grey and the magic is gone. Still, left alone, we might have worked it out as we stood face to face holding hands—almost a move of self-protection, at least it was for me—each trying to fathom the other's thoughts while guarding our own. Each afraid to let go yet unwilling to make a first move of any kind. Not even the sound of loud stomping steps on the walk outside as someone kicked snow from their feet fully distracted us though one back corner of my mind tracked the steps along the walk, to the porch door, to the kitchen door, and here is Peter.

His eyebrows shot upward, for him a great show of surprise as he took in the picture. Ember, standing hipshot, one foot high-heel booted, the other stocking-foot bare, the vagrant boot lying amid the wreckage of the light globe. Then he said mildly, "I thought you were alone, Em. When I heard what happened I came to see if you were okay."

He came damn quick was my uncharitable assessment!

She dropped my hands as if they were on fire—maybe they are—and ran to him just as she had in the store his first day here. As on that earlier day, he opened his arms to welcome her. I guess the right man had come. "Oh, Peter," she wailed into his jacket, then something more that mumbled out a little like, "What do I have to do?" Held against him she is so small—and yet—of the two I fear her the most. But it's a strange and tingly, almost anticipatory, fear mixed with many other emotions that have been clutching at me from the very first time I saw her—in the dark in a snow storm! My idea of her—the vision—is sometimes so much nicer than the reality.

I stepped around them feeling Peter's eye's boring accusingly into me over Ember's head as I left by the door he had just entered. If I get out of here quickly enough he might not realize how much he has interrupted but mostly I don't want to listen to the lies Ember will now have to tell him. It has worked out amazingly well for her, this must be very near to the best that she could have hoped for with Peter walking in on us at a very right moment. The timing of it all boggles the mind! How could she know for sure that he would come at all after his apparent indifference at the dance? Or when? Was I better bait than Nick? Maybe that's why she dumped him—no reaction from Peter. It must have all been an act played by ear just as Jan played out her act flawlessly the day of the Ski-doo party. A fellow could get hurt playing around with these Morrow girls! Many have! Nick did! And Alec? So, what else is new? I've known for years that they are dynamite on a short fuse. Beautiful, sexy and arrogant. They have grown up among a crowd of hard-working, healthy men mostly single and it has bent their thinking. Snap your fingers and any one of them is yours—punch him on the nose and he's gone!

What is new is my supporting role in her play for Peter and if he takes exception I may get my own lumps yet. I grinned bitterly though there is little humour in me right now. Let him try, he will find that while my legs may not be too agile my hands are. But my main advantage is in my head for I would feel no compunction to fight fair. Anything I can lay my hands on can be a weapon of some sort—a chair, a portable radio, an ashtray or bottle, all good clubs or missiles. Even a ballpoint pen used right and with the proper facial expression might set him back for second thoughts.

More dumb thinking! Chalk it up to the turmoil of the evening. He will never lift a hand to touch me—he will simply find some subtle way to make my life miserable if I let him. I tend to think of him as a physical type but that's only true when he's dealing with someone like Alec or Tom. The sadistic streak I have seen in him would be equally satisfied to dish out a beating of a different sort and I can cope with that too.

I must be the only one of my kind, I fumed. I doubt that any other man in the country has carried his girl over her threshold and then gotten off scot-free. And there lay my two major obstacles. First and foremost she is not my girl and I know it well despite tonight's antics. She has drilled that fact home to me at every opportunity. Almost as important it was, after all, her threshold and not mine. I don't think I suffer any qualms or delusions of pride about her being the boss's daughter or maybe even one of the owners. That doesn't bother me at all, if the bank so decides, she could be poor as a church mouse after the church has burned by this time tomorrow. And no less attractive. It's just that circumstances have made her tonight's aggressor, carefully calculating every move of every moment and that rubs a nerve end raw. I don't think it will do.

11

The first day of the new year and I spoiled it for all of us! The family gathering and dinner is to be held at Tom and Jennie's but unlike most of these family parties I'm not looking forward to it. Jennie, always stirring, will place me either directly across from or right beside Ember, a situation I usually find quite pleasant but not so today. Today I would just as soon not see her at all, for like her, I am not too proud of my conduct last night. Letting that remembered image from the first aid room ruin what had promised to be a beginning for us, letting Peter run me off without the least effort on his part. I am already willing to forget that I suspected her of carefully and coldly planning the whole incident. The memory of last night up to the time of Peter clomping in with his number twelves is just too enchanted to cloud with doubts.

I cleaned up my room a little while waiting for the right time to leave for Tom's place. I didn't overdo it though, I don't care for my surroundings to be too spotless, a little disarray left for seed is much more comfortable. Peter is reading in his room—with our doors both open I can hear him turning a page every once in a while. He has been quite abrupt with me this morning and that's different because he usually says what he thinks or hides it deep. But it's more like he is disappointed in me than angry so I guess I am to get off lightly for my transgressions of last night. He is a strange one in a strange bunch and my feelings toward him are equally strange. He is now my best friend and I don't understand how this has come to be. If it were not I might know better how to cope with him because at the same instant he is my worst enemy. I would trust him with my life but not with what he would demand of it once I owed it to him. I have fooled him into thinking there is more to me than there really is and it has backfired because he demands more of me than I want to give. There is no doubt in my mind but what he is the root of all my current troubles and I am only about half joking as I amuse myself turning over ways to bring about his untimely demise or at the very least, his departure for a distant address—Grise Fjord sounds about right. The problem with departure is double, first, even from the High Arctic he might come back or worse yet, Ember might go with him. So it will have to be demise. But we've already had one disappearance, if there's to be a second so soon it will have to be very smoothly done. Either an unquestionable accident or the body and all evidence must totally vanish leaving nothing behind except some plausible story. But how do you completely dispose of a human body short of having access to a super incinerator I pondered.

"The burner!"

I must have shouted it out loud because Peter's feet hit the floor and in a few long strides he was in my room peering out my window which, unlike his, faces toward the sawmill.

"What are you yelling about? You can't even see the burner from here with mall in the way. I thought the whole mill was on fire the way you were yipping."

"Peter," I said, scarcely daring to believe the flash of intuition that has struck and certainly unable to explain the line of reasoning that led to it. "Did you look inside the burner the day we searched for Jan?"

His first notion was to scoff but then all expression faded from his face and he answered tonelessly, "you have a point there. Get your boots on we'll have to check it out. What do we need? Shovels?"

I nodded, "There's no shortage of them at the mill."

The burner has two doors, one large enough to take in a front-end loader whenever the ash accumulation needs cleaning out but it's warped, heavy and always hard to open. We went in by the smaller, man-sized door that gives access to light the fire on the rare occasions it's allowed to go out. It's out now having been fed no slabs or sawdust for over a week. But there are still hot spots in the ashes that keep us wary and stepping carefully as we looked around inside this dark cavern where all the mill wastes end up falling from an overhead conveyor into the inferno that is normally where we now stand.

It's noticeably warmer in here, so the first thing I did was to shed my coat and toss it outside onto fresh snow well back from the bare dirt, sawdust and fly ash that surrounds the immediate perimeter of the burner.

"Looks like a big job for two guys, Byron, and maybe we need some light."

I looked up at the screened circular roof far above, it's small as compared to the floor area and I can see there's not a lot of mystery as to where the term 'tipi burner' has come from. In spite of the screen at the top and a lot of small holes and cracks scattered all around the sheet metal wall not much light filtered down to ground level. But we have just come in from a world of bright white snow to this one of sooty blackness and even as we discussed it our eyes are becoming accustomed to the gloom. "What we are looking for will be bone white and should show up plain enough," I said, instantly regretting my choice of words. "What we are going to need is dust masks," I added after turning a few shovelfulls of ash, The stuff is surprisingly hard-packed but a lot of fine dust rises from it just the same.

"I'll go for some," Peter volunteered.

By the time he got back my face already felt gritty and blackened with dust.

"You're stirring up an awful storm there, friend. She's only been missing a few days so if she's in here any bones should be right at the top." He is probably right, I have been digging like I was going to excavate the place. "Besides," he added, "it looks hot down there even though the mill hasn't run since Tuesday."

"Good thing it hasn't or we'd be on a wild goose chase. I don't know how much heat it takes to disintegrate bone but it must get hot enough to melt iron in here at times."

Ten minutes later he said, "We'll be at this all day and then some."

"We've got today, tomorrow, and Sunday before the mill starts up again."

"That's what I like about you, Byron, you always have a way of cheering me up." Then with only pause enough for a change of tone, "I think I've got something here!" What he has is a small pocket of very white ash, it's long and narrow and careful scraping uncovered more, but it's only fine powder and crumbly flakes.

"What is it, Byron, bone burned away to nothing?"

"I don't think it's anything from burning wood."

"Think there's enough left to tell what it is?"

"A laboratory could tell, I suppose. Maybe we need someone here who knows what he's doing. If this is what we think it is we might destroy it if we keep digging around."

"What's this over here?" While asking, he reached out to touch a small mound of ash and as it rolled over from the shovel's prodding it became very clear that we need look no farther. I have never seen one before but even though it shows hard usage I need no expert opinion to confirm that we are looking at a human skull. Peter sucked in one deep breath and without a word turned to march straight away to the clean white world outside. In spite of a faint hearted flutter in my midsection I had to have a better look before following him. There is no lower jaw in sight and the back half is missing but the upper front is enough intact to leave no doubt as to what we have found.

"You're a cool one," Peter complained as we walked away from the burner.

"Not really. After the first shock of recognition I just saw it as another old piece of bone like any you'd find out in the woods. The girl who used to live in it is long gone."

"Not for me she isn't. I watched that kid grow up and the last thing I expected from life was to have to attend her funeral. It just isn't fair, she was only beginning to enjoy living and suddenly she's gone."

"The twins have always enjoyed living," I said gently, "she has lived a fuller life than many people twice her age." For my part the last thing I expected from life was to have to watch this man break down emotionally and I think he's not far from it. "Do you think there's enough left for legal identification?"

"I don't know and I don't care," was his sullen verdict. "There's only one person missing around here so for my money it's Jan all right." A hard and suspicious edge came into his voice. "What I would like to hear right now is how come you knew we would find her in there?"

There really is no help for it. Anyway, a reckless mood has been hounding me all morning. "Ever since you walked in on Ember and I last night I've been trying to think up the best way to dispose of your carcass. The burner came to mind."

For the first time since I have known him he was set back on his heels and totally speechless. His mouth made a couple of starts but nothing came out the way he wanted until finally he said, "I guess I asked for that didn't I?" Then he got it all together and turned sarcastic, "I don't think I'll let you get behind me anymore when we're alone, at least not until you let me know I'm forgiven." The funny thing is, he seems now to be pleased with my answer. Like I said, he is a strange one.

We split up then, Peter going for Ember to accompany him to Pat and Alec's while I went to Allan's then Tom's to break the bad news. Then, after a while, I went to the office to call the police again. They are going to get tired of hearing from me I thought as I tried to get a connection. But the line is dead. Hard to say if the trouble is in our own phone, wiring or a bigger problem somewhere along the line. Not likely anyone will be out making repairs over this long holiday weekend either. I will try again later but for now we seem to be cut off from the rest of the world.

Eventually we all got together at Tom and Jennie's house and since we had to eat something sooner or later, Jennie served the meal that was intended for a happier day. There wasn't near the grief around the table that one would expect, so obviously I am not the only one who has been skeptical of the report we had been given about the blonde girl going to Jasper. We had, I guess, already gone through our initial period of mourning knowing in our hearts that she had to be dead. Today's discovery is only the confirmation.

Pat, who is really Jan, understandably shows the most strain and also an uncharacteristic desire to be near her brothers and sister. For the rest of us there is actually some relief in finally finding Jan, who is really Pat. Enough of that! I admonished myself feelingly, from now on this one is Pat while the one in the burner is Jan and I must not forget it.

Of course we discussed our discovery and there was ample speculation as to what might have happened but Pat is the only one with a possible explanation. "It's a long walk from the farm back home so when it's cold we always stop at the engine room to warm up. Once when the fire in the burner was down low we went inside but while we were there the pile of burning slabs toppled over and the fire roared up. If it had come our way we could have been injured or burned so we never went there again but she might have the other night." Then she told a story on herself, "I nearly went into the burner the hard way once. When we were younger we used to play around the mill while it was running and sometimes we would watch until a big slab or a cull plank was going up the conveyor then we would sit on it and pretend we were on a roller coaster. But this one time when I went to get off near the top my coat was caught in one of the conveyor chain links and I was stuck. Jan was pulling at me from the side and getting real scared but I managed to slip out of the coat and climb out onto the walk alongside the conveyor trough. Once I was out of the coat I was able to untangle it before it went over the end into the fire but I had to follow along right to the end of the wooden walk to where it's made of iron to stand the heat. Of course it wouldn't be any fun at all without that chance of danger."

"My God!" Allan snorted, "You girls were lucky to survive childhood." To judge by expressions around the table everyone would agree but it took Jo to ask the question that counted.

"How long ago did you last ride the conveyor?" From her tone of voice I have to think she knows something the rest of us don't.

Pat looked around the group defiantly then admitted, "A few weeks ago." I think everyone in the room cringed at least a little, I know I did.

"Well, there you are," exclaimed Ember, "she must have done it again and suffered a terrible accident." Heads nodded all around but I reminded myself that this girl we now know as Pat is the same one who so sickly peeled Gabrielle and I apart. She is a fast thinker and equally quick at putting thought to action. I see no guarantee that this story is not a well-ripened herring being dragged on a long string.

Around eight in the evening I said I was going home and immediately Ember jumped up to announce that she too was going home. With some trepidation I held her coat while she wriggled into it and off we went. It's been too cold to be worth starting a vehicle for such short distances on this day of no business pressure so we are all pedestrians tonight. It's hardly more than across the street to her house and we went halfway before either of us spoke.

"I'm glad it's all over," she said.

"I'm afraid it may be just beginning, there is sure to be a thorough investigation now."

She stopped dead in her tracks. "Investigation of what?"

"Of why she is in the burner. We have found her but we don't know the whys or wherefores, there have to be reasons." If she had shown less alarm I could have liked her more.

"I hope you aren't planning to say anything like that to the police!"

"I won't have to. I expect they will have plenty of questions to which the answers might be difficult for some of us."

"All we have to do is tell them the same as last time and they will go away like before only now we at least have her remains."

I nodded, my attention now divided between her and the uncomfortable knowledge that we are under a street light and in full view of everyone behind Tom's living room picture window. "It might happen that way if we are lucky. But we'll be no better off. We've still got someone running around causing us no end of trouble, cost, and heartache."

"That's a different matter, Byron, and there hasn't been anything done since the light plant was damaged."

"Maybe it's different and maybe it's all tied together, we just don't know."

"It might be better if we never learn as long as it has stopped. I think that when the phone comes back on it would be a good idea if you did not make that call to the police. We'll handle it ourselves."

"It bothers me no end the way you've all latched onto Pat's story like a badly needed crutch even though it may be nowhere near the truth. Jan might have been murdered for all that we know."

"Someone might be able to make it look that way," she agreed, "but there is absolutely nothing to gain by calling in the police. In fact they may do a great deal of harm." She had moved closer and spoken firmly and very clearly—glints of green beginning to sparkle in the grey. Remembering what happened the last time the green sparks flew I backed away step by step still too much aware of our probable audience. I had no answer for her so taking that correctly as refusal she followed me, two steps to my one, until I stopped and held my ground rather than be trod into it. Another inch and she is standing on my toes. "Byron, if you have any feeling for us—for Rainy Mountain, for me—then let it drop. In time you'll see it will be best if you don't call the police."

Anyway you slice it I'm caught between a runaway log truck and a bogged down bulldozer with my feet to the boot tops in gumbo. She has made no threat, given no order and promised nothing, yet I feel that everything I could wish for in my future is hanging on my answer.

Until this moment there has been only one person in the world for whom I would set aside my own stubborn principles. Her father. The man who after an honest hesitation welcomed me without obligation, not only to his town and table but into his family as well even though every sighting of me must have reminded him of his own dead son. Only since he has been gone have I started to see the enormity of my debt. Now it seems that somewhere along the way some strange form of osmosis has been at work extending that loyalty to the daughter as well. But loyalty is one thing, maybe triggered by obligation as much as more admirable motives, trust is something else and comes from deeper inside. There I seem to have the same problem with her as with her stepbrother, that is, I would trust her with my life but I would not want her given free rein to tamper with it.

"Okay. I just hope that, as you say, it turns out right." That's what I said but it's not all that I wanted to say!

"It will! I'm sure you will never regret this decision." With that observation she smiled, took my hand and led on. She knows me too well. She knows that having been cornered into making a promise I will keep it. To her way of thinking this little crisis is now past and already there is laughter trying to hide in her voice as she reassures me, "Don't worry, I won't drag you in and embarrass you again." But the look she gave me was full of questions and the green is gone.

So. Her passion tonight is only for her precious family pride and not for me. At her gate she let go and waggled her gloved fingers good night. At least there seem to be no hard feelings for last night.

I stood still and watched until she passed from my sight at the back of the house. Such a weird, mixed up procession of thoughts are working their way through my head. If only I could see that she disliked me I could have written her off and forgotten her long ago. Instead, I sometimes think she likes me rather too well considering circumstances. Certainly I am the one she looks to when she needs help— someone to be used to bring events around to her liking. She uses me as a cushion between herself and her brothers and sisters too and I have to admit they all get along better with a third party in the middle. She has led them into believing I am her one and only intended and the reason she does not pursue romance elsewhere. She also uses me as a pawn between herself and Peter. Not nice.

"Good night, Miss Ember," I said under my breath, "There is a day of reckoning coming up soon between you and I and friend Peter but since you may be the prize, don't expect me to play the game entirely by the book."

My intentions thus stated, be it only to myself, I feel I am entering a new phase of my life. For years I've been infatuated with the girl despite the danger to my peace of mind that she represents. But all to no avail. Then along comes Peter and that's the end of it. Right? Only it's not! It's more like the beginning. Because now, as I keep warning myself, she is playing games with me and the funny part is, trust her motives or not, I'm starting to like it. 'So watch out, Pretty Girl, I'm in this race too now!'

I had a passenger up to the train for a change later the same night. Nick, complete with two eyes wonderfully black in sympathy with his badly swollen nose. So much has happened since the dance last night that I had forgotten about him. It seems more like a week ago that I sweated blood watching him waltz Ember around the dance floor. I don't know what to say to him, I certainly feel no animosity now, in fact I feel he's been victimized as much as myself by our unfathomable Miss Ember. She certainly played a nasty game with him and I'm no longer quite sure if it was for Peter's benefit—or mine.

"It's broken," he said, indicating his nose, "I know it is, I'll need a doctor to check it or it might heal crooked."

"When will you be back?"

"I won't be back." When I didn't ask why, he continued, "How could I when I've been beaten and humiliated by a slip of a girl you would have to dip twice in the log pond for her to weigh much over a hundred pounds. Right in front of all my friends too! No, there are simply no words for it and nothing to do except to go some place where as few people as possible know me and let this all blow over. When it's a girl doing the punching a fellow just can't hit back. Anyway, by the time I could believe I was in a fight it was all over.

"The main reason I hired on last fall is I heard the girls out here were all pretty and half wild as well but no one warned me that assault and battery was one of their hobbies. What really spooks me though is the way she waited there all set to give me more had I been stupid enough to get up but so sure of herself that she was going to let me get up before nailing me again."

While we waited for the train I did my best to convince him that a run-in with a Morrow girl was nothing unique and not to be ashamed of. That no one before him had ever won a round with them either. I even promised him a raise in pay perhaps on a production bonus basis. Peter would be torn between laughing at me or skinning me alive if he could hear me now. A few hours ago I would gladly have packed this guy's suitcase for him if it would have guaranteed his absence. Now all I can think of is that the graveyard shift is going to be a sick goose without him. At least Ember should understand where the fault lies. He did get on the train saying, "maybe," and sounding less like the victim of a mugging.

Once home in bed I am finally free to consider the pact I have entered into. For possibly the first time in my life I am party to an act that has to be outside the law. It frightens and disturbs me just to think of it, I don't see how it can turn out for the best as Ember claims it will. The more I think of it the more sure I am that it was no accident, someone is getting off the hook here and I don't like that. I'm also sure that Ember and all the rest are afraid of an investigation simply because their precious family pride will take a beating if one of them is accused or suspected of murder. They are all tarred with the same brush to some extent where pride is concerned. Better to leave it as it is with the official opinion being that Jan has run off, and the acknowledged explanation within our own closed circle being that she has met an accident. I am the only one who will have trouble living with it. There is just one bright spot and that is there will be no inquest. If there were and each of us questioned then I reckon we would all commit perjury by lying while under oath.

It gradually comes to me that my promise to Ember isn't so all encompassing—I have only promised to not inform the police—I haven't promised to keep my own nose out of it. I have some solid evidence but it's no good to me without the services of experts in finger prints and ballistics and that means the police so I'm blocked there.

Or maybe I'm not! Only Ember knows I won't go to the police. Perhaps some bluff with the others will get results of a sort. I will have to try something for I will not be able to live with myself if I don't find out what has happened. It's curiosity sure, but it's more than that, I was born curious but I was raised to be law abiding and I'm heavily burdened with an oversized conscience to cope with.

As for Ember's statement that we would take care of it ourselves, I expect I know exactly who is going to have to do the dirty work in the morning. At least we were all able to agree that the next step must wait until morning because lights seen around the burner at night could spell lots of trouble for us.

In the morning, to my surprise I get all kinds of help. The store is to be open today but Jo takes care of that while Ember, who refused to be diverted from this and Alec gave me some very steady assistance in the burner collecting anything that appears to be bone remnants. It all goes into an intricately carved cedar box made years ago by Allan but supplied by Jan-Pat who wanted no part in this so is waiting at home for us to pick her up later. We are a silent threesome as we work—there is no unnecessary talk the way there was yesterday when Peter and I were here. Alec must be tormented with memories, doubts, and lord knows what. For Ember it must be hard too but she doesn't handle it as well as Alec, her cheeks are awash from the word go and her breath is a bit ragged at times. But they are a game pair and by the time we are finished I have more respect than ever for both of them.

The sawmill burner is in a good location for secrecy on a day like this when no one will be wandering around the working areas. Not a soul was near us when Alec loaded the box onto Cossack while I added a wadded up tarp carelessly tossed over it just in case. The three of us climbed in and I drove around to collect Pat then up to the switchback where there are already two pickups parked. This is asking for trouble, I thought, leaving our trucks parked here. But if the unexpected does happen and someone comes up the road maybe they will think we are honouring the family dead on this holiday weekend and leave us alone.

The high bank pushed up by the snowplow is so hardpacked that we left no footprints showing on it. When we jumped down the other side our wallowing trail in the deep soft snow is hidden by that same high pile that we just climbed over. We are that quickly in a different world, one of snowy trees leaning over a narrow unplowed road and the deepest silence I have ever listened into.

At the cemetery the others, except for Jo, still busy holding the fort at the store, are waiting for us their part of the job already done. Peter is off to one side at his parent's headstone—alone. There is hardly even a bump in the snow to show the place so he is there only because he knows where they are.

Despite the long spell of cold weather the earth is soft and unfrozen under the snow just as I had expected earlier when Tom asked me to tend to Lupe. For all that we have to put in the ground a full-sized grave is not needed anyway. I see they are going to put her right beside Terry and I wondered what Jo would say to that. Of course by the time Jo needs a place up here Terry should be ancient history in her life and that made me sad too.

Peter spoke quietly for us and did well while I, the unrepentant and suspicious sinner, managed to stand where I could watch them all. I watched for anything—any sign of guilt—not enough grief or too much. But as in the burner with Ember and Alec I saw nothing except what should have been. Every one of them was uncommonly sombre just as they should be except for Pat who trembled close to breakdown and that also seemed right. It looked right to me in more ways than one—a little care with the sod; a bit of wind and snow and no one need know there is a new grave in this snow swept, hillside meadow. We have tramped down and dirtied an alarming big area and looking around I can't imagine how we could have been so unthinking and careless. But it probably doesn't matter, the first snowstorm will blot out every track. No one else presently living in Rainy Mountain has kin buried here so small chance that anyone will come around. In the spring some tending should keep it reasonably concealed until new grass hides all sign. As time passes we can openly express doubts about Jan being alive and very properly erect a monument to her memory. No one but us will know that a twin really does rest here and only I will care that this is all very illegal. Yet even I am quite satisfied with what we have done.

Most of the men stayed to fill in the grave while Ember and I took Pat and Alec to their home. But we were too slow getting started—at the sight and sound of lumps beginning to fill in the grave Pat had fallen over an edge so that Alec had to carry her to the truck and from the truck to the house. Then I dropped a subdued Ember and Cossack at her place. She offered to make coffee for us—said she had fresh cookies and bread. And that's all it was—coffee, cookies and quiet talk. After a while Peter came in looking like he needed some friends so we drained the pot then another and it was quite a while before I hiked along to the office.

There I slouched into a chair and plunked my feet on the middle of the desk that gave the best view out over the mill yard. When I am alone here I never worry about whose desk I take over, I just pick the one with the view I want. I love to sit here, especially alone at night with the inside lights off while the mill and planer are working and the log yard is receiving and sorting. The two-way radio behind me alive with instructions, communications, and no end of idle if meaningful chit-chat. Watching that organized activity is good for the soul as long as I can do it at my leisure. It lets me think about how accidental it is that sometimes things go right, how incompetent we are in so many ways, how small we really are in the scheme of things. But now it's better yet with not a turning wheel in sight nor any machine making noise. To think that on Monday morning a handful of people who keep secrets to themselves including one who, I think, keeps a desperate secret—people who can hardly stand the sight of each other at times yet who each defend the others against any outside threat will gather here. They won't admit that their breakfasts were hurried or skipped as they growl good mornings, grumble what must be the right words to the foremen who come for orders and the whole thing is in movement. Beautiful concerted action that produces logs from the woods, rough lumber from the logs, finished dry lumber into the rail cars, and cheques in the mail. I find it awesome and when I am alone I can lose myself in the pure drama of it.

For someone like myself who has never wanted much from life—never been inclined to work very hard and when faced with a difficult choice always slips aside to whatever way is easiest—it is heady stuff. It wouldn't do to get hooked on it. What little I do I like to do well but I also make sure that's as little as I can get away with.

By the time the last misty wisp of my imagination drifts away the sun is gone behind the mountain that keeps us shaded for many hours of each winter day. From the blank spot in the back of my mind has come the understanding of what I must do. I must call a meeting—present my guesses as if I know them to be facts—make threats to the point of blackmail and see who breaks out in a sweat.

If that won't work then I am at a loss as to what might but this will have to do for a start, if more is needed I'll play it by ear. I neither need nor want everyone at my meeting. Ember must not hear of it for she would fight me every inch of the way. Jo is not needed because in my opinion she is not a suspect and might just decide to put a bug in Ember's ear. Jan/Pat is a suspect but I don't want her present. She is too smart for me and if she is guilty I think I can get at her through Alec. She's not likely to come anyway because she has not attended a meeting since signing over to Alec. I guess the brothers are too smart for me too but at least they have been dulled by overwork, worry and routine to a point where I like to think I can handle them. Tim also is not a suspect but it will be difficult to get Tom here without him now that they live in the same house and eat at the same table. But it's okay, Tim can come, he's not likely to do any damage.

The others are the ones I want, Allan, Tom, Peter and Alec, and the way to get them here will be to track each one down as late this evening as possible and tell them that we have a meeting at 9:30. Nine thirty because by then Ember will be gone home. Each of them will think that Peter has called the meeting and will come without question. Peter will be different, I will simply have to tell outright that for a change I am calling a meeting and count on him showing up to see what is happening. He is the only one I feel it necessary to tell that the women are not wanted this time.

Now that my plans are made the easy part is over and I find I must leave my comfortable nest to take care of another chore that right now appears to be necessary. One that involves calling at the homes of all my suspects, and will need some luck.

Alec is the first to show up for my meeting but Tom is only a few steps behind and as I expected, Tim is with him. Allan is so punctual that once again I have to suspect him of coming early so he can stand outside the door until the exact moment to enter.

Peter has these people so used to attending these impromptu meetings that so far no one has asked why we are gathering. After the events of the last few days, and knowing what is in store for tonight, sitting here listening to them crack jokes sets me very much on edge as I wait and wonder if Peter will show up. He had done no more than raise his eyebrows when I told him that I wanted his presence here tonight. Nor had he commented when I added that I didn't want any of the women to hear about the meeting. He just nodded his head to help hide the questions that had come on behind his eyes.

About the time I decided it's going to be a lame duck meeting without my #2 suspect, light steps of an easy walker in the hall came closer and materialized into Peter at the doorway. He looked around, saw that everyone expected is already here and closed the door behind him. "I don't know how you've managed to call a meeting without Ember getting wind of it but it looks as though you have pulled it off. She's gone home."

"A bit of luck," I agreed, not bothering to comment that Ember misses a lot of what is under her nose.

Before anyone thought to question that exchange he went on, "Since this is your meeting, you sit behind the desk where you can see us all and for a change of pace I'll stay out here in the audience." If he is having fun at my expense at least he held a straight face while I shifted myself over behind the desk. "Now maybe you can tell us what you have on your mind."

He could only have shown less interest if he had managed a

yawn right then so I snapped him out of it in a hurry. "Maybe we can start with you telling us what you had on your mind while you were sneaking around camp at two a.m. the night that Jan was killed."

His eyes came fully open and he jerked his feet in close as he came erect on his chair. I had caught the others napping also but they are all awake now.

"That's none of your business!" But he is so surprised at my nerve that he sounds quite meek—for him.

"That may be so," I admitted mildly looking around at the others, "maybe I'll apologize some day but don't sit there expectantly holding your breath. Now that I have everyone's attention I'll set out some guidelines for this meeting. By the time I finish here tonight some of you are going to want my hide, I'm hoping that others of you will see fit to defend me, otherwise I'll just have to do the best I can." As I said this I casually slid a twelve-inch crescent wrench out of my hip pocket where it has been riding with considerable discomfort and laid it within easy reach on the edge of the desk. Every eye in the room followed that movement but no word was spoken. I may be laying on the melodrama a bit thick but I want them in a mood to sit there and take it on the chin.

"Now, I'm going to lay it on the line for you the way I see it. I want a minimum of interruptions until I finish and then we'll talk it over. The subject is twofold—Jan and the damages we have been suffering lately to our equipment."

Hardly started and already Tim interrupts. "Are you saying you think Jan did all that?"

"Anything is possible but no, that's not what I'm saying. What I mean is I believe there is a connection, I think that Jan could have told us something and that's why she's dead. We know that she died Tuesday evening, maybe in the burner, maybe in the engine room but for sure somewhere around the mill."

"That's solved, Byron," Allan objected. "It's plain that she was fooling around the burner or the conveyor and got into trouble."

I shook my head, "That was a nice handy story Pat told us but it doesn't necessarily have any bearing on the actual situation. One of the very few things we do know about that evening comes from Pat and also Alec's mother who both say that Jan was nicely dressed and wearing her new coat. That says to me that she wouldn't willingly step into a sooty, smoky old burner or go joyriding on a conveyor chain. Together, the sky was the limit for those girls but alone, a rare occurrence until Pat's marriage, they tended to be more ladylike. Anyway the conveyor wasn't running that night because the mill was shut down."

Tom wasn't prepared to concede that point. "All you have to do is push one little button and the conveyor runs independent of the rest of the mill. She could have done that easily and there's usually no shortage of junk material around to throw in and take a ride on. I can remember doing things like that myself years ago.

"But only the light plant was running at the time, if one of the big mill units had been started we would have heard it all over camp. Allan?"

He nodded, "That's right, the light circuits in the whole mill can be, and often are, powered by the light plant but the motor circuits, and the refuse conveyor is one of them, require at least one of the big sets to be started."

"Okay," I said, gratified to see they are showing cautious interest. I think they wouldn't mind knowing the truth as long as it goes no farther than this room should it turn out one of their own is involved. Allan and Tom in particular seem interested in hearing more. "Jan is killed at the mill, I believe in or near the engine room on Tuesday evening." I didn't try explaining that the main reason I am mesmerized by the engine room is because of Pat's loss of mental contact at that point. I find it easy to accept and believe but I don't want to have to explain and defend it.

"Lupe is shot, also on Tuesday evening, as Tom walks toward the engine room. Actually he was going to the boathouse but that may not have been the way it looked to someone seeing him coming."

"We also know that sometime between Monday afternoon and Friday, Christmas Day, the last known act of sabotage was committed; once again in the engine room. I don't see it being too far-fetched to assume that all these activities are likely to be connected."

I held up a hand to stop the next interruption which I could see coming from several quarters. "As you all know, the light plant broke down because of antifreeze in the lubricating oil. What you may not realize is that all the oil stored in the engine room was okay on Monday. I know that because on Monday Albert Jacobs changed oil and filters in the light plant engine and it then ran nearly a week trouble-free so obviously nothing was in the oil then. Now, on Christmas Day, Albert added a gallon to the little electric set, drawing oil from the same barrel on the drum rack that he had used on Monday for the oil change. It must have been nearly straight antifreeze that he added because it was no time at all when the engine seized up. This happened Friday and must mean the oil has been tampered with sometime since Monday—why not Tuesday evening?"

"You're whistling in the wind."

"At least I'm whistling, nobody else is trying."

Allan broke in with his usual bit of foot-in-mouth disease. "If Jacobs poured the stuff in maybe he's our man, after all he should be able to tell the difference between oil and antifreeze." Everyone looked at him. "No! Forget I said that, we all know Jacobs wouldn't do anything of the sort but he still should have noticed the difference. He has to be guilty of negligence at least." Calm dependable Allan, always the first to put his mouth in gear without starting his brain. Just don't count on him being as simple as he makes himself look and sound.

"The light isn't too good in that back corner, Allan, once the oil is in the pouring can you don't see much of it with that funnel top and spout arrangement in the way. He would judge 'full' more by weight than by sight and the noise in there would keep him from noticing the different sound of the splash. Maybe the can would have filled faster than normal but it is warm there and the oil stays thin and fluid. Besides, Christmas dinner was waiting."

My defence of Jacobs was hardly needed, the man is held in high esteem here even by Peter who added, "I don't think Albert's eyes are too good at close range and he hates to put his glasses on."

"Now if we can get back on track here and confine ourselves to Tuesday night and concede that the oil has just been doctored by either Jan or an unknown person and then something transpires that leaves Jan dead. Either Jan poured the antifreeze and got caught or she caught the culprit in the act and paid the price."

"Wait a minute now," Peter said indignantly, "this sounds like you are connecting Jan's death with our troubles down river. Let's not forget that we're only talking about a few machines damaged and a little two-bit outfit that may or may not be up for grabs. Nobody, least of all the owners of L&N, would conspire to murder over a little deal like this."

"So, it's no big deal, is that what you are saying?"

"That's the way I see it. It might seem big to us but to them we are no more than a minor flea bite. At least that's the way I see it if you are thinking in terms of murder."

Not long ago I would have argued with him but since meeting the L&N owners on one of my town trips I have had to revise my estimate of them. I still see them as hardnosed, greedy business men but they are also the type who have a healthy respect for the law or better yet—a healthy fear of it. Their intentions may, in some roundabout manner, be responsible for our trouble but they would think hard before setting anything criminal into motion. I too am confident there will be no way of tying them to Jan's death. "I guess I have to agree with you basically as far as the L&N slant is concerned but we can't rule out the chance that monetary gain in some form is behind all this, directly or indirectly. How much is our timber quota worth?" He wouldn't answer so I told them, "I know it depends on the deal arrived at but I guarantee there are no peanuts involved when you calculate the value. We're talking millions if we get out of our present troubles to where we can talk turkey with a serious buyer. Many people have been killed for much less and she is dead or will you argue with that too?"

No one does.

"All right, we now have the oil adulterated and Jan dead on the floor. The next thing that happens is Lupe is shot as Tom approaches. Actually he was heading for the boathouse but whoever was in the engine room, by now with the lights turned off and the door open to look around, wouldn't know that so he or she panicked. And for good reason, there he is crouched over Jan's body still wondering what to do and here comes Tom. He could have shot Tom but that would mean double trouble, two bodies to get rid of and two people gone missing so he shot the dog instead and bought time by turning Tom back."

"Now suppose you end the suspense and tell us who is in the engine room doing all these fun things," Peter suggested.

"Unfortunately I can't do that, but I can tell you who the most likely candidates are and why."

"Maybe it would be better if you just keep it to yourself, things are bad enough now. Why make it worse?"

"Worse, Allan? It can't get worse, we have murder and sabotage aimed at breaking us. We've got to stop whoever it is before they stop us." I looked around at them a moment as though I couldn't believe what I saw. "Here we are! Your sister has been killed and you would have me believe you just want the whole affair hushed up? You don't want her killer caught?"

There was a long, long silence, even Allan thought it out before he said carefully, "What you don't understand is that it could be made to look like one of us is the guilty party, that's why it's best to leave it alone. No matter what we do we can't bring her back as much as we would like to. The next best thing is to cause a minimum of fuss and hope we can avoid further trouble. If the police are satisfied that she ran off to Alberta then let's leave it that way."

"You and Ember must be reading the same book," I muttered. "What if you are the next one we have to plant up on the hill? And maybe Erin and the kids with you?"

You could see it was a thought he didn't like but he played it down. "Then I should be able to rest in peace knowing that you will leave no stone unturned to bring our assassin to trial."

They are too much for me! They have already led me off on half a dozen tangents after I told them I would allow no interruptions. "I can't do it your way Allan, I'm not made like the rest of you, to me right and wrong and justice are big ticket items in my life. So is loyalty and there lies my problem, loyalty says to follow your lead no matter what." I nodded in general to the group, "You, collectively are my employer and individually my friends. I want what's best for you, that's why I've conspired with you to obstruct the police even though, paradoxically, it was me who thought it necessary to call them in the first place. But I've gone as far as I can, Jan too was my friend—if she was murdered then I want someone to pay. It's time for the truth."

Tim applauded. "Hear! Hear!" He jeered, but none of the others joined him.

After a moment I went on, "But there is some middle ground, a compromise is available to us. The guilty party can confess right here and now and explain the exact circumstances, then we decide if it's a family matter or one for the police."

"You're setting yourself up as a little tin god are you?"

"No, I'm not, Peter. I said we, not I. I mean this group decides whether to hand it over to the police or to sit on it."

"You have to be out of your mind if you think one of us killed Jan deliberately and even farther out if you expect, assuming that were true, that the guilty one would admit it.

"Alright, we'll take it a step farther and I'll show who had opportunity and motive. Opportunity is easy, every last one of you has access to a pickup day or night. No problem to run out the logging road any night there was no fresh snow to leave tracks in or enough coming to cover your tracks, do the dirty deed to some skidder or crawler and be back home in an hour or two. All you had to watch for was to avoid me while I was meeting trains."

"Motive is a little more complicated but every one of you is richer on paper than when Jan was alive. Except Alec," I amended. "I must confess to trouble seeing that as being the cause. I see it as more likely that one of you took matters into your own hands when you caught her red-handed or conversely, when she caught you red handed. That old Morrow code of self-help ethics might have called for instant justice."

I paused but no one picked it up. "I find it very interesting and significant that no one has suggested the culprit is a man from bunkhouse row or the married quarters perhaps hired by L&N to cripple us. I see that as tacit admission that we all know we are dealing with one of our own. But just to clear the air I'll touch on the subject of outsiders as I will call them even though some have been here a long time. In the first place, I've had a big change of opinion on that subject myself and I no longer see any credibility in the idea at all. I can't see any of them in such a position of trust to be hired by L&N for such an audacious affair. As Peter implied the directors of L&N are business men, and good ones, not criminals. They would never run such a risk for any kind of gain when there are more legal ways to crush us. All they need to do is to put their minds fully to the matter. Secondly, if an outsider were to do this they would have to run a terrific risk just going to the parking area and taking a truck, not once but many times. If anyone at all were to see them their goose would be cooked, while if any one of you were seen about at night it wouldn't be a bit out of order. At one time or another all of you except Tim have faced emergency situations that have kept you out and about all night or nearly so. If I were to see one of you bombing around in a 4x4 in the middle of the night I wouldn't give it a second thought. I might not even remember it later."

"There are exceptions though," I looked Peter in the eye. "When I find someone running about on foot trying to avoid discovery at two a.m. or thereabouts it rouses my curiosity."

"That was long hours after Jan was killed if your own timing is to be believed."

"Yes, but that doesn't let you off the hook because you could have been out taking care of unfinished business that you had no time for earlier." He gave me a wide grin that could mean anything. "As to motive, you told me yourself that the twins were your favourites or words to that effect, you care deeply for them by your own admission. You identify with, and are proud of them, but you also showed me that you could be disturbed beyond reason by their actions and apparent lack of morals. I'm now suggesting that their blatantly open two-way takeover of Alec has snapped your usually sensible mind and you have removed one of them to end the whole embarrassing affair."

The dead silence following that accusation was not broken until Peter grinned, a little weaker this time. "You'll have fun proving that."

"I may not have to," I told him and then forgot him for the moment. "I'm going to eliminate Tim quickly here because I see no motive, nor opportunity either since Tim running around at night would be as obvious as any of the outsiders.

"Tom—same thing as Tim where motive is concerned, I've never seen any indication that either of you care a hoot how your sisters run their lives. You had opportunity, perhaps the best of any of us since your position as woods manager gives you unquestioned access to every machine out there day or night. But you, Tim, and the twins were together on the sell vote so I can't see any conflict. Also, the fact that it was you and your dog who were shot at would seem to establish you as just another victim."

"Allan, I haven't heard you chastising the girls either but there was an incident right here in this room when you threatened to kill anyone who engineered a sellout. You might have gotten smarter since then, turned quiet about it, and have now started a program of elimination or reduction of those against you. Actually just the removal of Jan means that you have a secure majority in any future ballot without having to count on my vote which might be disputed." I can see the colour rising up his neck and into his face but he seems determined to wait it out and let me pass on to the next on my list. "Getting out to the woods would be a little more risky for you than the others since your job is supposed to keep you around the mill and planer yards but as long as you avoided my schedule and picked slack times on the haul road I see no great difficulty for you. Especially since all the new pickups look the same and the truckers and any night service crews are used to both Tom and Alec tearing around without calling their position over the radio."

"You're forgetting that I was here with you when Lupe was shot and Tom came to tell us about it." He kept his voice amazingly mild, he's not nearly as upset as I had hoped to make him. All these hot tempers and tonight, I can't rouse a one of them.

"That had me stumped," I admitted, "until I remembered Tom telling how he crouched beside Lupe wondering if there was to be a bullet for him too. Then how he started to the house to get you but when he was on your doorstep he remembered we would all be here in the office so he had to retrace his route. That would have given any or all of you plenty of time to make whatever detours were needed and be here long before Tom arrived,"

Alec has been sitting loosely in his chair but as the silence lengthened he pulled himself upright. "I guess I'm next, eh, Byron?" There is the shine of sweat on his face though if anything, the room is a bit on the cool side.

"I left you until last Alec because I think you are the man we want. I can't imagine what would lead you into the sabotage part unless it was the girls egging you on for their own reasons. But Jan's death has got to have resolved an otherwise impossible situation for you. At first it was probably fun and exciting having two pretty girls falling all over you but it must have paled rapidly as you felt yourself being pulled apart by them. To the rest of us they seemed to be willingly sharing you but I'm betting that in truth each of them would want all of you. You must have been living in agony at times, so much so that it would soon seem the greatest relief imaginable to be rid of one of them. The only question I have for you now is—did you know which one you were killing?"

He is a man in tumult, his eyes showed guilt if ever a man's did. The others saw it too and each showed his own individual reaction, disbelief, shock, angry wonder, and Peter—deadpan.

"I never did learn to tell them apart, they made certain of that. As far as I know there was never any trouble between them, just between them and me and you're right, I was at my wits' end, they were driving me crazy. In time I would probably have blown a gasket and done—something—to one or both of them. Jan's death tears me apart because morally I am guilty as sin. It makes me so glad that I cry and so sad that I laugh but I swear to you, Byron, I had nothing to do with any of it!"

I was afraid back at the beginning when I planned this confrontation that I would prove too soft-hearted for this role. Now here it is, he spoke with such imploring sincerity begging for understanding that I cannot bring myself to disbelieve him. To cover my own confusion I pretended to ignore his protest and pressed on with my next theory. "There is another possibility, remote but not impossible and that is that Pat did the job herself to remove the competition for Alec." I watched Alec carefully, quite sure that if this is the way it happened then he will know about it or at least have his suspicions and he is in a poor frame of mind right now to hide the truth. "All that togetherness we have interpreted as great love could have turned into equally great hatred and murder once the big chips fell into place. If she needed help she could call on Alec, after all, it solved all his problems too."

It's also possible that my good friend Ember knows a great deal more than she should about this but that's not for public discussion. If nothing works out here then I may or may not follow that line.

"You're a way out of sight," Peter declared, "you would have us believe the killer, assuming there is one, is huddled in the engine room with Jan's body before him and a rifle in his hands with which he has just shot Lupe to keep Tom at bay." He paused to let us get the picture and maybe to get it a bit clearer himself. "Now, in the little while, fifteen minutes at an outside most, that it would take Tom to get moving, go to the houses and back to here, you expect us to swallow the notion that he could come up with the idea of the burner, carry her body to where she would somehow wind up where we found her and still beat Tom to the office to be present for our meeting? Talk about risk! That sounds pretty far-fetched to me. As for Pat doing it she's not big and strong enough to have carried Jan any distance let alone uphill on the conveyor walkway."

"To that I can only say that the killer was desperate and thinking hard, adrenaline flowing freely and all that. Whatever else you may be you are all fast thinkers though some of you go out of your way to be sure other people miss that fact. The plan may already have been decided on before Tom showed up and only a little time was needed. As for moving the body, Jan, like her sisters, was small and light while you are all strong enough to throw her over your shoulder and probably trot up the walk to stuff her through the conveyor entrance near the top of the burner. The result would be finding the bones right about where we did. But if Pat did it alone there's still no great difficulty because she could have dragged Jan the short distance to the bottom end of the conveyor where it starts, actually below ground level, before leaving the mill building. She could have rolled the body into the trough, thrown some debris over top, then a few shovelfulls of sawdust and it's just a small pile of cleanup waiting for the mill to start in the morning. The chances of someone noticing and investigating a pile of junk on the refuse chain are so remote as to be laughable." As I say this it dawns on me that it couldn't have happened this way because the mill did not start the next morning since the crew was all shanghaied to run the planer an extra shift. The body would be left lying there yet. But no one else picked up on it so I let well enough alone. That should eliminate Ember too but as quickly as the thought comes it goes because at times I have seen that girl so single-mindedly determined that she could probably have thrown me over her shoulder and toted me uphill quite happily if there were a burner handy to toss me into. For her size she is incredibly strong. When it comes to moving or shifting heavy objects she is much stronger than I am, although I must admit to a lack of dedication for such activities. And neither Ember nor Pat were at the meeting so time was not a factor for them. Ember would never willingly go into the mill but she might have been deliberately following Jan with a definite purpose in mind. She wouldn't know the engine room from the saw-filing room or antifreeze from uncle thaw. But she did have the time to get there after closing the store and all night to take care of the rest of it. And she understands guns and like her sisters handles them quite well.

Peter asked, "At the meeting how many of us came less than fifteen minutes ahead of Tom?"

"I don't remember," I had to confess.

"Well I do, I was the last one in and I saw Alec just ahead of me. Tom came five to ten minutes later so you're saying it was Alec or me unless someone was just ahead of Alec."

Allan supplied the answer to that. "No. Tim, Byron and I waited together quite a while before you two came."

"Then it's Alec or me and I know it wasn't me so it must have been you, Alec." Only he didn't make it an accusation, he was amused.

Alec caught the mood and chuckled, "Sorry, Peter, it wasn't me either. Must have been Byron himself out on one of his jaunts that no one ever seems to notice."

"I think that's a pretty good notion, Alec, it looks to me like Byron has been casting accusations around freely just as a smokescreen for himself."

"Don't be ridiculous, Tim."

"No more so than you are, you above everyone have twenty-four hours a day opportunity to go anywhere and presumably to do anything. You have your own truck and if that isn't handy you are in the habit of grabbing any 4x4 around and everyone is so used to you doing just that that no one would give you a second glance." To my relief he finally stopped and looked around for support, maybe wondering if he had said too much.

"Go ahead, Tim, you're doing fine." Peter urged.

Encouragement was all he needed. "The reason for the sabotage could be because of better than four years of all hours of the day-slaving for this outfit for no financial gain and probably even less gratitude."

That's the way Tim would look at it alright and the farther he goes the more he seems to like the sound of his own voice. I can't remember ever being as dumbfounded, disgusted and dismayed as I am right now. I can't understand how anyone, even Tim, can see me as anything but harmless. The others should be laughing their heads off but no one is even smiling except for Peter.

"Jan probably wasn't as much interested in stopping you or turning you in as she was in blackmailing you. We all know you and Ember are thick as molasses in January but we also know that you don't mind letting her cool her heels now and then while you check the field for other girls. I'm thinking that either you gave Jan reason to act the way she did the other day when we went up to the lake on the Ski-doos or else she was already applying the pressure on you. You have to admit she owned you that day and I don't recall you objecting, at least not in public, in private the story looks somewhat different.

"Just what are you trying to say, Tim?"

"That she wanted you as a father for her child," he blurted. "You stepped right into a trap when she caught you doping or busting machines and she decided to blackmail you away from Ember. The simplest way out for you was to kill her."

"Utterly preposterous! Jan could have just about any man she wanted and she did not want me. Your imagination has gotten the best of you."

"If we have to answer to your accusations then you have to answer to mine."

"I don't have to answer to anything or anybody! I'm running this show so we'll do it my way!" I banged my wrench on the desk adding considerable to it's antiquity. He lost his air like a stabbed balloon and looked so crestfallen that I almost felt sorry for him. Seeing as I had control again I took advantage of it while they were all quiet. "Well, since no one is leaping up to take credit then we will discuss the evidence and maybe that will get some action."

"What do you mean by evidence? I haven't heard of any."

"Well, how about the bullet that killed Lupe? We can have it ballistic tested to every rifle in camp until we find out whose gun fired it."

Tom changed position in his chair. "That bullet is gone down the river, Byron. It's not going to be evidence for you."

"I have the bullet that killed Lupe," I stated flatly, hoping to see some reaction. All I got was a scornful look from Allan.

"That won't work. You can hand over any old bullet that suits you but don't expect anyone to believe it. That's not evidence."

"I still have the whole dog, Allan. Some police appointed expert can have the job of digging out the bullet." Seeing the look on Tom's face I stopped.

"But you put Lupe in the river, I saw your tracks myself!"

"You didn't actually see me throw him in though did you, Tom? Yes, I made tracks to the river but then I took Lupe somewhere else and hid him for future reference. And I did something else just in case anyone is jumping ahead to the next step. This afternoon while you were all occupied, at whatever occupied you today, I took the liberty of driving around, unseen and unnoticed just as you said, Tim, and I picked up every small calibre rifle and handgun that I could find in your homes. Your wives were home of course, a nod to Tom and Allan, but it's not the first time I've been around to borrow something and only some trivial excuses were necessary then they didn't even watch to see what I took."

"You son of a gun!" Peter exclaimed almost admiringly. "You got mine too, I suppose?"

"Of course. I've got them all safely hidden, you will get them back in due course."

"Now what was that in aid of?" Tom asked, more perplexed

than angry. Then he grinned a little as he added, "You must have had an armful going out of my place."

I nodded, "I knew you had a lot of firearms, Tom, but I only took the .22s—the more modern and likely to be working ones so that cut down on the volume considerably. Most were so loaded with dust that I left them alone. Because of the range involved I figure it had to be a rifle, maybe even scope-sighted but I picked up handguns too, they were all at your place and I took just the small-bore, usable looking ones. There too, only a few were dust free."

"As a member in good standing of the handgun club in town and a recognized collector, I have a permit for every one of them."

"Just so, Tom, no one is saying different." He obviously isn't worried and since he has by far the most guns involved that set the tone for the rest of them so once again I am left holding an empty bag. Eventually I answered his first question though they probably all have it figured out by now. "I picked up those guns in case someone should get the idea that one of their .22s should go missing. In case you think I may have overlooked some, I went through your 4x4s tonight and found a few more."

"This could be interesting alright but really, what do you expect to prove beyond the fact that someone didn't like Lupe?"

"I thought I had made it clear that when we find the owner of the rifle that killed Lupe we will have the man who was in the engine room, the one who killed Jan. If by chance it was Pat, then she probably had Alec's .22." I shrugged, "just one more detail to come out in the wash."

"If a man owns a rifle it doesn't necessarily follow that only he pulls the trigger on it."

"Okay. But it will be pointing a pretty big finger. There is also a little item that the killer or the saboteur, who I think are one and the same, forgot to take away with him and I expect to find fingerprints on it. Now that, I think you will agree, should be pretty good evidence especially if it points to the same person as the rifle's ownership does,"

While telling this I watched both Peter and Alec as closely as I could with my attention divided between them. I got absolutely nothing from either one. It's a good thing, I reflected, that I am not trying to earn my living as a detective or I would perish of starvation while searching for my welfare cheque.

Allan asked guardedly, "What did you find and why do you expect there to be fingerprints on it?"

"I found the can that was very carelessly left behind after being used to carry antifreeze from the shop, just a two-gallon can so maybe there was more than one trip made. At first I wrote off the possibility of fingerprints because everyone wears mitts while out and around now. But the drums of antifreeze are kept in the back of the shop where it may not be exactly warm but it is above freezing. The short haul to the mill wouldn't cool it much more and it's nice and warm in by the engines. So, what's the most natural first thing to do when you want to remove the caps from a can to pour some liquid out of it?" I looked around at them but no one is going to help me out. "The first thing I would do would be to pull off my mitts. So—no mitts—lots of fingerprints. The can is still at the mill but hidden where I can get it any time."

Peter was the first to speak. "May I ask what you plan to do with your so-called evidence?"

"I'm going to use it for blackmail. Tim thinks I'm a victim of blackmail, now I will show him that I am more likely to be on the other end of the stick."

They all exchanged glances wondering, I know, if I have suddenly gone daft.

"Just who are you planning to blackmail?" Peter is definitely showing more curiosity now than the others.

"You! Or more precisely all five of you. Here is my final offer since you are all declining to admit involvement. Whichever of you is the guilty party, or if any of you knows who is, I want to be told about it here and now otherwise I collect my evidence and hand it over to the police. Or I will as soon as the phone comes back on so I can reach them. Then you can try answering their questions."

After a full thick minute I had to break the silence myself. "So! Still no takers? Very well, you give me no choice, but in case you are merely bashful about speaking up in a crowd, here is your last opportunity. I want you all to leave now and I'll sit here alone for half an hour. If at the end of that time no one has come to talk turkey with me then the police get the dog, the can and my story."

They left me rather briskly I thought, Peter favouring me with a strange look as he pulled the door shut. A look that seemed to combine envy and apprehension but it had to be a trick of the lighting in that transition zone between this room and the hall. I listened to their footsteps along the corridor and out, then it got awfully quiet.

12

Half an hour is only thirty minutes, if you're having fun it's quickly gone. But now the seconds laboured past each one tied to a D7 Cat churning its tracks trying to go the other way. Though it took ages for that brief time to pass no one came near me. I am bitterly disappointed but after waiting an extra ten discouraging minutes I gave up. Since the phone is still not working I am at least spared having to walk past it wanting to make the call but bound by a promise not to. But I know one thing for sure and that is I have talked too much tonight. I feel the dog is safe from discovery but I've as good as said that the can is still in the engine room. If someone wants it to protect themselves or someone else then all they have to do is to give the engine room a good once-over. Whatever else I do tonight I must get that can hidden more securely before some smartaleck runs off with the better half of my trophies.

Once outside I stopped on the office steps. There is a lot of moonlight, so much that the overhead lights scattered about the mill yard and buildings seem faded and ineffectual. Even so the light is tricky, there are shadows within shadows, it took no time at all for me to convince myself I am being watched. There are so many trucks and machines parked around the shop yard an entire army could hide there till daylight. The log yard on my other side is even worse. I walked on trying to act normal but my eyes roved as far as possible to each side. I can see now that I am very foolish to be out here unarmed. Or out here at all! I've sure gone and set myself up as the next one to go missing and all I have in the way of a weapon is the wrench that I had in the office. It rides in a deep pocket of my overcoat, not much protection unless the action gets to very close quarters. Until lately I still enjoyed some leftover dregs of the old invisible man syndrome, always underfoot but seldom noticed. Now that desirable state of affairs is a thing of the past because I certainly got their attention tonight.

 I made it past the dangers, imagined or otherwise, of the shop yard but as I was nearing the bulk of the mill some urge made me turn to look back just as a figure darted from one parked truck to the next one nearer and I know now who is stalking me. It's the same movements, the same silhouette as the other night when I caught him trying to cross Ember's fence. I felt a shiver of both fear and satisfaction run down my spine for of them all I see him as the most dangerous, the one least likely to worry about tomorrow's consequences to today's actions. I also stand to gain the most if I can prove his guilt, it doesn't matter to me if he lands behind bars or simply picks up his pack and moves a long ways off.

 I have a good lead on him for he seems unwilling to leave his cover near the shop. Even when I have gone around the end of the green chain there is still too much open ground between us and he doesn't seem in a hurry to move any closer. As I pass through the engine room door and close it behind me I know that will be the signal for him to sprint forward but my plans are made. I will grab the can and duck into the dark labyrinth under the mill itself. No one knows the way around under there better than I do except for the millwrights who work there every day and maybe

Allan who helped design and build it. I can out-manoeuvre Peter there and work my way back to the mall where I will feel much better behind some doors I can lock around me.

The thought of locked doors distracts me and I glanced at the door I have just come through. There's no lock on it but it opens inward and the possibility of barring it is built in to the frame. There is no bar provided but within seconds I have a long section of black iron pipe that was lying on the work bench jammed into place. No one is going to open that in a hurry. A few more precious seconds and I have the opposite outside door jammed in a similar fashion with the long handled tool for running threads on pipe or iron rod. I've squandered a little time but I should gain considerable because when Peter hits that locked door he will have to retreat to the nearest outside entrance leading under the mill and I'm confident he has little knowledge of the building's layout for it's never been his habit to come around here. By the time he gets under the mill and finds some light switches I will be working toward an exit somewhere else. It's well lit in here but there are no windows so I'm not on display. As well as the two doors on opposite sides that I have jammed there is a large sliding door on the side away from the main building. It's intended for use when a forklift has to come in to remove or replace one of the engines. In summer it's often open for ventilation but it will not open now for the ice and snow frozen to it are as good as any padlock ever made. The only other exit is the man-size door leading under the mill where I will be going in a moment.

It's not really noisy in here even with the light plant, now repaired, pounding away. Its exhaust noise is vented far above the roof so only the whine of the generator, the hum of the cooling blower and the rattling knock of diesel ignition are noticeable. The can is still under the bench where I left it, I've caught glimpses of it while I've been locking doors but I delayed reaching for it for a moment. Peter hasn't hit the door yet so I am wondering what might be developing outside, maybe he is coming under the mill. It's becoming too obvious that, unless he is coming very slowly, he is not simply following me but is trying instead to outguess me and trap me in some manner, and that's more scary yet. I'm starting to think that I had better turn the lights off and try my luck out the river-side door, it will only take an instant to unlock it again. I started toward the work bench to get the can from under the shelf but my surprise came from inside.

"Looks like you're planning to hold off a siege, Byron. What's going on?"

It was Tom, stepping from behind one of the big electric sets, he may have been there all along or he may have just entered from under the mill. My thinking is all mixed up as I wonder what he is doing here. Was it him in the shadows at the shop? How could I mistake him for Peter and how did he get through under the mill so quickly? I can't be that slow! He must have been here all along and will be a welcome ally when Peter comes. But the expression on his face! My mind races back over the events of the last week or so trying to find something I have missed that might explain that regretful but stubbornly determined look.

"It was careless of me to leave that can behind but things got unexpectedly complicated when Jan walked in on me. So much so that the can slipped totally out of my mind."

My God! I've locked myself in with the murderer.

As that realization sank in I edged a step or two closer to the door I had just jammed shut. There is no possibility of me getting out quickly enough to evade him but still the movement alarmed him and brought his hand from his coat pocket and in it came a nasty-looking short-barreled .22 revolver. When I could pull my eyes from its threat I glanced longingly at the light switch beside the door but it's just out of reach. The switches at both doors are series wired so either one turns all the lights in the room on or off at one click.

"I guess you won't get out that door in any hurry now that you've jimmied it but just the same, don't get any closer to it."

How ridiculous that Tom should use a revolver on me when he

could break me in half with one hand tied behind his back and raise no sweat. He must be remembering the wrench I waved at them in the meeting room and doesn't want to come close, maybe it shows in my coat pocket. "I didn't realize you were in the habit of packing a gun in your pocket Tom."

"I'm not. It's usually locked in the glove compartment of my truck for casual target-plinking whenever I feel the urge for some diversion. You got the rifle from behind the seat but I've had this in my coat pocket all day. I doubt you would have found it anyway."

I nodded, it would never occur to me that anyone would carry a handgun around in their vehicle. No wonder he didn't look worried when I threatened them with ballistic comparisons, he knew I didn't have the gun that killed Lupe. There it is! It comes unbidden from some hindsight recess in my mind but much too late. "You shot Lupe yourself."

"That's right, the hardest thing I ever did in my life up till now. I hate to do this to you—you've been a meddlesome little cuss but I've always had a liking for you for some reason."

This is sounding far too much like an obituary to my notion and hearing it first-hand is no substitute for being around to point out its inaccuracy. I shuffled my feet and managed to get a few inches closer to the door.

"But first, I want that dog. I've waited here expecting you to come because I need to know where you've hidden him."

I shook my head and backed up a small step toward the door. Even I am smart enough to see that as long as I have something he wants he will be slower pulling the trigger. It's an awfully small hole in the end of the barrel and I looked at it morbidly wondering how much it's going to hurt and how many of those tiny slugs it will take to put me down. With Tom doing the aiming it will probably be over quick. "Why shoot your own dog Tom? I can't figure that part at all."

"That's neither here nor there, what counts is what you did with him. I see the can over there under the bench but there's a thousand and one places you could have hidden Lupe. This gun is registered and permitted to me so it wouldn't look good if it went missing under the present circumstances. That means I need to know where Lupe is because the bullet in him is dangerous to me. So—what have you done with him?"

"And then you shoot me," I stated matter-of-factly shuffling my feet again. I am now close enough to reach out and touch the door, if that will do any good.

He thought that over a moment. "Yeah, that doesn't leave you much room for optimism does it." He almost smiled then. "I'll make you a deal, your own curiosity can do the job for me. I'll tell you what happened and you tell me where Lupe is."

"And then you shoot me," I repeated for him, edging once more a few inches toward the wall.

"No, I guess not. It looks like I'm done here anyway. If it weren't for you I'd have gotten away with this so far. But if you go missing that will be just too much for anyone to swallow. Two in a row would trigger all kinds of trouble, most of it for me. So I'll just tie you up and leave you here on the floor. Someone will be around to check the light plant tomorrow so you will just be uncomfortable for a few hours."

"And what does that gain for you?"

"As I said, I'm finished here, I can see the writing on the wall. By morning I'll be gone, the train to town, a plane out from there. No one here will ever see or hear from me again. Satisfied?"

I nodded. I can't trust him I warned myself, tell him where Lupe is and Mrs. Smith's little boy won't be to the cookshack for bannock and beans again. But for the moment there's nowhere else to turn and for the life of me, I've got to hear his story. "Okay, Tell me about it. Why did you kill Jan?"

"I didn't kill her, Byron, and get that straight. It was an accident—sort of. But this starts away back so just be quiet for a while if you can.

"Last fall, when I started going to L&N to sound them out about sale possibilities it didn't take them long to spot me as the weak link. I'll make no excuses, I was always too deep in a bottle and needing money for the next one. As you know it's like pulling teeth to get cash from the office especially with my own wife working there. That's what they gave me—money under the table—when I suggested I could slow things down enough that we couldn't fill the quota. Then they could step in before spring breakup with the offer of a lot of help and all the strings attached they wanted. They could wind up owning control on their own terms.

"I guess I didn't do a very good job on the sabotage, I found my heart wasn't really in it. It seems I've spent too many years nursing our equipment through each winter to suddenly turn on it. Each machine out there is, maybe not a friend, but at least an acquaintance. That's when I found out I'm just another machine-loving Morrow. It's our own special curse and everyone of us is afflicted. I thought all I had to do was cripple a few of them and you'd be down for the count. I didn't realize there would be so much cash money coming in this winter that you would just hire more mechanics, buy more parts and put on an even bigger push for production. In past years, as you well know it wasn't like that, we never had enough money to fix things right. I couldn't understand that this year was going to be different or I might not have made such a fool of myself, after all, profits are what I want too."

"In the raid on the engines," he waved a hand toward the electric sets, "I expected to get one of the big units. I wanted it to break down during working hours while I was off in the woods beyond suspicion and with antifreeze doing the damage it might have passed as nothing more than internal leakage. It should have worked if Allan hadn't shut the mill down to run the planer instead. That was to be my last effort, make or break, I had decided if that didn't stop you I would quit causing breakdowns and stay with you for the rest of the ride. L&N wouldn't dare object, the money they gave me was no more than a speculation, they knew it might or might not pay off."

"Where does Jan come into it?" I prompted him.

"As you guessed she walked in on me while I was pouring the antifreeze into the oil drum, I didn't know she was within a mile until she looked around my shoulder to see what I was doing. The twins are no slouches around machinery, she saw it was antifreeze and she knew that wasn't good for engine oil. She put two and two together, came up with a great big four and turned her tongue loose on me. Now, when I first realized I was caught I just sagged inside, actually glad it was over and resigning myself to taking my medicine whatever that would be. But she wouldn't leave me alone, she cursed me out like I've never experienced before, I've never seen anyone fly into such a rage as she did. I tried to walk out on her but she followed me to the door giving it to me all the way. She was crowding me so close that when I jerked the door open in a sudden hurry to get away from her I bumped her and sent her off balance. She went over backwards, mostly from surprise I think and banged the back of her head on the corner of the channel iron part of the engine base there. She twisted around, gave a few jerks and that was the end of her."

"It wasn't murder then, Tom. Not planned."

"No. Not until I packed her up the conveyor walk and dropped her into the burner, it's not nearly so easy as you implied at the meeting but that's what I did. By then I was in such a state of shock and sorrow and regret that I knew I couldn't face any of you, or Jennie either, yet I had to and the sooner the better. Jan meant more to me than all the Lupes in the world but that was still about the hardest conscious decision I ever made in my life. I went to the truck and got the revolver—Lupe followed along like always."

He trailed off into silence and I supplied the finish for him. "So, you came back part way with Lupe behind you then turned around and shot him."

He nodded. "Then I had a reason for being so upset."

"You should have claimed some other cause for her being angry at you then we could have written it off as an accident. You could have cooked up a better story than this."

"Never mind, it's your turn now. Where is he?"

That's when I reached out and flipped the light switch to off. He fired twice immediately but I was already moving. He fired several more shots as I hurried along, I don't think any came near me but they certainly speeded up my exit. That answered one question for me—I have been wondering if he really would shoot.

He would!

I had sized it up while we were talking, now I went along the wall, one hand touching for guidance, until I reached the corner. Then I turned right for a few steps to the door leading under the mill, it's a spring-loaded door with no latch so after pushing through into frigid air smelling of sawdust and oiled machinery soaking in the cold, I eased it shut quietly behind me. So far I haven't worried about any noise I made, the thumping of the light plant has been enough to cover my minor scufflings but at the same time I can't hear what he is doing. It won't take long for him to find a light switch and get on my trail, my only chance is to put as much distance between us as I can before that.

All the lights throughout this building are normally left on twenty-four hours a day, seven days a week but they are off now. Either Tom turned them off for his own reasons or some conscientious soul is saving fuel for us over the long shutdown. Either way it suits me just fine. As long as he has the gun, darkness is my best friend. I turned right toward the town end of the mill thinking only of direct flight to locking doors and other people while hoping he will think me devious enough to go the other way. But it is dark with a capital 'd'! Not one forlorn hint of the moonlight from outside filters in. With my eyes not yet used to this total lack of light I'm running into timbers, beams and all manner of obstructions that I don't remember and I'm not making much progress.

The lights in the engine room came on again much too soon and the feeble glow as Tom pushed through the door to follow shows that I have not progressed nearly far enough. It took him a few seconds to find the switches for the lights in this part but that didn't help me much. I only had time to duck behind one of the twelve-by-twelve inch timbers that stand upright to support the production floor overhead before the whole area turned bright as day. I would much rather be farther along but there's still a chance he hasn't seen me and will go the other way.

The longer I stand straight and stiff behind that timber the more worried I get, I haven't heard a sound from him and I don't dare take a peek around my square post in case he happens to be looking this way. It's much too quiet for far too long but the quiet ends with a bang, literally. There's a sharp tug at the hem of my treacherous coat that has obviously been protruding into sight to betray me. As the echoes shake dust from somewhere over me I am left reflecting bitterly on the discovery of what a small bit of shelter is afforded by a twelve inch width of wood. Tom shot my coat again, this time barely ticking the back of my elbow on the opposite side of the timber. Then he put a couple of fast ones into the timber itself bringing on another small shower of dust that has survived all manner of mill vibrations but objects to this unusual treatment. He is teasing me, no doubt about it, all he has to do is walk forward and he's got me dead to rights. I have only one painfully thin chance left and that's my wrench. It's a mighty good chunk of iron for throwing and heavy enough to do the job if I can step out, throw fast and score a lucky hit. I've had my share of luck bagging willow grouse by throwing rocks at them but sometimes it took a dozen tries to make the hit, tonight I'll have only one throw. Right after his next shot I'll try—or when he comes closer, whichever he does next.

He did neither, he chuckled then said, "All over, Byron, you might as well step out, I still want to know where Lupe is."

So! We are going to talk again. Maybe! But it might be better at that than what I was going to try so I stepped clear of the timber with the hand that holds the wrench deliberately hidden from him. He is about twenty feet away, taking no chances but his attention is so firmly fixed on me, probably wondering about the hand that's kept behind my back, that he doesn't realize Peter is coming up behind him. This is the first time I have ever been so glad to see that man coming but my expression must have tipped Tom off too soon. He took a quick look over his shoulder, moved swiftly to one side to where he could better see both of us and stopped Peter with a motion of his revolver.

"Good thing for me that neither one of you is armed isn't it?"

Peter started toward him again, talking as he advanced. "You wouldn't shoot me Tom, we're practically brothers. Put that thing back in your pocket and we'll all go to the office and sort this out like Byron is always saying."

Tom raised the gun to sight directly at Peter's chest. His voice breaking with emotion he warned, "Don't come one step closer, Pete." Peter did not stop and I threw the wrench at exactly the same instant Tom squeezed the trigger. The hammer clicked down on a spent casing or an empty chamber just as the wrench hit Tom over one ear, a glancing blow but enough to stun him into dropping the empty gun. He collapsed to the floor alongside it after flinging his arms about trying to grab something to hold onto and finding nothing. There was the most surprised look on his face as his legs gave out under him.

Peter too was stunned but not because he was injured physically. "I didn't think he would do it," he muttered in disbelief.

With Tom still down I retrieved my wrench and picked up the gun. "Just in case he has more ammunition in his pocket."

"Yeah!" Peter agreed quickly. "You know, I feel like I'm starting a new life right this moment. The old one ended when he pulled that trigger even if the blasted thing was empty."

"How did you happen along just in time to save my bacon? Was that you hiding among the trucks at the shop when I came by?"

"Yes, and getting mighty cold in the bargain," he stopped and looked thoughtful. "It's every bit as cold here as outside but now I'm warm! Not every one has the experience of being reincarnated and still be able to remember the past life but that's what's happening to me." I can't hold it against him, I'm giddy from my narrow escape too. He went on, "I kept an eye on you because anyone who sets himself on a stick of dynamite like you did tonight is going to get the fuse lit sooner or later." He watched as I propped the unconscious Tom on his side, he's breathing heavily so I think he will be okay for now. "But somehow I got the message that it was Tom who was playing with fire. Anyway, I figured I had better keep an eye on you the rest of the night and see what kind of a hornets' nest you managed to stir up."

"How did you know it was Tom?"

"I didn't, as I just said, it was you that I was watching. If you will recall I was the last one out the door when we left your—ah—meeting and the others all scattered in as many different directions. I couldn't watch them all so I stuck with you fully expecting someone to come after your scalp, I didn't plan to put my own life on the line in the process though. But I goofed when I elected to come through the ground floor instead of following you to the side door of the engine room. It was so dark that I was soon lost and bumping into every timber and conveyor down here, I couldn't even go back the way I had come because I closed the door behind me so there was no light showing. The noise from the lightplant bounces all around and I was even having trouble tracking that down. When I heard the first shots I figured it was all over and you were history. I was still trying to work my way toward the location of the shooting when the lights came on."

"You didn't overhear Tom and I then?"

"No!"

I thought about that abrupt answer. He wants me to tell him and yet he doesn't really want to hear what I will say. He already knows enough and can guess for himself whatever he wants to, I will keep Tom's story to myself.

We got the awakening Tom sitting up then and I examined the cut on his head. There is a sizable swelling starting but no blood coming from inside his ear. His eyes and speech are soon clear enough so I am sure the biggest injury is to his pride. I have to confess to mixed feelings of my own, it would seem that I have succeeded admirably in what I set out to do but the end result is not what I anticipated. Peter is the one I wanted to catch but the tree just refused to fall that way. The very last thing I wanted was to wind up beholden to him for saving my skin but that is what has happened.

I get the feeling that Peter too is dissatisfied with the turn of events so that makes all three of us in similar patterns of thought because obviously Tom is not jumping for joy either. The only amusing note—annoying might be a better word—is Peter's illogical assumption that I planned all this deliberately. It's positively uncanny the way he insists on giving me credit when none is due. I can't help thinking there's some ulterior motive involved and I will find out all about it soon enough.

I'm not sure why we are going to the office but that was apparently our goal until Tom stopped near one of the overhead yard lights. "No farther, Pete, I'm not going to face the others, certainly not Pat, I never want to see Pat again, she's been the same thing as a ghost to me this past week or so."

"You should have thought that out sooner. Now things can never be the same again."

"Leave out the sermon, you're as bad as the old man sometimes. I'm not going an inch farther and that's all there is to it."

"What have you got in mind?"

"Let me go. I'll leave and I'll never be back. Jennie can have my share of the place, Lord knows she's earned it putting up with me."

"What about the kids, Tom?"

His answer came slower this time. "Yeah, what about them? Do you think they will be happier with their father in jail for killing their aunt or if he's just gone and soon forgotten? My marriage has been dead ever since the whiskey got to me—you wait and see, it won't take Jennie long to find someone to be daddy to them again."

They sound like brave words but he is not a brave man. He is very nearly a broken one trying to convince himself more than us that his family will be better off without him. I should have known that for a man normally arrogant and self-controlled, saddled with the strong Morrow sense of family, a turn of events like this could make him desperate again.

"But that's not the only issue, Pete, this will do in the old man. If Dad finds out I've killed Jan it will be a slow knife in his heart and then I will have killed him too. So, for his sake, walk away and leave me to my own means. The family might overrule you two anyway and tell me to get out no matter what punishment you two think I deserve."

"Don't include me in that 'you two' that you keep tossing around," Peter said irritably, "as it happens I am in complete agreement with you, I just need to be certain that you'll go."

I might have expected it but still I can hardly believe what they are saying and worse yet was coming.

"If we were alone, Tom, I would probably do my best to lock my thumbs on your windpipe until you quit kicking and then I'd toss you in the river."

Tom nodded, "It's what I would expect from you though I'm glad I don't have to face the treatment. Besides, Byron would hound you to death, he's the worst nuisance I've ever run afoul of." He looked at me almost fondly. This is getting so weird that I'm now doubting my eyes as well as my ears.

"So, what's your wish, Tom? Are you wanting to catch a train tonight?"

"That would be best, the longer I stay the harder it will be."

"Need any money? We can have Byron open the safe at the office."

Tom seemed to consider the offer but then said, "No, I have my own money, the blood money that L&N gave me, I'm not feeling generous enough to give it back to them. But I'll have to go and get it. I could use some help."

"Why? Where is it?"

Again Tom hesitated, as though wondering how far he could trust us. "It's in the river, under the dock in a watertight contraption I made in the shop. It's anchored to the dock by a cable fastened below the waterline. It's heavy and nearly impossible to pull out against the current now that there's ice just where it's not needed."

"Okay, we'll give you a hand." Peter doesn't know it but he is speaking for himself only. When I went down in the night to pretend I had thrown Lupe in I saw quite all I needed of that open swirl of water. Water that should be frozen solid but there it is, sucking greedily at the underside of the raft. It's simply not my cup of tea out there.

I followed them back toward the river but lagging behind as we went. I stopped altogether halfway down the bank where the road passes under the old jack ladder. I want to object to this so badly that the words are bottle-necked in my throat choking me up quite effectively. But I know it would be a waste of breath so I can only stay out of their way—it seems important to me that I lend no helping hand.

They are just silhouettes against the snow-covered ice alongside the brighter, black silver shine of the water while they appear to inspect the current at the end of the dock. In the next second they are scuffling, each seeming intent on flinging the other into the water. I knew instantly that the smartest thing for me to do is to make tracks away from here at my top speed. Like the old prospector who found a grizzly bear following him said—'you like my tracks? Okay, I'll quickly make you many more.' Because, like the old-timer, if Tom wins that struggle on the dock, I will have a grizzly on my trail.

But it's strange sometimes what a man will do against his better judgment. My wrench feels too small for this job and Tom's gun is no good to me without ammunition so I looked about wildly for a weapon. Here under the jack ladder I'm near the log infeed deck where the loaders drop tree length timber for the mill, there are always little bits and pieces of wood flying from the impact when the grapple loads are dumped. It took only a few seconds to find a section of frozen spruce limb about two inches in diameter and a couple of feet long. With that as reinforcement I hurried down the hill and onto the dock near the struggling pair. Peter has to win this battle or it's my turn next but, so help me, I can't do a thing to influence the outcome because they are flopping about so swiftly that by the time I am set to smash Tom's skull or break his arm they have turned so that I would have hit Peter. It would never do to hit the wrong one.

In a moment they were both on their feet and I winced just hearing the effort they put into the blows they traded. If size means anything Tom should have the best of it but stories I've heard from older days claim that Peter can hold his own with any of them, including Tom. I have to count heavily on that now.

I was scrambling to remain a safe distance from them yet close enough to step in if I got the chance so I didn't see what happened to cause it but suddenly one of them staggered backwards trying for balance but without a sound escaping him splashed into the water. Instantly the one still on the dock threw himself forward, for all the world, as if he too were diving into the river. But he landed short, still balanced over the edge of the dock, reaching as far out as he can. The one in the water broke back through the surface and momentarily hung still in the current at the edge of the ice.

For the rest of my life I am doomed to be haunted by moonlit scenes of high emotion. For as long as I live I will never lose the vision of those two hands reaching for each other—failing—then the extra effort to stretch a little farther and they clasp together. I felt relief and joy as much as the one in the water did—but, too soon—it's not over yet. The one on the dock is overextended, the current's implacable pull on the one in the water is going to have both of them. Despite his frantic efforts to grab something with his free hand and desperately digging his toes into the snow-filled cracks between the deck planks, Peter is being dragged inch by slow inch over the edge. Now that I am standing right over them I can see it's Tom in the water and Peter holding on to him.

I didn't move a muscle!

All I have to do is walk away and I will be rid of both of them, they will have killed each other with no doings of mine. I can see it! No more Tom to want my silence and no more Peter to stand between Ember and I. What a feeling of power and exultation in my chest! I can hardly believe my good luck. But all for nothing. I was reckoning without that perverse little devil who shares my innermost works.

Even with my weight on Peter's legs pinning him against the pull of the current it isn't easy, I can't release my hold on him and he can do nothing but lay there rigid. For a horrible moment I thought the river would have us all. It is now the enemy, we three are allies, all for one, all silent, not a word as we strain to cheat the current. Tom came hand over hand along Peter's arm and upper body to where he is able to grab onto a plank. Relieved of that burden and with an effort far beyond my normal ability, I hauled Peter with one swift jerk away from the water. It took both of us to drag Tom onto the dock for he suddenly seems unable to help himself. His strength is all gone as we flop him onto the dock like a big fish yarded through a hole in the ice. This cold air won't help him any either, I can already feel ice forming on the sleeves I soaked when plunging my hands down to get a better grip on Tom as he chilled and nearly slipped away from us. I don't remember pulling my mitts off but now I retrieved them from the edge of the dock and pulled them on my hands that are already stinging with pain from the cold.

"Byron! If it's within your power to run then for God's sake run and get us a truck down here!"

I ran! Like the wind! Spurred on by the sound of desperation in Peter's voice as he pulled, slapped, shook and yelled at Tom trying to get him on his feet. I was back quickly with a 4x4 from the shop but already the two of them had reached the top of the hill, Tom plunging along in pretty good form considering his apparent exhausted condition when I left them. I skidded to a halt and reached over to open the passenger's side door just in time for

Peter to shove Tom into the cab with a combination of splash and a crackle of ice. Peter crowded in beside him, slammed the door shut and I took off for the mall. As I started slowing for the office entrance Peter redirected me, "To our shack, Byron, to our shack!"

That's where we thawed Tom out and Peter too for he wasn't exactly dry either. With the doors to our rooms both shut the entry and washroom area rapidly overheated with the stove turned up. I soon had to open my door a little and retreat to some coolness and a chair to sit on. Peter supplied Tom with dry clothes that didn't fit too well but would do until his own dried on the lines over the stove. Then he started heaping verbal abuse on Tom and he got louder and more explicit until I was embarrassed to be listening in on them. He ranted like an irate father to an errant son and that's about the way Tom took it. Oddly enough he seemed to take no offense, in fact several times he nodded or made agreeable sounds. Once he said, "I was running on sheer desperation, Pete, you can't guess how good it feels now that it's out of my hands. It feels good to be alive too." But he turned his face downward as he said it.

"You have Byron to thank for that, if it wasn't for him we'd both be feeding the fish by now. Bless our lucky stars we have one man in this outfit who is always in the right place when he's needed."

I think they will need those lucky stars if they are to avoid some frostbitten fingers and faces from this episode, especially Tom who had to cling bare-handed to the raft until we got around to him. No wonder he was losing his grip by the time we pulled him out. These people leave me gasping at times. They did their level best to do each other in but then the river, an outsider, tried to take one, actually it nearly got them both but they fought it together and survived. Now there may still be difficult differences between them but I know that right now despite the verbal abuse they are closer to each other than ever.

Peter's mood is shifting, his anger has died away and as he

winds down there is more regret than any other emotion in his voice.

In the quiet that finally overtook them Tom asked, "Well, what now, Pete?"

"I don't see that anything is changed. If it were just me we might work something out but I don't think Byron will want you around after this night's work."

They were quiet again, Tom digesting this verdict while I gagged on it. Why should it matter whether or not I want him around? It must be Peter's way of putting the blame for a tough decision elsewhere.

"I'd like to back up a little on that first deal, Pete. Once I'm set up someplace I'm going to write to Jennie and ask her to follow."

"Of course. In the meantime, for anyone who wonders, we will explain that after a lengthy period of dissatisfaction you have finally pulled your stakes and moved on." Then, curiosity needling him, "is there really some cash under the dock, Tom?"

"No," he admitted, "what I haven't spent is in a bank in town. As you see I have enough money to get a ticket on the train and a bit left over." He waved a hand toward the contents of his wallet now spread to dry on a mitt rack over the stove.

"Then that's the way of it." Peter rose and came to my door. "How long till you go up to meet the trains?"

"An hour or so." How close they came to not being met at all tonight!

"Okay, take Tom up and see that he gets on. Then, can you come down between trains? I need to talk to you briefly before you meet Number 8."

"Ordinarily that would make it a bit of a rush. But according to the brakeman on the wayfreight late this afternoon, tonight's eastbound passenger was held up by a freight train derailment along the Skeena. It's running about eight hours late, I haven't got the phone to check on it but I can find out the latest from the crew on No. 9 as it passes westbound."

He mulled that over a moment his face showing some impatience. "Alright, no problem then. I'll see you when you get back down." With that said he wheeled around and went back past Tom and into his own room. It would be cold in there by now so he left the door open but we didn't have to be told to leave him alone. I made a pretense of reading for the next hour while Tom soaked up all the heat he could get from our stove. He changed back to his own clothes, loaded his wallet and stuffed it into a pocket then checked his coat. It seems to me there's not been time for it to dry but there was a look of satisfaction on his face as he draped it over the drying lines again and adjusted the fan to blow more directly on it.

When the time came I pulled on my own coat, mitts and toque. "I'll get the truck and pick you up in about five minutes, Tom."

"I might as well walk along with you, I've got all day tomorrow to warm up," he said reaching for his coat. We left without a word of farewell between Tom and Peter, another Morrow trait. There is no 'goodbye' when they leave and no 'hello' when they return, they just pick up where they left off as if there has been no absence at all.

Actually I am quite indignant as I drive Tom up to the railroad. How come, I wonder, is it suddenly safe for me to be alone with this man who, earlier this same evening, had it at least briefly in his mind to kill me? There is a good heavy wheel wrench under the seat of Nightrider and I itch to have it in my hand but pride will not allow me to reach for it. If Peter assumes the crisis is past then I must do the same.

As if it weren't already bad enough, tonight of all nights, the train had to be late. Not much but enough to fray my nerves until I became irrational. I must have because it's unmistakably my own voice I hear saying, "You know, Tom, you don't really have to leave." He looked at me in surprise as I went on, "I can't see that it will bring happiness to any of us to have you gone."

"But what about tonight? And what about Jan? You've made it too much of an issue at your meeting, everyone will be expecting you to follow up to the end."

"Tom, as far as I am concerned," I said slowly to let him know I meant it, "my efforts of tonight will be a fiasco of considerable embarrassment to me and a subject I will drop for all time. As for Jan," I sighed feelingly, "I see now that it wasn't murder at all despite your feeble-minded attempt to cover it up. It was no more than a tragic accident resulting from the hair-trigger temper you both fell heir to."

"That's so, you and I know it, even a jury might agree to some extent but that won't help me face the others in the morning."

"I can't help you there but you have been facing them every day right along so now that it's out and settled between you and I there should be less strain to get on with it."

"Maybe!" He said it doubtfully but hopefully too. He thought it over until the headlight glow of the approaching train was growing on us. By his next question I knew he had decided to stay.

"What about Pete? He's pretty keen on me going."

"Leave Peter to me," I said rashly, feeling braver than I should.

As often is the case Number 9 dropped only a bag of mail so Tom and I were soon headed back down to camp and that's when the biggest bomb yet fell on me.

"You've been pretty decent about this business, Byron. I guess I should give you some good news for a change and at the same time warn you about a phone call one day soon that will knock your socks off. Somehow you will have to keep the others from noticing or finding out."

Now what? I guess my surprised look at him was as good as asking out loud but I added, "who from?"

"From Jan."

"From Jan?" I'm thinking of Pat who once was Jan and is living with Alec down the hill from where we are this moment.

"Yeah, she's not dead. That's the good news. She's just—gone away for a while. Maybe quite a while."

I moved my foot to the brake pedal and slowed us a little. He looks okay. Actually more relaxed than I remember seeing him in quite a while.

"Care to explain that?"

"That story I told you wasn't quite complete—Jan didn't die—she was just knocked out for a bit."

"Oh! I'm glad of that." My voice came out unnaturally faint and Tom noticed.

"Having a little trouble believing me?"

"I'm afraid so."

"Yeah, I thought I spun you a pretty good yarn. Probably because it was true—up to a point."

"She did catch you with the anti-freeze then."

"Oh yes. Lupe has always liked the girls so much he didn't even warn me she was coming. She had me dead to rights. And I actually heard a bonk when her head hit the engine base. I didn't touch her, I just knew she was dead of a broken skull. I'm not trained in first aid like both Ember and Jo are so I panicked and took off for home. But I didn't get far before seeing that I had to do something so I stopped a moment to figure it out."

He swallowed and looked less than happy. "I had to go back and see if she really was dead and if so to get rid of the body and I thought about the burner. But when I got back to the engine room I found her sitting up feeling the back of her head. She was mad clear through when she saw me but it was different than before, a cold quiet anger that I sensed more than anything. She looked at me a couple of seconds then told me that I was going to pay for this, and the way I was going to pay was by getting her out of Rainy Mountain—now, immediately—with no one else knowing or ever finding out."

"When I asked how, she said that was for me to worry about, she wasn't even going to give it a thought because if she did her sister would come charging after us. Besides, her head hurt too much to think. So while she went home, which I took as meaning to Ember's, to sneak out a few things and a bottle of Aspirin I went to the meeting you guys were at and put on my act for you. The meeting ended soon after you left to take care of Lupe so I went straight home and loaded my new Ski-doo onto my truck and mixed some extra gas for it. I walked over to the office and phoned out for a train movement schedule then went back to my shop."

I opened my mouth to object to the phoning out then shut it when I remembered that this all happened before the phone quit.

"Jan was there, trying to sleep, partly to keep Pat from getting on to her and partly hoping to get rid of her headache. She had come dressed warm, wearing a hooded coat and carrying a few clothes and small things in a couple of shopping bags. I swiped a suitcase of Jennie's, which she will miss and wonder about someday, put Jan's stuff in it and gave her an outfit to wear over top her own on the snowmobile, all much too big for her but plenty warm. We drove out to the end of the snow-plowing on the dump road and took off from there on the Ski-doo. I didn't want to put her on the train here because even if you missed us she would be remembered. So we got up to the railroad from the dump, got between the rails and headed for McBride. Somewhere near Loos we took a logging road up to the new highway grade and went the rest of the way on it. There's enough detours around bridges that aren't built yet that it would have been faster to stay on the railroad but at least there weren't any trains to meet. The highway goes nowhere yet so we had it all to ourselves.

"It worked out pretty good because the eastbound passenger nearly caught up to us so we had hardly any wait before she was able to get on the train. We aren't known well in McBride because business always takes us to Prince George instead so there wasn't much risk. Anyway, she tied a scarf over her odd coloured hair when she put the hood down and it did change her looks—that and the loose outdoor clothing she was wearing."

So she's gone. Now Pat and Alec have a better go at it and Jan has a chance to make a life of her own just like I want to someday.

I had let Nightrider coast after rounding the switchback and we were getting up some speed. There are some serious questions Tom will have to answer before I start to believe him so I braked down almost to engine stall to give us more time before reaching camp and then for good measure, shifted down a gear.

"Does she have any money?"

"I gave her most of what I had—L&N money—and since I have no account in town, despite what I said earlier, that was quite a bit. I only kept what you saw drying out back in your shack. She's okay for awhile and if she's gone to Mom and Dad she'll be fine but I think she plans to strike out on her own. If so she will soon need either something on a regular basis or maybe a lump sum to get her into some business of her own. You will have to figure out how to do it without the others finding out. You're the one she will contact though I'm not sure how she will go about it to keep her identity secret."

"I can probably handle that," I said without having the slightest idea of just how I would do so. "But, Tom—the bones that Peter and I found in the burner! They were real weren't they?"

"Oh yes, they were real alright."

"Who for god's sake? And how on earth did that come about?"

He shifted his position and actually looked a little embarrassed. "You aren't going to like this, Byron." But I already knew that.

"That was Terry."

I closed my eyes—tight—and when I opened them we were still on the road! "Terry! I don't believe you, Tom. I simply can't believe you."

"Well, it was. I can't help it if you're having a problem with it. We needed his help, that's all—there was no other way to make it look like she was dead with no ands, buts or maybes. Can you think of a better way to put finished to it so her sister won't be trying to hunt her down?"

"Sheesh! Four years dead and still working for Rainy Mountain Lumber!" I marveled. Tom smiled as if that thought was good. Jo must never hear a murmur of this.

"It's impossible you know! You couldn't have done all that alone in one night!"

"Maybe, maybe not but I didn't have to because I had help and actually it didn't all have to be done at once."

"I suppose they were all in on it and I was the only one left ignorant.

"No, not all of them. Only one. The others know nothing and for the sake of Pat and Alec it would be best if they were a long time learning"

"Who helped you?"

"I don't think I should tell. I don't think he would want me to."

"I've got to know, Tom, and I've got to know how you did it. If I have to carry this on and take care of Jan I've got to know who my allies are, especially if you decide to leave like you've been threatening. I hope you realize that not a whisper of this can come out to anyone because if Jo ever hears of it she will be right broken up and soon on the prod for sure. For that matter, Ember too." Ember, though, after the initial shock might look more at the end results.

"I guess I can see that now that you bring it to my attention. Allan helped me, I went to him the next day and the rest was his idea more than mine. We dug up Terry's coffin in broad daylight though it was dark by the time we hauled him to the mill. The coffin was wooden, you know, made from the best of our own cedar planks and still in good condition. There were no hinges or handles so there wasn't a lot of metal to find around the bones. We scouted the place out to be sure we were alone then sent him up the refuse conveyor to the burner. Allan knew how to jump the electric circuit to run the conveyor without starting one of the big engines."

"And Lupe? Why Lupe?"

"That was tough but it was coming anyway. You must have noticed that he hasn't been with me much lately, he's been lying around at home or the office or the shop a lot. He was sick, dying actually. Shooting him was a kindness that I already knew I would have to do before the winter was over. That's just the way it is in a dog's world. Unless I've lost track, he was fifteen years old and that's pretty good for his kind. It turned out convenient to do it the night of your meeting then put on an act designed to lead you around to the engine room and eventually the burner."

"But that's crazy, it was the purest accident, nothing more than chance that made me think of the burner."

"Chance is a thing that can be worked on. We'd have dropped more hints as the holiday went by and if nobody tumbled to it Allan would have done a burner inspection before starting the mill. There would have been no chance involved because he would have found the bones himself if necessary."

"So we just have a little mess and mix-up to take care of at the cemetery?"

"Not even much of that because when we dug him up we moved the top part of his monument over a few feet and threw snow around it then tramped around a lot to make it look like we had dug alongside his grave instead of in it. When we reburied the ashes Allan and I made sure we were first ones up there and the new grave is actually the same old one. Terry is right back where he belongs. By now Allan will have been up and shifted the headstone back to its base so we just need some grass to grow in the spring."

I have been fed so many wild stories lately that I can't decide yet whether to believe this one or not. I think it's because I want very much to believe him that I ploughed on trying to trip him up. "How come all that bare earth didn't freeze solid on you while it was open to the weather? I mean you were still able to stick a shovel in it the day we buried the ashes."

"A couple of big insulated tarps, some old insul board, a propane heater and a lot of snow took care of that."

"That's why such a big area was tramped down."

"Yeah, it was kind of obvious but we couldn't help that. The trail in was our biggest problem—all those trips in and out and we had to keep it looking like just one or two passes the day of the reburial. That's partly why Allan and I had to be first ones there."

My next question might be a little dicey but it has to be asked. "At the mill tonight—you would have killed me if you could have."

"Aw—if I had wanted I could have hit you with every shot I

fired even when you snapped the lights off on me. A pretty good show that was though I didn't think so at the time because I really felt I had to get Lupe and that can to make sure my tracks were covered."

"You had me fooled."

"That was the main idea. You wouldn't have told me anything without being good and scared. As for shooting you—forget it. I wouldn't have even tied you up because that would have just spread the word to whoever found you. I wanted it kept quiet so we likely would have wound up talking just like we are now. And when Pete showed up I was all bluff because I knew the gun was empty. You should have too the way the hammer clicked down on an empty chamber after the last one I dusted you with."

He could have tried talking then, I'd have been no more skeptical than I am now but I didn't bother mentioning it. "I suppose there is some logical reason for that —um—tangle between you and Peter at the river?"

"Well— no. You've got me there. There never is much logic involved between Pete and I, those things just naturally happen, if I don't instigate he does. I have a problem where Pete is concerned. I've never once been able to beat him even though I'm bigger than he is so I have to keep trying. You've got to understand though—if I had gotten him into the water I'd have pulled him out the same as he pulled me out. It was a contest—that's all. But he was suspicious and ready for me so I lost again."

"But this was too close a call, Tom. I hope you both grew up a little tonight." I got no answer to that but at least there was no argument either. "I'm surprised you would go to such a complicated—uh—words fail me. I guess I'm surprised you would throw away your own chances here to help her get away and do such outlandish things to bring it about."

"Once I understood what she wanted I was all for it 100% because that's what I want too. A chance to get away. She didn't have to force me—I'd have done anything short of murder to help her get out of Rainy Mountain. As for the method— well—

maybe I overdid it but I didn't have the luxury of a lot of planning time—first thoughts had to fly. Each act led naturally to the next until it was done. Even you guys forcing me to leave tonight was okay because it fits my own long range plans. Only as the train was arriving I found I wasn't ready to go—not yet. I discovered that I want to see this winter through and then Jennie and I can boot it around a bit and make a decision."

After leaving Tom at his gate I plugged Nightrider's block heater cord in at the front of the office rather than monkey with the doors to the warehouse and then carried the mail to the post office. I wonder if I have heard the truth yet. What if it was the other way around and Tom caught P/Jan pouring the antifreeze and events unfolded from there? Maybe Pat woke up half way to McBride and Tom plans to take the rap for her so my curiosity won't lead me on to Jan/Pat as well and maybe Alec too. If that's so then there will be no more trouble from that pair as they will be much too puzzled and distracted over—uh—Jan's fate. I may never know the true details and maybe—like Ember says—it might be best.

I can almost smile over the twins' final deception—impersonating each other yet! And forever more if all goes well. Or until some far-off time when a reunion might be welcome. Even Tom, who helped, doesn't realize it's Pat—Alec's legal wife who has seized the chance to go—leaving Jan, the common-law wife to live with the unsuspecting husband.

I mentally kicked myself every step of the way to the bunkhouse. "I might as well change my name to Morrow," I muttered, "I'm worse than the worst of them." It's the only comment I intend to allow on my sudden flip-flop on policy, my much declared longing for justice. For the police to do it right. Has it triumphed tonight? Or taken a beating? I just don't know and that makes me angry enough to face Peter without qualm.

But the wind went out of my sails the instant I stepped into his room. He is sitting there with a magazine in hand calmly waiting for me but he is packed. I mean that his duffle bags are stuffed with his worldly belongings and not a trace of him remains loose in the room other than himself.

"Yes. I'm leaving," he smiled at me.

"You can't," I protested illogically. The words I had planned to say to him and all thought of Tom faded like smoke in the wind at this new development.

"Why not? Everything is lined out and running smoothly now. You, yourself, say there will be money made this winter. Big money! There's not a thing more I can do to influence whether we survive or whether we don't and for the first time in my life I feel like I have paid my dues so I want to get away while I'm ahead."

"What do you mean?"

"I mean that Rainy Mountain has led a precarious life since its very beginning and some of us have not helped. We've taken more out of it than we've put back in. John never did have the kind of backing needed to set up properly especially back at the start so he had to do it all on a combination of bluff, charm and a lot of luck. He was the right man for the times just like I was the right man for these times we have just passed through. All my life I was one of those who took but forgot to give until now. Suddenly I can say I have paid up just by reason of tonight's work. Keeping you alive if nothing else."

"You're leaving us with a lot of loose ends."

"Precisely, I never was much good with loose ends. Give me something I can jump up and down on with caulk boots—that I can handle but don't talk to me about details. These sneaky little aggravations that come creeping up underfoot getting bigger every time you look warily down until they trip you up. That's not for me."

"What aggravations?"

"You know what I mean, you probably know it better than I do. Everything is up in the air, someone is going to have to bring it down. It was all fine as long as John was here to run it—it was his outfit to do as he pleased. Now that he's gone everything changes—whose outfit will it be now?"

"A good question," I said, meaning more than he knew because I'm still half suspicious that he has signed John's bill of sale making Rainy Mountain his own. But, once again, he misunderstood me.

"Yes. Besides myself, the wild card, there are five surviving children of John and Lora's plus Jo. They can't all be boss and it's unlikely they will ever agree on one of their own to take over. Now we need someone we can trust who has a devious, slinky sort of a mind that can work around corners and meet all these new challenges that seem to be coming our way. It's fortunate and a good indication that Rainy Mountain luck is still alive and well in that the man ideally suited to lead the way through the next phase is already with us."

He has lost me, I can't think who he means because after all he did just say, and I agree with him, that the Morrows will be unable to select someone satisfactory to all. With Peter gone I can see each of at least two factions presenting their choice of manager and then the fun beginning.

"You are the only one of us who has the full confidence of everyone. It won't all be easy or much fun but I'm sure that your time will be long, like John's."

"Not a chance! Not me!" I blurted the words out as if I had been kicked in the stomach. "Never! Not in a thousand years will I be sucked into being fall guy for this crazy bunch."

This then is what he has been leading up to almost since the day he arrived. With his teasing, his way of handing out unearned praise like candy to a kid. And even with his long speeches which I mistook simply as a need to have an audience he has been preparing me for this day. Bending me to his style of thinking, training me, in his own odd way to be his successor. I've probably been targeted ever since he read of me in John's letter, which he must have, despite pretending to be unaware of my existence when he came. But even as anger at his presumption rages through me the voice of my cunning little sidekick is shouting at my inner ear. "Accept," he says, "Agree to anything Peter wants just to hasten him on his way. Then make your deals to get out of this.' Of course! All I have to do is to see us through the next year or two and by then there will be dollars enough to hire smarter people than I whose duty will be to see that we never operate at a loss again. And to find the options that will let us keep the town alive without cutting so much timber. No! I'm thinking slow! We already have one person who can run the company as profitably as any professional. She just has to be eased into it properly. Ember may not have done as well in school as Tim but she is shrewd and tough far beyond all her brothers and sisters. She is dedicated totally and can read trends into the future that none of the rest of us even notice. She might, where Rainy Mountain is concerned, be overcautious—too protective—but that might be good. She will think she needs help and that's fine—I will let her think I am helping as long as necessary. She will not be the first woman to run a forest company—nor the last. In the meantime, Peter is free to think he has hung it around my neck just as I am free to see that he does not.

"I knew you'd be thrilled," he grinned, "but you have no choice, just as I had no choice when John called for me. What this outfit needs—thrives on—is a benevolent dictator and you are elected. Never consult the others as I did—just act—and from you they will all accept it."

"Okay. But it will take some arranging won't it?"

He chuckled at that, "no problem there, you know those documents of John's giving me control? The ones I was forever waving in everyone's face to keep them in line?"

I nodded. "It's a wonder someone hasn't been asking for a signed copy by now. I mean the bank or the lawyer."

"I guess that shows how easy we are to forget about—out of sight, out of mind sort of thing and a good way to be."

"Lets hope they are slow remembering."

"Well, anyway, I've never signed them, they are still in the desk that's been called mine so legally the place is still John's. The thing for you to do is to say nothing, just get those papers and use them any way you see fit. We'll all be grateful and I will know that our interests are in good hands. I'm going east first to have a quiet visit with John and Lora. We won't talk business but in the long run I will have them knowing that all is well despite our loss of Jan. It would probably be best if they are never told the whole story about that but are left thinking that Jan has run off."

"Aside from that everyone we deal with, including the bank, already know that you are some kind of a wheel here so you will have no difficulties in that respect. Besides, with all those wild ideas you dream up it would be a shame if you weren't in a position to try some out just to see why they won't work."

"Okay." Two 'okays' in a row, I'll have to watch this, if I start sounding too agreeable he is bound to start wondering why.

"And, Byron?"

"Yeah?"

"You know that little metal box on the outside of the office where the telephone line comes in?"

I admitted that I did.

"If you rehook a disconnected wire there the phone should work again." He smiled widely at me as he headed out the door, "I'll be back in time to catch that train, I've got an errand to run."

"Wait!" I called as he went down the steps, "What do I tell the others about you disappearing?"

"Oh, I'm not disappearing. I have no doubt my lady friend will leave farewell notes that should explain matters to everyone's satisfaction."

The chill started at the top of my head and tumbled over me like a waterfall. He is taking Ember with him! Dazed, I went to my room and sat on the bed. What irony! Here I will be, stuck with a haywire sawmill operation to babysit for the benefit of others while the only reason I have stayed so long now will be gone. Yes! In this moment of stress the truth has finally come out to front and foremost. It completely escapes me now that over the years I have invented and used many excuses—first to come back to and then to stay in Rainy Mountain—but the fact now admitted only one has ever really counted — Ember.

I jumped up to follow him to thrash this out and I got halfway to her house before my senses returned. It will do no good to confront them in my present state of mind. Any rash statements on my part will almost certainly send her packing all the faster. I've got to wait and think this out. There is a lot more to this affair than I understand. I'm sure of it. They are the strangest pair of lovers that can be imagined because to my notion she is actually afraid of him. Yet at times she runs to him for comfort like a lost orphan. He must have some hold on her that is much more persuasive than an old promise between parents who by now have forgotten, indeed, half of whom are dead and the other half gone. I will wait for Peter to return—sooner or later he must come to me and then we shall see.

The night passed and no Peter. When the cookhouse opened I went over and halfheartedly picked at some breakfast but it was after six-thirty before he showed up. He came in looking like a man freed of all his cares, filled a plate and a coffee mug then came to join me in my corner. Dean and a couple of other early risers have already been and gone but no one else is up yet on this Sunday morning so we have the dinning area to ourselves except for a flunky who avoids us anyway.

Despite having half the night to plan this out I pulled Allan's trick and jumped on him with both feet in my mouth. "Just what is the score between you and Ember anyway?"

He turned that infuriating grin on me before he said, "I don't understand you, Byron, I've tried to tell you before that there is nothing between Ember and I that concerns you."

"You keep saying so but the evidence I see tells me different. Part of the time you have her frightened out of her wits, other times she can't get close enough to you. I want to know what it's all about and I'm all ears right now!" That's not the way to talk to Peter but I couldn't care less that his grin has turned to anger at my tone of voice.

The anger faded to consideration and then decision, finally he said, "Okay, I suppose you're right, maybe you should know about it. You might better understand what you've gotten into. For sure she will never tell you." He still took his time getting started but now I dare say nothing for fear of distracting him. "Em and I had a bit of an adventure in town the year she graduated. It's left scars on both of us but mostly on her. You've got to remember, my friend, that Ember, like her sisters, is a foolish girl. So proud of her family background and so spoiled that she can see no wrong in anything a Morrow might do other than to quit the bunch. And blessed—or cursed—with the innocent good looks and the occasional nasty twist of mind to cause more trouble in the blink of an eye than you and I together could dream up in a month."

"A matter of opinion," I growled, unable to take that quietly.

"Sure. But anyway, I was living in town that year too and working at a planer mill nearby. It was just a year or so after I'd split away from here and gone off on my own. I had a place rented where I lived but mostly I ate in restaurants. One of the fellows I worked with was a no-good, useless type, a lot like I was at the time and we had no end of fun together, drinking, burning gasoline as quickly as a fast car could and chasing girls. Jerry had double trouble—first he was alcoholic and second he was married. While his wife was less than the usual image of dutiful housewife—she was a dozen cuts above him and eventually she locked him out. It had happened before and according to Jerry it would probably happen again which I took to mean that he expected her to take him back again some day.

"He moved in with me and we carried on as if life were just a party we had crashed. Then he started going off by himself and staying almost sober of all things. He had found a special girl, a high school chum of his youngest sister and he simply went bananas over her. Her father owned a sawmill out somewhere in the boondocks and she was boarding in town to attend school. It was nothing to me, no bells rang, dozens of fathers owned small sawmills in those days. It was like owning a ranch down in the Chilcotin, most everyone local was into it one time or another and lots of them boarded kids in town.

"They suffered a setback on graduation night when Jerry met her father. He saw Jerry for exactly what he was and told him to shove off or maybe more direct words to that effect. But she still had a few more days to spend in town and after daddy was gone they cooked up a new scheme. She must have been as crazy about him as he was for her because she agreed to go with him when he started making plans. He told her that since her parents had misjudged him they would have to run off and they would marry later when her folks decided to accept facts. He laughed about it when he told me and added that she didn't know yet that he was already married and hadn't even considered starting divorce proceedings—didn't want to. The devil of it is—I laughed too.

"They planned to go down to Kamloops to start their life together and since I had a car while he didn't, he asked me to drive them to the bus depot. He had to borrow money from me too. So for the first time I was finally to meet the girl. When I followed his directions to the home where this girl boarded I was looking around thinking in a vague way that Em lived somewhere in this part of town but I had never been to the place. So you can imagine my surprise when he came trotting out carrying the girl's suitcases and I saw it was Em tagging along with him.

"I didn't take time to think up niceties when I jumped out to confront them, I just roared, 'Emmbuur, you're not going anywhere with this two-faced cheater!' Well, as you could expect, her temper popped too and we had a good old shouting match right in the street. Just as well it was a new subdivision still under construction and there were no close neighbours. I told her he was married and had a little daughter, and she told me I was a lying so-and-so. Jerry saw it was going his way and laughed at me. That was just about his last mistake because with my usual blunt line of reasoning I saw it would be far easier to beat him to death than to change Ember's mind.

"Byron, I have to admit that I gave him no chance, He didn't know he was in a fight until I had him flat on his back—he wasn't a fighter anyway and had no chance at all with me. I intended to kill him and I could have easily only I was too mad and distracted to go about it properly. I hammered on him until he went unconscious then I grabbed his hair and pounded his head up and down fully intending to break his skull open or snap his neck. Good thing for both of us that we had rolled down into the ditch and it was soft damp earth under us instead of pavement or even gravel. All this time Em was beating on me though I hardly noticed as long as she just used her fists. I only had to watch that she didn't get close enough to get one of her fancy holds on me. I always was too quick for her so when that didn't work she went hunting for one of her high-heeled shoes which she had kicked off at the start of hostilities—those horrendous spikes she always wears—and went to work on me with that. That got my attention fairly quickly because she got to me a few times and was gouging little patches right out of my scalp every time she connected. I could push her away but she would jump up and come right back." He chuckled in reminiscence, "My blood was running down over my face and onto Jerry giving him a well and truly done in look so I left him be, brushed Em off and went away. With my shirt wrapped around my head, I drove straight to the planer where I worked and went to the night shift first aid attendant. I told him almost the truth—that I'd been in a fight over a girl until the girl took the other side—and sat still while he patched me up enough to stop the blood flow. Then I went home, no police there yet, cleaned up, changed clothes, threw all my gear in the car and took off west on Highway 16. I've got the scars yet from that night all over my head but they're covered with hair now. Em's scars don't show either but they go a lot deeper.

"I knew I would be run down or stopped in a roadblock before I got far but I didn't care, I was just out enjoying one last fling in a good car. Once Burn's Lake was behind me I started to feel let down and when I got past Smithers, over two hundred miles, without hearing so much as a peep about it on the car radio I knew I had done a poor job on him. At Terrace I went to work in the most remote logging camp I could find and I stayed there for longer than any other place before or since."

He stopped a while, getting his words together. I can see that, despite his smiles and occasional chuckles, these are not all pleasant memories for him. "In a way you are right, Em has always been special to me but for a reason you would never guess. I suppose it's why she hates to love—or loves to hate me so much.

"It was a long time before I found out what happened to her after I left. About a year or so later I sat down one night in camp and very painfully composed a long letter to her, carefully avoiding mention of our past but telling her all the things I have been doing lately and I asked her to write and let me know how she was. I expected her to be off with Jerry someplace but I addressed the letter to Rainy Mountain hoping they would forward it to her. She answered fairly quickly—from home—she also said nothing about our wild night in town but took a couple of pages to say that everything was fine. She mentioned that she was meeting the trains at night and that gave me an idea. I hate writing letters but telephoning comes easy for me so I decided to try to get her on the phone in the middle of the night when no one else was around the office. I knew the train time and about how long it takes to drive down from the railroad. So one night on a long weekend when I was in Prince Rupert, thinking of home and just about dying of loneliness, I sat in a hotel room and kept asking the operator to ring the number here until Em was in the building after parking her truck.

"Something happened to both of us when we made voice contact. After an uncertain moment all the old dams and walls in her broke down. She was so glad to hear from me that she laughed and then cried and then laughed again and I think I was no better. It was some conversation! We said things to each other that we could never say in person. In a letter that no one else would ever see she was unable to talk to me but over the phone, a party line at that, with who knows how many between here and town able to listen in if they were up that time of night, she poured out her heart. She told me about Jerry, how she called an ambulance then climbed right in and went to the hospital with him—it seems that good looks and brass will get you anywhere. In Emergency they washed my blood off him and found there wasn't much wrong other than a probable mild concussion and the odd bruise that you would expect after a fight. She sat beside his bed waiting for him to wake up but in comes a nurse to ask who she is and then to say that she will have to leave. It seems he has a wife and now the wife has come. Someone in the office must have gone through his wallet for identification and phoned the next of kin listed there.

"Em was appalled, she hadn't believed me, now she had to accept it. In fact she bumped into the wife at the door as she fled and Lise was coming in. Em put the old nose up in the air and tried to ignore her but Lise, looking tired and worried, had the last scornful word. 'So! You're the latest homewreaker! Funny—you don't look the part—I can't see what he finds so great about you.'"

"Em caught the first train home swearing never again to fall for another man. Then, despite her good intentions she admitted to—bragged of actually—doing just that. But of course this one was different; 'yes,' she admitted when I teased her with questions, 'He drifted in for the work but he's here of his own choice now and will stay—ye-ss—I suppose you could say he is the hungry, skinny, haunted type. So what?' Yet she no longer trusted her own judgment so she wanted a lot of time for this one to grow or fade on her and what did I think of that?

"Well, in the headiness of the moment I thought she would be receptive to a joke so I growled, 'Embuur, if you have gotten yourself into another mess like last time, I'm going to come home and do a good job on this one.' From nearly six hundred miles away I felt the icicles suddenly hanging on the wire between us. There were a few seconds of dead silence then, bang! End of conversation! I called right back but she wouldn't answer so I had no choice but to shrug it off. Later, maybe much later when I was in

Terrace for a weekend I tried again but a man answered the phone, probably you, so I mumbled something about wrong number and hung up. I never tried phoning again and I felt I had hurt her enough so I didn't write either, she'd probably have torn it up without reading it anyway. Unlikely as it sounds she had legitimate reason for concern because Jerry was not the first of her boyfriends that I disapproved of and ran off or beat up. She had no way of knowing he would be the last."

I am deeply moved by his story but it's too much an insight into the lives of both of them for me to handle right now. Especially since it does not come within a miles worth of cross ties stood end on end of explaining why she should drop everything she has worked for and go away with him. I looked at my watch, though it's still dark it won't be for long. "We've got to get rolling, we may have to wait up there a bit but the engine crew will be trying to make up all the time they can." I was developing a distinctly antsy feeling and that might mean the train is getting close. We could 'miss' the train—that would give me another day to work something out—but I think not. More time is not what I need. What I need is the nerve to say some things to each of them—in the presence of both. Some things I would rather not have to say because I am afraid of what the reactions will be. Anger is about the best I can expect—laughter would be the very worst. I guess what I really need is a lot of luck!

My mind is whirling, trying to come up with what to say and how to say it. It seems that a direct appeal is the only chance remaining— instinct tells me she simply will not buy any roundabout subterfuge. It will not do to criticize her choice or point out what I imagine to be Peter's faults. I will have to tell her no less and no more than the truth, that Rainy Mountain needs her, will in fact die without her. That so do I and so will I. At the station, when the train is arriving, surely she will be torn and undecided—wanting to go and wanting not to go. That will be the time. If she is still determined to climb on the train then counting on her strong sense of duty and family, her conscience and pride I can turn bitter and lay a load of guilt on her so deep and heavy that she will not wriggle beyond the borders of our camptown for years to come.

But I'm not sure I can do that, it might be better in the long run to let her go. It will be a last resort—we'll see.

Peter threw his gear on the back of Nightrider, "You can put my guns back in the house, I won't be needing them until I'm home again some day. Or use them yourself." Then as he climbed into the cab he surprised me by continuing the story I thought he had finished. "There's not much more to tell," he said. "When I finally did come home I was more than a little concerned as to how she would receive me although that part turned out okay. But I could see she was scared silly that I was going to beat up on anyone who smiled twice at her and it didn't take long to figure out that you were the one she was worried about. I'm afraid I let my wonderful sense of humour take over and I've had no end of success making life miserable for both of you. And if you think I'm apologizing, forget it, I've had far too much fun for any regrets. Just a bit of payback for the anguish—and bruises—that Em has caused for me over the years.

"If Gabrielle hadn't decided you were such a nice fellow we might have gone on indefinitely. For a pair of otherwise intelligent people, you and Em are both remarkably thick between the ears in some respects. There have been a lot of men in her life and she has selected and controlled every one, except maybe Jerry but it seems she hasn't a clue how to approach or what to say to one she really wants. It's the first time I can remember seeing her uncertain about something. She's always positive about everything she does—confident should have been her middle name—but she's unsure of you."

"There was nothing between Gabrielle and I. Mine was just the first friendly face she saw here so she sort of attached herself to me till she got her feet muddy."

"That's exactly what scared Em and it gave her the courage to buttonhole me one day, the night of the concert actually, before we realized how serious Jan's disappearance might be. She demanded I quit running her life. I told her I had no such intentions and didn't realize I had done anything to make her think that I was doing so," he smiled wryly. "She then asked if I still had objections to her choice of boyfriend and I told her to perish the thought, all she would get from me in the future would be best wishes. Then she was really mad at me and said, among other things, some not nice, that because of me she was losing you to Gabby and she demanded that I help straighten matters out."

"I laughed at her and said, 'you have no problem, Em, just take him home some night and he'll be proposing before the sun comes up.' She didn't stay mad, she just turned real serious and told me that, despite what everyone thought, that was not her style and I should know that. Besides, she wanted you to think it was your own idea. So I told her the next best would be to come out less quick with her 'no' the next time one of the boys from bunkhouse row asked her to a dance. I told her to go with the guy and let you see that she had other interests and that should bring you smartly to heel. But that one backfired though it was Nick who caught the backlash," he chuckled, "sure wish I could have seen that. Then I walked in before she got the first part of my advice into action. I'll admit I didn't expect her to take me literally, I just enjoy shocking people though it's hard to shock Em."

I had to interrupt him, "Do you mean she was unaware that Gabby had taken up with Tim?"

"She was so worried about you that she didn't notice that and I was certainly not about to tell her and spoil the fun." By now we are turning into Morrows' street, Ember's house is the first on the left but I drove right on by without slowing until I reached the path to Jo's front door where I stopped. He grinned, relishing his hold over me to the very last second, "Finally figured it out did you?"

I blinked hard and again I see the moonlit pillow in the first aid room. Again I say to myself, 'no one has hair like that but Ember.' And Jo! I almost shouted it aloud. Who knows why they chose to go there. Certainly not deliberately to be discovered by me. Not even Peter could predict that I would see Jo, assume the worst and think it Ember. Probably it was no more than the nearest warm place with privacy—they forgot about me being around after meeting the trains. Then the night I caught Peter walking about in the early a.m. when he took such exception to my running him down that he tried climbing over Ember's fence. He was not up to anything sinister nor had he been at Ember's, instead he was coming from Jo's and his natural perverse character led to him trying to hide from me.

Jo could be seen through the front windows of her house as she moved around putting the last minute touches to her departure. She knew we were waiting because twice while Peter talked to me she put her face to the window and shaded out the back light with her hands.

Peter's voice changed perceptibly, "There's one other little detail I might as well tell you about as long as we are having old home week and true confessions rolled in one. I would rather you heard it from me because you will hear it or guess it sooner or later." I looked at him, wondering what more might be coming. He spoke in a flat voice entirely unlike him, toneless, detached and completely neutral. "Ember says I am her brother or possibly her half-brother. She says all one has to do is watch Allan, Tom and I together with her dad and it's plain as a bump on a log that we are three brothers with our father. She could see it when we were still kids. In fact more so then." He shrugged, "She could be right, back in the days when my parents were married, couples expected to start raising a family right away. Those who produced no children were soon pitied by their friends because it could only mean that one of the unfortunate pair was unable to be a parent. My folks were married nine years before I was born. My mother was an attractive woman and she worked in the office with John just as Erin and Jennie work there now.

"Even so, Ember believes it more likely that Lora is my mother since there is nearly a four year gap between Allan and Tom that I would fit neatly into. But I'm not comfortable with the thought of having been given away even to lifelong friends. I'd almost sooner the first scenario were true."

"When I walk around this place I seem to be looking at it through John's eyes, it's like standing back and seeing him in my every move. That's why Em is so special to me, it's why I've always looked out for her—my little sister—and why sometimes I managed to hurt her when I thought she was making mistakes. She was always a holy terror with her boyfriends—book-of-the-month sort of thing and it's often been near war between us because of that. With the twins it was better because they are younger and I feel I helped to raise them."

"I like to think it's true, my friend, because it means I've got brothers and sisters, even if I can't speak out and claim them. One can only guess what secret misgivings there must have been in the hearts of two of the four parents who made the pact between Ember and I. If all four were in on the secret of my origins then this arranged marriage stuff must have come to a life of it's own as a rumour as we grew up probably because of the way I looked out for her and acted as if she were mine. But sometimes things turn out right no matter how wrong they start." His voice came suddenly back to normal. "Jo, now—now here's an ember that has turned to a steady flame," he said it appreciatively watching her struggle to us with two big suitcases. He got out to throw them on the back and boosted her up into the cab.

As I jockeyed to turn around she exclaimed, "Boy! Some honeymoon! Here I am packing my own luggage already!"

"It's okay, Jo, I was just explaining the facts of life to Byron and not much time left for it."

"That's good! And about time too! "

"You think they deserve each other do you?"

"Absolutely! I'd sure hate to watch them go separate ways and wreck two families." She gave me an elbow in the ribs that made me glad it's still dark in the truck cab. So she knew all along that Peter was having his fun with Ember and I. She is excited and gay and I think more than a little frightened of this new adventure in store. I am surprised to find I feel envious—more than just a little—she has been like a partner to me—a confidant—almost a fellow prisoner who is escaping first and with a new partner. She has stood for me against the others and even shielded me from Ember's wrath more times than I can remember. And more, she is one half of the image I fell in love with at first sighting, in fact—she's the one I saw first in broad daylight.

I can tell she is not joking as she says, "Hold the house for me, Byron, in case things don't work out well with this lout. And take care of it will you? Most of everything I call mine is still in it." She bumped him in a friendly way that said a lot but I know what she means. As long as her house is empty it will remain 'Jo's house' and she has a home here no matter where she roams. But once someone else moved in it would no longer be 'Jo's house'. It would be cutting one of the ties that bind her to us.

By the time we reached the railroad day is breaking noticeably as I parked Nightrider a bit beyond the station for receiving the mail and et cetera. I doubt we were there more than ten minutes when we were startled by the whistle of a train that has snuck quietly up on us and here is Number 8 bearing down from the west, its triple headlights bright even in the growing morning light. As we collected the luggage I asked Peter, "Will you be coming back?"

"Talk to my friend the north wind, perhaps it can answer that."

For him that remark is so out of character that I have to think he is already feeling the freedom of release from a time not to his liking.

"That was good timing," Jo said as we walked toward the station where the coach steps will likely be when the train comes to a stop. "It must be true—what they say about you—that the train won't come until you are here to meet it."

"There's some more good timing," I pointed to Ember arriving with her Cossack. She drove right to us at the station and joined us as the iced and steam-sweating coaches jolted to a hissing rest.

"You two are pretty sneaky," she said, sounding jaunty even though clouds of concern for them showed in her eyes. "Good thing I wasn't sleeping sound when Byron drove by the house after doing a noisy job of turning around at your place. With all that baggage on the back I knew something was in the wind besides snow." She embraced Jo and then hugged Peter before we left them to the trainman waiting with the boarding step. But none of them said goodbye so I didn't either.

I heard someone shouting my name and looking along the train I saw the man at the express car wanted my truck moved. I waved then ignored him, he can move it himself, dump our stuff on the ground or bring it back next trip, I'm busy right now.

We stood in the cold with the first lazy flakes from a storm that's darkening our new day drifting around us. Through the coach windows we saw Peter and Jo as they dropped their luggage at an empty seat then hustled along the aisle toward the tail end of the train but Ember and I stayed where we were. My heart is light, I no longer envy Jo. This is her train out. In my own case I can see now that as long as there is a Rainy Mountain or any vestige of it, there will be no train out for me.

But—thinking of Jo—I must have unconsciously leaned toward the rail cars, perhaps took a little step because I felt Ember stiffen, sensed her alarm, she is standing that close. At some point she has taken a hold of my coat sleeve and my first thought was of the collar and chain that Peter once spoke of—but it's okay, this gentle tug feels good. We exchanged cautious glances that seemed to reassure—perhaps it's been true all along—and she needs me as much as I need her.

I suppose this means I'm in trouble again. Perhaps deeper than ever before in my life but as someone suggested recently—pleasant trouble.

Maybe!

It caused quite a delay, not appreciated I'm sure, for someone to move Nightrider to where they wanted her. They had some impatient and caustic comments but still managed to wave at us as the train pulled away accelerating to regain minutes lost. By then Jo and Peter had reached the railed-in observation platform on the end of the last coach and they were there waving to us as the train moved swiftly out wreathing them in swirling snow.

We waved and waved till the train went around the bend already lost in a snow cloud of its own making.